Mermaids in the Basement

Mermaids in the Basement

MICHAEL LEE WEST

AVON

An Imprint of HarperCollins*Publishers*

This book was orignally published January 2008 in hardcover by HarperCollins Publishers.

HarperCollins books may be purchased for educational, business, or sales promotional use. For information please write: Special Markets Department, HarperCollins Publishers, 10 East 53rd Street, New York, NY 10022.

FIRST EDITION

Designed by Kara Strubel

Library of Congress Cataloging-in-Publication Data is available upon request.

ISBN 978-0-06-098507-3

10   11   12   13   ID/RRD   10   9   8   7   6   5   4   3

For Annabel Arnett

I started Early—Took my Dog—
And visited the Sea—
The Mermaids in the Basement
Came out to look at me—

—Emily Dickinson

Esmé Vasquez Lures Director with Siren Song
Gossip Swirls on the Set of Ulysses

"Enquiring" minds want to know if man-eating actress Esmé Vasquez, 27, merely has a taste for Guinness, or if she is on the prowl for a new boy toy. Last week, Vasquez was spotted at McKenzie's, a popular Dublin pub, with award-winning director Ferguson Lauderdale, 38 (see full story and color photos on pp. 24–25). Scottish-born Lauderdale has been on location in Ireland since last September, filming a big-budget remake of James Joyce's *Ulysses*. Vasquez, who snagged the role of Molly Bloom, recently split with her latest love, a German-born underwear model. Known as a "serial on-set seducer," Vasquez has been romantically linked with her costars, notably Tom Cruise, Jude Law, and Leonardo DiCaprio. Lauderdale reportedly has an ongoing relationship with screenwriter Renata DeChavannes, 33, the stepdaughter of the late Randolph "Andy" VanDusen of VanDusen Films. Lauderdale and Ms. DeChavannes have cowritten several screenplays, including last year's hit *Bombshell*.

In an exclusive interview, an unnamed source reported that Vasquez and Lauderdale spent three hours at McKenzie's Pub. "Mr. Lauderdale bought a round of drinks for everybody," said the source. The couple reportedly ducked out of the pub after midnight. The insider added, "She was all over him, but he seemed to like it. In fact, they seemed to click."

Unfortunately, the same thing cannot be said for Lauderdale's ambitious project. *Ulysses* has been plagued by injuries, foul weather, script problems, overworked vocal coaches, and rising tension between cast members. Originally budgeted at $122 million, the costs have reportedly risen to $215 million. Last month production was halted for over a week after a food poisoning incident, when the cock-a-leeky soup was laced with angel dust. Lauderdale was reportedly hospitalized with hallucinations.

Noted for risk-taking and genre-jumping, Lauderdale made his directorial debut in 1997 with the independent film *Just Walk Away, René*, collecting accolades across the globe. His career went into high gear after filming big-budget hits, most notably *The Clone, Made in Japan,* and the megagrossing *Bombshell,* which earned three Academy Awards, including Best Director, and raked in over $1.8 billion in ticket sales, making box-office history.

Last spring, after *Bombshell* snagged five Oscar nominations, Lauderdale announced his plan to film *Ulysses. Variety* reported that Esmé Vasquez had beat out Nicole Kidman for the much-coveted role of Molly Bloom. Vasquez, who is barely fluent in English, is best known for her simmering roles in art house films (*Mile High Club; Miss Bubbles' Bed and Breakfast*) and a small but memorable role as the lost Chihuahua, La Bonita, in the popular animated film *It's a Dog's Life.* Last year, Vasquez lashed out at the tabloids via an interpreter when she was voted "Hollywood's Worst Boob Job."

Vasquez's publicist attempted to release a comment but could not find an interpreter.

Chapter 1

❀ ❀ ❀

RENATA DECHAVANNES SAYS, ONE SIZE FITS ALL

*I*f I had not read the cover story in the March 2, 2000, *National Enquirer,* it's doubtful that I would have gone to Alabama and ruined my daddy's engagement party, much less sent the bride-to-be into a coma. Just for the record, I don't go around hitting other women, even if they are all wrong for my daddy; I don't read tabloids, and I certainly would never steal one, yet that's exactly what happened.

For the past six months, I'd been staying at my late mother's cottage on the Outer Banks of North Carolina, eating salt water taffy, forgetting to shave my legs, and plotting my next trip to Ireland. Days ago, my sweetheart, Ferg Lauderdale, had called from his Dublin hotel room, and, in between sneezes, he'd mentioned that he'd lost his sweater at a pub. "Could you pop a cardigan into the mail, love?" he asked. "Or better yet, could you deliver it in person?"

After we went through our five-minute ritual of saying good-bye, I drove to Jockey's Ridge Crossing, where I bought a pound of pecan divinity at the Footgear, then looked at a flying pig whirligig at Kitty Hawk Kites. Finally, I wandered over to Black Sheep, an eclectic wool store that sold dhurrie rugs, Flemish tapestries, Aubusson pillows, cashmere sweaters, and assorted one-of-a-kind clothing.

A bell tinkled over my head as I ducked into the store. A woman with short gray curls and horn-rimmed glasses sat next to the checkout desk, dipping French fries into catsup. She directed me to a polished maple display table that was piled high with cashmere. I hadn't seen Ferg in five weeks, and the notion of hand-delivering a care package was quite appealing. I selected three blue crew-necked sweaters that were exactly the color of his eyes, and a heavy, oatmeal-colored cardigan with deep pockets.

"Don't forget to look at our fifty-percent-off counter," called the clerk, lifting a plastic cup.

Tucking the sweaters over my arm, I wandered to the sale bin. A white poncho was spread out like gull wings over a half-price bolster pillow. With one hand, I lifted the poncho, and the macramé fringe, which was knotted with aqua beads, clicked and swayed. I had an image of myself wearing this poncho to Ireland. I'd jump into Ferg's outstretched arms and wrap my legs around his waist—well, maybe I wouldn't leap, and I certainly wouldn't do any sort of leg wrapping. A salt water taffy binge had left me with ten, or maybe twenty, extra pounds.

Setting down Ferg's sweaters, I slipped the poncho over my head, taking care not to snag my dangly seashell earrings in the fringe. The poncho felt a bit snug, and on my way to the three-way mirror, I caught the clerk's attention and said, "Does it come in a larger size?"

"I'm afraid not. One size fits all," said the clerk. "Unfortunately, that doesn't mean it flatters all." She waved her hand, knocking over the plastic cup. Ice and cola slid across the glass counter, then cascaded over the sides, pattering against the industrial-grade carpet. The clerk threw down several paper sacks, then bustled off to the stockroom for a mop.

I parked myself in front of the mirror, glancing over my shoulder, trying to see if the poncho covered my rear end. It didn't. Grasping the fringe, I tried to stretch the garment over my elephantine self. My head jutted out of the poncho, resembling the handiwork of a South American head shrinker.

I turned away from the mirror and bumped into a hospitality table that held a coffee urn and Keebler oatmeal cookies. A thick stack of fashion magazines and tabloids toppled to the floor. I hunkered down, gathering them into my arms, and happened to glance at the cover of the *National Enquirer*. It was upside down, but I recognized the couple in the photograph.

The laughing, dark-headed woman was Esmé Vasquez, the star of my sweetheart's new film. Her tight black pants showed the outline of aerobicized thighs. She leaned sideways, her breasts spilling out of a V-necked blouse, a smoky topaz necklace shining against bare skin. Her manicured hand gripped a man's thigh—Ferg's thigh. He was wedged against her, gripping a pint of ale. Behind his familiar wire-rimmed glasses, his eyes held a bemused expression.

I'd helped Ferg select those glasses after he'd stopped wearing contact lenses. His hair looked shorter and redder than I remembered. If he'd altered his hairstyle, what else had changed? The old Ferg had coppery, ropelike natural curls that sprang out all over his head. I remembered how he used to sit on the floor between my knees, a towel draped around his shoulders while I shaped and scrunched his hair with my unglamorous, unmanicured hands.

Me, I was the antithesis of all things Hollywood. One year ago, when he gave his acceptance speech at the Academy Awards, the camera had panned over to my row. I started to shrink down, but I was seated next to Susan Sarandon, who'd been nominated for best supporting actress in *Bombshell*. Susan grabbed a handful of my black gown and held me aloft. Later, when we made the party rounds, she pointed to my feet—one navy pump, one black. I waved my hand, and explained that the shoes were Prada, identical twins except for the color: the navy kid leather was almost black. I had borrowed them from my late mother, a self-professed shoe-a-holic. When Shelby VanDusen fell in love with a shoe, she bought them in multiple colors. "Just go barefoot," Susan suggested, "unless you're trying out for Fashion Victim of the Week in the tabloids."

"But I'll get my feet dirty," I said.

"That's all right, love," Ferg said, handing his statue to Susan; then he swept me into his arms. He smiled. "I'll carry you."

I always thought his hair went with his smile, a wide-mouthed, open grin. I'd worked with him three years, lived with him for two; but the longer I stared at the picture, the more alien he seemed. If it wasn't the camera angle, only one explanation made sense: I had never really known him. He was a stranger with even stranger hair.

In less than four minutes, my own hair was about to undergo a radical transformation, and not by choice.

Chapter 2

❀ ❀ ❀

A Redneck Mullet Isn't a Fish

*L*eaning against the hospitality table, I studied the grainy tabloid photo, my seashell earrings clicking violently. The shakes had started months ago, after my mother and stepfather had died in a plane crash off Nantucket. Trying to keep my hands steady, I shoved the *National Enquirer* under the poncho, then hurried into the dressing room and bolted the louvered door. Taking a deep breath, I lifted the poncho and yanked out the tabloid.

Vasquez's publicist attempted to release a comment but could not find an interpreter.

Comment my foot, I thought, and tented the magazine over my face. "Breathe," I whispered to myself, then wiped my eyes. Back in Hollywood, it was common knowledge that Esmé Vasquez wouldn't speak English—not because of a learning disability, but because she thought a language barrier was cute. During interviews, she'd laugh and twirl her hair and say, "No comprendo." However, I'd watched her audition for the role of Molly Bloom. She'd put on a wig and a nubby vintage suit. When she spoke, I listened, transfixed. Later, a reporter from *Variety* said, "Good God, man. Vasquez as an Irish woman?" Ferg defended his choice. "She nailed her lines," he told the reporter. "She summoned the voice and essence of Molly Bloom."

When it came to Hollywood, I myself was a bit foreign. I'd been raised in

New Orleans and coastal Alabama, to be exact. My paternal grandmother, Honora DeChavannes, used to say that I possessed more "hell" than "belle" in my backbone. Although she still lived in Alabama, I could almost hear her slightly nasal voice, chastising me for falling apart over a tabloid story. "Shame on you, Renata DeChavannes!" she'd say. "You aren't a wilted gardenia, you are crabgrass! You are kudzu!"

Well, I'll just tell you. Sherman may have burned the South, but kudzu will engulf it. Maybe I'd been away from Alabama too long, but it seemed to me that one could be weak *and* weedlike. Then I wondered if Ferg preferred women who spoke with strong accents, because I spoke (and thought) with a heavy southern drawl. Back in L.A., people still asked, "Where are you *from?*"

Now I leaned against the louvered door and slid down. "*Siren Song?*" I whispered to myself. "*Gossip Swirls on the Set?*" Did the alliteration mean something? I threw down the magazine and started to jerk the poncho over my head, then I felt a bolt of pain as the tassels and beads snagged in my hair and left earring, and also in the dressing room doorknob. With one hand, I reached up and gingerly patted my earring. It was entwined with hair and threads. Afraid to move, I shifted my eyes toward the mirror. The poncho covered the left side of my face, and white yarn zigzagged through my hair, around the earring, then stretched in a taut line to the doorknob.

The clerk heard my cries and came running. The doorknob rattled, then the clerk began tugging the door. With each jolt, the macrame tightened, yanking my head and ears. "No, stop!" I cried. "Get away from the door."

I explained that I was hogtied, then reached up to grab my earlobe, trying to keep the metal hook from ripping through the plump flesh. The clerk's face appeared over the louvered door.

"Oh, dear," she said, clucking her tongue. "You're in a fix."

"Maybe you should call the fire department," I suggested.

"I can handle this." She dropped to all fours, displaying surprising agility for a woman of her vintage. She slid under the door, reached into her pocket, and whipped out pinking shears.

"No, not that," I said, cringing.

"Just a snip or two," she said, and with a flourish, she cut me loose, neatly bisecting the poncho. Unfortunately she also chopped off several inches of my hair. On the left side. I peered into the mirror, thinking she'd given me a one-sided mullet, the favored hairstyle of redneck southern males.

"Shall I cut the other side, too?" She waved the shears.

"Just cut my throat and be done with it." I stared down at the carnage.

"I'll just go find you a hat. You can't go outside in this condition." She bustled off. I picked up the tabloid and stuffed it into my tote bag. On my way out of the shop, the clerk said, "Wait, I found you a hat! And do you still want to buy those sweaters?"

"I'd rather have my hair." I tugged at the shorn locks. Then, blinking back tears, I reached into my bag and pulled out the tabloid. "But this will do instead."

"Wait!" yelled the clerk. "Put that down. I haven't read it yet!"

"Weight broke the elevator down," I said and charged out the door, tucking the stolen magazine under my arm, thinking the worst was over. Unfortunately, it was just beginning.

Chapter 3

◉ ◉ ◉

A Phone Call to Dublin

I drove home in a daze and bolted from the car. My purse banged against my legs as I ran over the dunes, onto the beach. Choking back tears, I stood at the water's edge.

The late-afternoon sun fell in long, burnished strips along the shore, and a cold March breeze was blowing from the south, twirling what remained of my hair. I tried not to think about Esmé Vasquez and her glistening black curls or her expressive, heart-shaped face; but it was impossible not to. She had a way of lowering her chin while simultaneously glancing up through her eyelashes. She had worked with A-list actors, married and single, and each one had found that look irresistible.

Three years ago, the day before Lent began, I had found Ferg Lauderdale irresistible. I'd gone to a small party at my mother and stepfather's house in Malibu and spotted a tall, redheaded man standing on the deck, staring out at the ocean. I pulled my stepfather aside and pointed. "Hey, Andy, who's that guy?"

"Ferg Lauderdale. He's the director of *Just Walk Away, René*." Andy bit down on his cigar and peered down at me. "Wish you'd work on the screenplay."

"I'll think about it." I gave Ferg another look, then headed over to the bar. The house was filled with VanDusen executives, and one of the vice presidents stepped over and said, "Andy tells me you're going to write the screenplay."

"Well, I—"

"Congratulations," he said, shaking my hand, then bustled off.

An older woman with red hair turned and nodded in Ferg's direction. "Honey, he's gorgeous. You should grab him before Hollywood ruins him."

"Good idea." I wandered outside to the balcony and leaned against the metal railing, which was built to resemble the railing of a cruise ship, with long, lacy bromeliads trailing down. When it came to flirting, I was a failure, mainly because I couldn't get past my shyness. Tonight, however, I was bolstered by a stiff vodka tonic, along with a makeover, courtesy of my mama. Knowing my tendency to underdress, she'd bought me a black Oscar de la Renta dress and four-inch Manolo Blahnik heels. Everything matched, by the way. She'd made me sit on a stool for twenty minutes while she'd arranged my hair into a messy knot, securing it with diamond-encrusted mermaid clips.

Now, I leaned into the wind, and a mermaid clip loosened. A panel of hair swung forward, tumbling over my forehead. With one hand I reached up, smoothing back my hair, fastening it with the clip. From the corner of my eye, I watched Ferg Lauderdale push away from the rail. As he stepped over, the white wine swayed in the oversize goblet.

"You've got stars in your hair," he said. Behind thick eyeglasses his irises were an intense blue, spangled with cobalt; the colors reminded me of a van Gogh painting.

"Better in my hair than in my eyes." I gulped down my drink and leaned into the wind, hoping he hadn't seen my flushed cheeks.

"Ah, you've got three of them." He said "three" with an Irish lilt—*dree.* He lifted his hand and pointed to each clip. "Here. And here and *here.*"

"Are you Irish?" I smoothed back my hair, feeling the vodka buzz.

"No, Scottish."

"Sorry, I'm terrible with dialects; but I shouldn't be, considering that I'm a native southerner—and I don't mean the southern hemisphere. I'm from the kudzu, choke-you-with-kindness American South." I looked into my glass and cringed. It was the alcohol talking.

"I've never met a southern girl before." His lips parted, showing a slightly crooked eye tooth. "By the way, I'm Ferguson Lauderdale, but everyone calls me Ferg."

"I'm Renata." I looked up into his eyes.

"Wait, are you Andy VanDusen's stepdaughter?"

I nodded.

"Fine man, he is." Ferg lowered his glass, clinking it against mine. "Here's to southern women and their alluring voices. Sirens of the modern world. Hard to handle and even harder to resist."

Now I reached inside the tote for my phone and called Ferg's hotel. It was 4:30 p.m. in Nags Head, so it would be 10:30 p.m. in Dublin. At the sound of his sleepy hello, my throat tightened. "Hey," I said.

He didn't respond, and I had the feeling that he hadn't recognized my voice. So I added, "It's me, Renata."

My plan was to chitchat for a minute, and then calmly ask about the tabloid. Instead, I blurted, "What the hell is going on with you and Esmé?"

"Me and *who?*" He yawned.

"The article in the *National Enquirer.* You and Esmé are on the cover."

"What article? I've no bloody idea what you're talking about."

I reached into my tote bag, pulled out the magazine, and read the headline and first paragraph. "Shall I continue?" I said.

"This is unbelievable, isn't it?" He sneezed. "It's simply not true."

"The picture's graphic, Ferg. She was groping you!"

"Darling, please listen to me. The whole cast was at that pub, and Ms. Vasquez had too much to drink. She was grabbing everyone. Renata, nothing is—or was—going on. Absolutely nothing. Except I left my sweater at that pub."

"Why did you take it off in the first place?"

"I was sitting next to a rip-roaring fire—"

"I'll just bet you were."

"—and it was stuffy," he finished. "You know how hot-natured I am."

"Thanks for reminding me." All my life I'd been waiting for a man like Ferg. He was everything my cold, selfish father wasn't. Or so I'd thought.

"Damn that bloody tabloid," he said. "Damn the paparazzi."

I leaned over and picked up a broken scallop shell. I almost believed him; at least, I wanted to. He'd never lied before, not that I knew of, anyway. Besides, if he were embroiled in an affair, wouldn't he have called her Esmé, and not Ms. Vasquez? Or maybe that was his strategy. My head filled with giddy, S-shaped alliterations, and I thought, *Somewhere in the haze a skanky starlet is stealing my sweetheart.*

"Renata, maybe you should fly over and see for yourself. I'll put you to work—I could use your help on the script."

"That's not terribly romantic." I dragged my toes through the sand, making giant X's.

"Sorry, it's too early. My brain hasn't woken up."

"Then go back to sleep, " I said irritably, tossing the shell into the water.

"No, I want to—" His words snapped off as a wave rose up behind me and slapped hard into my rear end. I lurched sideways, knocking the phone out of my hand. The water took it with a slap, then the phone dropped off into the swirling blue.

Chapter 4

❦ ❦ ❦

A Sacrifice to Cupid

When I reached the cottage, I mixed a vodka tonic. I hadn't eaten since early this morning, so I fried a pound of sugar-cured bacon. These days, cooking was the only thing that soothed me. I'd been preparing meals with a Celtic twist: lamb stew, steak and Guinness pie, corned beef and cabbage; but this afternoon, I was in the mood for a BLT, just the thing for a botched haircut.

I fixed another drink and assembled the sandwich—curly lettuce, bacon, glistening tomatoes, all laid out on French bread, which I'd slathered with Duke's mayonnaise. Next I set the table, adding one of my mother's checkered seafoam napkins. I set the tabloid next to my plate, studying the picture, then I dipped my finger in mayonnaise and drew a mustache across Esmé's eyes. My own eyes were nearly swollen shut from crying.

Halfway through the sandwich, the bread stuck in my throat. I put one hand over my mouth, then ran to the bathroom and threw up. Ferg's possible defection was just the latest trauma. I had been working on a screenplay for Caliban Films, and the executives kept asking for rewrites. It was that most dreaded of subjects—a coming-of-age story about a southern girl overcoming her fear of water. The working title was *Hydrophobia*. The studio had offered sound advice, including a new title, but in my present mind-set, I just didn't know how to fix anything. I'd just completed my fifth revision. It was sitting on the knotty pine desk, but I was closer to a breakdown than a breakthrough.

I wrapped my arms around the base of the toilet, tucking my legs to my chin, waiting for the nausea to pass. Somehow I managed to pull myself off the blue tile floor and stagger into the kitchen. In the back of the refrigerator, I found a box of Phenergan suppositories. The name on the prescription label was "Andy VanDusen." I couldn't make out the expiration date, but the directions were clear: "Take every six hours for nausea." So that's exactly what I did.

Later, while I cleared the table, the Phenergan collided with the vodka. I gripped the counter. Outside the window, past the checkered curtains, I couldn't see the moon, but it must have been full or three-quarters because I could make out the heaving sea, all black and silver. In my confused state, it reminded me of aluminum foil, something you'd peel off a barbecue grill.

As I passed out of the room, I snatched the stolen *National Enquirer*, thinking I'd do a little bedtime reading, and search for overlooked clues that would exonerate my sweetheart. The last thing I remembered was slipping a Counting Crows CD into the player, then crawling up the stairs, into my room, falling face-first onto the bed.

J woke up at daybreak. Pulling the sheet around me, I propped myself up on my elbows. Through the long windows, first light was breaking over the ocean. Above the dunes, smoke drifted toward the water. The wind picked up, bending the sea oats, and the smoke blew in the opposite direction. Then I remembered the tabloid and how my emotions had set off a gastronomic storm.

I slid off the bed and knelt beside the window, pressing my face against the cool glass. My mother and I had spent many summers here together after she'd married Andy VanDusen back in 1979. Since my real daddy, Louie DeChavannes, owned the Gulf of Mexico, it only seemed fair that my mama got to claim the Outer Banks.

Andy had bought her the cottage to celebrate their first anniversary. In those days it was an old, unpainted house named "Chambres de Sirene." At first I was frightened of the water because it was different from Honora's place on Mobile Bay, with its scruffy, driftwood-strewn beach and oyster-colored water. Here in Nags Head, the Atlantic seemed athletic and unpredictable, even more subject to the whims of nature. I would climb up to the widow's walk and watch the surf zigzag. There were no trees, just wind, sand, and water. Mama said it reminded her of her favorite movie, *Summer of '42*.

Every summer we left the glass house in Malibu and came to Nags Head. In those days the Outer Banks were quaint and unpretentious, wild around the edges. By the time Mama and Andy died, they had been married twenty-one years, and they not only thought alike, they had started to resemble each other—the same beaked noses, thin upper lips, and gray-blond flyaway hair.

I hunkered beside the window for a minute longer, holding back tears. Then I padded down to the kitchen and made a pot of coffee. The headache had worsened. While my temples pounded to the beat of "In-a-Gadda-da-Vida," I rummaged the cabinets for the Excedrin. I had always found this room soothing, but when Mama had redecorated, she'd added a bit of whimsy along with the modern culinary touches. In addition to the six-burner Viking cooktop and Sub-Zero refrigerator, she'd set a concrete alligator next to the back door. Seven white scalloped dishes hung in a pleasing arrangement on the celadon walls. Arranged on top of the creamy glazed cabinets were antique sailboats, baskets, and an old aqua jar filled with shells.

While the scent of coffee curled in the air, I wondered if anything that smelled this good could be healthy. I leaned across the counter, breathing the alluring fumes, musing about discipline and impulse control. If I couldn't resist a cup of coffee, how could I expect Ferg to behave himself around a world-class man-eating beauty? Then again, just because I loved him didn't mean he'd stopped looking at the opposite sex.

I picked up the pot and started to pour coffee into a mug, but my aim was off, and hot brown liquid splattered onto the counter. Throwing a tea towel over the mess, I grabbed another mug and promptly dropped it. As I blinked at the shattered crockery, I heard three short raps on the back door. A moment later, Edna Pierce, my elderly next-door neighbor, poked her head into the kitchen. Edna reminded me of my paternal grandmother—both were elegant, mannerly ladies with gravelly southern voices and a penchant for snooping.

"Hi, sugar," Edna said brightly. She squinted at my lopsided hair and then pointed at the side window. "I poured a little water on your bonfire. It was still smoldering."

"What fire?" I leaned toward the window, pushing back the curtain. The morning sky curved, all pink-tinged at the edges. The beach was empty, except for a pile of charred wood.

"Why, the one you built last night on the beach," she said. "I just figured you were roasting clams or S'mores, and my feelings were kinda hurt that you hadn't invited me. You'd been right neighborly up to that point. Anyway, when I carried out my trash, I saw you wandering around in the dark, holding two big FedEx envelopes. You couldn't find your car. Even if you were a little tipsy, the car was parked in a funny spot. You were in no shape to drive. So I offered to take the packages to the FedEx drop box. I went to the one by the bank."

"Hold on a minute, Edna. What packages?"

"Maybe this'll jog your memory," said Edna. "One packet went to Ireland, and one went to California. I couldn't help but see what you'd scrawled on the California envelope. I'm no prude, but I doubt if FedEx will deliver something with profanity written on it. The one to Ireland wasn't much better. You wrote 'SKANK' on it. It was addressed to Esmé Vasquez, in care of the Grand Hotel in Dublin, Ireland. Isn't she an actress?"

"Yeah. But why would I send her anything?" I pulled out a chair and sank down.

"You didn't say. But the envelope felt kinda powdery and had a burned smell. I sneezed my head off. The second package, the one you sent to California, was squishy and smelled like homemade yogurt. And you kept talking about Ozzy Osbourne, something his wife mailed to somebody, maybe? You weren't making good sense."

I shut my eyes. Ozzy Osbourne's wife, Sharon, had once placed excrement into a blue Tiffany box, then sent it to a rival. I was far more timid than Sharon, and less original; but I would have loved to send Esmé a package of poop. I glanced at the desk where I kept FedEx envelopes, my laptop, and the latest— and only—version of my new screenplay. I kept it in a sea-grass basket. From here, the basket appeared to be empty, but I could only see one edge.

"Honey, you look pale," said Edna. "Can I do anything for you?"

"I just need a little rest," I told her.

After she left, I tore my desk apart looking for my manuscript, but it was gone. I thought about the bonfire and cringed. Nothing could have made me burn that screenplay. It was flawed, to be sure, but I had done an old-fashioned edit with a lead pencil and hadn't yet keyed in the changes to WordPerfect.

I pulled out the drawer; wedged in the back was an aqua envelope. Across the front, in my mother's back-slanted handwriting, was written *"Do Not Open Except in an Emergency."* If this didn't qualify as one, then I didn't know what would. I slit open the envelope with my fingernail and pulled out the engraved stationery. Mama had died on October 31, 1999, to be exact. This letter, dated a week earlier, had been written at the knotty pine desk in Nags Head, days before she and Andy had left for New York.

Shelby VanDusen
October 24, 1999
Nags Head, North Carolina

Dear Renata,

If you're reading this letter, I'll be dead. And I didn't get a chance to tell you my dark, dirty deeds before I became the divine Mrs. Andy VanDusen. Okay, stop laughing. If you are reading this and I'm alive, then I just forgot to tear up this letter. Chalk it up to bad housekeeping or menopausal forgetfulness. Seriously, I've written you a letter before every trip that Andy and I have taken. But I've always made it back to dispose of them.

In fact, I've come to see these missives as talismans. So here I am, writing you another letter that you will (hopefully) never read.

As you know, Andy and I will be flying to Egypt, and on the off chance that we're run over by stampeding camels, I thought I'd better mention a few things. First, your inheritance (Andy says to tell you to please buy furs, diamonds, and Gucci—with his blessings). Second, I promised I'd tell you the truth about me and your father. Just on the off-off chance that something does happen in Egypt, and I take my secrets to the grave, I want you to call Honora and Gladys. They can fill in the missing pieces—and no, it won't be as juicy, but maybe that's a blessing. Of course, I plan to defy the Fates and to personally tell you all of my dirty secrets.

I will always love you. And if I really am gone, don't eat chocolate and mope. Just know that wherever I am, my thoughts are with you, and that I am thankful for every day that your beautiful soul touched my life.

Mama

Inside, a smaller envelope held a few black seeds. Written across the front in Mama's handwriting was "Zinnias." Picking up her letter, I read it again, trying to imagine my mother writing the note at this rickety oak desk, then fitting in the seed packet and sticking the whole thing way back in the drawer.

*F*oul weather blew in from the Atlantic, and while I searched the cottage for my screenplay, a heavy mist settled over Nags Head. In every room the celadon walls turned muddy green. I couldn't concentrate; my thoughts finned off into the gloom.

I grabbed a teal-plaid mackintosh and an umbrella, then bolted to my Jeep. I drove over to Something Fishy This Way Comes, and a waitress led me to a blue booth. While I waited for slaw and crab fritters, I sipped hot tea and thought about my mother's letter. What did she mean, call Honora and Gladys? What did they know?

I drove home and stepped into the kitchen. A red light blinked on the answering machine. My finger trembled as I hit the replay button. The first message was from a Caliban executive, threatening to report my vile, unsanitary package to the authorities, adding that I would never again write a screenplay for their studio.

The next message was from Ferg. "Renata? Are you there?" A pause. "Well, I guess not. Please call when you get home, love. I just got a frantic call from Ms. Vasquez's assistant. Actually, I laughed about the skank business ... but what's with the ashes? How many tabloids did you burn? Still haven't seen the offensive article." Ferg laughed. "I'll be waiting for your call, my little fire-bug. I love you—do not forget that."

I sat down in a chair and put my head between my knees. Last night, while under the influence of a dead man's Phenergan, I must have burned my manuscript and then somehow poured the ashes into a FedEx envelope, which I'd inadvertently addressed to Esmé "SKANK" Vasquez.

But what had I sent to Caliban Films?

Chapter 5

○ ○ ○

HONORA DeCHAVANNES SAYS, EVERYBODY LOVES A SCANDAL

I never dreamed I'd turn into a little old lady who carried a dog in her pocketbook. I'd known people like that, and to tell the truth, I found it a tad eccentric. Yet here I was, Honora DeChavannes, an eighty-year-old dog worshipper, sneaking my Yorkie into Fairhope, Alabama's premier salon.

I shifted in the blue vinyl swivel chair, then peered down at my oversize Kelly bag. The object of my affection, a six-pound Yorkshire terrier named Zap, peeped back at me, watching the beautician touch up my white roots.

Zap's nose twitched, then he barked. Candice, my beautician, hunched over and started barking, too. Candice had a nose ring and a snake tattoo on her upper right arm, but could she ever do hair. She scowled at Zap. "That damn Yorkshire terrorist is gonna bite me one day."

"He's not a terrorist," I said. Zap showed his teeth, then dove back into the Kelly bag, emitting warning growls.

"I don't know if I should show you this, Honora." Candice opened a drawer, sending plastic curlers crashing to the floor, and pulled out a magazine.

"Show me what?" I asked, wondering if she was going to show me a new hairstyle. For weeks, she'd been trying to talk me into a short cut like Halle Berry's old look, but I just didn't have the bone structure for it. Candice held up the magazine. "I'm sorry to report this, but your granddaughter's boy-friend is a front-page scandal."

"What're you talking about?" I put on my reading glasses and glanced at the cover. It showed a redheaded man with round John Lennon glasses being squeezed up one side and down the other by a pretty (if tarty) black-headed woman. I'd never met the man, but I knew about him. Ferguson Lauderdale was Renata's sweetheart.

Several women leaned out of their hair dryers to listen. "Why, I don't know what you mean," I said, trying to catch Candice's attention and make her hush, but she sashayed between the swivel chairs, flashing the tabloid at every customer. People in Point Clear, Alabama, loved a good scandal, and a lurid one was even better. The hairdressers turned off their blow dryers, and all of the customers stopped talking. I was tempted to pour a little Frivolous Faun on Candice's head.

Mrs. Jennings, the owner of the shop, was sitting in the chair beside me; she craned her neck and stared at the picture. "Honora, do you really know this guy?"

"She certainly does," said Candice, holding up the magazine for all to see. "This is a picture of Ferguson Lauderdale, everybody. He made that hit movie last year. I'm sure y'all have seen it. Raise your hands, anybody here who hasn't seen *Bombshell*? I didn't think so. Well, anyway, Ferguson is—or maybe I should say *was*?—in love with Honora's granddaughter."

"I remember Renata," said Mrs. Jennings. "The last time she visited Honora, I gave her highlights. The most stunning gray eyes I ever saw, except for her mother's. Lord rest her soul, Shelby was gorgeous. And she had natural curl to *die* for. But good hair won't protect you from love troubles."

"You ought to know," I snapped, but Mrs. Jennings just laughed. She'd just gotten married for the fourth time, and to a much younger man who gave scuba lessons at the YMCA.

"And so do you, Honora. So do you. Why, I remember when your husband Chaz died. You were burning something in your barbecue pit. I could see the flames from my shop."

"Candice, honey?" I glanced up at my beautician. "Can we hurry this up? Because if you don't, I am going to use a curling iron on Mrs. Jennings's tongue."

"Now I know the answer to that blind item that ran in last week's *Star*," Candice said, digging through a pile of magazines beside the dryers. I leaned back in my chair and squinted down at the tabloid.

"What does Renata's boyfriend see in that Spanish harlot?" Mrs. Jennings reached into the space between our chairs and patted my hand, her way of letting me know that my secrets were safe with her—at least, until I left her shop.

"I know," said Candice, walking back to my chair. "Renata's gorgeous."

"And talented," I said, leaving off the neurotic nail-biting and her tendency to overindulge in all things chocolate. On the other hand, she adored Ferguson, and losing him would be a harsh blow. "She has no idea that she's beautiful," I added.

"It helped having Shelby and Louie for her parents." Mrs. Jennings smiled. "And you for the grandma-ma!"

"Oh, pooh." I waved my hand; but to be perfectly honest, Renata hadn't been a pretty newborn. She was what my late husband, Chaz, would call an F.L.K. He'd been a neurosurgeon, and I still remembered the medical lingo. F.L.K. stood for Funny Looking Kid. Renata's daddy had been one, too. True, they'd transformed, but only on the exterior. Not that Renata cared about such things.

I opened my bag and reached under Zap for my wallet. Then I passed around my granddaughter's pictures. While the beauticians ooh'd and ah'd over her eyes and cheekbones, an argument broke out over her hair color. Candice said it was a level 6; Mrs. Jennings said it was a 7.

"I would *love* to give Renata a few strategic highlights," said Candice.

A little strategy was just what I had in mind, but I wasn't sure where to begin. If I weren't so old—and if I could take my Yorkie with me—I'd fly over to Ireland and hunt down Mr. Lauderdale. I would just love to shake that boy really hard, or give him a tongue-lashing. It would be worth breaking bones to knock sense into that Scotsman. Not that I was a stalker or the meddlesome type. Heaven forbid I should stoop that low. I'd never stalked anything, man or beast, not even asparagus (did I ever tell you about the time Euell Gibbons was my houseguest? No? Well, I'll just save that for another time). That said, I had been known to interfere in matters of the heart. Which was not the same as stalking.

I slid out of the chair and grabbed my Kelly bag, then hurried toward the back door. Zap ducked his head, and only his topknot was visible. "Wait, Honora," Candice hollered. "Don't run off, I need to rinse you."

"I'll just have to rinse myself." I stepped out of the shop into the windy

March afternoon. I reached inside the bag and patted Zap, who was digging in the bottom of the purse, making odd little growls, then I hurried out to the Bentley.

When I got in the car, I set the bag on the seat, and Zap hopped out, wagging his stubby tail. He glanced at the bag, then at me. That dog knew the routine better than I did. Every time I went to Fairhope—or just anywhere—I took an extra pocketbook, maybe a Jackie O Gucci or a Dior saddlebag, and I tied a little notecard to the strap: "Free to Good Home." Then I released it into the wild. That was how I thought of it, releasing designer handbags into the wild. Today, I'd planned to give up this green ostrich leather Kelly bag. It was very dear, and I loved it. But I was in no shape to set foot in public, what with my hair and all. My friend Isabella believed that I was crazy to release handbags. She couldn't understand that the handbags were better off being loved and used by a stranger than collecting dust in my accessory closet.

"That's just plain silly, Honora," Isabella would cry. "Sell them on eBay! You'll make a small fortune." I tried to explain that it wasn't the money, that it was the joy of giving away a Gucci. Hoarding it on a shelf in my closet only led to a handbag's decline. Well, it really did. They lost their shape and acquired odors.

I drove home and swung the Bentley through the gates. Gathering the Yorkie into my arms, I hurried into the house, thinking about that article and wondering how Renata was holding up. She had just lost her mother, and now she'd lost her sweetheart. She was my only grandchild—well, the only legitimate one. Considering my son Louie's libido, only the Lord knew how many little DeChavanneses were running around greater New Orleans and the Gulf Coast, if not the entire American South. Maybe the world. I just didn't know.

I felt terrible because I hadn't called Renata in weeks, mainly because I'd been planning a big engagement party for her daddy. Louie was getting married for the umpteenth time, and after all Renata had been through, well, I just didn't have the heart to explain. Her relationship with my son was, at best, stilted—but Louie held me at a distance, too. Both Renata and I had been much closer to Shelby. Long ago I had made her a promise that if anything happened during her globe-trotting, I would bring Renata back to Point Clear and attempt to fill in the missing pieces of her childhood.

When I made a promise, I kept it. I might take my time, I might get distracted, but in the end, I would come through. Inside the house, I snatched the portable phone and dialed the cottage in Nags Head. Then I reached up, patting my head, and wondered if the dye would rinse out or if my hair would just break off.

Renata's answering machine clicked on, and I listened to her voice, wondering what in the world I'd say. Probably it was best to keep it light, something like, I am thinking about you, call when you get a chance; but what came out was, "Come home, Renata. You may not have much of a family left, but we love you. And—well, your mother wanted me to tell you some confidential information. Things she meant to tell you. Even if you don't want to hear it, I'd still love to see you. So please, my darling, come home to Point Clear."

Chapter 6

● ● ●

WELCOME TO ALABAMA

I'd just broken one of my ironclad drinking laws, which was never to order an old-fashioned anywhere except in the Deep South, much less thirty-five thousand feet above it. Another was never to exchange sad stories on airplanes, but it looked as if I might smash that rule, too.

From my seat in row five, seat A, I tried to ignore the panicky redheaded woman beside me. The poor thing had downed her second gimlet and had ordered a third. While she waited for the stewardess, she raked magenta fingernails through her hair, which was extremely short and had been dyed a violent, almost hurtful shade of mahogany. Then she reached into the seat pocket and pulled out the laminated US Air safety brochure with its cartoonish illustrations.

"God, I hate flying," she said, fanning herself. "Any minute now we're going to crash."

"No, we're not," I said in a soothing tone. I had an emergency Xanax in my purse, but pure selfishness prevented me from offering it. I might need it later. In the latest tabloids, Ferg and Esmé's romance was being compared to the infamous Burton and Taylor affair. I had seen the magazines at the airport bookstore. Ferg and I weren't engaged, but didn't our three years together count? Well, no. Not in Hollywood, and not around Esmé Vasquez.

Now I straightened my floppy black hat, hoping my hair wasn't visible. Stop dwelling on the past, I told myself. Engagements and marriages broke up every day; people fell in love and died in plane crashes. It wasn't bad luck, it was just part of the phenomena we call life.

*D*uring a two-hour layover in Atlanta, I wandered into a gift shop and stood in front of the candy counter, trying to decide between Skittles and Reese's Pieces. My gaze wandered over to the magazines. The old *National Enquirer* was prominently displayed, showing the infamous thigh-squeeze. I paid for the Skittles and Reese's Pieces, then hurried out of the store, bumping into a pudgy tourist with a camera dangling from his sunburned neck.

"What am I—invisible?" he cried.

"I wish," I muttered.

His eyes narrowed. For a moment, I thought he might slap me. Instead, he raised his camera with one hand and snapped my picture. I apologized, then hurried toward the escalator, toward my gate. The plane was already boarding, and I stood in line, eating Reese's Pieces. When I finally boarded, I was happy to see that my seatmate was an attractive middle-aged woman in a navy business suit. During the short flight, she worked on her laptop. I did not order an old-fashioned. The stewardess threw down little bags of pretzels, then offered lemonade or bottled water.

Before the plane landed in Mobile, the cabin seemed to fill with pungent aromas: chicory coffee, mildew, Tabasco, and Jax beer. Once you inhale the air in the Deep South, you'll never forget it. Maybe it's the moss and brackish water, but the entire region gives off a seminal odor.

Honora stood by the gate, a Louis Vuitton bag slung over her arm. "Darling!" she cried in a Barbara Stanwyck voice. "Over here."

I wrapped my arms around her, pulling her close. "I'm home," I whispered.

"Yes, my darling, you are." She patted my arm.

Two women wearing Talbot pantsuits stepped over to me and shook my hand. "We feel like we know you, Renata," they gushed, slinging their Aigner handbags. "Your boyfriend must be a fool, chasing after that silly woman. She was just horrid in that dog movie. Well, anyway, God bless you. And God bless your sweet little mother, too."

Mother? I thought, then smiled. Honora kissed the women good-bye and escorted me to baggage claim, chitchatting about the Bay Cotillion Club and how she'd just finished the latest John Grisham novel. In typical Honora style, she slipped in a recipe for a five-mushroom tart, then moaned about a strange fungus that was blighting her Siberian irises.

"Don't try to distract me." I laughed, happy to be distracted from my own sordid troubles. "Who were those women in the terminal, Honora? What did you tell them?"

"Hardly anything at all." She smiled. "You would've been proud. I left plenty to the imagination. Speaking of which, I need your ideas for my party. The forsythias have stopped blooming, but you should see my lilacs. They'll look regal in tall crystal vases. We'll just put key limes or maybe brussels sprouts in the bottoms to anchor the stems. Oh, won't it be lovely to have everybody together again?"

I let that pass, because having "everybody together" was impossible. Once, I'd dreamed of bringing Ferg to Mobile Bay and showing him around my grandmother's gardens, taking him floundering along the shore, feeding him authentic southern food. My fantasy had included my mother. All my life, she had tried to make up for my father's lack of interest. In the weeks following her death, I'd hoped to grow closer to my father, but he became even more distant. That was saying a lot. I hadn't thought I would make it after my mother died; losing Ferg this soon after her passing was more than I could stand. Not wanting to upset my grandmother, I turned my head, as if admiring the view, then reached up and wiped away tears.

By the time we'd gathered the luggage and found Honora's Bentley in the parking lot, I was dripping wet. Perspiration slid down the tip of my chin. A warm, gasoline-smelling wind rushed up my nose. Beneath my floppy hat, I could almost feel my damp, butchered hair starting to curl and fray.

This morning, when I'd left Nags Head, a chilly breeze had wafted off the Atlantic, and I'd grabbed a heavy wool turtleneck. Here in Alabama, it was practically summer. On the *Southern Living* map, the state had three different gardening zones. Mobile Bay, along with the entire Gulf Coast, was a sub-tropical Zone 8, which basically meant that everything grew larger: roses, tomatoes, termites.

My grandmother drove her car around the concrete loop, taking up two lanes. She paid the attendant, then headed toward the Eastern Shore. "Do you want to just go home, or shall we sightsee?" she asked. "We can swing by the USS *Alabama*. You're here in time to see the Festival of Flowers, too."

"Let's go home," I said.

"Fabulous idea." Reaching into the backseat, she pulled out a wicker picnic basket. Inside were two crystal glasses, a cold, preopened bottle of Dom Pérignon stuffed into an insulated bag, a tiny Evian bottle, and a tin of Tabasco pecans.

"Will you do the honors?" she asked. "Just water for me. At my age, I can't talk my way out of a DUI. Are you starting to cool down? Add a little ice to your champagne. Speaking of ice, I just reread Dante's *Inferno*."

She leaned forward and twisted the air conditioner knob, then turned up the radio. While Simon and Garfunkel sang "Bridge over Troubled Water," Honora chatted about the weather. "In the last two weeks we've had cold snaps and heat waves. Gladys says that when the humidity rises, the tree frogs speak in tongues. Doesn't that sound just like her? She can't wait to see you ... don't worry about that water, darling. I've changed my mind. Be a dear and fix me a teeny glass of champagne."

"Why didn't Gladys come with you?" I poured a glass of Dom and handed it over. Gladys Boudreaux had been my nanny, but now she worked for Honora.

"She's dog-sitting. I swear that woman never ages," Honora said. "And she's older than me! She's thinking of taking a Pilates class."

She took a sip of champagne, then began to hum. I started to relax. She hadn't mentioned the tabloid, and I wondered if she'd forgotten about it.

"By the way," she said, "I burned that heinous picture of Ferguson. I burned the whole damn *National Enquirer*, and I took great pleasure in it. It's Dantean, the depth people will sink, just to sell a story. But that's just one example of the modern world gone awry."

I poured a dollop of champagne into my glass, and the bubbles tickled my nose. When I was a small girl, I'd felt seasick, listening to Honora's swaying sentences, but now they soothed me in a way I could not explain.

"Don't fret," she said. "I won't badger you about Ferguson." She fiddled with the radio until she found a station playing the standards. When Julie London started singing "Cry Me a River," my grandmother sighed. "Oh, I *do* miss the fifties, even though we didn't have good antibiotics back then. Now, we have better drugs and desserts. That reminds me, there's a new bakery in Fairhope that makes key lime pies with a nut-and-candy crust. The beignets are sweet and dense and chewy. Just the way you like them. Perfect with chocolate almond coffee. We'll go there tomorrow or the next day. I thought about having that bakery cater your daddy's party, but I'd already hired the Grand Hotel."

By the time we reached Fairhope, with its year-round white Christmas lights and red verbena baskets, I'd finished my champagne and was feeling quite cheerful. The same gnarled oaks dotted the road, and I even thought I recognized the people standing on the community pier, waiting for sunset. Behind them, gulls wheeled over the rippled, bronzed water, and farther out, a barge puttered toward Mobile, its engines leaving a wide, foamy wake.

The Bentley sped down the road, past the boutiques and art galleries. Through openings in the trees, I caught glimpses of dark, verdant streets with azaleas poking through wrought-iron fences. If we turned down any of those roads and kept on driving, within minutes we'd be engulfed by wild tangles of kudzu. Just outside this civilized southern town, with its church spires and Dollar Generals, the bayous twisted off like spilled cane syrup, and the thick, moss-choked woods formed a canopy over poisonous snakes and man-eating alligators.

I looked off into the distance and saw the large sign outside Honora's favorite restaurant, Fisherman's Wharf. But the sign read: "GOOD LUCK, RENATA & FERGUSON." Now that's odd, I thought. Odd and disturbing. I couldn't believe that anyone still remembered me, much less had followed my disintegrating romance in the *National Enquirer* et al. My cheeks burned, and I bit down a sharp comment about meddling grandmothers. It was just like Honora to misinform the local gossips, telling them that I was freshly engaged and coming to town with my boyfriend. Then she'd admonish them not to spy on us, because we would be in seclusion at her bayside estate.

Honora gunned the Bentley around the restaurant, and I saw that I had misread the sign. "GOOD LUCK, REGGIE & FERN ANN," it really said. My anger segued into embarrassment as I leaned against the leather seat and wondered if the universe, along with Fisherman's Wharf, was trying to tell me something. Could the sign be a sign? Or maybe I just needed glasses. More likely

I had lived in Hollywood too long, and I'd become like everyone else: I was always on my mind.

Honora was chatting about her garden when the Bentley rolled up to fourteen-foot-high black iron gates. The ironwork was intricate, featuring a hairless donkey and the words *chauve* and *ane*—a motif Honora had devised to counteract her ancestor-worshipping in-laws, who'd insisted they had descended from French royalty.

"These gates get more decrepit each year, but I'll never part with them." She laughed. "They are perfectly over-the-top, and utterly define Chateau DeChavannes, don't you agree?"

"Yes, ma'am," I said, remembering that the house had been named by her social-climbing mother-in-law, Solange DeChavannes, who had clawed her way into the old-money set on the Eastern Shore. All these decades later, Solange's touches remained. I rolled down my window as the Bentley cruised past the sun-spattered green lawn, past hundreds of azaleas. The estate was grandiose and excessive, dwarfing the quieter, more laid-back houses that were visible through the loblolly pines. Tall statues were ensconced in high boxwood niches. The surrounding gardens were French and formal. They had been patterned after Versailles but on a much smaller scale, of course; in the old days, the upkeep had required five full-time gardeners. Several cast-stone fountains had been shipped to Alabama from the Loire Valley, including a statue of Circe that spilled water from her bowl, into a koi pond.

Honora turned up the oyster-shell drive, and I saw the house, beige stucco with green shutters. It wasn't my grandmother's taste. Over the decades, she had tried to obliterate the formality of the old manse. One year she'd added striped awnings, and another she'd planted messy cutting gardens. All renovations had been done under the watchful eye of her old friend, Sister DeBenedetto, a New Orleans interior designer. But no matter what they did, a pretentious aura hovered.

We got out of the Bentley, and I followed her down the walkway, curving around to the stone terrace. The smell of coastal Alabama blew all around me. It was the scent of my childhood—pine needles, sunlight, and sour, brackish water. I took a deep breath, feeling mildly disoriented. After coming from the Outer Banks, Honora's waterfront estate seemed tame and structured, but just the least bit naughty. It wasn't the sort of place where you could start a bonfire and burn your Life's Work, even if it was a shoddy Life's Work. It was the sort of place where you sat in white wicker or Adirondack chairs and got politely (and just barely) drunk on French wine and talked about gardening and hummingbird feeders and the recent Bay Cotillion Club meeting and who wore what and who was sleeping with the tennis pro and who was spending too much time with Jim Beam.

When I started up the terrace steps, I caught my first glimpse of Mobile Bay. The sun almost touched the water, turning it brassy and gold. These shallow waters were at the mercy of every weather system that traipsed through the Gulf of Mexico, but the sight of it could just about break my heart. "Three weeks ago it got down to twenty-eight degrees," Honora was saying. "Gladys and I scrambled to cover up the daffodils, and still, we lost a few."

There, at the end of the terrace, I saw Gladys Boudreaux standing on the pier, tossing French bread up to the gulls. As long as I could remember this dock had been patrolled by the birds. They would materialize during meals, hovering from a discreet distance, waiting for us to toss up a biscuit or hunk of corn bread. Honora's neurotic Yorkie walked on his hind legs, snapping at the gulls. When he saw me, he let out a howl and ducked between Gladys's legs. She tossed a handful of bread into the air, and the gulls descended. It could have been a scene straight out of a Hitchcock film. Gladys threw up more bread, and her yellow floral dress rippled around her knees. Her hair was dark and undyed, and it fell stick-straight in the same short pageboy she'd worn for the last twenty years. No one really knew Gladys's age, but she'd once admitted to being older than my grandmother.

She opened her arms, and I ran down the pier. Zap barked and ran in circles. Gladys tugged the brim of my black hat, then rubbed her rough hands over my shoulders.

"It's so good to see you, baby," she said.

Honora came up the dock, and the little dog lowered his head and sped over to her, a black-and-tan streak across the grass. The wind sucked up my hat, and it cartwheeled along the terrace, into the yard. Zap leaped into the thick St. Augustine grass, and snatched up the hat and shook it.

Honora's eyes rounded as she watched me run my fingers through my hair.

"What got hold of you?" Gladys reached out to touch my hair, then drew back.

"A freak accident," I said, and told them about the scissor-happy clerk at Nags Head, followed by my lost cell phone, the midnight bonfire, and the mixed-up FedEx envelopes.

"Don't you fret," said Honora. "Andy and Shelby left you comfortable. You won't have to write any more screenplays."

"Well, I'm *going* to." I tried to smooth back my hair. "If I remember how."

"You'll remember." Honora whistled to the Yorkie. His ears perked up, then he dragged the hat over to her. She bent down and straightened his top-knot. "Give it to Renata, that's right, good Zapper."

"He don't understand a word you're saying," Gladys scoffed.

"Au contraire," said Honora. The Yorkie stepped toward me, then glanced back at my grandmother. She nodded, and he trotted over, dropping the hat at my feet. I wiped off the spittle, then jammed the hat over my head.

"Much better," said Honora. "And the extra weight suits you."

"Speaking of which, I made your favorite supper," said Gladys. "Shrimp creole and rice and garlic French bread."

I put my arms around them, happy to be home, where food obsessions and animal worship seemed normal. They cooked the way they lived, with abandon, verve, and a bit of mystery. No telling what these women might serve—shrimp, scandals, long-lost secrets. I was ready for anything.

Chapter 7

✹ ✹ ✹

A Pretty Face

I stepped into the kitchen and smelled contrasting aromas: lemon, garlic, shellfish, and browning bread, all of it floating in a cloud of well-seasoned tomato sauce. Honora had remodeled the room two years ago, after Hurricane Georges sent a tree crashing through the roof. I ran my hand along the weathered, celery-washed kitchen cabinets. Fashioned to resemble old armoires and chests, the cabinet doors were fitted with heavy bronze hardware. They had been made in England, banged up with chains to give the "aged" look, then shipped across the water. For a week they were accidentally quarantined, but everyone agreed the cabinets had been worth the wait.

While Honora slipped a Cole Porter CD into the player, I followed Gladys into the dining room, helping her light candles. She had set out the Limoges and the Francis First silver. "I have missed you so much, baby." Gladys blew out the match, then pulled me into a hug. "Did Honora tell you that we burned that damn gossip magazine? The one with your honey in it?"

I laughed. "So did I."

"That fool boy." Gladys bristled. "Well, you're home now, and it's best you just put him right out of your mind. We won't even say his name. Let's get Honora in here before she feeds all the shrimps to that damn dog."

After supper, Honora set out a carton of Ben and Jerry's vanilla bean ice cream. While it softened, she poured espresso beans into a grinder.

"Before I leave Point Clear, I'll weigh a thousand pounds," I said.

"Already talking about leaving, and you just got here." Honora chuckled. "Your mother loved this dessert. She used to serve it at dinner parties. It's not low-calorie, but it's simple yet elegant."

She piled the ice cream into three crystal bowls and sprinkled the espresso powder over the top. Then she licked the spoon, leaving a white streak on her tongue. "When Shelby was pregnant with you, she craved ice cream and fried okra. Not together, of course. Your daddy kept her well supplied. Now *that* man has no favorite foods. I swear, Louie will eat and drink anything. Did you know that he's learned how to make pepper jelly in his old age?"

I shrugged. I hadn't heard from him in months.

"I shouldn't be surprised," said Honora. "He always loved to cook. When you were little and got a cold, he'd make a huge pot of chicken soup. He'd chop the garlic and onion real fine, so you wouldn't make a fuss. You just hated vegetables!"

After dessert, Gladys couldn't stop yawning, so she kissed us good night and went upstairs. Honora poured Courvoisier into crystal balloons, and I followed her into the mahogany-paneled library, the dog's toenails snicking on the wood. This room had been added by my great-grandmother in 1942, the year my father was born. It was dark and forbidding, even with lamps burning. I sank down on the green chintz sofa, tucking my bare foot beneath my hips. Then I hunched my shoulders, waiting for her to start quizzing me about my troubles with Ferg. I had been expecting her to pounce ever since she'd picked me up at the airport. Zap jumped onto the sofa and flopped his head onto my knee, his brown eyes gazing out from tufts of tan-and-silver fur.

Hoping to distract my grandmother, I rubbed the dog's ears, then said, "When I was little, this room horrified me."

"It had the same effect on your father." Honora touched the glass to her lips. Then she walked over to the carved Jacobean table where silver-framed photographs were artfully arranged on the polished wood. She leaned over, staring down at the pictures with the same intensity I'd seen her give cantaloupes at the A&P.

"Gladys and I were cleaning the old wine cellar, and we found a box of pictures," she said. "Water had ruined some, but I was able to restore most of them." She lifted a small, ornate frame and brought it over to me. "Have you seen this one? Your father was two days old when it was taken. My mother-in-law hired a portrait photographer from Mobile. That was vintage Solange, excessive in every way. It was against the hospital rules for anyone to get near the newborns. Solange just bribed the nurses. But the picture didn't turn out, so she must have hidden it."

She sat down on the edge of the sofa, and I leaned over to study the photograph. My two-day-old father glared back at me with puffy eyes. One dark eyebrow stretched across the elongated forehead. His tiny fists were pressed against his ears, as if trying to shut out a disgusting conversation. Thick black hair stuck out in tufts all over his head, and his tongue protruded from swollen lips.

"Wow," I said, "are you sure this is my daddy?"

"Positive," said Honora.

"He looks absolutely—" I broke off, searching for the right word.

"Ratlike?" Honora lifted one eyebrow.

"No, I was going to say furious."

"I loved him the minute I saw him, but Chaz cried. My sister-in-law thought the nurses had mixed up the babies."

"Aunt Na-Na would think that," I said.

"It was those strong DeChavannes genes." She set down her brandy, then slid off the sofa and walked to the bookcase. Opening a cabinet, she reached into a crevice and pulled out a white leather album. "Our Baby" was written on the front in gold letters. She carried it over to the sofa and sat down next to Zap. The leather spine cracked when she turned a page. Baby Louie's milestones were documented in Honora's spidery handwriting, augmented with black-and-white snapshots.

"I haven't looked at this album in years." She stared down at a picture, then quickly turned the page. I caught glimpses of Honora's entries—"First Solid Food—Gerber strained peaches, December 12, 1942, 7:30 A.M." Immunizations were listed, dated, and annotated. "Cried all night and ran 100.2 temperature!"

"It's so detailed," I said. "Like a documentary."

"Louie hated it. I kept it hidden, or he would have thrown it into Mobile Bay."

"Seriously?"

"He didn't see it as a doting mother's memory book. He saw it as the record of an ugly-duckling childhood."

"Daddy wasn't ugly. That old baby picture doesn't count."

"He was an intense-looking baby, fierce and Gallic." She flipped to the middle of the album and pointed to a dark, thin boy-child kneeling in front of a Christmas tree.

"*That's* Daddy?" I asked.

"He was three years old and still quite strange looking. Those dark eyebrows dominated his face. Nowadays they call it a unibrow."

She turned a page and rubbed her finger over a picture of an older Louie posing next to a bicycle. "When he was four years old, he fell off this bicycle. The training wheels got caught in a hole, and flipped him over. He landed on his forehead. It knocked him out. Chaz and I rushed him to the hospital. They x-rayed every inch of that child's body. The skull wasn't broken, but he'd suffered a concussion. A week later he was running around like nothing had happened, except for one thing—he stuttered. The accident had somehow hurt his brain, and he stuttered for the next sixteen years, even with the best speech therapists. Chaz said it was an injury to the frontal lobe."

"I've never heard so much as a blip in his speech," I said.

"No, he conquered it by singing his words. Now, when he's tired, he'll stutter a little. If you didn't know better, you'd think he was drunk."

I pointed to a photograph of a dark, skinny teenage boy. "This doesn't even look like my father," I said.

"It's the strangest thing," said Honora. "When Louie went through puberty, his face changed daily. The teardrop nose dwarfed the rest of his features. Or it was dotted with blackheads. One summer he grew five inches, and it was all in his legs. The stuttering reached a crescendo. And of course, he couldn't even talk on the phone. He still doesn't like talking on it. Girls didn't like him. But he did manage to get a date for the senior prom. Then the girl came down with mononucleosis and couldn't go. Louie went by himself. A lot of boys would have stayed home, but not Louie.

"Everything came together when he turned twenty-one. Nothing magic about that age, by the way, it was just his time to be gorgeous. The funny-looking child had vanished. Louie had my father's aristocratic cheekbones mixed in with the DeChavannes Frenchness. His dark looks juxtaposed against his white uniform was striking. It was more than the average woman could bear. Yet it was more than looks. The old manners of his childhood were perfected. Opening doors, pulling out chairs, ladies first. The women went wild, phoning him all hours of the night, waiting outside the hospital. Begging him to have a drink, even offering to have his baby."

"Daddy had groupies?" I smiled.

"Did he ever. Especially after *New Orleans Life* put him on the cover of their magazine. The caption read, 'Crescent City's Heart Throb: Dr. Louie DeChavannes Is More Than a Pretty Face.' When the article came out, he acted like it didn't exist. Everybody thought he was humble and gracious, but I knew the real story. When he looked in the mirror, he'd frown, as if he saw nothing but eyebrows."

"I had no idea," I said.

"Most people don't." She turned the page, then bent closer to a faded color photograph of four women. She slid her fingernail down the sides of the picture, loosening the glue, then pulled it up and handed it to me.

"I don't know how this got in here," she said. "It's me, your mother, Gladys, and Isabella."

"Y'all look so young." I turned over the picture, and someone had written, "Beached Mermaids, 1977." Each woman sat on a different color beach towel—three blondes, with Gladys the lone brunette. Behind the beach, Chateau DeChavannes rose up, resembling a giant sand castle. The women smiled straight into the camera. I couldn't remember them sunbathing, but I did know how they acted when they were together. They talked nonstop, their voices distinct as thumbprints.

"We were young," said Honora. "Time is a bitch."

I bent closer. Honora wore a black one-piece suit and a black straw hat. Her skin was pale, and her large breasts spilled out of her cleavage into a V. Mother's yellow polka dot bikini barely covered her dainty parts. Her long blond hair was pulled into a ponytail, and it streamed down her right shoulder. Gladys wore a pink floral housedress and looked grumpy. Isabella D'Agostino wore black sunglasses, a red two-piece, and all of her jewelry. Her hair was pulled back with a red geometric scarf, and she held a cigarette in her left hand. Isabella had always fascinated me. She was a native of Fairhope, Alabama, but she'd gone to Hollywood in the 1960s and gotten famous. She'd enjoyed brief popularity costarring in romantic comedies alongside Doris Day, Rock Hudson, and James Garner. Isabella specialized in playing stodgy, insufferable bitches, but at the height of her fame, she came home to Alabama, married a wealthy Alabama man, and abandoned her career.

Finally I said, "Who took the picture?"

"Why, you did, baby doll," she said. "You did."

Honora shooed me upstairs to the New Orleans Room, with its muted yellow walls and lilac silk curtains. On the night table, Gladys had set out ice water in a crystal carafe, along with pecan pralines wrapped in cellophane and tied with a purple bow. My luggage had been unpacked. My clothes were neatly stacked in the drawers, with rose petal sachets tucked between the layers. A white cotton nightgown with pink ribbons was laid across a chair.

As I got ready for bed, my head swirled with brandy, shrimp creole, lost love, tabloid stories, and my father's baby book. After my parents were divorced, Honora had apparently taken my mother's side. "You'd think Shelby and Honora were mother and daughter," Daddy would complain.

When I'd gotten older, I'd demanded to know what had happened, but my mother would always put me off, saying she'd explain one day. In some ways her life and mine seemed to begin after she married Andy VanDusen and we moved to California. Every summer, she sent me to Point Clear, Alabama, to visit Honora, but I rarely saw my daddy. Louie was a cardiovascular surgeon in New Orleans, and a gifted one. He blamed his absences on his profession. Honora refused to accept my father's lack of interest and badgered him with phone calls and letters, setting up father-daughter dates. Louie would promise to pick me up at four p.m., and I would sit on Honora's marble staircase, my petticoats itching my legs. Outside, through the beveled glass doors, the sky would change from blue to gray to navy, then black. The whole time, Honora would be calling his answering service and every hospital and bar in New Orleans.

If he'd been left to his own devices, I wouldn't have ever seen the man, but he was more afraid of angering his mother than he was of being a terrible father. He would eventually show up—sometimes with a woman, sometimes alone, and always full of I'm-sorrys and plausible excuses. He'd bring a bouquet that he'd hastily bought at Delchamps, or a couple of helium balloons painted with garish cartoon faces and printed with inappropriate greetings, such as "Get Well Soon!" or "Congratulations on your baby boy!" His every gesture said, *See? I'm trying to love you, trying to pay attention*; but my cruel, childish self knew that he longed to be elsewhere.

I only heard from him at Christmas, and I was always the one who phoned. On my birthdays, I received a gift and a card, but I recognized Honora's handwriting. For my sixteenth birthday, he'd presented me with a pearl necklace that my grandmother had personally selected, but I treasured those pearls. Honora described my daddy as loving but neglectful. He was a workaholic, a backsliding Catholic, and a sports fanatic. He had season tickets to the Saints games and never missed a home LSU game if he could help it.

Me, I despised golf, tennis, soccer, football. If it had a ball, you could be sure I'd hate it. I preferred to read Nancy Drew or to rearrange my grandmother's majolica dogs, or to help Gladys plant herbs or deadhead the five-acre rose garden. Not only that, my mother and Honora dressed me in pastel voile. My wardrobe must have been a subliminal blow. My big, dark, masculine father holding an ugly, squirming baby girl, dressed head to toe in ruffles. I knew this was true, because I had seen pictures. I really was an odd-looking girl-child. My mother's dainty features had blended unhappily with the thick, Gallic DeChavannes bone structure. I was only five feet four, but I had enormous feet with little crooked toes shaped like overripe blueberries. My fingers were fat, and I had a broad, ugly chin; but the finishing touch was the famous teardrop DeChavannes nose, which was too big and witchy for my childish face.

After my father's third marriage broke up, I stopped going to Alabama, and I spent blissful summers at Nags Head. I would introduce myself to the summer children—and later, to boys—as Renata VanDusen, eliminating the DeChavannes. However, my mother refused to let me drift away from my daddy's people. She invited my grandmother, Isabella, and Gladys Boudreaux to join us at the Outer Banks.

People often mistook us for a real family, and we never corrected them. The fact that Mama had been married to Honora's son didn't matter to Andy. Anyone my mama loved, Andy automatically loved, too. Honora, Gladys, and

Isabella would roar up the sandy driveway in the old Bentley that resembled a tank. Andy would put on an apron and boil a pot of crabs. He and Isabella would exchange gossip and tell outrageous stories about famous actors.

"Let's toast Hollywood," she'd say, raising her drink.

"To Hollywood," Andy would say, clinking his glass against hers.

"Are you sorry you left Hollywood?" I asked her.

"Me?" Isabella laughed. "Not one little bit. Why, if I hadn't retired, I wouldn't have returned to Alabama, and your mama wouldn't have met Andy."

"Let's drink to fate," he said, raising his glass. "Fate and true love and happy ever afters."

Chapter 8

@ @ @

GRITS AND REVELATIONS

he next morning I examined my haircut in the bathroom mirror. Short, cowlicked hairs stuck out of the left side of my head, making me think of an old movie, *Ryan's Daughter*. I resembled the actress Sara Miles after the Irish villagers had whacked off her hair for sleeping with the peglegged (but gorgeous) English officer. The right side of my head looked the same as always, a sort of dark blond, shoulder-length Bride of Frankenstein.

I found scissors in the vanity drawer and went to work on the lopsided Mohawk. Then I squirted grapefruit-scented mousse into my palm and rubbed it over the spiky tips. Satisfied with my handiwork, I changed into gray sweatpants and a white cotton shirt that smelled faintly of Ferg—Aramis, tobacco, and single-malt whisky.

On my way out of the room, I bumped into the carved French dresser, overturning a silver picture frame. It was an old photograph of me and my daddy. I looked to be three or four years old. I wore a stiff, frilly pink bonnet that tied under my chin.

Tilting the picture closer, I searched for details. Inside the bonnet, dark blond bangs covered my eyebrows, and my eyes held the same fierce glint that I'd seen in my daddy's baby pictures. He was kneeling beside me, his hands gripping my chest, as if restraining me; perhaps he was steadying himself. Parked between us was a straw Easter basket, brimming over with green shredded cellophane grass, all of it dotted with pastel eggs, jelly beans, and Elmer's Gold Bricks.

I traced my finger over Daddy's hair, a 1970s style with heavy bangs that fell over his eyebrows. His smile was crooked, sardonic, and utterly familiar. I was looking at the photographer, but my father was staring at something or someone just off to the side. Behind us, the sun hovered over Mobile Bay, staining the water orange. Oh, Daddy, I thought. Why couldn't you love me? What did I do wrong?

I set the frame on the dresser. Reaching into my tote, I pulled out my mother's aqua letter, leaving the small packet of seeds; I slipped it into my pocket and headed downstairs for coffee. Gladys and Honora were sitting at the cherry table, morning sun spearing through the beige floral curtains. My grandmother traced a bottle of Elmer's Glue along the edges of a white card. Gladys lifted a coffee cup and turned a page of the *Mobile Register*. Next to her elbow was an untouched bran muffin and an eviscerated grapefruit half. She wore the same frayed chenille robe that I'd given her in 1975; but Honora was dressed in a beige Chanel suit. I glanced over her shoulder, watching her press the white card into her book. It was the invitation to Daddy's party.

• PLEASE JOIN US FOR COCKTAILS •
In Honor of

Dr. Louis DeChavannes and Miss Joie Mayfield

Friday, March 14, 2000
Seven O'Clock
at the home of Honora Hughes DeChavannes
394 Scenic Highway
Point Clear, Alabama
RSVP

She glanced up, scowling. "Goodness, your hair is so short," she said. "Did the rats chew it off in the night?"

"Well, I think it's cute," said Gladys. "Did you go to an all-night salon and get fixed up?"

"Good morning, lovelies," I said, pouring coffee into a donkey-shaped mug. For the first time in days, my hand was steady. Coming back to Alabama was going to be a tonic.

"It makes your eyes show up," said Gladys.

"I wouldn't go that far," said Honora. "Renata, let me call Salon du Jour. A few highlights around your face would make a world of difference."

"There's nothing to highlight." I tugged at the ends of my hair, then carried my mug over to the table. I sat down and glanced at Honora's book. "What's that?"

"The invitation to your father's engagement party." She tilted the book in my direction.

"Nice paper, but the wording is cryptic," I said.

"Isn't it though?" Honora smiled, then laid the book out in the sun. She got up from the table, pausing to smooth down my hair, then pulled a bulging black Hefty bag out of the pantry and dragged it over to the door. Zap shot out from beneath Gladys's chair, head ducked, and trotted over to the bag and lifted his hind leg.

"Don't you dare pee on my designer handbags," Honora scolded, and he slunk off.

"Are you still releasing pocketbooks into the wild?" I asked.

"They're handbags, not pocketbooks." Honora opened the refrigerator, shifting a few bottles, then reached for a yellow plastic squeeze lemon. "If you won't let me call the beauty parlor, then squirt lemon juice on your crew cut and go sit in the sun for a few years."

"I haven't had breakfast." I yawned.

"I'll bring you a bowl of Special K."

"I was hoping for cheese grits and sausage."

"How about a omelet?" Gladys asked. Zapper stood on his hind legs, his dark eyes watching her hands. She pinched off a piece of muffin and dropped it on the floor. The Yorkie snapped it up.

"She'd be better off with Slim-Fast," said Honora. "With hair that short, the girl needs diversionary tactics. Like cheekbones."

"Or a wig," said Gladys, throwing down another hunk of muffin.

"Don't you want to look fabulous tomorrow night for the party? Of course you do. So, run on outside and douse yourself in lemon juice. Gladys will bring you a healthy breakfast. I'd love to chat, but I'm late for my canasta game." She glanced at her watch, a vintage Cartier Tank. "Where is that damn Isabella? She was supposed to be here fifteen minutes ago."

My grandmother tugged at her suit, then picked up a beige Ferragamo bag and slung it over her wrist. "Did I hear Isabella's car drive up, or did I imagine it? She's going to make us late."

"No, I'm afraid she's here." Gladys rolled her eyes.

Zap spun in circles, then trotted over to the French doors. He stood on his hind legs and sniffed as the doors whooshed open, and Isabella D'Agostino McGeehee stepped into the room. The breeze stirred her long paisley skirt and sheer, bell-sleeved blouse.

"You look like a Roberto Cavalli model," I called.

"I'm tall enough for one," she said. Tossing back her long blond hair, she strode over to me, her alligator pumps clicking on the limestone floor. She gripped my elbow and air-kissed my cheeks. "You look pretty damn good for someone who's in the middle of a scandal."

"Thanks."

"Tell me *all* about it, dahling." Isabella smiled. Back in the late 1950s and early '60s, her full curvaceous lips had bewitched American and European film audiences. Then she gave it all up and came home to Alabama to marry the very rich, but sickly Dickie Boy McGeehee.

"Y'all don't have time for chitchat," said Gladys.

"Just one question for Renata. Has Honora filled you in about your father and his new lady love?" Isabella raised one dark blond eyebrow. "Her name is Joie Mayfield; and when you meet her, *do* take care how you pronounce her name. You say it like the French textile, *toile du joie*."

"You make her sound like a tart," said Honora.

"She *is* one," Isabella sniffed.

"Joie is a perfectly respectable third-grade teacher over in Pensacola. And she isn't a gold digger, either. Her daddy was one of the wealthiest men in the Panhandle. He owned M. B. Mayfield Produce and Seafood."

"But isn't she about five years old?" Isabella lit a cigarette.

"In dog years," said Gladys.

"Well, you've got to admit that it looks odd when any twenty-something girl shows up on the wrinkled arm of a fifty-nine-year-old man," said Isabella. "I bet Louie's taking Viagra like M&Ms."

"Maybe she's feeding it to him." Gladys laughed.

"We'll discuss this later." Honora pointed to her watch. "I wanted to release a couple of handbags before the canasta game, but now we don't have time."

"I'll make time." Isabella pointed to the Hefty bag. "Grab your booty, and let's go."

After Isabella and Honora drove off, I gathered up the squeeze lemon, then wandered outside to the sunny terrace and sat down in the chaise. I had a view of the narrow beach, where sandpipers ran along the surf. Farther out, a blue heron stood in the shallows.

Gladys stepped onto the terrace, gripping a black tole tray. She set it down with a flourish on the iron table. I leaned over, breathing in the fatty aromas. Melted butter skated over the grits, next to fat, red sausage hunks. Two biscuits lay open like clamshells, each half drizzled with cane syrup. The little Yorkie ran over to the table, lifted one paw, and sniffed. He gave an impatient snort, then danced around my chaise, his pink tongue sliding between his incisors.

"You doing all right, baby?"

"Not really," I said, then I burst into tears. "Oh, Gladys, I'm so worried about Ferg. I waited so long to find him, and I'm afraid he's gone."

"Don't cry, baby." She drew me into her arms. "No man is worth all these tears."

"You don't know Ferg."

"I know *you*." She stepped back, squeezing my shoulder. "And you are your mama made over. You will find a way to get over this."

"That reminds me," I said, and pulled my mother's letter out of my pocket. When Gladys saw it, her hand slapped against her bosom, feeling for her reading glasses, which hung from a beaded chain.

"Your mama always meant to tell what happened to her and Louie." Gladys looked off toward the bay, then reached up and wiped her nose. "She meant to explain, but she was fierce about protecting you."

"Protect me from what?" I asked.

"Pain, honey. Nothing but pain. It goes back to her girlhood. She and her sister had burdens no children should have. Shelby swore that you wouldn't be pulled down by her mistakes."

"Whoa, hold on, Gladys. I think you're confused. Mama didn't have a sister."

"Yes, she did." Gladys nodded. "An older sister named Abigail."

"You're getting Mama mixed up with somebody else." I reached for the bowl of grits, wondering if she'd suffered a light stroke.

"I'm not mixing up a thing. I'm just trying to fill in the background. Shelby's childhood marked her. And it shaped how you was raised."

"If Mama had a sister," I said, spooning grits into my mouth, "she wouldn't have hidden her, she would have told me."

"She wasn't hiding her. Abigail died before you was born."

"This doesn't make sense. I would have seen that name in the family Bible."

"Abigail *was* in the family Bible. The one at your Granddaddy Stevens's house over in Covington. I know this for a fact. See, before I raised you, I raised your mama and Abigail. And I also took especial care of Shelby's crazy mama."

"Wait a minute, back up." I waved my spoon. "I'm confused. First, you tell me I've got a dead aunt and then you say my mama's mama was insane?"

"I know it's a lot to take in. But the important thing is this: if Shelby had told you about Abigail, then she would have been forced to tell you the rest of the story. Your mama's big fear was that she'd turn into *her* mama." Gladys slipped her hand around my shoulder. "Hearing it from me won't be the same. Your mama would have told it better, and truer; but she can't. That leaves me, baby. I'm ready to talk—if you're ready to listen."

Chapter 9

⊙ ⊙ ⊙

GLADYS BOUDREAUX SAYS,
IT ALL STARTED WITH A BEAR

I came into Shelby's life in 1954, after my husband, Dolph, shot a black bear up near the Mississippi state line. Two witnesses seen it happen, and they wrote down my husband's license tags. By the time the police and game warden showed up, Dolph was long gone from those woods. And so was the bear. A week later they tracked Dolph to our shotgun house. He was sitting on the porch, cracking pecans for a pie I was making. The police didn't give him time to put on his shoes. They handcuffed him and then threw him against the squad car. Split his lip and blacked both of his eyes.

"What bear?" Dolph kept saying while they punched him. "I don't know about no bear."

I asked around, and people told me to hire Thaddeus Stevens. His law office was over the Western Auto. It was late August, hot as blazes, and when the secretary showed me into the office, I was pleased to see a rotary fan riffling the papers on Mr. Stevens's desk. He was talking on the phone, and he lifted one finger, as if to say, Be right with you.

I glanced around at the knotty wood paneling where dozens of mounted animal heads and humongous fishes stared down at me. I knew then I'd found me the right lawyer. I opened my purse and dug out all the money I had—fifteen dollars and sixty-seven cents from cleaning rooms at the Driftwood Motel over by the lake. I had give the rest to Dolph, but the police had tooken it.

"I don't need any money," said Mr. Stevens. He'd never known anybody who'd killed a actual bear, and it tickled his fancy. He told me not to fret, he'd take care of things. "Just tell me one thing," said Mr. Stevens. "Where's the bear?"

I played with the handle of my pocketbook, twisting it back and forth, wondering if I could trust him, this gray-eyed man. Nailed to the wall above his head was the biggest catfish I ever saw. Next to it was a twelve-point buck. Its glassy eyes looked sad.

Mr. Stevens watched me stare at the dead animals. Then he said, "Anything you or Mr. Boudreaux tell me is privileged. That means that as your lawyer, I cannot—and will not—tell anybody. Believe you me, it's in both our interests for me to keep this information confidential."

I told him that Dolph threw the bear into the back of his truck and drove it to his sister's house in Mississippi. She didn't want to put the bear in her deep freeze, but Dolph made her.

Mr. Stevens whistled, then he leaned across the desk. "Must've been a big freezer?"

"Yes, sir. When all this blows over, Dolph wants to make a bearskin rug, complete with the head and teeth."

"I want to see this rug," said Mr. Stevens, laughing.

The judge scheduled to hear the case was Mr. Stevens's fishing buddy, but he had pneumonia, and they brought in a judge from another parish. He ordered Dolph to say what he'd done with the bear carcass. Dolph said he reckoned another wild animal dragged it off. Then he said it could've been another hunter. He got sent to Angola Prison.

Mr. Stevens felt terrible and offered me a job. "I've got two little girls, and my wife is sickly," he said. "We could use live-in help. I'd pay you good, and you could stay in the guest room. Well, just think about it. But I'd sure appreciate any help you could give."

I wanted to ask what kind of sickness she had, and if it was catching. I dabbed my eyes with a handkerchief. "Well, I reckon I could go with you," I said. I followed him out to a green Cadillac. He drove one block away from Lake Pontchartrain and turned into a sandy driveway, all strewn with pine needles. I saw a red brick house with white shutters, not any flowerbeds.

Maybe they did need help. I could stay here awhile and save my money. Plus, I could walk to town on my day off.

He led me into a sunny yellow and purple kitchen where checked curtains sucked against the screens, bringing in the heat and smell of late summer. A wooden footstool was pushed up to the sink, and I wondered if the wife was also a short woman. Down the hall, I heard the TV. Roy Rogers and Trigger was having an adventure. Mr. Stevens waved his arm. "My wife loves the colors of Mardi Gras."

"It's lively, all right." I glanced at the purple dishes stacked in the cabinet. "And clean."

"My daughters see to that." He poked his head into the hall and whistled out. "Girls? Come on out, I want you to meet somebody." He turned back to me. "The extra bedroom might need airing out. Just tell me what you need in the way of sheets or pillows. Or if you want to paint the walls, just say the word."

Two little blond-headed girls appeared in the doorway. "Girls, I want y'all to meet Mrs. Gladys Boudreaux. She's going to take care of things." The taller girl, Abigail, wore thick eyeglasses; the short one, Shelby, had round gray eyes and a little turned-up nose. The girls shook my hand and said pleased to meet you and whatnot, real polite but in a weary, grown-up way.

Mr. Stevens led me down the hall. Here, it was dark and smelled dank. I stepped past pecan shelves that was crammed with books and silver trophies and pictures of a pretty blond woman in a tiara. A banner across her chest read, "Miss Louisiana." He stopped at a door and knocked twice. "Emma Gail, honey? I found somebody to help around the house, and I'd like to introduce y'all. Can you come to the door a minute?"

Inside, I heard a scrabbling noise. I just stood there, looking straight ahead. The door cracked open, and the stench of cigarette smoke and Vicks VapoRub hit me. A woman stuck out her head. It was X'd with pincurls. She looked thin, all weak-eyed and sickly. Behind her, the room was piled high with junk and clothes. There was no room to walk, just little pathways to the bed. Mr. Stevens made the introductions, and when I shook his wife's warm, damp hand, I did not think she was long for this world. Those poor little girls would soon be motherless.

After Mr. Stevens drove back to his office, the little girls helped clean my room. They bustled around like grown women, dragging out the Electrolux, flinging open windows, ripping off the sheets. A sick parent will do that to a child. Later, we walked to town and bought a cartload of groceries. The girls showed me how to charge it to the Stevens account.

I found a pressure cooker in a cabinet, and I made a pot of chicken gumbo. I fixed a right nice tray for Emma. Shelby wanted to take it to her mama, but I said, "Maybe she can join us in the kitchen."

"Mama can't leave her room," said Abigail.

"I can carry her. I'm a stout woman," I said, wondering if Mrs. Stevens had been struck with polio. "Let's find her a comfortable chair."

"It's not that." Abigail stared at the floor. "She can walk. She just likes to stay in her room."

"All right, then," I said, but I didn't understand. Abigail picked up the tray, and from outside, I heard music. I peeked out the window and saw a white ice cream truck with a great big fake Creamsicle on the roof. "Y'all better hurry up and get y'all a Popsicle," I said.

Shelby's cheeks turned red, and Abigail said, "We can't eat sweets."

"Plus, we don't have money," Shelby added.

"How much is it?" I reached for my pocketbook.

"A nickel," said Abigail, setting the tray on the table. "But I already told you Mama doesn't allow desserts."

"Once won't hurt," I said, and pushed open the screen door with my hip. "Here's enough money for you both—but hurry! Y'all are going to miss him. You better run!"

They walked into the yard all stifflike, but when they saw that the truck was leaving, they broke into a run. The truck wheeled over to the side of the road. I went back inside, picked up the tray, and carried it down the hall, trying to walk slow to keep the dishes from rattling. Her door wasn't pulled to all the way. "Mrs. Stevens, I brought you some chicken gumbo," I called.

"Come in," she called.

I nudged the door with my shoe, and it swung open. I stepped into that smelly sick room. Golden light seeped through the venetian blinds, spearing through cigarette smoke. She was stretched out on the bed, the sheets mismatched and wrinkled.

Above the bed hung a picture showing a mermaid sitting on a rock, combing her hair.

"Just set the tray on the dresser." Mrs. Stevens lifted one bony hand and pointed. "And thanks. What did you say your name was?"

"Gladys Boudreaux." With my elbow, I pushed aside empty teacups and made a place for the tray. I tried to guess her age—thirty-five? Forty? But that couldn't be right, not if she was the lady in the Miss Louisiana picture.

"I'm Emma. And don't worry, you can't catch what I've got," she said. "My trouble is in the brain."

"A tumor?" I asked, then clapped my hand over my mouth.

"Heavens, no." She fingered a pin curl. "I just have conniption fits when I leave this room. I can't stand open places. I'll shake and vomit. Actually, I'd rather have a tumor."

"Yes, ma'am."

"You don't understand, do you? Well, I'll explain. First, you have to know how a small town works. The worst thing you can be is crazy. Tuberculosis, they understand. So, a long time ago, I started a rumor on myself, and now everybody thinks I've got a fatal disease. Sickness doesn't cause vicious gossip if people know what you've got."

"Yes, ma'am," I said again. It wasn't my place to judge, and I didn't. She kept on talking, claiming she'd been drove crazy by Mr. Stevens himself. When he wasn't at his law office, he was at the hunting camp or fishing down at Grand Isle. He would go off with judges, lawyers, buddies from high school. He hadn't been present at the birth of either child. With Abigail, he was quail hunting, and when Shelby was born, he was deep-sea fishing in Biloxi. He couldn't remember Christmas presents, Easter baskets, birthdays, anniversaries. He was no good in bed, couldn't get it up half the time, and when he did, it was over in three minutes.

From the hallway, I heard a sniffling noise. I turned and saw the girls. Abigail was licking her Creamsicle, but Shelby had finished hers and was chewing the stick.

"I've told y'all not to eavesdrop!" Emma clapped her hands. "And where did y'all get that ice cream?"

"I bought it for them," I said.

"Gladys, you shouldn't have." Two lines creased Emma's forehead. "My girls aren't allowed to eat sweets."

"Please don't talk ugly to Gladys," said Shelby.

"I wasn't talking ugly, and even if I was, I can't help what I say. I'm a lunatic, my mama was a lunatic, and so was her mama. Before it's over, you girls will be just like me."

"I'll never be like you!" Shelby threw down her Popsicle stick, then took off running.

"Oh, yes, you will," called Emma, the veins standing out on her neck. "You can't escape it."

I measured time by the holidays. Not only did Halloween pass us by, so did the trick-or-treaters. For Thanksgiving, I pan-fried quail that Mr. Stevens had shot. Christmas almost rolled by, but not before I made him buy those girls a tree. They'd not had one since they were itty-bitty babies. By Easter the girls' faces had filled out. Mr. Stevens took Emma's old wood-paneled station wagon off the concrete blocks, where it had been setting in the side yard for Lord knows how many years, and taught me how to drive. I had never drove Dolph's old truck, and even if I'd wanted to, the police had done towed it off for evidence.

Driving sure did come in handy, because every week the Stevens girls got one invitation or another. This surprised me, but Emma explained that Mr. Stevens's family was old and respected, and just because she was an invalid, it didn't cast a full shadow on those girls. They didn't have overnight guests; in fact, they didn't have no company. But they was invited to birthday and slumber parties, hayrides and scavenger hunts. I was evermore driving them to one brick house or another. Mr. Stevens used to take them, and it wore him to a frazzle.

I knew better than to ask if the girls had ever had a birthday party. They couldn't invite children to the house. So I got me a idea. During the week, when the girls was at school, I made Emma my especial project. Every day I'd make her take one step farther from her room. At first, she hollered and slapped me upside the head. But I kept at it. She got to where she could stand in the hall for a minute, then five minutes. I'd stand there, holding her hands until she stopped shaking.

By Memorial Day she could sit in the living room and watch *Wild Kingdom* with the girls. On July 4, she joined us in the kitchen for a hot dog supper. But no amount of coaxing would make her step outside the house.

When I'd worked there a little more than a year, I sent the girls into the attic for their sweaters, and they brought down a dusty Royal typewriter with a missing N key. It had a wrinkled piece of paper jammed inside it. Abigail squatted on the floor and started banging keys, then she hit the silver bar and it made a *ding*.

The noise drew Emma from her room. She stared down at the machine, smoking fiercely for several moments. "What is it for, Mama?" asked Shelby.

"For? Your grammar is offensive, my dear," Emma said, then she began to circle the machine, her house slippers flapping against her heel. "It's a relic from my days at Newcomb."

She sent the girls to town for crisp white paper, a typewriter ribbon, and a eraser. After they left, she hoisted the Royal onto the kitchen table, then lit a cigarette and blew smoke over the machine. Dust swirled up, hanging in the air. I sneezed into my apron.

"Sorry about that, Gladys. Actually, I'm sorry about a helluva lot. Did I ever tell you that I was an English major at Newcomb? My junior year I heard that a New York publisher was having a contest, so I sat down and wrote a novel in three months. I didn't go to class, didn't eat, didn't comb my hair. I still made straight As." She reached up and patted the spongy, home-bleached curls. "My poor hair was never the same, but my novel won the contest. The publisher flew me up to New York City, and they took me to the Rainbow Room."

"So what happened?" I lifted the teakettle and poured steaming water into the china pot. The only book I'd read was the Bible. Many a time I had dusted the Stevens's crowded pecan bookcases, and never once did I guess that Emma had wrote one.

"Do you know what autobiographic is, Gladys? Well, it's a true story. A lot of people chalked it up to a vivid but twisted imagination. But other people knew better."

"What was it about?"

"A Tulane English major named Bethany. Only I changed Tulane to Toulouse University. I was—I mean, Bethany was in love with a porter at the Fountainbleu Hotel."

"She was really in love with a porter?"

"Actually, *I'm* Bethany. And I never got over him. I'd hoped the book might be a catharsis, but it only brought it all back. I dropped out of school three months before graduation and went home to Alexandria. My mother and Aunt Abby had been scandalized by my novel, and they insisted I redeem myself by entering the Miss Louisiana pageant. I won it, but Atlantic City was a washout. I did a dramatic reading from my book. A big mistake.

"So I came home, and as the reigning Miss Louisiana, I had all these silly official duties. They sent me down to New Orleans to shake hands with the customers at Maison-Blanche. That's where I met Thaddeus Stevens. He had on a white short-sleeved shirt and a maroon bow tie. But he was looking for a pin-striped suit. He thought I was a saleslady and asked if I'd help. He'd spent the last year in the law library and hadn't even heard of my book. However, he'd watched the Miss America Pageant. He'd rooted for me. Two weeks later, I married him at City Hall. We moved across the Pontchartrain to Covington to his hometown. His daddy set him up in a law practice, and I started having babies. But I still thought about Shelby and wondered where he was."

"Shelby?"

"That was my porter's name. But in the book, I changed it to Samuel."

"Did you ever find out what happened to him?"

"No, but I named my baby daughter after him." She lifted one eyebrow. "If you tell anyone, they won't believe you. What a strange world this is, Gladys. The truth is perceived as a lie, and lies are taken as the gospel. Maybe I should write about that. If I remember how."

When the girls got back with the supplies, she let them pound on the machine. Then they got bored and ran off. Emma pulled up a chair and rolled a new white page into the Royal. Then she set her trembly fingers on the keys. The clacketing started up, and in all capital letters she typed, "DAUGHTERS OF REVOLUTION, A Novel by Emma Stevens."

I grabbed the feather duster and tiptoed into the dark living room. The curtains were pulled tight and gave off a mildewy stench. What this house needed was a good scrubbing with Bon Ami. Then I would open every window and let the stink blow out.

She wrote her book in four months. It was the story of a ex beauty queen who married a sports fanatic lawyer but got her revenge by seducing a whole slew of married men. She put the loose papers in a blue Madame Alexander doll box and sent me down to the post office. "You take good care of this," I told the clerk. "It's going all the way to New York City."

Before the book came out, Emma started practicing to be a famous writer. She went to the kitchen door and just stared through the screen mesh. Then she pushed it open and stepped outside. First, she started shaking, then she vomited in the lilies. It looked like a real illness to me, one that had swooped down and just sucked the breath out of her little body. I ran outside and put my arms around her. "Gladys's here," I said. "Don't be afraid. Gladys's here."

"My heart is whirling out the top of my head," she whispered.

Every day she stepped a little farther into the grass until one day she made it to the mailbox. "I might beat the crazies," she said. "If I make any money, I might leave this damn town and move to New York. Do you want to go with me?"

"No, ma'am," I said. "There is Mafia up there."

"There's Mafia in New Orleans," she said.

"I don't go there, either," I said.

By the end of summer she was strong enough to visit Mr. Pierre's Beauty Shoppe in downtown Covington. I stayed with her while Mr. Pierre detangled, trimmed, and conditioned her hair. We even got her nails painted. Then we drove over to Taylor's Mercantile and bought her some knit suits and low-heeled pumps. She did not shake or vomit. She even made small talk with Mr. Taylor. If you didn't know anything about her, you would take her for a regular Covington housewife.

We stepped out of the store into the sharp, Pontchartrain-scented light. She lifted her face up to the sky. "I'm going to be all right, Gladys," she said. "Really, I am going to be a whole woman."

Then the book came out and the town was all abuzz. Emma and I set up a little card table at Piggly Wiggly with her books all piled up, ready to be signed. She didn't intend to sell them. They was extras from her publisher, and Emma said they was free.

Ladies with snot-nosed children walked right by the table, not even glancing our way. Emma sent me to buy a box of pinwheel cookies, and we set them on the table. That drew a few people, mainly kids. Now and then she'd see one of her neighbors, but she was too shy to holler at them. They'd just pass on by, going out of their way to look in the other direction.

"Now I know how the Invisible Man felt," she said. "Don't these ladies realize that I never did all those things in the book? I never cheated on Thaddeus! Why, I never left my house!"

In the first book, Emma had told the truth but nobody believed it, and in the second one, she told lies and people thought it was the gospel. It takes a lot for a small southern town to cast aside its good manners. The politeness is buried deep. But *Daughters of the Revolution* was more than the good people of Covington could stand. Housewives thought the book was a tell-all, that Emma had faked her illness, that she'd sneaked out in the night and had snookered all their husbands. Some folks thought it was a attack on the DAR. Others thought it was a military book about a real war.

Hair-pulling arguments broke out at bridge clubs and ladies' cotillions, the women wondering who Emma had fornicated with. All over St. Tammany Parish, marriages were slung onto the rocks. Several churches had sermons about the evils of adultery. Emma's books were pulled off the library shelves at the local card and stationery store. And in the courthouse parking lot, one copy was set on fire by unknown culprits.

The *Times-Picayune* called the book "the romance novel that ate New Jersey." Mr. Stevens handed me the paper, wondering if he should show her. I shook my head. Far as I could tell, New Jersey hadn't been mentioned in that book. He burned the paper in the barbecue pit, then threw on some charcoal and grilled hot dogs. He'd planned to run for judge, but he'd laid them plans aside. He knew that book wasn't true, but he took a lot of ribbing at the courthouse. He'd just laugh off the rude comments. "The girls and I are so thankful that she's gotten her health back," he'd say.

One afternoon we was sitting in the front yard, watching the girls run through the sprinkler, when a beat-up Plymouth drove up and two boys throwed a headless mannequin into the yard. It had a sign taped to its chest—"Emma Stevens, Whore of Babylon." The girls stopped skipping. One of the boys throwed out condoms.

"Get out of my yard!" Emma yelled.

"Slut," hollered a boy. "Teach you to mess with my daddy."

The Plymouth roared off. I gathered up the girls, wiping their tears with my apron. Emma ran into the house, then marched out, holding the Royal typewriter. She lifted it over her head and threw it against a pecan tree as hard as she could. "And the truth shall set you free," she said, then she walked into the house.

And didn't come out for the next ten years.

Chapter 10

◉ ◉ ◉

LOVE AT THE FUNERAL HOME

*T*hat whole night I lay awake in the New Orleans Room, going over Gladys's story. It had shaken loose a memory of a green shotgun house near a park where people rode horses. Every weekend my daddy drove us across a long bridge, then he'd pull up to a red brick house. Grandfather Stevens squatted on the sidewalk and picked me up. He had silver hair and a nose shaped like a strawberry. Mama said he was a judge, and he decided who went to jail and how long they stayed. Everybody called him "the Judge," even my mama.

I remembered being led into Grandmother Stevens's shadowy room and how the cigarette smoke burned my nose and I burst into tears. "Oh, no, I've made the baby cry," said Grandmother Stevens. "She sure is pretty, but just take her out. I'm sorry."

While the grown-ups opened oysters in the backyard and drank sour-smelling drinks, I hid under the redwood patio table and hung on to my mama's leg. Above me, my daddy and Grandfather Stevens laughed. They talked about hunting and where to buy the best oysters. I had no memory of anyone mentioning Abigail. I just recalled laughter and the clink of shells.

*N*ow, I turned over, pulling the sheets around me, watching the pear trees throw shadows on the walls. I was still awake when first light broke through the trees and birds started chattering. Maybe they were telling stories to their babies: *You think I'm bad? You should have known my mother. She was real flighty.* If a bird could tell her sad, secret history, then why hadn't my mother? I pressed the pillow to my head and tumbled down into a sweet, sticky, dreamless sleep.

I awakened to a loud, rhythmic banging, followed by Zap's barking. Then I heard Gladys and Honora's voices. I threw back the covers and sat up, tilting my head. The thumping sounded like a demolition crew, and it appeared to be coming from downstairs. It would be just like Honora to add another wing to the house, a shabby-chic wing. Then I remembered my father's engagement party. It was this evening. The caterers were probably downstairs, setting up.

I pulled on my blue jeans and a sweatshirt, then hurried down the curved staircase, into the kitchen. It was empty, except for Zap, who ran in circles, biting his stubby tail. When he saw me, he ran over, licking my feet. As I bent down to scratch his ears, I heard another thump. Zap barked and raced over to the wine cellar door. It swung open, and Gladys stepped out, her reading glasses dangling back and forth from the beaded chain as she hoisted an old steamer trunk into the kitchen. A moment later Honora appeared, pushing the trunk into the center of the room.

"Did y'all just wake up and decide you had to clean the wine cellar?" I laughed.

"We're not cleaning," said Honora. "We're excavating. I thought we'd put the trunk in your room. Can you give us a hand?"

"Ugh, it's filthy." Gladys reached for a dish towel and began swatting the cobwebs.

"My room?" I stepped back as dust spiraled up. It wasn't Honora's nature to make a mess right before a party.

"Gladys and I have discussed this," said my grandmother.

"Argued is more like it," said Gladys.

"This was Shelby's chest," said Honora.

I knelt down and raised the domed lid. It creaked, then fine particles drifted up, backstroking in the light. Inside, the trunk was heaped with objects and yellowed papers. I picked up a lace shawl, and a gold necklace dangled from the fringe. Honora leaned over and pulled out an empty bottle of Dom Pérignon. "Consumed on honeymoon" was written on the label in faded ink.

Beneath the bottle were water-stained invitations, newspaper clippings, and a hardback book, its pages stuck together. In the right-hand corner of the trunk, I saw a glint of old silver. I pulled out a small tarnished bracelet, the charms gently clinking: a tiny crab, pelican, mermaid, conch, lighthouse.

"Shelby left it here when she and Louie were divorced," said Honora. "I forgot all about it until Hurricane Danny. That was in 1997, the summer a fishing boat washed up into my yard. The wine cellar flooded, but Gladys and I managed to put the trunk on a shelf."

"Humph, it still got wet," said Gladys. "Twenty-five inches of rain in seven hours. You should've known better than to dig a hole just to keep your wine bottles."

"It wasn't my idea," said Honora. "My mother-in-law cried for that wine cellar. A whole slew of architects and structural engineers told her not to add a below-grade room. But Solange DeChavannes believed that people who live on the Coast are a tough breed."

"And we are," said Gladys. "Even though Hurricane Danny was wicked. It stalled over Mobile Bay for I don't know how long. And wrecked our pier, too."

"No, that was Georges," said Honora. "Danny crashed a tree into the boat-house. Both times the damn insurance company tried to get out of paying. We're just lucky we didn't float away. Renata, be a dear and grab the other end. I'd like to get it to your room before the party. It's tonight, in case you've blocked that information."

I was only half listening. I couldn't stop looking at the trunk. I ran my hands down the bumpy metal sides, then reached inside and pulled out an old *Mobile Register* clipping.

Thursday, September 18, 1966

DeChavannes–Stevens Engagement Announced

The Honorable Judge and Mrs. Thaddeus Stevens of Covington, Louisiana, announce the engagement of their daughter, Shelby Ann, to Dr. Louis Charles DeChavannes, Jr., son of Dr. and Mrs. Louis Charles "Chaz" DeChavannes of

Point Clear, Alabama. Miss Stevens is a sophomore art history major at Sophie Newcomb College. Dr. DeChavannes is a graduate of Tulane University and Vanderbilt Medical School. He completed a four-year surgical residency at Rice Medical Center in Houston, Texas, and has been accepted as a cardiovascular fellow at the Ochsner Clinic in New Orleans. The couple is slated to be married at All Saints Cathedral in Covington on December 29, 1966.

"Let's take a little walk, you and I." Honora patted my shoulder.

"Good idea," said Gladys. "I'll just clean up this old trunk."

I pressed the clipping inside the trunk, then I followed my grandmother outside. We didn't speak until we'd reached the pier. I held her elbow as she climbed down the wooden stairs, then I said, "Thank you for unearthing that trunk."

"Don't thank me yet." She tucked her arm into mine. The tide was coming in, pushing seaweed onto the sand. My first apartment in Los Angeles had been located near a major thoroughfare, but after a glass of wine, I could pretend the traffic was a kind of surf.

"I've really missed this place." I reached down to pick up a tiny shell. "Mama and Daddy met here, didn't they?"

"No, they met at a funeral. Shelby's sister had died. Gladys told you, right?"

"Lord, did she ever. If Mama had lived, I don't think she would have explained all that. It sounds freaky."

"I hate to say it, but you're probably right. Shelby feared that she'd turn out like her mother, but she didn't. She built a new life and beat the crazy curse." Honora turned her face up to the sun. "Why dredge up these hurtful things? In fact, are you sure you want to hear the rest of it?"

"You know I do. Tell me about the funeral."

"Well, it was 1966—Good Friday, as I recall. Abigail was a nursing student at Baptist Hospital. She was driving on the causeway, from Covington to New Orleans. Bringing Easter baskets to the children's ward. Witnesses said her tire blew out, and she lost control of her convertible. It crashed through the guardrail, right into the Pontchartrain."

"That's awful." I shuddered, imagining those plastic eggs floating in the rough water.

"A tragedy." Honora patted my arm. "Abigail had been engaged to a vascular surgery resident at Ochsner. He was inconsolable. Two friends had to prop him up at the funeral. One of those friends was your father. Apparently he couldn't take his eyes off your mother. He called me up and said, 'I've met my future wife.' "

I stopped walking and touched her arm. "Did he ever say why? I mean, was it her looks or something else? What drew her to him?"

"You should ask him. You'll see him tonight."

"But it's his engagement party. I can't mention Mama."

"Of course you can. How can you ever hope to create a lasting relationship with your Hollywood director until you make peace with your father?"

"The only lasting thing about Ferg is that tabloid photograph."

"Then you're going to punt him?"

"Punt?"

"You know, kick him out of your life. Free yourself to meet another man."

"With this hair?" I raked my hand over my scalp.

"Yes, with that hair. It'll grow. And you'll find another man. That's how life works."

"Not my life," I said. "Not anymore."

"Talk to your father," she said. "He might surprise you."

"I've tried. And he just freezes or makes a joke."

"Well, that's true." She shifted her gaze to me. "I don't like to speak for Louie. But your mother had the most breathtaking gray eyes. Nowadays people can get that look with contact lenses, but in 1966, it was exotic. And she had a long blond braid that almost hit her waist."

"A Heidi braid?" I smiled.

"Don't be silly. She looked just like Glynis Johns in *Miranda*. Shelby had a solemn, watchful air. She wasn't a nervous chatterbox, and she didn't seem eager to impress me and Chaz. She possessed a maturity that was absent in girls of her era. Everybody was running around in miniskirts and go-go boots. Shelby wore Villager dresses. This set her apart from your father's usual women."

"So Mama was old-fashioned?"

"Nothing about her was old except her spirit." Honora squeezed my arm, and we started walking again. "But that was from her difficult childhood." Honora tilted her head. "When she and Louie got engaged, I gave them a fabulous party. I hired an orchestra from Mobile, and all of the guests danced on the lawn."

"What about the wedding? Did Grandmother Stevens go, or did she stay in her bedroom?"

"No, she went. Gladys made sure of it. They sat together in the front pew. I thought Gladys was an aunt, not their housekeeper." Honora glanced down at her watch. "We better head on back and get ready. The caterers should be arriving now—damn, I forgot to pick flowers!"

"I'll do that."

"Nonsense, I don't want you digging in the garden. I want you to look gorgeous."

"That's impossible." I laughed and tugged at my hair. "Will you settle for gamine?"

"Oh, poo. Just put on your pearls and an extra dab of mascara, and you'll look splendid."

Chapter 11

* * *

Honora Says, There's More I Haven't Told

Gladys had filled my bath, adding jasmine oil and fresh gardenia blossoms. I sat on the edge of the tub sweeping my hand through the steam. Then I slipped off my robe and eased down into the water. Zap pushed open the door with his nose, then trotted over to the tub, licking water off the tile. "Hello, gorgeous," I said, then felt foolish for talking to a dog. There was a banker's wife in Point Clear who kept a ferret in her coat pocket, and not only that, she dressed it up. If she wore a blue sweater, so did the ferret.

As I sank into the oily water, my flabby old arms dislodged a clump of gardenia petals. I didn't know where Gladys had found them, because my bushes hadn't yet bloomed. I breathed in their smell, then peered over the edge of the tub. Zap grinned up at me, his pink tongue curling. "Where am I going to put you during the party?" I asked, and he cocked his head. I couldn't believe I was talking to a damn dog. Well, I was just getting senile. But I didn't know what I'd do without him.

Soon I needed to show Renata her parents' wedding pictures; but knowing my granddaughter, she would rather hear what happened after they got married. If her memory loss was a form of protection, then had I done her a disservice by dragging that trunk out of the basement?

Shelby was gone, and I lacked proper guidelines. How much to divulge without causing pain? I scooted down into the water, feeling it ruffle around my chin, and breathed in the scent of gardenias. Whenever I thought about Louie and Shelby's early days, I always thought about that gardenia bush that bloomed under their bedroom window in their old shotgun house near Audubon Park.

I remembered a hot August night when Shelby and Louie drove over to Point Clear to watch the Perseid shower. I remember how happy we all were. Shelby was eight months pregnant, and her stomach curved beneath the blue voile dress. While shooting stars fizzled into the bay, she stretched out on a chaise longue and Louie massaged her feet. Chaz opened a bottle of champagne, and each time a star etched over the bay, we made a toast. We toasted the baby and the beautiful summer night. A while later, we heard big band music drifting up from the Grand.

The next morning, Shelby put on a navy blue maternity suit and swam out into the bay. She rolled over and spread her arms, floating, the waves breaking over her dark stomach. Inside that belly, my grandchild no doubt turned somersaults in the salty amniotic fluid. On either side of Shelby, dolphins cut through the shallows, leaving behind little commas of foam. Closer to shore, another group of dolphins swam around their babies, keeping them afloat.

Louie walked past me, wearing cutoff jeans. "Lovely day," he said, then headed down to the beach. He waded into the water, then swam out to Shelby and drew her into his arms. I turned away, embarrassed that I'd witnessed such a private moment, but grateful that God had placed this much beauty in the world.

A month later, Shelby went into labor. Louie called us at three o'clock in the morning from the Ochsner Medical Center. He kept stuttering, and Chaz said, "Slow down, what's the matter?"

"S-shelby's in l-labor," he said.

Chaz and I got dressed and drove straight to New Orleans. When we arrived at Ochsner, Louie was sitting in the expectant father's room, surrounded by empty Styrofoam cups, the type with little green leaves along the rim. When he saw us, he scrambled to his feet and wrapped one arm around Chaz, the other around me. "She's been in labor eighteen hours, and she's barely dilated," he said.

"Shelby's a strong girl," I said, trying to comfort him; but as the night dragged on, and the sun rose over New Orleans, I began to worry. Lamaze was all the rage in France, but here in the U.S., the mothers were strapped down and gassed. She was determined not to put drugs into the baby's little system. Oh, how that girl suffered. I stood outside the delivery room, keeping an eye on Chaz and Louie. The door opened, and the RN brought out the baby, wrapped in a bloody receiving blanket. Louie ran over and pulled back the blanket, counting Renata's fingers and toes. The nurse laughed and said, "Let me get her cleaned up first."

Above the door, a red light began to wheel, then a buzzer went off. "What's the matter?" I grabbed Chaz's arm. His eyes met Louie's. The buzzer echoed in the corridor; nurses skidded around the corner and burst through the delivery room door. I caught a glimpse of Shelby. Her legs were in stirrups. The obstetrician, Ned Thaxton, was working between her knees, and his scrub suit was splattered with blood.

"I'm going in there," said Louie. He pushed open the door, but a squatty nurse blocked him, screaming about the room being a sterile environment.

"That's my wife," said Louie.

"Is she all right?" I asked the nurse.

Ned Thaxton's head rose up between Shelby's thighs. He hollered out that Shelby's uterus had prolapsed, and she was hemorrhaging. He needed permission to do an emergency hysterectomy.

"Do what you have to," said Louie. "Just save her."

"It might not come to that," Ned hollered back. "I'm doing everything I can."

The nurse began to close the door, and Ned bent back down to his work. Before the door closed, I saw that they'd tilted Shelby's head toward the floor, with her feet pointed toward the ceiling. A nurse swabbed Shelby's stomach with a brown antiseptic. Chaz said it was Betadine. Somehow Ned Thaxton stopped the bleeding and put her back together. But she could never have another baby.

After they'd settled back in New Orleans, Shelby's daddy, Judge Stevens, found a woman to sit with Emma, then sent Gladys to New Orleans to be the nanny. I remember she planted red tulips in the front yard, and a gardenia bush. Every sunny day, the two women strolled the baby down to Audubon Park. Shelby put her whole heart into mothering that child. She'd hold the baby in her lap, staring with unabashed love into Renata's dark, monkeylike face, but I knew she saw nothing but beauty. Money was tight in that household, but Shelby made certain that her baby's life was rich in other ways. She got a library card and checked out children's books; she took the baby to the French Market and taught her child the name of every fruit, vegetable, and flower.

One day I drove over to New Orleans to see the baby, and while we sat on the floor, helping Renata stack her blocks, Louie rushed into the house, his handsome face split into a smile, saying he had a surprise. He'd bought them a cottage over in Covington so Shelby could be near her people. Her bottom lip trembled and her eyes filled. Louie thought she was overcome with joy. He started to put his arms around her, but she pushed him away.

"What's wrong?" His eyebrows slanted together.

"I know you meant well, but I don't want that house," she said. "Is it too late to back out?"

"I signed the papers last week. It's ours."

"I refuse to live in Covington."

"But it's where you grew up."

"I belong in New Orleans with you."

"I thought you'd be so pleased. And it's not that far, just a little drive across the Pontchartrain."

"It's not little. My sister died on that bridge."

"Baby, I know. But I just don't want to raise Renata in New Orleans."

"I hate Covington." She was crying so hard, she was having trouble breathing.

"Just give the house a chance, that's all I'm asking. If it doesn't work out, we'll sell it."

"Louie, please. Don't do this."

I hated hearing them argue like that. And I was shocked by Shelby's hatred of her hometown. Louie tried to sell the house; but he'd paid too much for it. Prospective buyers kept making low offers. It sat empty for six months, with Louie checking on it every week, driving back and forth across the lake, and falling in love with the area. Meanwhile he was paying the mortgage on the Covington house, and also paying rent on their little shotgun house near Tulane. Finally, when a woman in their neighborhood was beaten to death by a drug addict, he put his foot down.

"We're moving," Louie said. "And that's the end of it."

But it was just the beginning of the end. Love can twist back on itself; and no matter what you do, no matter how hard you work to repair the damage, it's never quite the same. All that's left is the memory of a hot summer night, of stars tearing loose from the sky, of gardenia blossoms breaking away from tender flesh and blowing heaven knows where.

Chapter 12

⊙ ⊙ ⊙

PARTY GIRLS

From my grandmother's terrace, I watched waiters from the Grand Hotel spread out like a battalion. Men in white uniforms marched through the rooms carrying champagne flutes on silver platters. Bars had been set up at three strategic locations, including a wine-tasting area in the glassed-in conservatory. Here on the terrace, the caterers arranged food on a long, skirted buffet table. The air was heavy with the mingled scents of Sterno, citronella, and brackish water.

I hadn't eaten all day, so the minute the caterers left, I grabbed a plate and started at the left end of the table. Boiled jumbo shrimp lay in a pinwheel pattern on a deep bed of crushed ice. My hand hovered over the design while I tried to decide if my love for shrimp outweighed the worry over messing up the concentric circles. Deciding that it did, I took some and moved down the table, reaching for less artistic compositions: canapes, sushi, crabmeat-stuffed eggs, and smoked honeyed chicken wings. At the end of the buffet, I saw a mound of chocolate-dipped strawberries. Since I didn't have room on my plate, I slid a berry into my mouth.

"Save me a strawberry, dahlin'," said Isabella, walking up. She wore dangling onyx earrings, and her black dress was slit up the side. Her hair was pinned into a shiny knot.

With two fingers I removed the berry and twisted it by its stem. "This is my first. But not the last. I can't resist food art."

"Only a fool would resist beauty."

Maybe it was due to my pre-party glass of Veuve Cliquot, or it could have been my frayed nerves, but I felt wicked. I dangled the strawberry above my head, then bit down and flung the green cap over my shoulder.

"That looks like delicious fun. But I have a better idea." Isabella picked out a strawberry, then slid her other hand into her pocket and pulled out a tiny blue pill. "Valium," she said, and deftly pushed it into the berry, then turned back to the buffet and slipped it onto the mound. "Wonder who'll get it?" she whispered. "Or maybe I should do another one?"

"Don't do that," I hissed.

"Oh, lighten up. I always insert a little fun into parties. One time my late mother-in-law ate a psychotropic deviled egg." Isabella giggled. "I stuffed it with Librium. And one Thanksgiving, I put ipecac in her oyster dressing. Another Thanksgiving I slipped Ex-Lax into the sweet potatoes."

"You should be ashamed." I blinked down at the buffet. All the strawberries blended together. Until she'd hidden the Valium, I'd been on the verge of challenging Isabella to a strawberry-eating contest. I heard a familiar bark, then turned back to the French doors. Honora stepped onto the terrace, hugging the Yorkie to her chest. He wore a small tuxedo, with a white bow tied in his topknot.

"I've been looking everywhere for you," she called, extending one hand. "Your father and Joie have finally arrived."

My hands started trembling; a shrimp rolled off my plate and hit the ground. I wasn't looking forward to seeing my father. He had a way of using humor as a barrier, and even though he never failed to make me laugh, I always felt a little sad, too. Long ago I'd lost hope of repairing our father-daughter relationship.

"I'll take that plate," said Isabella.

"Be good," I told her.

"Not for a million dollars," she said. "But I might consider it for five."

Honora pulled me into the living room, cutting a serpentine path through the crowd. The Yorkie's ears swiveled like tiny satellite dishes, as if tracking conversations. "Louie's in a cheerful mood for a change," she said, then squeezed my hand, indicating that she was speaking in code, one she'd perfected for parties and public functions. It was a language I'd learned from birth. *Behave yourself,* said the code. *Don't needle him, and don't you dare mention his heinous baby pictures. Above all, don't reveal your shock when you meet Joie.*

She towed me into the living room, over to a green marble desk with gold dolphin legs, where my father was popping the cork on a '63 Dom Pérignon. Foam gushed down the sides of the bottle, and he deftly blotted it with a white linen napkin. Beside him, a short, birdlike blonde turned and smiled.

"You must be Renata," she said in a breathless voice. She tugged at a zigzaggy scarf then extended her hand. "I'm just so pleased to finally meet you!"

"My God, what happened to your hair?" Daddy said. Still gripping the champagne, he pulled me against his shoulder. I smelled Aramis, Dial soap, and Irish whiskey. At fifty-nine, Louie DeChavannes still turned women's heads. He pushed back a lock of iron-streaked hair.

"It's the latest style in L.A.," said Honora.

"Actually, it's not," I said.

"Well, *I* think it's stunning," said Joie. Now her voice sounded unnaturally high-pitched, like she'd been breathing helium.

"Icebergs can be stunning," said Daddy.

"So are stun guns!" Joie giggled. "Listen, I'll see y'all later. I've just *got* to get me a chocolate strawberry."

A former Alabama state senator clapped my father's shoulder. "How's the heart business, Louie?"

"Can't complain," said Daddy, his eyes tracking Joie. "How's politics?"

"Crooked as the Mississippi River, and just as polluted," said the former senator.

While Daddy made the introductions, people streamed into the room, toward the bar, pushing me against the fireplace. A waiter glided by, and I took a flute. Then he melted into the crowd, holding the silver tray aloft. I stood on my toes and searched for my father. The ex-senator said something, and my daddy threw his head back and laughed. I drank my champagne, then had turned away from the fireplace to set my empty flute on a table when the bride-to-be crashed into my shoulder, dumping a plate of chocolate-dipped strawberries against my black dress.

"Oh, no! I was just bringing Mama over to introduce you. Now look what

I've done." She stepped back as the crushed berries slid down the front of my dress. Then she waved one hand at an older blonde. "Mama, run and get her some club soda."

"Hi, I'm Faye Mayfield. Joie's mama?" The woman was dressed in a black, voluminous dress, and she spoke with the same squeaky voice as her daughter. She grabbed my hand and shook it, her gold bracelets clattering.

"I've ruined your pretty dress," cried Joie. "Is it a Betsey Johnson or a Cynthia Rowley?"

"I'm not sure what it is." I glanced down at the stained bodice. I couldn't remember which year I'd bought it, much less the designer's name.

"Hold on, sweetie. I'll fix you right up." Faye held up one hand, and I blinked at the sudden flash of diamonds and aquamarines.

She elbowed her way through the crowd, working her way over to the bar. I started to look away when I noticed a diminutive bald-headed man. His eyes were level with the counter. Faye didn't seem to notice him. But he'd noticed Faye. He gave her the once-over, then reached for his scotch, his Rolex sliding around his tiny, hairy wrist.

Joie frowned at my dress. "I'm just mortified," she said.

"That's all right, Joy."

"No, no, it's not Joy!" Her tiny eyebrows slanted together. "It's Joie, like the *toile du joie* fabric."

"I'm sorry."

"Well, that's all right. Lots of people screw it up. I don't know what's keeping Mama. I'll just go get a paper towel. Don't you move!" Joie fluttered off, her small, apple-shaped buttocks moving beneath the clingy dress.

Honora was working her way over to me, trailed by my father, who was holding the Yorkie. Now that's odd, I thought, until I saw that Honora was clutching a damp napkin and a bottle of soda.

"Baby girl," said Daddy, "I've told you time and again not to play with your food."

"Can't resist," I said.

"Here, let me clean you up," said Honora, then she gave my father a sharp look. "Step back a little. Don't let Zap lick the chocolate."

"Is the little fellow allergic?" Daddy laughed.

"For your information," Honora said through her teeth, "chocolate has caffeine. And even small doses can be fatal. I should think a cardiologist would know these things."

"I'm a people doctor." Daddy winked. "Not a vet."

"Too bad." She lifted one eyebrow and continued to scrub my dress.

Just a few feet away, Isabella was holding court with several young men. "Hollywood casting directors taught me to be strong," she told them. "Also, I had great legs. That helped."

"You were an actress?" said a man with blue eyes.

"You haven't heard of me? If not, then shame on you! You have missed some great romantic comedies starring me, Doris Day, Jim Garner, and Rock Hudson. Everybody said I'd never make it in Hollywood 'cause of my round face? It just didn't lend itself to the silver screen. Hollywood's idea of beauty leaned toward the classic, not the cherubic. Of course, I looked into surgery, but the doctor explained he could not change bone structure. Well, they couldn't in those days. Now you can change anything, even eye color. But the doctor suggested that I lose weight. So he wrote me a prescription for Dexedrine. It just made my head spin and my heart race something awful. But within days my cheeks began to deflate. I went off to film a movie with Rock Hudson, and everybody told me how gorgeous I looked. Well, it was true."

Daddy switched Zap to his other arm, and leaned closer to me. "The real story is, the pills turned Isabella's brain into a sieve and she forgot her lines. The director lost his patience, and the next thing you knew she'd been replaced by Doris Day. So she flew down to Alabama and helped Honora plan dinner parties."

"How come I've never heard this story?" I asked him. "You're making it up, aren't you?"

"Nope, it's true. Just ask Honora."

"It's ancient history," said Honora. "And you're rude to bring it up."

"It's the truth," said Daddy. "What we need is more champagne. Can I get you ladies a drink?"

"Not me," said Honora. "A good hostess never drinks until after the party's over."

"You and your rules," Daddy said, but his voice was kind. He placed Zap in my grandmother's arms, then winked at me. "How about you, babe—another glass of champagne?"

"Think I'll pass, too."

"Maybe you should rescue that little man from your future mother-in-law," said Honora, nodding toward the bar. "She's just insulted him by making a reference to pygmy goats."

Chapter 13

✦ ✦ ✦

WOMAN ON TOP

After Daddy left, Honora lowered her voice. "Poor Louie has a penchant for choosing odd mothers-in-law. Faye cleans up nice, but she's still rough around the edges. She worked at Mayfield Seafood Cannery when she caught the owner's attention. Old George Mayfield got her pregnant—he was married, of course—it was the talk of Pensacola. His wife went to her grave claiming that their Mexican divorce wasn't legal and that Joie was illegitimate."

"But that's Pensacola gossip. How'd it reach your ears?"

"Because of the drumbeats, dahlin'. The South is full of drumbeats. Now that Faye's a widow, she's gone wild, and there's no telling what kind of stunt she'll pull tonight. And she's famous for pulling them."

"It's a fabulous party, Honora, and nobody's ruining it."

My grandmother had a knack for building unique menus and guest lists. So far, I'd spotted a Louisiana artist, a TV chef, and politicians from Louisiana and Alabama.

"I've had better," she said. "I don't know, something's off-kilter tonight. Maybe I'm getting too old for parties."

"That'll never happen," I said. It was easy to think she hadn't aged. She was still a beautiful woman, and her mind was younger and quicker than mine; still, I couldn't help but notice that she walked slower these days.

"I'd always hoped your father would retire in Point Clear, but he's a confirmed New Orleanian. You'd never know he was raised in this house.

Personally, I think the Eastern Shore is too quiet and elegant for him. I don't suppose you'd someday want this house?"

I wasn't sure how to answer. Her home was beautiful, but it was far too grand. The taxes and upkeep would send me to the poorhouse. Her forehead wrinkled, as she glanced toward the French doors, which stood invitingly ajar, so that guests could wander onto the rock terrace. Across the bay, lights glimmered, and the moon floated low between the Spanish oaks.

On the other end of the room, Isabella's voice was rising. "I live next door to Honora," she was telling the men. "Have you ever built a house? Well, I'll tell you, it's not for the fainthearted. It's one of life's big stresses, right up there with death and divorce. I nearly lost my mind. All those decisions nearly broke me. I mean, really. Who pays one bit of attention if doorknobs and hinges match? But for an old-age nest, it's all right."

"You're not old," said one of the men.

"That reminds me," I said, turning back to my grandmother. "Don't eat the strawberries. Isabella tampered with them."

"Damn her." Honora rolled her eyes. "What was it this time, Ex-Lax or Benadryl?"

"Valium."

"I'm shocked. Normally she hoards nerve pills."

"She only put it in one. At least, that's what she said."

"And you believed her?" Honora made a face and stopped scrubbing my dress. She glanced toward the foyer, into the dining room, where faux clouds seemed to waft on the dining room's tall, barrel-vaulted ceiling. The butler's pantry door swung open, and a harried caterer shot out, holding a tray of puff-pastry hors d'oeuvres.

"Maybe you should run upstairs and change clothes," she said.

"I didn't bring anything dressy enough. And besides, at the rate people are drinking, pretty soon they won't notice."

"I don't know. Drunk people might mistake the strawberries for blood. A stampede might break out. We could end up on CNN. You need more napkins."

She pointed me toward the kitchen, gave my bottom a pat, then turned back into the living room to keep the party moving. I didn't get that gene, but I hoped to acquire it. As I pushed open the door to the butler's pantry, I spotted Joie. She gripped a paper towel roll in one hand and a cell phone in the other. The phone was bubble-gum pink, all trimmed with rhinestones, or maybe it was diamonds. When she saw me, she clicked off the phone and snapped off a paper towel.

"I got sidetracked, but I knew you'd find me." She handed me a towel, then shoved her lilliputian hand into my face. "See the ring your daddy gave me? An old-fashioned Tiffany setting suits me just fine. I don't remember how many carats, but it's not vulgar in the least."

"Daddy has excellent taste in jewelry," I said, fingering my chocolate-stained pearls.

"Yeah, he does. Did you know that we saw *Bombshell* on our first date?"

"Really?" I said, trying not to seem impressed, but I was flat-out bowled over.

"Yes! Isn't that cool? He told me you helped write that movie with your boyfriend. Is he still your boyfriend?"

I blinked.

"Well, listen, if you dump him, I wouldn't blame you one bit. Some men just have roving eyes. Better to find out sooner than later, is my motto. And you don't have to tell me about your father. I know all the stories. Now that he's older, he's quieted down. In fact, he's ready for us to marry and start a family. Although I'm not eager to have kids. Have y'all made any other movies?"

"Some independent films."

"Indy what? Is that, like, a rehab thing, like in codependent? Never mind, I'm not really into movies. But I've been wanting to talk to you and get your opinion. See, I haven't decided if I want to be a summer or a fall bride. My birthday is September fourteenth, and I don't want to get married anywhere near that date. Or Christmas. Christmas is the worst time of year to have an anniversary because you get shortchanged on gifts. You know how men just hate to shop? They'll buy you a combined Christmas-anniversary gift every year. Ditto for birthdays and anniversaries. You might want to keep this in mind, unless you're breaking up with . . . what's his name again?"

"Ferg."

"Oh, I just don't see how he could cheat on you. Because you're such a doll. Honora said I'd love you, and you know what? I do! Isn't that wonderful?

Oh, just listen to me blathering. And here I've ruined your pretty outfit." She shoved the paper towel into my chest, then turned back to the granite counter and plucked a chocolate-covered strawberry from a tray.

"Please don't eat that," I said.

"Don't worry. I can eat anything I want and never gain an ounce. My smallness has other drawbacks. I never learned to drive a car. I'm not teasing. I can't see over the steering wheel. Thank goodness men prefer tiny women."

"You can't be serious."

"Why, no. It's true. Men worship tininess."

"No, I mean, you *do* drive, don't you?"

"Never in my life. I know it sounds odd, but I am really too little. And besides, I just don't like the pressure. It's got too dangerous to drive in New Orleans, or anywhere. Before my daddy died, he made me swear that I wouldn't go near I-10. So he hired me a driver, and that was the end of that. Want me to get you something to eat? I swear, I could eat my weight in chocolate-covered strawberries."

"I wouldn't advise it." I folded the paper towel into a crown and set it on her head, then I ducked out of the room. I stopped by the grand piano and listened to a man in a tuxedo play "Moon River." A champagne cork popped, followed by applause. After a while I stepped onto the patio. The wind swept through the oak trees. The air felt cool and smelled salty. Over by the water, I saw bars of light whirling from the spidery Mobile Bay lighthouse. It lent an eerie glow to the Spanish moss—which wasn't a parasite, like most people thought, but it did cause damage by blotting out sunlight. Just like gossip, it spreads small seeds into the wind and takes root.

It was eight o'clock. So that meant it was two a.m. in Ireland. I wondered if Ferg was sitting in a pub. If so, I would read all about it in next week's tabloids. I hated a liar more than I hated a cheat, and Ferg had sworn that nothing was going on. I eased back into the house, climbing the back stairs up to my room. Then I sat down on the bed and pulled the phone into my lap, dialing Ferg's hotel. The line made a strange, potty sound. The operator answered in an alert, cheerful voice and said he was sorry, but Mr. Lauderdale had a Do Not Disturb notice until seven a.m. Did I wish to leave a message?

I did not. I went back downstairs. When I opened the kitchen door, I smelled oysters en brochette. Joie was sitting on the counter, leaning against my father's right arm. She tossed her head and laughed at something he'd just said, causing the tassels on her scarf to swing back and forth.

"Are y'all hiding in the kitchen?" I asked.

"Best place in the house." Daddy winked.

"Mind if I join you?"

"Sure, babe." This was how our conversations usually went, no more than two or three syllables, although with everyone else, he was quite talkative. I remembered how he'd loved to mingle at parties, and I found it odd to see him hiding in the kitchen. But maybe Joie felt intimidated. Honora had invited the crème de la crème of coastal Alabama and every southern state that touched it.

The butler's pantry door opened, and Honora and Gladys swept into the kitchen. "I've been looking everywhere for y'all," said Honora. "The mayor wants to meet Joie."

"How many mayors are here?" Joie laughed. "I've already met one."

Honora leaned over the counter and began rearranging the tray of oysters en brochette, stuffing parsley around the edges. Joie watched for a moment, then tucked her small-boned hand into the crook of Daddy's arm and smiled up at him, her heart-shaped face smooth and radiant.

"Louie, baby, we better get out there and mingle. After all, we are the guests of honor."

"Indeed we are." Daddy smiled, his head tilting to one side. As he led her out of the kitchen, the pendant lights picked out gray hairs. He looked handsome and distinguished, every inch the successful heart surgeon. I wondered what had shaped him, what had made him into a self-absorbed god. Had Honora been a doting or a neglectful mother? Would either extreme have made a damn bit of difference?

Before the door whooshed shut, I saw Daddy and Joie step into the living room, waving to a few guests. I fought an impulse to pull him back.

"He looks like a toad with a baby tadpole," Honora said.

"Tadpole, hell," said Gladys. "She's a shark."

"I never realized that Louie was that huge," said Honora. "It looks like he'd squash that poor girl during sex."

"Not if she's on top," said Gladys.

Chapter 14

⊙ ⊙ ⊙

STRING OF PEARLS

The party was showing no signs of slowing down. Honora dragged me into the living room and introduced me to the former lieutenant governor of Mississippi. Then she pulled me over to meet members of the garden club. Even though it was clear that they had heard about the *National Enquirer*, several ladies acted confused and wanted to know if the engagement party was in my honor. It was a silly, southern ploy to acquire information, but my grandmother wasn't fooled.

"No, it's for Louie." Honora smiled. "Renata's boyfriend is in Ireland. He's bringing *Ulysses* to the silver screen."

"But, sugar," said a lady in a green dress, "didn't Arnold Schwarzenegger immortalize that role?"

"No, I'm talking about James Joyce's *Ulysses*," said Honora.

"Oh, that's right," said the lady in the green dress. "Arnold starred in that Conan movie."

"Wait," said a woman with cake crumbs on her chin, "I saw *Ulysses* way back in 1955. Kirk Douglas was just divine."

"That was Homer, not Joyce," I said, and all of the women stared.

The cake-crumb lady turned to Honora and said, "I thought the book club was going to read Joyce."

"Joyce Carol Oates," said Honora.

I was looking around for my daddy and Joie, but I couldn't see them anywhere. Faye was pressing the short man against a table. His shoulder knocked against the fishbowl; it tipped sideways and rolled over, spilling water and the fish to the floor. On that side of the room the conversation dimmed, and several people turned.

"Ooooo, just look at it flopping around. Somebody step on it, quick," yelped Faye.

I bolted across the room and scooped the fish into my hands, then rushed to the kitchen. Honora was right behind me. She filled a Pyrex bowl with tepid water and set it on the counter. I dipped my hands into the bowl; the fish spurted between my fingers, listing on its side a moment, then began to swim in tight, angry circles.

"I've got a bigger vase in the garage," said Honora.

"I'll get it," I said. "Just tell me where to look. You get back to the party."

"Look on the shelves, way down on the bottom row. Get the great big brandy snifter." She opened a cupboard, pulled out a whisk broom and a dustpan, then headed back into the living room.

As I cracked open the garage door, I jumped a little when I saw Joie. She stood next to Honora's Bentley, cradling a platter of chocolate-covered strawberries, her pink cell phone tucked between her chin and shoulder. "I love *you*, Billy," she crooned, popping a berry into her mouth. "Nobody but you. And don't you worry, baby doll, I'll see you real soon."

When Joie saw me at the top of the staircase, she slapped the bejeweled phone shut.

"I was just looking for a vase," I said, and started down the steps, acting as if I hadn't overheard the conversation. All I had to do was fetch the vase, make a little small talk, and return to the party. But I couldn't. I had my grandmother's meddling gene, and there was no going back. "By the way," I said, "who's Billy?"

Joie looked up at the ceiling, then staggered backward. Honora had painted the ceiling black, to match her Bentley, and here and there she'd hung cast-off chandeliers. Only my grandmother would decorate her garage. Joie reached for another strawberry and slipped it into her mouth.

"Don't let me interrupt your snack," I said, kneeling beside the shelves. I wondered if she'd found Isabella's tainted berry—or berries, if Honora's prediction was accurate.

"I'm sure you're wondering about Billy," Joie said, then bit into another strawberry. "He's my . . . You know what? I don't have to explain what Billy is. It's none of your business."

I didn't respond; I grabbed the fishbowl and cradled it in my arms. Giving Joie a wide berth, I circled back toward the stairs.

"You've no idea who Billy is," she cried. "You'd die if you knew."

"I'm all ears."

"That's not all you are, darlin'," she said in a tipsy, slurry voice. She raised a strawberry to her mouth, but her aim was off, and the berry glanced off her cheek and hit the concrete floor. She reached for another and held it over her head. "Take my advice and go on the Atkins Diet before it's too late. Because you're over thirty, at least, you look it, and if you don't get control of your figure now, that's it, you'll never be thin. When you die, they'll have to get you a plus-sized casket."

"I resent that," I said, trying not to laugh. "I wear a size eight. That's hardly endomorphic."

"I know what that means." She put her hands on her hips and blinked.

"If you'll excuse me," I said, "a fish is waiting for me."

"What fish?" She blinked. "Are you speaking in code?"

"Fish is a four-letter word for fish. As in goldfish." I couldn't believe my father saw anything in this overwrought child-woman. Had he lost his mind? More to the point, what kind of school would allow this pea-brained woman to teach? I thought of at least ten insults, but growing up in Hollywood had taught me to choose my battles and to keep my powder dry. But nothing my father had ever done made a bit of sense. I started up the stairs.

"What four-letter word?" she called. "Oh, I get it. You're just trying to change the subject."

"As I said, fish has four letters. You ought to know that, Joie."

"What are you getting at?" She pushed the last berry into her mouth and bit down. Then she set the empty platter on the floor.

"Someone knocked over Honora's fishbowl. I'm just trying to save the poor creature."

"Are you making an allegory, or whatever? Fish out of water? Shattered lives?" She opened her mouth, revealing a chocolate-streaked tongue. "Wait, don't go. I'm not finished talking to you."

"Too bad," I said. "Because I'm finished with you."

She let out a strangled cry and grabbed my collar; I felt her tiny fingernails scrape the back of my neck, digging into the flesh. The pearls cut into my throat, and my head bowed. She yanked them hard, and the strand rolled over my Adam's apple. Gripping the fishbowl with one hand, I reached up blindly with the other, groping for her fingers.

"Stop it, Joie," I cried in a raspy voice.

"No," she said. "You stop."

The necklace broke, and my pearls hit the steps, pinging across the concrete floor. Still gripping the bowl, I threw out my elbow, and it hit Joie's shoulder. Her mouth opened, and she toppled backward. She didn't fall far, just two steps, and she landed on her hips.

"Well, thanks a lot," she cried, and yanked her dress over her right knee. I didn't see any blood, just a red spot on her shin.

"Are you all right?" I asked.

"No, but I will be, just as soon as you get your gigantic self out of my face." She licked her finger and rubbed it over her knee. "But go ahead, tell the world what you *think* you heard. I don't care."

I set down the vase and eased down the steps and began gathering loose pearls, dropping them into my pocket. "Are you sitting on any pearls?"

"What if I am?" she snapped. "Don't worry, I'll buy you a new necklace."

"These pearls are sentimental," I said. "My father gave them to me."

She rolled her eyes and scooted to the left. Several pearls rolled out like freshly laid, lilliputian eggs. She reached out and grabbed them.

"Here, take my hand," I said. "Is your knee okay?"

"Oh, shut up. Get away, don't touch me." She held out her hand, the pearls rolling on her palm. "Take them gently, no grabbing!"

I could imagine her speaking this way to her third-grade students. I gingerly picked up the pearls. "Come on, let me help you," I said.

"No, just let me sit here a minute, Miss Know-It-All. I'm truly sorry about your necklace. I'll look around and try to find stray pearls. Like I said, I'll even buy you a new strand. And I *know* it won't be the same, but it's the best I can do."

I scooped up another pearl. I didn't trust her to pick them up. In fact, I just didn't trust her at all. I couldn't decide if I should pull my daddy aside and tell him about Billy, or if I should just let it go. He was a grown man, and surely it wasn't my place to tell him that he'd picked the wrong woman—again.

"So, can you just leave?" Joie cracked open her Judith Leiber bag and pulled out a lipstick and tiny mirror.

After I rescued the fish, I wandered outside and found Honora and Gladys sitting on the stone terrace. "Come on and sit with us," Honora said, petting the Yorkie's head. "I was just telling Isabella about the Mayfields."

"It's juicy," said Gladys. "Apparently the mother was a skank."

"Faye was especially fond of portrait photographers," said Honora. "And she had many suggestive pictures taken of Joie. When she lived over in New Orleans, she dabbled in voodoo. And she stalked two prominent women."

"Surely not," I said.

"No, Faye herself told it. She has to be the center of attention, even if she's ruining her reputation. A lot of people dismiss these stories because Faye isn't a drinker, and she doesn't smoke. Except for decorating herself with jewelry and haute couture, she seems rather normal—until she opens her mouth. She can't carry on a normal conversation without bending it in her direction."

"Has Daddy heard these stories?"

"He'd never admit it to us," said Honora. "Besides, Faye has fooled him. She flatters and cajoles and pampers. Louie eats it up. Surely in a past life, he was an emperor. Because your father understands the language of a good merlot, oysters en brochette, and Italian silk suits. He prefers women who burp their men."

"And Joie does this?" I said, trying to imagine it. The girl who'd broken my pearls hadn't seemed like much of a nurturer.

"Honey, oh, *honey*. She can do it with a smile and never lay a hand on him. She's a pro, just like her mama. But she's also quite gifted in the laying on the hands, if you get my drift. Or so I've been told."

Isabella stepped out of the house, gripping a white coffee mug, and sat down next to me. The smell of bourbon drifted over.

"Fab party, Honora," she said.

I tipped back my head, then glanced toward the buffet. The mound of strawberries had diminished, thanks to Joie. I hadn't noticed any other dazed guests, but then I'd consumed several glasses of champagne, and I was feeling a tad groggy myself. The night air felt cool and refreshing, and a low mist blew over the water. I wondered if I should mention the mysterious Billy.

"Find a cute man and talk to him." Honora pushed my arm. "Go on."

"That's the last thing I need." Southern men were emotionally stunted. Most were helpless. Why on earth would I want one? Unlike my father, if Ferg was hungry, he'd fix a sandwich; but my father would give the women a sheepish look and say, "I'm starving. Will you fix me something, and a drink too? Bring it to me on the patio."

Not only did my daddy expect pampering, he was vulnerable to flattery. When his patients or the hospital staff praised him, he believed every word, never thinking that they might have secondary gain. Ferg saw through the bullshit of Hollywood. He had built-in radar for silly, phony goo-goo talkers. He focused on his work. But then, he'd hired Esmé Vasquez to play Molly Bloom, and despite her acting skills, she had a reputation. Maybe deep down, he was more like my father than I'd thought. I heard a shout from inside the house. Turning around, I saw guests squeezing through the French doors. "Probably another broken bowl," said Honora, hoisting herself from the iron chaise longue.

The clacketing of Faye's bracelets announced her arrival before I actually saw her. Then I saw her push through the crowd. "Get out of my way," she said. "I've got to find my daughter."

"Find her?" Honora's brow furrowed. "Where'd she go?"

"Haven't you heard?" cried Faye, her eyes glittering. "My baby has gone missing. Somebody has stolen my Joie."

A spot of blood, studded with a pearl, marked the bottom step in the garage. The second splotch stood a few feet away, next to a crushed strawberry. More splatter marks led to a zigzag shawl, which lay crumpled on the concrete, then out the side door, where the garden dropped off into darkness.

There was no sign of Joie.

Faye gripped my father's lapels, her bracelets clicking, and gaped up at him. "Is that *her* blood? You're a doctor, surely you can tell?"

As Honora and I approached the crowded doorway, the short Rolex man stood back to let us pass.

"One of the caterers went into the garage for a cigarette," he said. "When she saw all the blood, she screamed. Dr. DeChavannes heard the commotion and came running. That's when he saw the scarf. I believe it's his fiancée's."

Honora walked down the garage steps and stared at the blood. Then she followed the spatter marks, which curved in a jagged arc around the storage shelves. "Maybe she's in the Bentley," she suggested.

"Already checked," said Daddy.

"Perhaps she's somewhere in the house? Have you tried the powder room?" Honora walked back to the steps and picked up the bloody pearl.

"Yes, and I looked upstairs, too," said Daddy. "I can't find her anywhere."

"We'll just have to look again. It's an enormous house."

"Whose pearls broke?" Faye leaned over the railing. "And why is there so much blood?"

"Maybe Joie took a tumble and broke her necklace," said the short man.

"Not on your life." Faye's head whipped back and forth, but her hair didn't move a millimeter. "Joie hates pearls. Trash from the sea, she calls them. Maybe we should call the police. Where's your phone?"

"In the kitchen. But let's don't be hasty. I'm sure there's a logical explanation." Honora's hand closed over the pearl. "Let's keep searching, shall we? Is anyone else missing? No? Well, let's look outside, too."

Isabella lit a cigarette. "Maybe it's time for an Amber Alert."

While Daddy went looking for Faye, the short fellow assembled a search party. He sent the Louisiana congressman, the mayor of Point Clear, and me to look outside. He dispatched Honora, Gladys, and Isabella to check the upstairs.

"I'll search the library," said Daddy, leading Faye back into the kitchen, guiding her to a straight-backed kitchen chair.

"I can't call the police, I'm too upset," she said. "Call them for me, Louie baby."

I grabbed a flashlight from the shelf and stepped outside. Fog drifted past the cypress trees. My shoes squeaked on the grass as I walked down the yard. It was difficult to see anything, but I clicked on the light and swept the beam back and forth, picking my way down to the pier and the boathouse. Behind me, my companions had fanned out in the yard, peeking under the azaleas. "Joie?" they called. "Honey, are you out here?"

The screen door creaked, and I glanced inside the boathouse. My worst fear was that she'd walked into the bay and drowned. I swept the light around the little house. Empty. Then I stepped back onto the pier. Earlier, after my little altercation with Joie, I hadn't seen any blood. Her knee had looked bruised, but the skin wasn't broken. Maybe after I left, she'd gotten up and tripped on a loose pearl. This time, she could have fallen hard, maybe cutting her lip or gashing open her arm. Even if she hadn't eaten one of the tainted berries, she'd had enough champagne to make her woozy. She could have staggered outside, into the bay. On the other hand, maybe she'd staged this little drama, leaving behind blood and pearls, hoping I wouldn't tell my father about the mysterious Billy.

Again, I swept the light over the planks, searching for blood; I didn't see anything but a clean expanse of pressure-treated wood. I stepped over to the edge. Water slapped against the pilings. I could hear the music playing at the Grand Hotel, and way off in the dark, I knew that people were dancing in the pavilion.

An owl hooted, and something rustled in the tall weeds. My companions were in the gardens, their flashlights illuminating boxwoods and hemlock. Those lights reminded me of hot summer nights when the tide comes in and the wind blows east, setting into motion an event called a Jubilee, when fish leap out of the water, flopping onto the sand. People spread out on the beach, their flashlights bobbing, while they gather crabs and flounder.

The men kept calling Joie's name, followed by a pause. If she was outside, she didn't—or perhaps couldn't—answer. I hurried off the dock, following the flaky stone path into the house. Faye was lying on the sofa, a rag over her eyes. Honora stood beside the window, holding the dog against her shoulder. Daddy sat at the massive ormolu desk, running his hands over the green marble inserts, explaining the situation to the 911 operator.

"It looks like Joie bled all over the garage banister," said Isabella, stepping into the room. "Could she possibly be having her period?"

"What are you saying?" Faye shrieked. "That my daughter slid down the banister without a Kotex?"

"Of course not," said Isabella. "Besides, Kotex is obsolete. Wouldn't Joie use a tampon?"

"Maybe she's taking a walk," Gladys suggested. "Or she could've left. Is her car still parked out front?"

"She doesn't drive. She came with me and Louie." Faye exhaled, and the rag rippled. "My baby isn't gallivanting. Somebody did this to her. Somebody with cheap pearls."

I cupped one hand over my bulging pocket. Then I sat down in the plaid silk chair. The pearls oozed between my fingers, running down the silk brocade, then pinging to the floor, rolling between my father's feet.

Chapter 15

ⓞ ⓞ ⓞ

Circe's Bowl

A t first I didn't think he'd noticed. He hung up the receiver and sank his elbows into his knees. Then he looked up. "Renata, do you want to explain how your pearls got broken?"

I wanted to say, "Ask Billy." Instead, I said, "I need to talk to you alone."

All the women turned and stared. Gladys's mouth fell open.

"Forget it, you're about an hour too late," Daddy said.

"Well, *I* want to hear what she did," said Faye. She flung the washcloth across the room. It hit the French door with a splat. Then she got to her feet and pointed at me.

"Start talking."

I touched two fingers to my lips. My hands shook, distorting my lips and chin, like I was rubbing off lipstick. I thought that made me look guilty, but I couldn't hold still. How to explain without enraging Faye? How could I just say that I'd interrupted a phone call between her daughter and somebody named Billy? There's a fine line between lying and being tactful; I don't know why I cared, but I did. I folded my hands and pressed them into my thighs.

Daddy's jaw twitched. He pushed away from the desk and started toward the kitchen. Halfway, he stopped and turned. "You are just like your mother," he said, and pushed away from the desk.

As my eyes filled, Honora grabbed his arm. "Where are you going?" she demanded.

"To find Joie," he said.

I heard the front door slam. Minutes later, headlights swung around the driveway, and I heard the low rumble of his Jaguar.

"Well? Don't just sit there like an I don't know what," Faye cried.

"Renata, tell us again what-all happened," Gladys said.

"Give her a second." Honora said, staring hard at Gladys. "Can't you see that she's upset?"

"Riddles," said Faye. "Nothing but riddles."

"My pearls broke," I heard myself say, "but Joie didn't get hurt."

Faye's face contorted, then she lunged toward me, fists raised. Isabella grabbed the woman from behind and led her back to the sofa. "She did it," Faye sobbed.

"Do not judge until you know the facts," said Gladys.

"Oh, shut up, you, you Catholic swamp thing, you!" Faye squirmed out of Isabella's grasp. "I know all about you people. Joie was scared to death of y'all."

Honora sat on the edge of the sofa and put her arms around Faye. "Honey, you've suffered a shock, and you're looking pale, mighty pale. Let's lie down, shall we?"

"I'm fine," Faye yelped.

"Can I call your doctor?"

"No, you may not," Faye snapped. "Louie takes care of all my prescription needs."

Honora didn't flinch, but I knew she was opposed to him, or any doctor, writing prescriptions for family members. She wouldn't take even an aspirin from him.

"Besides," Faye added. "He's gone, isn't he? Leaving me here with y'all."

"We won't bite," said Gladys.

"Well, not hard," said Isabella.

"I can't stay here another second." Faye shrugged off Honora's hands, the bracelets rattling, then she struggled to her feet. "Where are the police? Maybe I should call them again."

"The phone's on the desk," said Honora, giving Isabella a scolding look.

"Faye, dahlin', why don't you have a nice glass of wine instead?" asked Isabella.

"I don't want anything except my daughter," said Faye.

"Of course you do," Honora said. "That's what we all want, for our loved ones to be safe and happy."

"Can we get you anything other than Joie?" Isabella raised her eyebrow. "Like a Valium?"

"You are a witch, and a drug addict," said Faye, with a freezing stare. "I just want to be with Louie. He's the only one I trust. Besides, I know y'all are going to protect *her*." She pointed one red fingernail in my direction.

A baggy-eyed policeman showed up, demonstrating a decided lack of interest in the missing bride-to-be, along with the hysterical ravings of her mama. Faye pointed a fingernail in my direction. "Ask that young lady about her pearls. Ask how they got broke."

"You can file a missing person's report, but not for forty-eight hours." The policeman coughed into his hand.

"In forty-eight hours," Faye said, "my daughter could be in the Caribbean, sold on the white slavery market!"

The policeman handed my grandmother a card, then excused himself. The guests were gathering their coats, thanking Honora for her hospitality and offering their heartfelt prayers to Faye.

I walked onto the terrace and looked up at the stars, wishing I'd never left Nags Head. Behind me, I heard the clink of metal as the caterers emptied the buffet. From the far side of the house, I heard shouting, and the short man ran up the path, his eyes shining. "We found her."

*R*ed lights swirled in the trees while the medics pushed the gurney toward the ambulance. Joie was strapped to the thin white mattress. She looked unconscious, or maybe even dead. Blood had caked on her nose and forehead, and a small knot protruded through her scalp. Her dress was wet and muddy.

A crowed had gathered around the ex-senator as he explained how he'd found her lying faceup in the koi pond. It was his opinion that she had started to climb the garage steps, then tripped and fell backward, smashing her nose against the banister. At some point she must have gotten to her feet and wandered outside, dazed and disoriented, until she toppled over into the pond, under the Circe fountain. More blood had been found on Circe's bowl. It looked as if Joie had struck her head against the thick limestone, then hit the water. "The gods must have been watching," said the ex-senator, "because she landed sunny-side up. Otherwise she would have drowned."

One of the medics helped Faye climb into the back of the ambulance. Mascara had gathered under her eyes and run down her cheeks. Her poofy hair was dented on one side. There was something pitiful about the tendons that stood out on her neck, and the loose folds of skin that hung from her chin. Faye looked old and frightened, and right before the ambulance doors slammed shut, she fixed me with an evil stare.

I rushed over to one of the drivers. "Is she all right?"

"Ma'am, I don't know yet. Are you a family member?"

I started to nod yes, but I caught myself. "She's my daddy's fiancée."

"Well, she's unconscious, and I think her nose is broken, but that's all I can say."

I thanked him and stumbled over the grass, back to the other end of the terrace, where guests had gathered around a blue-haired lady who was lying down in one of the lounge chairs. She sat up, holding her head in her hands. "I've never fallen asleep at a party in my life!" she said. "And it was such a nice one, too. The chocolate-covered strawberries were divine."

I found my grandmother in the living room, lecturing Isabella on the evils of food tampering. Isabella listened without comment, blowing a smoke ring into the grainy dark. When she saw me, her eyes rounded. "Is Joie alive or what?"

"Alive, but knocked out cold," I said.

"Knocked," Honora whispered, as if awestruck.

"What could've done it?" Gladys asked. "Or should I ask who?"

"Maybe she ate a tainted strawberry," said Isabella.

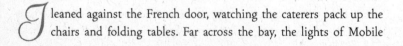 leaned against the French door, watching the caterers pack up the chairs and folding tables. Far across the bay, the lights of Mobile

winked. Warm air pooled in the shadows. I picked out the Big Dipper, and Mars drifted toward the west. I thought I saw a star drop out of the sky and sizzle down into the bay; I made a wish—*Please let Joie be all right.*

Behind me, the door creaked open. Gladys grabbed my arm and towed me into the living room. "Honora's got your dad on the phone. He wants to talk to you."

Honora raised her eyebrows as she stepped back from the green marble desk and held out the receiver. "Be calm," she whispered. "Because he isn't."

The phone felt heavy as I raised it to my ear. I inhaled, then released the air through my teeth. "Hello, Daddy."

"I'm on my way to the hospital, and I don't want to see you there. I just want to know what you did to her."

"I didn't do anything," I stammered. "She broke my pearls."

"Joie wouldn't do that."

"Yes, she did. She broke them, then she tripped. But she only fell down two steps, and she hit her knee, not her head. Daddy, why don't you believe me?"

"Fine. When she wakes up, I'll ask her what really happened."

"Do that," I said, and my hand began to shake. "One more thing, Daddy. Why did you make that comment about my mother? You said I'm just like her. What did you mean?"

"It wasn't a compliment, kid. But I don't have time for that. All I care about is Joie and what you did to her."

"I did nothing. But when she wakes, maybe you should ask her about Billy. She was talking to him—no, cooing to him—on her cell phone."

Daddy was silent. Then he said, "Billy is her dog. A freaking Chihuahua."

I sucked in air, then shut my eyes.

"First Shelby," he said. "Now you. If God isn't punishing me, I don't know who is. Never mind. I'll be at the hospital with Joie, but like I said, do not come near her."

I set down the receiver, then put one hand over my eyes. Tears spilled through my fingers, hitting the table.

"Renata?" said Honora. "I know you're beside yourself . . . but I get the feeling that you haven't told us everything. Who's Billy?"

I spread my fingers and looked up at her.

"An old lover?" Isabella nodded sympathetically.

I swiped a finger under my eyes and said, "Billy's a Chihuahua."

"Oh, dear. I'll put the kettle on," said Honora. "A good, strong cup of tea is what we need. My mother used to say that tea soothes just about any upset."

"I'd rather have champagne," said Isabella. "And two Tylenol, if you have it. My head is bursting. It feels like somebody put those growing Magic Rocks inside my brain. I don't think I can walk home."

"Not in them high heels," said Gladys. "Take them off, girl."

"Honestly, Gladys," said Isabella. "If you weren't my best friend's maid, I'd bite you."

Chapter 16

❀ ❀ ❀

A CUP OF CHAMOMILE TEA

*T*he scent of chamomile drifted above my head while I told the women about Joie's phone call and how I'd assumed Billy was her lover. While I talked, Honora turned on the stereo, and Vivaldi's *La Tempesta di Mare* began to play. She poured another round of tea, then passed the sugar bowl.

"If only you hadn't left behind that damn pearl," said Isabella. "Then I could call Robert Stack—is he still alive? Well, never mind, I could ask him to put Joie on *Unsolved Mysteries.*"

"Humph, we can figure this out ourselves." Gladys put her chin in her hand. "When Joie broke your necklace and fell down them stairs, could she have hit her head?"

"I don't think so." I stirred my tea. "It happened so fast. But no, it wasn't my impression that she hit her head. She did scrape her knee, but it didn't even break the skin."

Isabella made no comment. She lifted her cup, her pinkie crooked, and took a swig of tea.

"Maybe after you left," said Gladys, "she started back up the stairs and just tripped on the pearl and bashed her own head in? And she was all confused and just wandered outside."

"Lured by Circe?" Isabella looked over the rim of her cup.

"She could have drowned in that fountain," I said.

"She didn't," said Honora.

Gladys grunted. "She could be dead now, for all we know."

Honora reached for the phone. "Maybe I should call Louie."

"He said he'd call," Gladys pointed out. "We better just sit tight."

"I'm not." Isabella lit a cigarette. "I refuse to sit here and hold vigil for that miniature tart."

"Oh, don't speak ill of the unconscious," said Honora.

"If you talk to him," I told Honora, "ask him why he thinks I hurt Joie."

"Because of them pearls," said Gladys.

"It's not just that," said Isabella. "Louie's a teetotal jackass when it comes to women."

"But I'm his daughter. He knows I'm not capable of hurting anyone."

"Honey, that doesn't matter," said Isabella. "To him, any woman he *isn't* screwing is the enemy. Besides, I don't want to talk about Louie or Joie, I want to hear about your director. Are those stories true? And if they are, will you dump him?"

"Of course she will," said Gladys.

"You're better off with someone outside show business. I mean, really. Directors are a tad vulnerable to ambitious starlets." Isabella lifted one hand and rubbed her temple. "And I should know. I was one myself."

"Ladies, let's stick to the topic." Honora opened a bottle of apricot brandy and tipped it over her friend's cup. "Joie was found all splayed in my fountain. My granddaughter has been implicated by a pearl from her own necklace, a piece of lovely jewelry, if I *do* say so myself."

"Louie was awful quick to blame her," Gladys said.

"Louie's just upset. And of course the pearls didn't help," said Honora. "I'm not defending him. I'm just stating a fact."

"You are too defending him," said Isabella. "Louie is a self-centered bastard, but he sure is a handsome one."

"He's not thinking straight," said Gladys. "He's crazy in love with that Joie."

"What if she dies?" I asked.

"He'll call the minute he gets news, good or bad," said Honora. "Even if it's just to rub it in, he'll call."

We sat there a minute, sipping tea. Honora said, "Your father loves you."

"Yes, that's right," said Isabella. "It's just more soothing to him if he pretends otherwise."

"Oh, for heaven's sake, Isabella." Honora scowled.

"No," I said. "Isabella has a point. How do you tell if someone is pretending not to love, or if they have no feelings? Isn't the end result the same?"

"You're being too cerebral." Honora smiled. "He's just afraid. Love cows everyone, even locally famous heart surgeons."

"But he said I'm just like my mother."

"That's a high compliment," said Honora.

"But he sneered when he said it," I pointed out. "What was so wrong with her? He didn't want her; she made a new life without him. And managed to do it without ever saying an ugly word about him, and you know it."

The women exchanged glances. Honora was the first to speak. "Shelby was like a daughter to me. And you're right, she never spoke ill of Louie to anyone, especially not to you, darling. Shelby's goal in life was to make sure you grew up happy and well adjusted."

"Then why is he badmouthing her? He knows I'm grieving for her."

"We all are, honey." Honora reached out to pat my hand.

"What did she do to him that was so terrible?" I asked. "She never came out and told me anything about their marriage, but I heard things. He was the one who left her, right? They got a divorce and were about to reconcile when he up and married that blond lady from Tennessee."

"Her name was Bitsy," said Honora.

"Why does he hate my mama?"

"That's easy," said Isabella. "He doesn't really hate her, but he got really mad when she—"

"Don't you say another word," Honora cried. She got to her feet and pointed toward the hall. "Hush, or leave this house."

"All right, then. I'll leave." Isabella grabbed her Chanel bag and stood up. "If I have a stroke, I hope you feel guilty. But Renata deserves the truth, and nobody but me has the decency to tell her."

"You mean, there's *more*?" I cried. "Wait, Isabella. Don't go. Tell me."

Keeping her eyes on Isabella, Honora said, "Now is not the time."

"You have kept their secrets too long, Honora," said Isabella. "It's time to drag them out of the basement."

"I just don't think my grandchild should hear this rubbish."

"She's not a child," Isabella said. "She's a grown woman, in case you haven't noticed. And it's not rubbish."

"But your timing couldn't be worse, Isabella," said Honora.

"When would be the right time? The girl has a right to know."

"Know what?" I asked.

"The truth," said Isabella. "The truth about your mama and your daddy and the passion that tore them to bits. You need to hear the real story of your life. The missing pieces, the parts you don't remember, the parts they covered up. Why, if Honora and Shelby had worked for Richard Nixon, Watergate wouldn't have happened."

"Stop being melodramatic," said Honora.

"Me?" Isabella rubbed her left temple. "I don't have a dramatic bone left in my body."

"Me, neither," said Gladys. "The only bone I've got left is backbone."

Chapter 17

◉ ◉ ◉

MARRIAGE, MURDER, COVER-UPS, AND AFFAIR-ETTES

I took Isabella home. As I helped her upstairs, she talked nonstop. "I go to the Birdcage Lounge every afternoon," she was saying. "That's over at the Grand? You ought to join me sometime. The bartender gives me free drinks, seeing as I'm a local celebrity and all. Did I ever tell you why I left my glamorous career?"

"Yes, ma'am," I said, thinking back to what my father had whispered.

"It was a mistake. Because I exchanged one shallow, inbred society for another. Hollywood isn't a zip code, it's an airborne virus. Don't let anyone tell you that showbiz is fair. It's all about who you know. It's about vendettas, favors, debts."

"Tell me about it," I muttered.

"It takes courage to stay in the business. I fled to the Gulf Coast, only to discover the good-ole-boy network in Alabama was not only alive, it was as strong as its evil three-piece-suit counterpart in L.A. Why, I could have stayed in L.A., and only the cuisine and landscape would have changed. Backstabbers are the same everywhere."

"No, the accents are different." I guided her over to the bed, pulling back the covers. The sheets felt silky and looked custom-made. Isabella glanced up as her bony hips dented the mattress.

"You keep staring at my bed. Why? Do you like it?"

"I was just admiring the linen." I walked over to the windows and began shutting the heavy draperies.

"Honora believes in thousand count linen. And it really does last a lifetime, if you care for it properly. Naturally Honora does." Isabella rubbed her hand over the sheet. "My husband died in this bed. You don't remember Dickie Boy, do you? Well, he was a little too Old South for my taste, but he was so rich, I forgave him. His moods were entirely dependent on the stock market. A one-percent shift could make or break the man's day."

"I've heard Honora mention him," I said, heading out of the room. "Do you want the door closed?"

"Stay a while, don't run off." She yanked the sheet up to her chin. "Sometimes I get so lonely I just want to check out of this crappy life. It's been worse than a three-star hotel in Austria. The Europeans have different standards, you know."

"Yes, ma'am."

"That's right. Louie has taken you everywhere."

"No, he didn't. My mother and Andy took me to Europe, and when I got old enough, I took myself."

"That's the spirit." Isabella clapped her hands. "I am woman, hear me roar!"

I just stared.

"Well, at least you got to go. That's the important thing, right?" She smiled and pointed to a dresser. "See that crystal decanter? Will you be a dear and pour us some whiskey?"

I found two glasses in the bathroom. While I poured, she patted the sheet. "Bring that over here and come sit with me awhile. I'll tell you a few tidbits about your mama. I have seen her roll up her silk sleeves—yes, *silk*—at parties and wash dishes. During parties, she'd get in Honora's kitchen and help the caterers."

"Why?" I smiled, remembering how my mother had never liked large gatherings. "Was she avoiding the party?"

"Heavens no. Shelby was a marvelous cook. Louie was better, of course. Shelby was more adventurous than your father. Growing up in all that craziness gave her a tougher hide. But if she liked you, she would do anything. You had a friend for life. Whenever Honora threw a party, Shelby would cook one special dish, and it was always a hit. She would have made a stunning chef on Food TV, a blonder, thinner version of the Barefoot Contessa."

Isabella took a sip of whiskey, then raised one finger. "I just remembered something else. Years ago, I used to have Yorkies. In fact, Zap is from my line. Once I was staying at Chateau DeChavannes, and my favorite Yorkie, Bebe, ran out during a tropical storm. It was night, and the wind was gusting forty miles per hour. Everybody said, Oh, don't worry, Bebe will come back. But the little thing only weighed four pounds. She wasn't any match for that storm. Your mother put on a raincoat and grabbed a flashlight and went outside looking for my Bebe. She was gone so long that we nearly had to send a search party for her, too, but she came back holding my little Bebe. They both looked like drowned mice. Your mother took bronchitis, but Bebe was fine. That's when I started liking your mother."

"Before then you didn't?" I laughed.

"Well, you know how I distrust pretty women. But Shelby was such a good mother. She'd get down on the floor with you and spend hours building Lego cities. You had thousands of books, and she'd curl up in your little bed and read aloud until her voice was hoarse. You demanded it, of course. The same stories over and over. But I'm sure you remember that part. I'm just telling you this so you won't turn on her later on."

"Turn on her?" I leaned forward. "Why would I do that?"

"When you hear the truth."

"What truth?"

"Me and my big mouth. Honora will skin me alive if I don't shut up."

"I won't tell."

"She's a witch. She'll know." Isabella paused. "Did I ever tell you about Dickie Boy and me? How I killed him and all?"

I choked on the whiskey. "You killed him?"

"Well, sort of. It was accidental. Besides, his days were numbered. He had liver cancer. And no matter what his mama said, if he'd lived, he would have suffered. But he went real easy. Well, I think he did. Actually, I'm not one hundred percent sure. Your father helped me cover it up. We were having the most divine affair. Well, it was more like an affair-ette. Short but intense. Did you know that he was a virgin until his junior year at Tulane? Don't tell Honora I said this, but she was way too overprotective. She almost ruined him."

"Wait, back up." I set the whiskey glass on the table. "You and my father were lovers?"

"Does that shock you? Don't let it."

"Was he married to my mother at the time?"

"No. Well, just barely. Dickie Boy died right before your parents divorced. So I didn't break up that marriage. Your father only slept with me to punish your mother."

"Punish *her*? Whatever for?" I shook my head, wondering if she'd already had a stroke, and she was confused.

"Because of what she did to him." Isabella paused. "She fell in love and she had great sex and she caused a scandal. Not in that order, of course."

"She didn't love anybody except my father."

"Oh, yes, she did. She cheated on your father, and it turned him into a cad. Well, maybe it didn't turn him into one. It was already coiled up inside him, just waiting to get out. But I can't help but wonder what would have happened if she hadn't broken his heart."

"It's the other way around, Isabella."

She raised one eyebrow. "And you're getting your information from whom? From someone who painted your childhood pink and then glued lace to the edges? Because that's what Shelby and Honora did. They redecorated the past."

"They did no such thing."

"Think what you want, but you grew up in a structured world." She yawned, then put her empty glass on the night table. "You were fed a script. And you believed every word of it."

"What script?" I said, reaching for my whiskey. "If you really slept with my father, why wouldn't I have heard about it?"

"You haven't heard a lot of things."

"But if you really slept with my father—that's pretty juicy, considering you're my grandmother's best friend. Does she know?"

"She suspected."

"And?"

"We never discussed it. She was my friend, and no matter what, she forgave me."

I thought she might be drunk or cuckoo, but one thing stuck in my mind, and I had to clear it up. "He really was a virgin that long?"

"Yes," Isabella said without opening her eyes.

I didn't believe it for one second. But I wanted her to say more. "Why hasn't he ever told me?"

"Don't be silly. That's the sort of thing lovers tell each other, not fathers and daughters." She fell silent, as if her mind was folding up like a daylily. "I'm tired of all this talking. I'm sleepy. Be a dear and lock the door on your way out."

When I stepped into Chateau DeChavannes, I found a note propped on the counter: "Try to get some sleep. Here's an Ambien if you need it. Love you, Honora." I barely made it upstairs before the drug collided with Isabella's whiskey. I collapsed on the bed and fell into a dreamless sleep that poured over me like an oil slick.

Chapter 18

✦ ✦ ✦

ARTIFACTS

J awakened to the sound of screeching gulls and the clanging buoy, thinking I was in Nags Head. I remembered how, depending on the time of day, the light in the cottage changed the walls from pale celadon to dark sea foam. When Mama and Andy had been in residence, they'd flown an aqua flag embellished with a tiny green mermaid. Inside, the aqua rooms were filled with overstuffed checkered sofas and honeyed wicker armchairs. Andy and I had helped her place the sisal rugs, the old pine tables, and the knotty shelves that overflowed with books and baskets of shells.

Unfortunately I wasn't in Nags Head, I was in Alabama, the land of magnolias and crystal meth. Pulling up on my elbows, I glanced at my travel clock. It was a little after one p.m. Which meant it was seven o'clock in Dublin. Ferg didn't know I was in Point Clear, and I probably should have told him, but I'd only been here a few days. Maybe it would do him good to wonder. In my mind's eye, I imagined him dialing the Nags Head cottage, then my drowned cell phone. What if some stranger had found that phone in the sand? Renata who? they'd say. You've got the wrong number, buddy.

I slid off the bed and knelt beside the trunk, sifting for clues. If Isabella's stories were true, then the evidence had to be here somewhere. Still, I couldn't imagine my mother having an affair. Isabella was just theatrical, and she was noted for embellishing stories. I reached into the trunk and pulled out the lace shawl. An invitation floated to the floor, and I picked it up.

Dr. and Mrs. Nigel DeChavannes

request your presence at a

• BIRTHDAY DINNER & GOLFING WEEKEND •
Celebrating Dr. Nigel's fifty-first birthday

Friday, August 14, 1972,
Dinner at seven o'clock p.m.
Pinehurst Hotel
Pinehurst, North Carolina
RSVP *Black Tie*

Nigel was my grandfather's brother. Now, he was nearly eighty and lived in a condominium in Naples, Florida. I didn't know if the invitation had ended up in my mother's trunk by accident, or if it was another puzzle piece. I shook out the shawl and draped it over my shoulders, wrinkling my nose at the moldy smell, then tucked the invitation into my pocket and went looking for my grandmother.

I heard voices coming from the sunroom, and I headed down the hall and turned into a sunny, glassed-in room. Honora was sitting on one of the wicker sofas, serving tea to a balding police officer. When she saw me in the doorway, her eyes clouded, but she quickly recovered.

"Detective Bass, I'd like you to meet my granddaughter, Renata DeChavannes."

"Pleased to meet you, miss." He stood up, briefly scrubbing his hand on his gabardine trousers before he extended it. I gave it a firm shake, then looked at Honora for further directions.

"Faye sent the detective to ask a few questions about Joie's accident," said Honora, gesturing for me to sit down in the brocade chair.

Detective Bass cleared his throat. "I understand Miss Mayfield tripped on your pearls?"

Honora caught my eye and gave an imperceptible nod, tugging at her shell necklace.

"Yes, sir," I said. "Joie broke my necklace, and then she tripped."

The detective opened a spiral notebook. His pen scratched across the paper. Then he looked up. "Miss DeChavannes, may I see your pearls?"

Honora got to her feet. "I hardly see what this has to do with—"

"Well, ma'am, it's like this," said the man. "I'm afraid I have to take your granddaughter's pearls into custody."

"Whatever for?" Honora's eyebrows slanted.

"Evidence."

"Look here, Detective," said Honora. "Joie's fall was an accident. No one in this house laid a hand on her."

No, I thought, but someone *outside* the house had slipped Valium into her strawberries.

"I could get a warrant," said Detective Bass.

"I'll just get the pearls," I said, and hurried into the kitchen. I picked up a green Limoges bowl where I'd stashed the loose pearls. Tucking it in the crook of my arm, I hurried back to the living room. The detective shook out what appeared to be a small bag and tipped the bowl over the edge. The pearls slammed against the paper like gunfire.

"One more thing, Miss DeChavannes," he said in an offhand voice. "How long will you be in town?"

"A week," I said. "Maybe two. Why?"

"I'd appreciate it if you'd inform us of your whereabouts. I might need to bring you downtown for questioning."

"Questioning!" Honora cried. "If this isn't the most ridiculous thing I've ever encountered."

"I might need to get a statement from your granddaughter, is all."

"Can't you get it now?"

"We're waiting for test results," said the detective, looking uncomfortable.

"May I ask for what?" Honora snapped.

"I'm not at liberty to say, ma'am." He picked up the bag. "Now, can you show me where the crime occurred?"

From the kitchen doorway, Honora and I looked down into the garage, watching the detective set up little numbers beside each blood spatter.

Then he pulled out an ancient camera and took photographs. The way his eyes darted into nooks and crannies, I could tell that he was looking for the object that had bashed in Joie's head and bloodied her nose. Finally, we followed the detective outside to the Circe fountain. "Maybe I'm slipping or something," he said, bending down to snap a photograph, "but Miss DeChavannes's story doesn't match the evidence."

"Why don't you give her a lie detector test?" Honora said, her voice icy.

"Look, miss, I just said her story didn't match. I didn't accuse her of nothing."

"Because she's innocent," snapped Honora.

After he left, she went straight to the phone. She called the mayor and the district attorney; both men had been guests at the party. Then she called my daddy but was forced to leave voice mail.

"Louie, this is your mother. I thought you'd like to know that Renata's pearls have been arrested. Of course, your daughter is still free; but the minute that changes, I'm disinheriting you."

Later that afternoon, Honora stood beside an iron table that was crammed with orchids, jade plants, and African violets. She tipped a watering can over an orchid. Zap paced behind her, sniffing the brick floor. The windows were open, and I heard gulls crying in the distance. Gladys was stretched out on one sofa; Isabella was curled up on the other with a washrag draped over her eyes.

"I'm just so woozy," she said.

"How much did you drink last night?" Gladys asked.

"Hardly any," said Isabella.

"We need to call Dr. Bryant," said Honora.

"No doctors until I've had lunch," said Isabella, lowering the rag. When she saw me, she smiled. "I *heard* about the police confiscating your pearls. But before we start plotting, make your grandmother feed us."

"How about a fried oyster sandwich?" asked Gladys.

"I gave up oysters years ago. They're polluted." Isabella raised her arms over her head and stretched. "I'm positively starving. In fact, I could eat a zebra. Don't laugh. I ate one in Kenya."

Gladys disappeared into the kitchen, and I flopped down on her sofa. I looked over at Isabella, hoping she would have more stories about my father, but she put the rag over her eyes. Honora glanced over at me and winked.

"Has Daddy called?" I said.

"Haven't heard a peep," said Honora. "I left two messages with his answering service."

Gladys returned with a pot of jasmine tea, four mugs, and a plate of gingersnaps, all of it balanced on a red tooled-leather album. She set the tea and cookies on the wicker coffee table, then carried the album over to the sofa, sat down beside me, and opened the book.

"I don't know who these people are," Gladys said. "Honora, get over here."

"Where did you find that?" Honora set the can on the iron table. Her shoes scratched over the bricks as she walked over to the sofa. I leaned against Gladys, staring down at the pictures. They were black-and-white, the old-fashioned kind with crinkled edges. Honora sat down on the other side of Gladys, and Zap shot across the room onto the sofa, then flopped his head on my grandmother's leg.

"This album reminds me of how old I really am," Honora said, glancing over at the book. "Why, I'm an artifact."

"Speak for yourself, darling," said Isabella, picking up the teapot.

"When was this taken?" I pointed to a creased snapshot of Chateau DeChavannes. Honora and Chaz were standing next to the rose garden.

"That's me and your grandfather right after we got married," she told me.

"Chaz was a bore," said Isabella. "I hate it when widows canonize the dead."

"I wouldn't dream of canonizing Chaz. Ah, here's one of you, Isabella," Honora said. "It was taken before you went to Hollywood and got famous. You were dating that optometrist. What was his name?"

"I never dated any optometrist. Let me see." Isabella walked over to the sofa and peered over Honora's shoulder.

"Didn't his girlfriend jump off an observation tower in Louisiana?" asked Honora. The Yorkie flipped over on his back and touched Honora's arm with his paws, inviting her to play.

"I don't remember." Isabella shrugged.

"The tower was in a state forest," Honora said. "In fact, I might have a clipping somewhere."

"Oh, yes. *That* optometrist." Isabella waved an imperious hand, dismissing the album. "Gladys, what prompted you to drag this up?"

"I'm trying to jog Renata's memories," said Gladys.

"Well, for heaven's sake. You don't need pictures. I can tell her what she needs to know."

"First, tell us about the optometrist's girlfriend," said Gladys.

"It wasn't my fault she jumped," Isabella said. "I didn't even know the woman."

"Well, she knew *you*," said Honora, scratching Zap's belly.

"That was never proved," Isabella said.

"They said she left a cart full of groceries at the Fairhope A&P," Honora said. "Just ran off and left her ice cream to melt and then hightailed it to Louisiana and climbed that tower and jumped."

"Stop it, Honora." Isabella frowned. "If she'd wanted to die, she could have stayed in Point Clear. She didn't need a forest. She had an entire bay at her disposal."

"But you have to admit, it was a horrible way to die," Honora said.

"How would you know? When did you become a self-proclaimed expert on fatal falls?" said Isabella.

"My husband was a neurosurgeon," said Honora. "That's why."

"What happened to the optometrist?" I asked.

"I left for California." Isabella shrugged. "But I heard that he fell into the most dreadful funk. Nowadays I believe they call it depression. Anyway, I lost track of him. Men are such flippant creatures. Easily bored, easily distracted."

"They're predators," said Honora. "But darling ones. Men haven't changed since the days of the Neanderthal. But we females are constantly evolving. In the old days, all a woman needed was an apron and a Betty Crocker cookbook. Today's woman needs good genes and a plastic surgeon."

"Ain't nobody cutting on me. I like myself the way I am," said Gladys.

"And *I* happen to like younger men." Isabella bit into a gingersnap.

"You should read today's horoscope," said Honora. "You're a Taurus, right? It says a sacrifice now will benefit your love life later."

"I haven't had a love life since 1978. Or was it '79?" Isabella folded her arms and gazed off into the distance, wildly tapping her fingers. "But you've got a point. Maybe I'll start trapping small animals and offering them up to the gods."

"You can buy hamsters in bulk at PetSmart," said Gladys.

"She'll need more than hamsters," muttered Honora. "She might have to start mutilating cattle."

Gladys flipped the pages, stopping near the middle of the album. "Oh, look. Here's you and Shelby sitting on the dock. It was right after the divorce."

"Y'all were living with me," said Honora.

"Do you have any pictures of Uncle Nigel?" I asked, and Gladys gave me a sharp look.

"I'm sure I do," said Honora. "Why?"

"I found this in Mama's trunk." I reached into my pocket, pulled out the birthday invitation, and handed it to Honora. Zap lifted his head and sniffed.

"We all went to that party," said Honora.

"Why was the invitation in the trunk?" I asked. "Did it hold a special meaning for my mother?"

"Maybe, maybe not." Honora pushed the invitation into my hands. Gladys twisted a button on her dress and wouldn't look at me.

"Is somebody going to fill me in?" I said. "I'm not a child anymore."

The three women stared at each other. Finally Gladys said, "I think she meant to tell you, baby. She didn't believe children should hear sad stories."

"I'm thirty-three," I said. "What was she waiting for, *my* fifty-first birthday?"

"It wasn't like that," said Honora. "Shelby didn't know she was going to die so soon. She was waiting for the right time."

"But it never came," I said.

"Well, she'd built a new life with Andy," she said. "He loved you, Renata. And in many ways he was more of a father to you than Louie. Can't you see why your mother wouldn't have been eager to dredge up the past?"

"No, I don't."

"I wish you didn't view the world in such stark contrast," said Honora. "Bad guys in one corner, saints in the other. How can you write screenplays with such a narrow view of human nature?"

I flinched. Long before I'd burned my screenplay, the Caliban executives had pretty much said the same thing. I'd chalked it up to lost mojo, but maybe it was something more. I squeezed my hands together. Then I said, "You could have told me."

"No, I couldn't. It wasn't my place to tell."

"That's a mother's job," said Gladys.

"Is it a father's?" I asked.

"Louie's not much of an historian, and you know it." Honora flipped to another page that showed wedding pictures.

"But your mother never loved Kip," said Gladys.

"Kip?" I sat up straight.

"That's who your mama had the affair with," said Isabella. "He was a beautician."

Gladys got to her feet and shook her finger at Isabella. "You just couldn't wait to tell, could you? And you promised not to."

"I lied," said Isabella. "Listen to yourselves, how mysterious y'all sound. The girl needs to hear the truth about her mother and Kip."

"What, did he give her a bad haircut?" I laughed and pointed to my head.

"No, dahlin'," said Isabella. "Kip Quattlebaum had a way with women. He couldn't be beat giving permanents. Plus, he gave Shelby more time than your father ever did."

I just sat there, shaking my head. This was the most ridiculous story I'd ever heard. "Let me get this straight," I said. "My mother slept with her hairdresser?"

"Actually, he was mine," said Honora. "And a damn good one."

"He broke up Louie and Shelby," said Isabella.

"I always blamed myself for inviting him to Nigel's party," said Honora.

"If it hadn't been Kip, it would've been somebody else," said Isabella.

"Wait a minute. We're talking about *my* mother? Better known as Miss Death Do Us Part?"

"She wasn't always that way," said Isabella. "Before she married Andy Van-Dusen, she was sort of fun."

"I can't listen to this." I bolted off the sofa, and the invitation fluttered to the bricks.

"Sit back down. You asked for the truth," said Isabella. "You said you could take it. Obviously you cannot. *There's* your reason why your mother didn't tell you."

"I know it's hard to believe," said Honora. "It shocked all of us."

"I wouldn't of believed it, either," said Gladys. "But I was there. I saw them fall in love."

"It wasn't love," insisted Honora.

"Maybe not," said Gladys. "But it was something close to it. It's a long story. We'll need more tea."

"Tea, hell," said Isabella. "Illegal substances won't be enough."

"Start talking." I picked up Gladys's hand. "Tell me everything."

Chapter 19

❂ ❂ ❂

GLADYS SAYS, THIS IS HOW IT STARTED

*M*y mama used to say that a poppy seed would tell if someone was unfaithful. Take the seed and lay it on your left hand, then hit it with your right fist. If the seed pops, your lover has been unfaithful. Dropped scissors is another sign that your sweetheart has been untrue. But neither seeds or scissors was involved when Shelby fell in love with that man-hairdresser.

Louie, he worked all the time at Ochsner, learning how to cut up hearts and sew them back together. He'd bought Shelby that little house in Covington, where her people lived, so she wouldn't be so lonely. It was a square blue house with curlicue trim work and a big yard with two pecan trees that dropped nuts on the garage roof.

Shelby hated that house. She didn't want to look at the lake where her sister had died. And to reach New Orleans, they had to cross the Pontchartrain twice, going and coming. She couldn't make Louie understand. To make things worse, he started taking little jobs on the weekend. Moonlighting, he called it. Every weekend he would be gone from Friday morning until late Sunday evening. The rest of the time he was working, leaving her alone with me and Renata.

Shelby and I passed time by planting a little garden, mainly tomatoes and cucumbers. She would set the transistor radio in the grass, then walk out to help me weed. Seems like all the stations was playing "You Can't Always Get What You Want"—I forget who sings it—and she'd yank them weeds with a vengeance. She jerked up crabgrass, then threw it in the trash can. "Do you know what I've done?" she asked me. And I said, "Pulled a weed?" "No," she said. "I have married a man just like my father. But instead of hunting, Louie is addicted to hospitals. He's a workaholic."

She sat down in the grass, big old tears hitting her knee. "Oh, Gladys, I'm so afraid I'll end up like my mother. Turning my loneliness inside out the way she did."

I didn't know what to say, so I just put my arms around her and rocked back and forth, like she was a baby. "I know his work matters," she said, wiping her nose, "but if he's going to be gone all the time, I'd rather live in New Orleans."

"Baby, have you talked to Louie? Told him how you feel?"

"About a thousand times." She didn't want to worry him, didn't want to nag. She'd seen firsthand how Emma had drove Thaddeus away. Despite her unhappy childhood memories and a deep-seated hatred of Covington, Shelby tried to make the best of the situation, but it wasn't easy. Those rare days when Louie was home, the telephone wouldn't stop ringing—patients, nurses, other doctors. He wore a contraption called a beeper, and it would chirrup when the hospital needed him. He never took it off except when he undressed. Sometimes he'd lose it and tear the house apart.

"Shelby? Have you seen my beeper?" he'd ask, opening a drawer, riffling through the silverware. He tore the garbage bag, spilling coffee grounds on the floor. "Honey? Did you put it somewhere? Come on, Shel, help me look."

"I am not your beeper's keeper," she said.

Well, I'll just tell you. Marriage is too hard without adding telephone calls and beepers. Before my husband Dolph went to Angola, his mama like to drove me crazy. Called on the phone four or five times a day, but I knew better than to disrespect the woman who'd birthed him. Dolph bitterly complained about those calls, but he couldn't make her stop. So he took it out on me, griping about my cooking, or how I kept house. Every marriage needs peaceable moments—no talking, just being. Floating together in sweet silence. It took Angola Prison to stop his mama, but I am drifting.

Back to Shelby. She was determined not to repeat her parents' mistakes, so she poured herself into child rearing. Renata was three and a half, and she was a mama's girl all the way. Shelby hired a man to plow the sunny side yard, then she and the baby planted a fairy-tale garden: Wizard of Oz poppies, Jack's beanstalks, Sleeping Beauty's rose trellis, and Johnny Appleseed trees. They'd read every children's book at the St. Tammany Parish Library, and Renata knew most of them by heart. Shelby printed simple words on index cards and practically taught that baby to read.

On the few occasions that Shelby and Louie went out to dinner, Renata would burst into tears and beat against the screen door, begging her mama not to leave. I tried everything I knew to distract that child, but she wouldn't budge from that door until her mama returned. Shelby got to where she didn't like to leave the baby, and in a scary way, she became the very thing she'd tried to avoid: she'd turned into her own mama. Shelby wasn't housebound, but she was baby-bound.

Honora drove over once a month to see the baby, bringing wine, champagne, and some toys that made the awfullest racket. Shelby loved anything that Honora did. They were closer than any mother and daughter, and it wasn't because of their shared love for Louie or Renata. Emma Stevens's illness may have had something to do with it, along with Thaddeus's absences.

For whatever reasons, Shelby and Honora just tooked to each other. They walked in downtown Covington, sharing a vanilla ice cream cone, or painting each other's nails. If a person didn't know that Emma Stevens existed, they might have thought Honora was Shelby's mother, not that they looked alike in the least. Honora was tall, with dark eyes and straight chestnut hair, and she wore tailored clothing. Shelby's sun-streaked head barely came up to Honora's chin. But they was alike on the inside. Those two could carry on conversations in their thoughts, finishing each other's sentences aloud.

It was a especial kinship. I don't think they understood it. Some things, and some friendships, just *are*, you know? And to question them is a invitation to the devil.

During one of her visits, Honora made me hold the ladder while she hung shell chimes on the screen porch. Shelby stood in the doorway, the baby on her hip, and complimented them. And once they were up, they did make a nice tinkle. Then Shelby set the baby in Honora's lap. Renata had a head full of taffy-colored curls that made me think she'd be a blonde someday.

We went inside to fix a pitcher of whiskey sours. Shelby turned up the radio. Louis Armstrong was singing about two to tango on the jazz station. Which was the very thing fixing to happen to Shelby. Inside the kitchen, she had the morning mail stacked on the counter. Sitting on the top of the pile was an invitation. Honora's brother-in-law, Nigel, was throwing a birthday party over in North Carolina at some famous golfing resort. He could afford it, I suppose, him being a general practitioner over in Gulfport, Mississippi.

All of us was being dragged to the far-off party, including me and one of Ida DeChavannes's longtime maids, Loretta, who said it was our job to take care of the crazy rich people and make a good impression. I didn't work for that woman, but Ida bought me a especial black gabardine uniform and a little white hat that looked like something petits fours come in. "Don't you dare wear that," said Shelby, pointing to the suit. No one, not even my own self, could have guessed that she would act up like she did and cause a uproar, bringing all that misery on herself and Louie.

It started at the Mobile airport even before the plane took off. All of the DeChavanneses were sitting in the chairs, laughing and carrying on. In one row was Miss Ida, Dr. Nigel, and their spoiled son, Chauncey. In the next row was Honora, Dr. Chaz, and their actress friend Isabella D'Agostino-McGeehee. Behind them sat Mary Agnes DeChavannes, better known as Aunt Na-Na. She was Dr. Chaz and Dr. Nigel's crazy sister. Beside her sat the "quiet" brother, Dr. James DeChavannes, who lived in Pass Christian, Mississippi, and didn't have one drop of personality; but he was the only neurologist between New Orleans and Mobile. Next row after that was Louie, Shelby, me, Renata, and old Loretta.

Then a good-looking man walked up, carrying a brown leather bag. Honora introduced him as Kip Quattlebaum of Fairhope, Alabama, where he owned a beauty shop. Loretta said that Kip was Honora's beautician; his daddy was the lieutenant governor of Alabama, and his mother was a fool, but Lord have mercy, you never saw a more handsome fellow in your life. He was hairy everywhere except for a bald patch on his head, which was slick and glossy and red-tinged from too much sun. And his eyes were a pretty purple-blue.

He kept glancing at Shelby's legs and her blond hair. "Ain't no good going to come of this party," said Loretta, looking up at me with muddy, half-blind eyes. "Ain't no good at all."

We climbed on the plane, hogging every seat in first class, and still, there were some of us left standing. The stewardess said she was sorry, but two of us would have to sit in coach. She asked for volunteers. Nobody raised their hand. Miss Ida said, "But I made reservations for everybody in first class."

"Huh," said Loretta. "Reservations for everybody but me and you."

"I'm so sorry," the stewardess said, "but there appears to be a misunderstanding. We don't have enough seats. Two passengers need to move to coach."

"I demand to see the head of this airline," said Ida.

The stewardess ignored Ida and looked at the rest of us. "You all decide among yourselves."

We were in the aisle, holding up traffic. People were pushing from behind, trying to get into their seats.

"I'm not going back there," said Miss Ida.

"Oh, for heaven's sakes, I'll go," said Shelby, picking up her flowery tote bag. She stepped sideways down the aisle and headed toward the back of the plane.

"I need one more volunteer," said the stewardess.

"I can go," I said, shifting little Renata to my other hip.

"Are you and the baby together?" asked the stewardess.

I nodded.

"Then you need to stay here." She pointed to Chauncey. "You, go sit in coach."

"I will not!" Chauncey's face reddened.

"Let's draw straws," suggested Dr. Chaz.

"That's okay, I'll go," said Mr. Kip. We all turned to stare. He gathered his leather garment bag and frowned, as if he'd made a sacrifice to sit back in coach with Shelby, and her wearing a blue dress cut up to here.

Miss Ida, she looked relieved. She sat down in her seat and crossed her legs. "Bring me a glass of champagne," she told the stewardess. I leaned my head into the aisle and watched Mr. Kip ease on down the aisle. He stopped at Shelby's row. His shoulders hunched, and his lips curved into a shy half smile. She said something—I couldn't hear what. Then he sat down. I could just see the top of their heads. What happened after that was a mystery. The stewardess drew the curtain, and the engines started to hum. I put my hand on the baby's head, thinking the grits was fixing to hit the fan.

We changed planes in Atlanta. In Charlotte we climbed off the plane and all of us piled into a little twenty-five-seater that rattled and smelled of gasoline. This time Dr. Louie and Shelby sat together. Renata sat with me, next to the window. She stood up on her seat and jumped. "Up!" she cried, stretching her arms. "Up, up!"

"Make that baby sit down and be quiet," said Miss Ida, turning back to glare. I took Renata's hands, told her to climb down from there and act like a little lady. After a while, the engines started whipping around. Through a part in the curtains, I saw the pilots. They wore dark blue trousers with knife blade pleats, and blue short-sleeved shirts. I even saw their elbows, all red and scaly, and for some reason this scared me. I started sweating, and my heart beat so fast that Renata reached around and pressed her little hand on my chest.

"What's in there?" she asked me. "A bird?"

"It's my heart, baby," I said. "It's nothing but Gladys's heart."

I silently praised God when the little plane touched down hard on the tarmac. We climbed down and saw the tiny little airport. The pilots helped unload the luggage and golf clubs. The baby was dragging my hand, but I was waiting for Shelby.

I heard Dr. Nigel say that rich businessmen flew to Pinehurst in the morning, played eighteen holes of golf, then climbed back on the plane and flew off. He said the average guest spent $500 a day.

"Nothing but crazy people," Loretta whispered, waving one brown, bony hand. "Crazy coming and crazy going."

A charter bus drove us to Pinehurst. Miss Shelby sat up front with the DeChavanneses, all prim and proper, but it was hard to tell what she was thinking. The bus pulled up to a long white hotel, and doormen in red coats rushed forward. Get you this, ma'am? Don't you lift that, let me take it, ma'am. Dr. Nigel and Dr. Chaz climbed out of the bus. They'd been drinking and had that shiny look in their eyes. Dr. Nigel pulled a handful of dollar bills out of his pocket and rushed around, crushing them into everybody's palms. He even gave one to a short man with curly black hair and thick glasses. "I don't work here," the man said, shoving the money back at Dr. Nigel.

"Sorry, pal," said Dr. Nigel. "Take it anyway."

The curly-headed tourist tucked the money into Dr. Nigel's pocket, then walked off into the trees, shaking his head. "What's his problem?" Dr. Nigel asked the doorman, who was too busy sorting our luggage to answer. Then Dr. Nigel looked up at the sky and asked it the same question, only louder.

"Guess he wasn't your pal," Ida said.

On the way to our rooms the porter asked me who we were, and I told him all about the birthday party. After he stacked our suitcases in the room, I laid a dollar bill in his hand. After he left, Ida pulled me aside and whispered, "Don't be so friendly with the help, Gladys. This is not the Deep South."

Just how deep was it? I wondered. Skin deep? Hip deep? And was other parts of the South shallow? The rest of us got connecting rooms. Except for Aunt Na-Na, who put a Do Not Disturb sign on her knob, the DeChavanneses left their doors open, and the people ran in and out, like this was summer camp. Down the hall, I heard Dr. Nigel just a-carrying on, telling Loretta to order sandwiches. Then Ida told him to leave the food to her, and she'd leave the bourbon to him.

"Order hors d'oeuvres, Loretta," said Ida, "not sandwiches. Order cheese straws, sausage pinwheels, boiled jumbo shrimps. Charge it to our suite."

"Who going to eat this food?" asked Loretta.

"Guests," said Ida. "Guests and family of the birthday boy."

The DeChavannes brothers crowded around Nigel, teasing him about getting old. Kip Quattlebaum walked around them, and never looked once at me or Shelby. He wasn't prissy like you'd expect in a hair man. He went straight to his room and shut the door.

While all this was going on, little old Renata fell asleep on my bed. The DeChavannes men kept wandering from room to room, ice clinking in their glasses, gathering up their tees and hats, ready to play golf. Then I heard Dr. Chaz scream at Honora, "You forgot to pack my golf shoes."

I stepped out into the hall, not to see if a fight would break out but to watch Honora turn him inside out. He was a bully, but she knew how to get to him.

"I didn't forget your shoes on purpose, darling." She pointed to his legs. He wore blue plaid golf shorts, with two hairy, slightly bowed legs sticking out. "Have you seen all those broken veins on the backs of your legs? My goodness, Chaz. You're riddled with varicose veins. My mother had them, but not quite this bad."

"Where?" He twisted his head, trying to see.

"You need to get off your feet. Just prop them on a couple of pillows," Honora said. "I could run down to the gift shop and see if they sell any support hose."

Louie must have heard his mama and daddy carrying on, and he ran out into the hall. "Don't worry about it, Daddy. I've got an extra pair. They'll fit you."

"Why, I didn't know you wore support hose, too," said Honora. "I guess varicose veins and the DeChavannes men are star-crossed."

"I was talking about shoes," said Louie. "Daddy and I both wear 10-D."

Now I will just tell you. Louie was easy on the eyes, all that thick brown hair, high cheekbones, and that famous DeChavannes nose; but if he didn't watch out, he'd end up shaped like his daddy. Dr. Chaz was built like a manatee, swelled in the middle, tapered at the bottom. Renata ran out of the room and held up her arms. "Dad-dy, pick me up!"

"Hey, sweet pea," he said, absently touching her head.

Dr. Chaz craned his neck, trying to glimpse the backs of his legs. They did have a lot of veins. He was the most famous brain surgeon in southern Alabama and had cut up many prominent brains. But he was proud. You could see it in his strut, the way he stopped in front of a mirror, looking this way and that way; sometimes he'd lift his arms and make a muscle. He didn't know he was puny. Psalms 94:11 says, "The Lord knoweth the thoughts of man, that they are vanity."

"I'll just buy a new pair at the pro shop," said Dr. Chaz, and he headed toward the elevator. "Coming, Louie?"

He trotted off like a wind-up toy, and I thought, Lord, when I get old and if my heart gives out, hide me from this man. Find him an ocean. Find him a woman manatee. Let him swim with his own kind.

The other DeChavannes men stepped into the hall and, except for James, clapped Louie on the back. Shelby stepped into the hall, watching them leave.

"Don't forget the birthday dinner tonight," Louie called out.

"I wouldn't for the world," she said sweetly, leaning against the doorjamb, one hand high over her curly blond head. She was still wearing that short blue dress and heels, but Dr. Louie hurried down the hall, chasing after his drunk uncles and his vain, brain-handling daddy.

Shelby went back into our suite and shut the door to her room. Isabella opened her door. "I don't know why Honora invited Kip," she said, lighting a cigarette. "When he isn't riding his Harley, he's fishing in the bay."

"Or fixing women's hair," I said.

"A lot of people who don't know him might think that a male stylist might not be masculine, but that just shows their ignorance. Heaven help the woman who needs her hair colored or trimmed during quail-hunting season, because Kip can't be found. He's also quite the ladies' man."

Our door opened and Shelby came out, wearing a yellow shift and white sandals. "Could you keep an eye on Renata?" she asked me. "I'm going shopping. I forgot to buy Nigel a birthday present."

"Of course I will," I said, thinking about that gift-wrapped box I'd seen in her suitcase.

"Mmm-hum," she said dreamily. Then she stepped out into the hall. Mr. Kip was waiting. He'd changed into a madras shirt. He lifted one hand and waved to Isabella and me, and I thought, Now that man is handsome. It must be something about the swamps in our part of the world, something that gets into their blood. Makes the women sassy, the men so pretty it breaks your heart. Together they walked off. I did not know where they went or what they did.

They didn't return for a long time. I couldn't shake the feeling that something was fixing to happen. Three hours later, it sure enough did.

Chapter 20

* * *

IT'S HONORA'S TURN TO TALK

That birthday party was in the evening. So Isabella and I spent the afternoon lounging around the pool, looking at architectural drawings of her new house. She and Dickie Boy had bought the summer cottage next door to me, then bulldozed it. Isabella wanted a miniature Château de Chambord, including a rooftop terrace with sweeping views of Mobile Bay.

Two hours before the rehearsal dinner, we rolled up the blueprints and proceeded into the hotel. We knocked on Kip's door, hoping he'd fix our hair, but he wasn't in his room. So we wandered over to Louie and Shelby's suite. Gladys had Renata in her lap, trying to brush the baby's wispy hair into a topknot, but it kept springing loose.

"Is Shelby getting ready?" I said, glancing toward the bathroom.

"Haven't seen her all afternoon," said Gladys, her lips shut with bobby pins. "Not since the men went golfing."

"Did she say where she was going?" I asked. It was unusual for Shelby to leave the baby.

"No, ma'am." Gladys put a pin into the topknot, then frowned when the hairs sprang free.

"Oh, dear." I touched Renata's curls. "Kip could fix this."

Isabella stretched her arms over her head. "I told you we couldn't rely on Kip to fix our hair," she said. "He's selfish."

"Oh, he's not," I said.

"His mama bought him that beauty shop," said Isabella. "Then she bought him a brick house over in Pine Shores subdivision. It has the cutest mosquito netting around the bed."

"Oh?" I raised one eyebrow. "Don't tell me you've seen it."

"Many times, dahlin'." Isabella lit a cigarette. "We had a little fling last summer, but his selfishness got in the way, and I dropped him."

"I don't want to hear it," I said. Laid out on the bed was a pink organdy dress and white patent leather Mary Janes. Next to that was a uniform that Ida had insisted Gladys wear. I thought this was presumptuous and offered to let her wear one of my dresses, but Gladys just shrugged. "I don't care what I wear tonight," she said. "This uniform says more about y'all than it does me."

While I cast about for a reply, the door opened and Shelby rushed into the room. Renata struggled out of Gladys's arms and screamed, "Mama!" Shelby leaned down and lifted the baby into her arms.

"There's my angel," she said, kissing Renata's neck. "You smell good!"

"Where have you been?" I asked, then flinched. It sounded a bit accusatory, even to my ears. Maybe she just needed time to herself. But it was not like her to neglect her baby girl.

"Shopping," she said.

I glanced at her empty arms and raised my eyebrows.

"I'm not *that* late, am I?" She grabbed a green dress off the hanger, then ducked into the bathroom. The door clicked shut. I knew she was upset with Louie over his work schedule, and I didn't blame her, but no one could talk sense to that boy. I kissed my granddaughter, then hurried to my room.

At a quarter to seven, Chaz and I went downstairs. Louie was waiting outside the dining room with Gladys and Renata. He lifted his hand and glanced at his watch. When Shelby finally walked up, he roughly grabbed her arm. He didn't say, You sure look pretty. Didn't say anything complimentary. Instead he started fussing. "That dress is way too short. Go back upstairs and change."

"I will not." She jerked her arm free, then stared him down.

"Don't make a scene. Look, I'll go with you."

"This dress is fine. I bought it at Gus Meyer, and it's perfectly fine. Why don't you just go inside and order a drink."

I drew in my breath. I had never seen her act this way, and I had been around them plenty. Little Renata looked up at her daddy, then at her mama. Her dark eyebrows pushed together. She looked just like her daddy; I glanced up, wondering if her parents had noticed. Their eyes were locked on each other, and not in a romantic way. Chaz broke the spell when he opened the door. "Ladies first," he said, sweeping his hand.

We were seated at the head table, and everybody made over Renata so much that I was afraid she'd put on a show. The child had been known to tap-dance on tables, she ate up attention. The introductions went all around the table. Nigel gestured to me and said, simply, "My brother's lovely wife, the former Honora Hughes." When he reached his sour-faced sister, Na-Na, he looked puzzled, like he didn't know who she was. While she glowered at him, he just snapped his fingers and said, "Wait a minute, it'll come to me, just a sec. Are you a nun? Where do you go to church—Our Lady of the Imbeciles?"

She picked up her fork and made a jabbing motion. "Oh, hell," Nigel said, "can't you take a joke? Come over here and give me a kiss."

She put down the fork and pecked his cheek; but the damage was done. Na-Na's face swelled and turned red. Then Nigel started to introduce Shelby, but she wasn't paying attention, she was looking at the double doors, where Kip had just appeared, his violet eyes lit up from within, like tea candles burned inside them. Even in his rumpled tuxedo jacket, he looked unbearably handsome.

As he walked to his table, he passed right by us. He smelled good, too, of bay rum and whiskey. I held my breath, waiting to see if Shelby would look at him. She didn't, but he gave her a long glance. Uh-oh, I thought.

My oblivious son sat across from me. He shook out his napkin, and started making small talk with Aunt Na-Na. He had forgotten to comb his hair, and it was sticking up like a hedgehog. At the other end of the table, Ida chattered about the food she'd special-ordered for the dinner. The men relived their golf games, talking about birdies and eagles.

Ida's maid, Loretta, snorted. "Why, you'd think they'd gone hunting, not hitting a little white ball with a stick."

I tried to engage Na-Na in polite conversation, then gave up in frustration and listened to the men. I put my chin in my hand and smiled over at Chaz, listening to him tell about his hobby—Civil War reenactments. Two seats down, Shelby busied herself with Renata, cutting up her veal and feeding her tiny pieces. Chaz ordered whiskey sours for Gladys and Loretta, then brought me a martini.

After the dessert, there was dancing. Right in front of our table was a marble dance floor, although I hadn't noticed it earlier. The orchestra was playing "I'm Getting Sentimental Over You."

A half hour passed. Shelby danced with Chaz, Nigel, and Chauncey. Louie sat off to the side, talking to his uncle James. Kip came over to Shelby and touched her shoulder. He bent down and whispered something in her ear. I couldn't believe his gall, and I prayed she'd shoo him away. But she smiled, then nodded. He helped her up from her chair and they walked toward the orchestra. I glanced toward Louie. His head swiveled as his wife and the hair-dresser stepped out onto the dance floor and put their arms around each other—not too close, but not too far apart. Kip was tall, broad-shouldered, and her head barely reached his chin, but anybody with eyes could see how they'd be a good fit. He touched her gently as if he was handling a delicate weave and not a woman.

The music changed to "All the Way." Shelby clutched Kip, and he kept holding on to her. I liked that song, and I am a fool for Frank Sinatra, but if you ask me, the Duke played it better. Louie gazed at the dance floor, his face calm and amused, as if this dance meant nothing. Na-Na watched, too, and two lines creased her forehead. Beside her, Ida opened a diamond pillbox and put a white tablet on her tongue. "Gladys," she said, "that's the second dessert you've let Renata eat. Every tooth in her little head will rot out."

I poured a glass of wine, then glanced back at the dance floor. Shelby looked up dreamily into Kip's eyes and smiled. All night long, they danced without stopping. Spinning around that floor, moving their feet to "Moon River" and "Secret Love." One song after the other. This music was written way back when I was a young girl, and it still applied today. If people didn't care about romance, why would there be all these songs?

The orchestra started playing "Summer Samba," one of my favorites. It was so snappy, I couldn't stop my foot from tapping. Even Renata was tapping away. "Don't scuff your patten leather shoes," Gladys said, and Aunt Na-Na leaned across the table, her heavy crucifix banging into her wineglass.

"It's *patent* leather," she snapped, spittle flying out of her tight lips. "Patent. Not patten!"

"Don't be rude, Na-Na," I said, and she flipped her hand and scowled. I turned my chair away from her, toward the dance floor. Shelby and Kip were dancing to a slow song. People flowed around them, smiling and looking amused. Nobody at our table looked particularly happy. I leaned across Gladys and pulled Renata into my lap. The baby put her sticky fingers all over my silk gown. Ida leaned across the table and in a slurry, drugged voice said, "Why, I never knew Kip could dance." Then she winked. "You ought to nip that in the bud, Honora."

"Is it time for another pill?" I said, and started playing patty-cake with Renata.

From another table, someone called out, "Play 'Jailhouse Rock,' " but this was a five-star restaurant, not a honky tonk. They would play what they wanted. Nigel kept ordering bourbon, adding ice and water from everybody's glasses. Ida was drinking something that had floating cherries and orange slices. Loretta tapped my shoulder and whispered, "See Dr. Nigel over there, sitting kind of lopsided? Any minute now, he going to keel over and hit the floor."

"Ida doesn't look good, either," I said.

"She'll pass out next," said Loretta. "Miss Ida can't take the pain of being unappreciated."

A woman with a voice like Peggy Lee was singing "Come Rain or Come Shine."

An older couple was dancing with their hands locked high over their heads. They sauntered over to Shelby and Kip. "Are you newlyweds?" the old woman asked in a loud voice. I could hear it from here. Every head at our table turned. Even Renata sat up on her knees and stared.

"No, ma'am," said Kip, and in his voice there was a hint of something sad. He stared into Shelby's eyes. It was the look of a man who was captivated, maybe not for long, but certainly for the evening.

The band started playing "The Devil and the Deep Blue Sea." That song struck a nerve, and Louie stood up, all stiff and evil-eyed. Then he walked over to Gladys. "It's past Renata's bedtime."

"She's doing fine," I said.

"No, she's not," he said. "Gladys, get the baby and leave, please."

"But she's being so good." I wrapped my arms around the child. Renata was his spitting image. She was watching the dancers, her head swinging from side to side, trying to snap her fingers.

"See?" I pointed to the baby. "She's having a fine time. She—"

"I don't want her to see what I'm going to do to her mother," he said.

I turned my head, gazed toward the dance floor. Shelby and Kip were fast-dancing to "Don't Be Cruel." Her hair spilled over his arm, gleaming under the strobe light.

"Please go now, Gladys," he said. "Take my daughter and go."

"Oh, really, Louie," I said. "This is Uncle Nigel's party. Don't ruin it."

"Some party." Louie shoved his hands into his tuxedo pants.

"Why don't you just cut in and dance with her yourself?" I suggested.

His jaw twitched, and I wondered if he was going to make a scene. The DeChavanneses just hated scenes of any kind. I had to admit that Shelby looked fetching in that pretty green sequined dress. Louie pursed his lips and blew out air. He had dark eyes, his daddy's eyes, and they shifted back and forth, as if trying to decide whether to punch Kip in the face or to ask a strange woman to dance. The band started playing a Judy Garland song, "More Than You Know," which was a good song for husbands and wives. So much is unsaid in a marriage. Kindness gets lost in the day-to-day worries and squabbles.

Finally, he said, "Well, all right. I'll give it a try."

"Good." I smiled. "A new song is starting. Don't wait too long, or the moment will pass you by."

I gave him a little shove, and he tottered forward, the strobe light whirling around him on the floor, little splintered pieces flowing over his face.

Chapter 21

✦ ✦ ✦

Hunt Scene

A rusted paperclip held together an old wrinkled newspaper article and a photograph of my mother and father. They held shotguns, and spread out on the ground between them were seven dead quail. Behind them, sunlight glinted through tall loblolly pines. I smoothed the clipping with my hands.

ST. TAMMANY *Citizen*
November 24, 1972

PROMINENT ST. TAMMANY JUDGE WOUNDED IN HUNTING ACCIDENT

The first accident of quail season occurred last Saturday near Independence, Louisiana, when Judge Thaddeus Stevens was accidentally shot at his hunting lodge by his son-in-law, Dr. Louis C. DeChavannes. Also present at the camp was the judge's daughter, Shelby DeChavannes, and a friend, Mr. Kip Quattlebaum. Judge Stevens was rushed to Parish Memorial Hospital, where he was treated and released. No charges have been filed.

Later that morning I found Gladys and Honora sitting in the den, watching the Weather Channel. "There you are," said Honora. "A storm's on the way."

"No, it ain't," said Gladys. "I won't let it. I got too much gardening to do."

From the television, a man in a black suit said a tropical depression was brewing off the coast of Cuba, then the picture changed, showing rain falling into the streets of Havana. In the background, the weatherman said, "It's three months early for hurricane season, but this system looks wicked."

The French doors blew open, banging against the wall. Zap jumped off my grandmother's lap and ran out to the terrace. A breeze ruffled his fur, stirring the potted lemons and sweeping over the glass table. The striped umbrella tilted sideways, and Zap lifted his right paw and sniffed the air. I wondered if the wind had traveled all the way from Cuba, bringing with it smells from every city it had touched. Havana, Miami, Tampa, Panama City, Destin, Pensacola, Mobile. I breathed in a mélange of scents: orange peels, coffee grounds, conch fritters, key lime pie.

Honora got up to shut the doors, snapping her fingers at the dog. He ran inside, over to Gladys, and plopped his head on her foot. I walked over to her chair, handing her the photograph and clipping. She reached for her glasses. "What's this?"

"I was hoping you could tell me." I sat on the floor, scratching Zap's ears. Honora crossed the room and leaned over the back of the chair.

"I didn't know Louie could hunt," she said. "Much less that he'd shot Judge Stevens."

"Me, neither," said Gladys.

"My mother could have worked for the CIA." I sighed.

"Why don't you call your father?" Gladys suggested.

I rolled my eyes. "We aren't speaking, remember?"

"Call him anyway," said Honora. "I'm dying to know what happened. Here, let me pour you a strong cup of coffee."

"Humph, she'll need something stronger than Community Coffee."

"You can do it," said Honora, putting her hands on my shoulders. "Just practice breathing."

It took two hours and four cups of coffee before I worked up my nerve. I was more frightened of my father than anyone. We talked so rarely that I always cut and measured my words, striving to keep them small and precise, all the while worried that I might say something that would alienate him forever. With Ferg, I could say or do anything. I could even wear mismatched shoes to the Academy Awards and he didn't judge. Well, at least he'd been that way. Maybe all relationships were more fragile than anyone knew, and the slightest things could swerve them off course.

Honora opened a Godiva box and parked it beside my elbow. "Here, have a few chocolate truffles," she said.

I bit into the candy, then dialed my father's cell phone. He answered on the third ring.

"Daddy, it's Renata."

"What?" he said. I glanced over at Honora for help, but she made the okay sign with her thumb and finger.

"I was just calling to check on Joie. How's she doing?"

"Comatose. Any other questions?"

"Will she come out of it?"

"Maybe."

"Daddy, I know you think I had something to do with her accident, but I didn't."

"Well, whatever." He exhaled. "Thanks for calling."

"Wait—don't hang up. I want to talk to you."

"Why? So you can run back to Honora? Her gossip cuts two ways. She told me that Caliban Films fired you."

I glanced at my grandmother and rolled my eyes. *Honora Tells All*, I thought, but I said, "Yes, I'm unemployed."

"Didn't your stepfather leave you his millions?"

I didn't respond. My grief was still too raw to discuss Mama and Andy, much less share the details of my inheritance. Finally I said, "Reason I'm calling is, I found an old picture of you and Mama. Y'all had been hunting. It was attached to a newspaper article. Something about you accidentally shooting Grandfather Stevens."

"Where'd you find that?"

"It was . . ." I paused, afraid to tell the truth. I didn't want to implicate Honora. "It was with some of my mama's things."

"What do you want to know?"

"The things that weren't in that article."

"Like?"

"Kip."

"Do not speak that name to me."

"But Daddy, I know about him and Mama. And I want to hear your side."

"She told you? Before she died, I mean?"

"No."

"Who the hell have you been talking to? Don't tell me—Honora and the witches."

My right hand began shaking so violently I had trouble holding on to the phone. Honora reached out and steadied it. "Daddy, I didn't mean to upset you—"

"No, you're an angel. A real, head-bashing sweetheart. My fiancée is in the ICU with God knows how much brain damage, and you want to dredge up the past? You want *me* to tell you about Shelby's lace-drawered boyfriend? I don't have time for this bullshit."

"Did Kip—I mean, did he have anything to do with the shooting?"

"Hell, no. It was an accident." He paused. "Anything else I can help you with, my darling daughter? Or can I get back to my brain-damaged fiancée?" He hung up with a decisive click, but I held the receiver to my ear for a moment longer, hoping it was a mistake, and I'd hear his voice saying, *I'm sorry, baby girl, it's just too painful to remember your mama. But I'll try—for your sake, I'll try. Just tell me where to begin.*

Chapter 22

● ● ●

SPORTSMAN'S PARADISE

After I hung up on Renata, I stopped by the ICU and checked on Joie. She lay there on the bed, bloody hair spread out on the pillow. Tiny bits of her scalp showed where the emergency room physician had shaved and sutured the wound. An endotrachial tube jutted out of her mouth, taped around her neck, and off to the side, the ventilator rhythmically whooshed. Joie's eyes were taped shut, and a lumpy bandage covered her nose.

The chart was hooked to her bed, and I picked it up, flipping pages. I'd pulled strings, gotten the best neurosurgeon in case she developed a subdural hematoma. The MRI and CAT scan had shown a slight amount of blood inside the cranium; the good news was, her brain had stopped swelling, and in the next day or two, they'd start weaning her off the respirator. Chances were good that she'd breathe on her own. Whoever had hit Joie had half killed her. If Renata hadn't done it, who had? And why?

Faye had freaked out after the toxicology screen was positive for a benzodiazepine. This could have been Valium or Xanax. "Joie doesn't take nerve pills," Faye had insisted. "I know everything she puts in her mouth."

Not everything, I'd thought, shifting uneasily in my chair. "Maybe she was nervous before the party," I suggested.

"Joie doesn't get nervous. She was fine, perfectly *fine*." She daintily blew her nose into a lace handkerchief monogrammed "FM."

"I'm not accusing your daughter of anything," she continued, "but the circumstances are suspicious."

"We'll get to the bottom of it," I'd told her.

Now I laid down the chart, thankful that Faye wasn't in the room, so I could have a moment alone with Joie. I pulled up a chair and reached for her hand. Even in this condition, she had a look of Shelby, way back when she was young and tender. I didn't know how that clipping came into Renata's possession, but I could guarantee you that Honora was behind it.

Last October, when Shelby's plane crashed, Honora had been after me to bond with Renata, to clear up all the misinformation that Shelby had disseminated over the years. I wouldn't tell it right, and even if I could, it wouldn't change anything. Hell, I didn't want to dig up those years, much less annotate them for my daughter. Tough break, kid, I thought. Her favorite parent was dead, and she was left with me.

After the divorce, those damn women had sided with Shelby. Blamed me for pushing her into Kip's arms. What did that beautician have that I didn't? Better scissors? The whole time we were at Uncle Nigel's birthday party in Pinehurst, I didn't suspect anything. Man, I was stupid.

That night, after the party, I took her to our room and laid her on the bed. I pulled her dress over her hips, then I licked my finger and wrote I ♡ Shelby on her stomach. We rolled over, and she climbed up on top of me, her hair brushing against my face. I felt her heart thudding against my ribs. "Please, please, can we move away from Covington?" she whispered.

"Anything you want," I said, shutting my eyes. "Anything."

When we got back to Covington, I took a moonlighting job at a little hospital near St. Francisville. It was the quickest way to get money for a down payment, in case the Covington house didn't sell right away. Shelby pitched a fit and wouldn't talk to me. "I'm doing this for you," I said. "I'm trying to save enough money so we can buy a house in New Orleans."

"We don't need to buy anything. We can sell this cottage and rent something," she said. Money wasn't the only reason I'd taken that job. I just liked being inside a hospital. I liked how they smelled, and how the PA system crackled and a disembodied voice would page the doctors. I got a rush when I heard my name. I knew I was gone too much, but I thought Shelby would eventually understand, the same way my mother had come to accept my daddy's absences.

Right before Thanksgiving, Shelby bought a full-grown dog, a Rottweiler mix. According to her former owner, the dog's name was Grendel. It hated kennels, dog food, and the hand of a stranger unless it was firmly between her teeth. "And she just loves to run in the woods," Shelby said. "She's a good squirrel catcher."

I got the feeling that she'd bought it for protection, seeing as I was gone every weekend. She even let it sleep on my side of the bed. Gladys didn't like the dog and wouldn't let it get near Renata. I got a kick when she'd take a soup bone and lure the dog onto the porch. Grendel would stretch out on the wooden planks, the bone propped up between her paws, long ropes of saliva hanging from her jaw. Whenever Shelby walked by, Grendel would drop the bone and scramble to her feet, pushing her muzzle against the screen and whining.

"Poor baby," Shelby would say, then she'd go outside and sit with the dog. I wasn't a bit surprised when she insisted on bringing the animal with us to Point Clear. Honora was having a big Thanksgiving dinner, and the whole DeChavannes clan was invited, plus Mama's friends.

"I don't know about that, baby," I said. "Honora doesn't like dogs in her house."

"She lets Isabella's Yorkies run all over," she said.

"Yeah, but they're little. Grendel is big as a donkey."

When we got to Point Clear, Grendel snapped at Aunt Ida, and Chaz put the dog in the pool house. Shelby didn't like it, but she didn't say anything until we got ready for bed. We were leaving early in the morning to go quail hunting at her daddy's camp near Independence. I'd never shot a gun, but here lately, it was all that Shelby talked about.

My family didn't hunt—they went boating—but most everyone hunted quail from Thanksgiving until Christmas Day. They treated their guns like members of the family, passed down each generation along with the sterling silver and jewelry. Like Judge Stevens said, "Louisiana is Sportsman's Paradise, no matter what you are hunting."

Honora had invited so many people for Thanksgiving, she'd set up a buffet in the dining room and placed card tables in four rooms. Shelby and Renata sat with Honora and Chaz; I was seated in the library next to Isabella, who'd brought a sweet potato casserole. I ate three helpings, which just tickled her to pieces. Later that night, my stomach began to cramp. Shelby put on a pink baby-doll gown, then grabbed her pillow and turned out of our room. "Where you going?" I called.

"The pool house," she said. "I can't let Grendel sleep all by herself."

"What about me? I'm sick." I rubbed my stomach.

"What's the matter, honey?" She sat down on the edge of the bed and placed a cool hand on my forehead.

"I ate too much of Isabella's sweet potatoes," I said.

"Oh, Louie, no." Her eyes widened. "Didn't you hear what she did last Easter?"

I shook my head.

"She mixed Ex-Lax into the chocolate mousse. Apparently some of the guests couldn't make it to the bathroom and they ran out into the bay."

"That's terrible. Why would she do that?"

"She was trying to make her mother-in-law sick," said Shelby. "That's what I heard."

"Wish you'd said something earlier." I fell back against the bed, one hand over my eyes.

"There's Pepto-Bismol in the bathroom." She blew me a kiss, then hurried out of the room. The next morning, I was still queasy when we packed the car and drove over to her daddy's hunting lodge. From the backseat, Grendel whined, then began to pant, sending fishy smells in my direction. When I twirled the dial on the radio, she whined and circled the seat a few times.

"She wants you to turn it down," said Shelby, reaching over to snap off the radio.

Grendel's pink tongue slid back and forth in the groove between her incisors. She was breathing so hard, the windows were fogging up.

"Maybe you should turn on the defrost?" Shelby drew her finger through condensation on the windshield.

"Look, do you want to drive?" I frowned. My knuckles turned white as I squeezed the wheel. It was a long way to Independence, and I wished I'd just stayed in Point Clear and let Mama feed me broth and dry toast.

"Sorry, baby," she said. "I don't mean to be a backseat driver."

I hunched toward the dashboard and stared at the highway. Actually, I was feeling pretty bad and was halfway hoping she'd drive. I glanced in the backseat, watching Grendel pace. The gray hairs on her muzzle pleased me in a perverse way. I cracked open the window, and the car filled with the scent of pines and creek water.

"By the way," she said. "Kip Quattlebaum is joining us."

"Who?"

"You remember Kip. He was at Uncle Nigel's party."

"That hairdresser?" I laughed. "Can he hunt?"

"What does it matter?" She shrugged. "You don't."

Shelby had been hunting many times with her father, but I'd never gone. I didn't see the point of killing birds. I glanced over at her, but she turned around, staring out the window. I wanted to ask why the hell she'd invited that hairdresser. Then I remembered how they'd danced, and I wondered if this was serious. Had she been in contact with him? And if so, for what purpose?

Without taking my eyes from the road, I lifted one hand from the wheel and squeezed her hand. "You're awfully quiet," I said, glancing sideways. She didn't respond, so I put my hand back on the wheel again, and Grendel grunted, breathing hard against the glass.

"You think your daddy will approve of Grendel?" I asked, stifling a belch.

"Sure, he likes dogs."

It was dusk when I turned the Triumph down a rough paved road. The ground looked dusty, as if it hadn't rained up here in weeks. Then I pulled into a long gravel driveway. Farther down the drive, lights burned in the windows of a white clapboard house. Judge Stevens sat on the front porch, cracking pecans. He set down the bowl and got up from the swing. A yellow tomcat followed him down the steps, his furry belly swinging back and forth.

"I was starting to worry about you all," Judge Stevens said, shaking my hand. Then he hugged Shelby. "Louie, you still planning to go quail hunting tomorrow?"

"Yes, sir."

Shelby ran back to the car and opened the car door for Grendel. The dog hopped stiff-legged into the gravel and eyed the Arabian mare in the pasture. The mare had a five-month-old filly by her side. The hair along Grendel's back lifted. She started running along the fence, barking, and the horses cantered into the trees.

"You stop that, Grendel!" Shelby clapped her hands. The dog turned away from the fence and growled at the cat. It leaped to the Triumph's roof. After a moment, it lifted its paw and licked the fur in short, bone-smoothing strokes. One ear was scabbed on the triangular point.

Grendel started barking again, running in circles. The tom seemed insulted; he stopped licking his paw and stared. Grendel paced back and forth, whining, then she spun in circles, chasing her stubby tail, biting air.

"Grendel! What's the matter with you?" called Shelby. "Bad girl. Bad, bad girl!" She isn't the only one, I thought.

I awakened before dawn to the smell of biscuits. My stomach churned, but I somehow got dressed and stumbled into the kitchen. Judge Stevens stood next to the stove, holding a stick of butter.

"There you are, Louie," he said. "Sleep well?"

"Yes, sir." I pulled out a chair and sat down, peering into the tidy kitchen. A yellow dishrag lay folded on the sink. A sweet potato sat in a Ball jar, its roots forked out in cloudy water. Judge Stevens came up to Independence every weekend, even when it wasn't hunting season. His wife always stayed in Covington. He opened the oven, grabbed a potholder, and slid out the biscuit pan. He'd built a little world here without Mrs. Stevens.

"Coffee's almost ready," said the judge, setting the pan on the counter. "Shelby told me that you like your coffee first thing of a morning."

"Normally I do," I said, rubbing my stomach. "My gut hasn't felt right since the big feast."

"There's Alka-Seltzer in the cabinet." Judge Stevens started buttering the biscuits. "Me and Emma just ate turkey pot pies for Thanksgiving dinner."

I lowered my head, ashamed that we hadn't invited them to Honora's dinner; but Shelby's mama was taking powerful psychiatric medicines, and they were affecting her in strange ways. Ever since I'd known Emma Stevens, she'd been a shut-in, but the new drugs made her sleepwalk. Although I didn't know the details, the last time the Stevenses had visited Point Clear, Emma had apparently messed up Honora's gardens.

Shelby walked into the room and sat down, lacing her boots. She looked over at me and waved her hand. "Is that what you're wearing?"

I nodded, glancing down at my green corduroy slacks, new Justin boots, and a green flannel shirt. But I'd heard something in her voice. "Do I need to change clothes?"

"No, you're fine." She picked up a biscuit and bit into it. Butter dripped down her chin, and she wiped it off with her sleeve. I knew she was still mad about my moonlighting job. Behind her, the windowpanes were beaded in moisture. Way over the trees, the sun broke open like an egg yolk, running into the ground.

Grendel sulked around the room, sniffing those biscuits. Then her ears perked and she growled. A moment later, I heard gravel spitting, and I pushed back the curtain. A brown truck lumbered up the driveway, with two dogs hanging their heads out the window. A man climbed out and walked toward the house. He wore a hat, faded jeans, a camouflage jacket, and a vest.

"Is that your friend?" Judge Stevens asked Shelby.

"Yes, sir." She nodded. "That's Kip Quattlebaum. He's a fine hunter."

"And a beautician." I dropped the curtain, and it swung over the glass.

My father-in-law laughed and poured coffee into a mug. "Louie, sure you don't want coffee? It's good and hot."

"No, thank you."

The door opened, and Kip stepped inside the kitchen, bringing the smell of cold air and damp pine needles. He stamped his feet against the chill. His eyes looked strange, too colorful, almost like a woman's.

"He pulled off his cap, and curly auburn hair flopped over his collar.

"Daddy, this is Kip Quattlebaum."

"Nice to meet you." Judge Stevens handed Kip a mug of coffee. "Shelby's been bragging about you. Says you're a fine hunter."

"No, sir. I've just got good bird dogs." Kip sipped the coffee, and a wisp of steam curled above his head.

"Shelby's a good little hunter," said Judge Stevens. "She was six when she shot her first dove. She can't be beat skinning quail."

"Oh, poo." She laughed and waved her hand. "He's exaggerating."

"Don't be modest." Judge Stevens tipped his head back and smiled.

I reached down and rubbed Grendel's neck. "You ready to hunt, girl?"

"You can't take that dog!" Two patches of color spread across the judge's cheeks.

"Why not?" I looked down at Grendel. "She's a good squirrel dog. Isn't she, Shelby?"

My wife looked out the window. Judge Stevens and Kip exchanged glances. "She isn't a bird dog," said my father-in-law. "And pardon me for saying so, but she doesn't look like much of a squirrel dog, either."

"Well, she's supposed to be." I looked down at Grendel, then grabbed her head. "Aren't you a hunting dog, girl?"

She responded with a growl, then snapped at my hand. Judge Stevens's forehead puckered. He scratched the side of his neck and looked at me. Kip turned toward the counter and poured another cup of coffee. He glanced over at me. "A well-trained bird dog is worth thousands of dollars," he said.

I looked down at Grendel but said nothing. Shelby had to know this. What was she trying to pull?

"Have you ever, you know, shot a gun?" asked Kip.

I hated to lie, but I said, "Sure I have."

"What kind of gun?"

I wasn't sure what to say. My daddy had started to collect guns from the Civil War era, and he let me shoot some type of musket at a reenactment. He belonged to a society of Civil War buffs and spent hundreds of dollars on memorabilia and elaborate costumes. Three times this year he'd taken off for one battlefield or another and pitched a tent, cooking his food over an open fire and pretending to be General DeChavannes. My mother refused to attend these events and thought my father lived in a fantasy world.

Judge Stevens was waiting for an answer, but I couldn't lie. He sat down at the table and rubbed his chin. His hand whisked over the gray stubble. Behind him Kip leaned against the sink. "Are you talking about a BB gun or a shotgun or what?"

"It was a Civil War gun," I said, and Shelby put her hand over her mouth.

"You're teasing, right?" Kip laughed. "You couldn't of fought in that war."

"My father collects antique guns," I said.

"All right, then," said Judge Stevens. "Then you probably know the basics. But in quail hunting, there's ethics and rules involved."

I chewed the inside of my cheek. I was starting to get mad, like the three of them had ganged up on me.

"Well, that's all right," said the judge. "We'll give you a crash course later on."

"Don't tell me—gun safety?" I said.

"Well, that, too. But there's other things. For instance, did you know it's unethical for a hunter to shoot a quail on the ground?"

"I thought quail lived in the bushes."

"Well, they mostly do, but no hunter worth his bullets shoots anything, and I mean anything, but an airborne quail. Ever. And on a covey rise, one hunter takes the left field, the other takes the right. A third hunter takes the center. We rotate singles. That's going to be Shelby's job. She keeps up with singles."

"Singles?" I asked.

"It's one bird." Kip smiled.

By the time we reached the cornfields, it was daylight. Kip's dogs loped ahead, scattering and sniffing the brush. The field shimmered beneath a layer of hoarfrost. Late November in Louisiana wasn't normally this cold. This far south, there was no seasonal change; the trees on Judge Stevens's farm were mostly pine in the highlands, but nearer the swampy areas, the hardwoods began: water oaks, hickory, and gum.

My father-in-law handed Shelby a shotgun. Behind her, the sky was turning blue, and the air felt so cold our breath rose in white threads. I looked at the polished wood, the hollow black barrel. The judge and Kip gripped Winchester pumps.

"Don't I get a rifle?" I stifled another belch.

"You'd best not," said the judge, straightening his LSU hat.

"It's not a rifle," Shelby whispered into my ear. "It's a shotgun."

Straight ahead, the largest pointer froze in front of a group of bushes; the dog's tail jutted straight out, his front paw lifted toward his shoulder. Kip walked over to the first bush and started kicking underbrush. Shelby had told me about this—it was the moment that always set her pulse to hammering, flushing the birds, waiting for the sudden flight of the covey. The dog held the position while Kip continued to stamp. There was a deafening noise as the quail ripped away from the bush. Shelby pointed her gun toward the left field. Keeping both eyes open, she looked down the barrel, picked out a bird, and squeezed the trigger. The blast echoed. The bird dropped to the ground, a dark speck moving against the blue sky.

Judge Stevens and Kip were still firing. From the woods, a flock of starlings squawked. The smell of gunpowder was strong.

"Did you see where that single went?" Kip asked Shelby.

"Toward the woods. Right there."

"Did you get one, honey?" I asked my wife.

"Of *course* she got one." Judge Stevens laughed. The dogs raced across the yellow field to retrieve the fallen birds. The setter dropped a quail at Shelby's feet; the big pointer loped forward, his mouth slightly open, but there was no sign of the quail.

"I'll be damned," said Judge Stevens. "Did he eat them, or what?"

The dog walked up to Kip and dropped four good-sized quail beside his boots. He reached down, stroked the dog's head.

"How'd he fit four birds in his mouth?" I asked.

"Atta dog, Duke," Kip said. "That's a good boy."

"Didn't leave a mark, either." Judge Stevens reached in his jacket and pulled out .20 gauge shells. "That's one helluva good dog."

After the judge and Kip collected the birds, securing them in their waist pouches, Kip held up a whistle and blew. The dogs cocked their heads, waiting for a hand signal. He shifted his palm left, and the dogs immediately turned, taking up the scent.

It was afternoon when I made my first kill. The dogs pointed at a thicket. Kip started kicking the bushes, and Judge Stevens coached me. "No, son," he said. "Don't squint. Keep both eyes open, son. That's right, you've got it. And when you get ready to fire, squeeze the trigger."

Kip stamped another bush. He jumped backward when the bobwhites ripped away from the thicket, tiny feathers wafting in the air.

"Now." Judge Stevens stepped back. "Pick out your bird and fire."

The report knocked me backward. To my surprise, a bird fell straight down. I whirled around, clutching the gun, looking for my wife.

"Shelby! Did you see? I got one!" As I stepped forward, my shoe caught on a hickory root, and I tumbled forward. I threw out my hands to break the fall. The gun hit the ground and discharged. The blast hit Judge Stevens.

"Daddy!" cried Shelby.

Judge Stevens fell to the ground and didn't move. I got up and ran over to him, searching his clothes for blood. The left shoulder of his jacket was turning red. Shelby pushed me away and lifted her daddy's head.

"Daddy?" she kept saying. "Open your eyes, Daddy."

Kip hunkered next to her, cutting open the judge's sleeve with a pocket-knife.

"Am I still alive?" Judge Stevens coughed. "Damn it, my arm. Did he blow it off, or what?"

"Sir, it just nicked you." Kip pulled off his jacket, then the quail-studded vest, and wrapped his shirt around the judge's arm. "You were lucky."

"Oh, Daddy," Shelby said, then she gave me a hard look. I bit my lip, and a moment later I tasted blood and iron.

It was almost dusk, and night was filling up the air. We'd long since returned from the emergency room. Judge Stevens's shoulder and arm were bandaged and put into a sling. He had fallen asleep on the porch swing, a mug of Jack Daniel's gripped in his free hand. When I tried to lift it, he clamped down on the handle.

"I'm not sleeping," he murmured. "I'm just resting my eyes, is all."

Grendel reached around and bit the fur above her stubby tail, grunting hard. Her fingernails clicked on the plank floor. After a minute, she lifted her head, sensing, perhaps, that I was staring. The dog gave a disgusted snort, then looked past the swing, past the screen mesh. Her ears twitched when the old tom leaped off Kip's old truck and walked toward the barn.

Shelby pulled on a sweater and ducked outside to secure the horses for the night. She knelt down to stroke the old tom; he rubbed his head against her leg. Then she crossed the driveway, toward the barn, clucking to the horses. They stopped grazing, ears perked, and trotted toward the paddock. After she locked the gate, I walked down the porch and followed her into the tack room, watching as she dumped sweet feed into the bins. The horses whinnied as the grain rattled; they trotted restlessly back and forth in the paddock.

"I'm sorry about your daddy." My stomach growled, and a moment later, I tasted bile.

"It was an accident, honey." The filly dipped her nose into a bucket. Shelby touched the forelock, threading her fingers through the coarse hair. The filly was starting to turn dapple gray, and her hind legs were still spindly, delicate as wineglasses.

Over by a dusty window, Kip stood in front of an old table, cleaning the game. From the portable radio in the tack room, Pure Prairie League was singing "Amie."

"Is the judge all right?" asked Kip. Behind him, the tom leaped through the window, cobwebs sticking to his fur. A bare lightbulb dangled from its wire, swinging back and forth over the wooden table. The table was covered with newspapers. A bottle of Wild Turkey, half empty, stood on a shelf. Shelby walked past me, and I smelled gunpowder. Quail were heaped on one end of the long table. On the other side, closer to where Kip was working, lay a pile of bloody feathers. The feathers were brown, spotted white, now thickly matted. He pulled off a bird's head and began peeling down the skin. The smell of blood and whiskey rushed up my nose. My stomach turned over, and I felt something hot spurt into my throat. My hand jerked up to my mouth, and I lunged forward, vomiting into the feathers.

"Damn," said Kip. "I thought he was a heart surgeon."

"He is," said Shelby.

"Sorry," I said, and wiped my mouth. "I've been fighting nausea all day."

"We ate at Honora's yesterday," Shelby said.

"S'okay, boy," Kip said, gutting the bird with a knife. "Hope you didn't eat any of Isabella McGeehee's cooking. She's lethal in a kitchen."

"He gorged on her sweet potatoes," Shelby said.

"Boy, you like to live dangerously." Kip shook his head.

Shelby picked up two skinned quail and carried them to the old porcelain sink. She held them beneath a stream of water. I coughed and bent over a bale of hay, retching again.

"Louie?" Shelby frowned. "You look pale. Are you all right?"

"I've got to get air," I said. "I've got feathers up my nose." I stumbled out of the barn. If I could just lie down with a cold rag over my head, I'd feel better. Midway toward the house, I broke into a run. Mr. Stevens's rocking chair was empty. I yanked open the screen door and shot inside the house. Before the door slapped shut, Grendel ran down the steps and squatted in the yard.

I sat down at the kitchen table, running my hand through my hair. I'd made a fool of myself in front of Kip and Shelby. I wanted to explain that it wasn't the blood and feathers. Hell, I'd handled hearts in my hands, stitching together arteries and minute vessels. Then I wondered if I'd lost my nerve. Maybe I wasn't such a tough guy, after all. The operating room was a controlled environment. There was no smell, except for the faint, burned odor of the cautery machine. The nurses wore masks, gloves, scrub suits, and paper caps; they draped the patient with sterile green cloths. It was easy to forget that a human being lay beneath those cloths. I would lean over, holding the scalpel, and without hesitation, I'd make an incision. Blood welled up, and a gloved hand reached out with gauze and blotted it. I'd tell the nurses what instrument I wanted, and they'd get it. They did anything I asked. Which was the exact opposite of how I got treated at home.

At dusk, I walked back to the barn. I didn't see Shelby or Kip. The table was littered with blood and feathers, and from the radio Jim Morrison was singing "The End." Over my head, in the hayloft, I heard floorboards screek, and I thought I smelled alfalfa. The tom stalked mice along the rafters, shrinking back as cold air blew through the loft, riffling his fur in the wrong direction.

Outside, a horse neighed, and I recognized Grendel's high-pitched yowl.

Above me, I heard a scrabbling nose, followed by my wife's voice. "I don't like the sound of that barking," she said. A minute later, she and Kip climbed down the ladder. Hay was stuck to their backs and elbows. Kip's shirt was unbuttoned.

"What the hell is going on?" I said. Outside, Grendel yelped, and Shelby ran out of the barn. Kip and I followed. By the time we reached the paddock, Grendel was limping toward the fence, holding out her front paw. Her mouth was rimmed with blood.

"Grendel?" I called, thinking the horse had kicked her. The dog ignored me and hopped toward the fence, over to Shelby. In the security light beside the barn, I saw the filly. She was lying on her side, blood spurting from her hind leg.

"Shit! Shit!" yelled Kip. He climbed the fence and leaped to the other side. The mare stamped toward him, flattening her ears against her head. She pawed the ground, threatening to strike with her front hooves. Kip pulled off his undershirt, squatted down beside the filly, and pressed the shirt to the wound. The cloth bloomed with color. The filly kept trying to get up, bracing her hooves in the dirt, her head arched forward. Shelby skidded under the fence and ran over to the filly. I started toward Grendel. She growled, then crawled under the fence, stretching her hind legs as she scooted forward, then she limped toward the house.

"Hold pressure on it, just like this." Kip pressed Shelby's hand over the shirt. Then he slid under the fence and ran over to his truck. He reached into the back, pulled out a flashlight and a battered first aid case, then ran back to the paddock. I started toward the fence—hell, if an artery had been severed, I could suture it. I was Dr. DeChavannes, I could do anything. I started to climb over the fence, and Shelby hollered. "Stay back, Louie," she called. "You're not feeling well."

I ignored her, hopped onto the fence, then dropped to the other side, my shoes sinking into mud. I jogged over to the filly. Kip was trying to clamp a hemostat over the pumping arterial bleed, but I could tell that he didn't know what he was doing. I elbowed him aside, then flung off the bloody shirt and plucked the hemostat from his hands.

"Hold the flashlight over the filly," I told him. "Shelby, open the first aid kit and see if you can find suture materials."

Her hands fumbled on the clasp, then she flung open the kit, rummaging inside. "I don't see any."

"Run inside and get a needle and thread," I told her. "And antiseptic, if you have it."

She looked up, her hair streaming down. Her eyes were gunmetal gray, and cold. I wondered what the hell she and Kip had been doing in that hayloft. Then I looked down at her hands.

Blood pumped through her fingers, little commas splashing onto her shirt. I knew she was afraid to move, afraid the filly would bleed to death.

"Get the thread, honey," I said, then I nodded at Kip. "Give me some light, buddy."

He clicked on the flashlight and aimed the beam over the filly's leg. Shelby let go, and a jet of blood spattered my sweater. As she ran toward the house, I clamped the hemostat over the artery, and blood stopped pumping.

"Shoot, I coulda done that," said Kip.

I started to say, I can cut hair, too. But I held my tongue and waited for Shelby. I saw a shadow moving around the paddock, then she ran over to me, slinging down a sewing box and a bottle of rubbing alcohol. They restrained the filly while I threaded the needle and splashed alcohol over it.

I felt Shelby's breath on my neck as I tied off the artery, removed the hemostat, and sutured the skin back together. Over Shelby's bowed head, the moon wafted over the pines, and way out in the woods, a pale quivering sound started up, *Bob-white! Ah-bob-white!*

"You saved her," said Shelby, but Kip glared.

Yeah, I thought. I saved the horse, but sure as I was sitting here, I was going to lose the girl. Maybe, just maybe, I already had.

Chapter 23

❖ ❖ ❖

TEARS OF A HUNDRED LOVERS

All night the wind blew over Alabama as the tropical depression moved into the Gulf of Mexico. For several hours I had sensed a change in the barometric pressure, a prickling along my spine and static electricity in what remained of my hair. Inside, I felt just as volatile. One minute I wanted to fly over to Ireland, and the next I wanted to stay in Point Clear and set free a couple of Gucci handbags.

Up in my room, I opened the casement window. Night air stirred the gauzy curtains, carrying the scent of mock orange. I couldn't see the bay, but I could hear waves smashing against the pier. Somewhere in the dark a storm was gathering strength. My thoughts drifted back to Ferg. I missed the way he'd push my hair out of my eyes and how he'd show up with a bottle of merlot and a cheese ball. I missed how he held me in the night. But I couldn't allow myself to think about him. If Ferg didn't want me, fine. The last thing I wanted was to end up like my parents.

I shut my eyes, imaging the bay tossing foam and shells and tiny blue minnows onto the sand, then sucking everything back again. I pressed my face against the feather mattress, the smells and sounds of water blowing around me. Just as I fell asleep, I thought I heard my mother whisper, *I will always love you. I will always be with you.*

When I woke up, it was dark outside. I heard rain ticking against the trees, a fine-grained sound like grits poured into a saucepan. I threw back the covers and slid out of bed. Then I bent over the trunk, peering inside. Near the

bottom right-hand corner, wedged against the brittle paper lining, I pulled
out a wrinkled page from the Pensacola newspaper.

Pensacola SUN
January 15, 1973

WOMAN FALLS THROUGH PARTIALLY FROZEN BAY

The Perdido Key Fire Department pulled a Louisiana
woman, Shelby DeChavannes, 31, from Wolf Bay last Saturday evening at 6 p.m. She was taken to a local hospital and
treated for frostbite. The bay was partially frozen due to
record-breaking temperatures that swept through the Panhandle last week. The local Audubon society rescued hundreds of shorebirds from Wolf Bay after their feet adhered to
the ice. The Perdido Key Fire Chief, Eddie Coggins, advises
residents to avoid inland bays, and under no circumstance
should they attempt winter sports, such as ice skating. "This
isn't Maine or Wisconsin," said Chief Coggins. "This is the
Gulf Coast, and inland waters might look froze, but it's just
on the surface. If a person falls through the ice, they could
be dead in ten minutes." Information about water safety and
frostbite is available at the Perdido Key Fire Station.

I tucked the article into my robe pocket and walked down the hall into Honora's room. Sunlight forked down the creamy walls, illuminating dozens of
family photographs. The air smelled faintly of cigarette smoke and Robert
Piaget's Fracas. Unlike the rest of the house, her bedroom was quiet and
restful, with tone-on-tone beige. She had taken great care to add textures: a
rough jute rug, a white wicker chaise with a silk plaid cushion; an ivory porcelain vase holding a dozen lilies; an ornate shell-encrusted mirror hanging
over a painted dresser. The bed was an old iron four-poster, draped in muslin
panels. An overstuffed ivory chair was angled beside the window, giving long
views of the bay.

    "Honora?" I called. "Are you decent?"

I leaned toward the window and pushed back the curtain. There, far out in the bay, I saw a small, capped figure doing the breaststroke. Honora was swimming. I started to turn out of her room, but couldn't leave without taking a peek inside her closet. In the old days, it had been a "new baby nursery" with adjoining rooms for a nanny; but Solange DeChavannes's architect had transformed the space into a "wardrobe room." In fact, it was rumored that *Vogue* had patterned their famed "cupboard" after Solange's gargantuan closet.

Now, I stepped into a room with white, furniture-like cabinets, housing furs, ball gowns, and suits. Deep drawers lined the lower part of the cabinets. I slid one open—sunglasses. Another held gloves. An armoire held great stacks of orange Hermès boxes. Directly over my head, a twelve-armed crystal chandelier tossed out a confetti of colors.

This room opened into a hallway with four doors on the right-hand side: the first led to a "spring/summer" room; the second was dedicated to fall/winter items; the third opened into a jewelry room, where everything from necklaces to bracelets to earrings dangled from small gold hooks. The heirlooms were locked into a freezer-sized vault. The fourth door led to a handbag room, its walls lined with cubbyholes and hooks. They were subdivided into summer and winter. Before I left the room, I ran my hands over a vintage Jackie O Gucci, a Chanel bowling bag, and several Hermès bags, along with a jeweled Leiber "sleeping cat" minaudière. The vintage bags had belonged to Solange. My grandfather, Chaz, had been raised to believe that every woman loved designer bags, and he'd never stopped to think that Honora might prefer something else for Christmas and Mother's Day. Now, many of the cubbyholes were empty, thanks to Honora's weekly bag-releasing runs, but she still had an enviable collection.

I walked downstairs and sat on the kitchen counter, waiting for the coffee to brew. Gladys ran a feather duster over the tables, humming "My Heart Stood Still." From the counter, the little TV showed a white circle bubbling in the Gulf like a pot of gumbo, full of rice and shrimp and crab claws. According to the weatherman, the tropical depression was headed straight for Gulf Shores.

"Humph," said Gladys. "Maybe it is, maybe it ain't. Them weathermen can't predict doodly."

Even though I'd spent the better part of my life in California, I always panicked when storms blew into the Gulf of Mexico. My mother would call Honora and Gladys a dozen times, making sure they were all right. She used to say that tropical depressions could spring up overnight. Any storm that moved into the Gulf could stir up trouble. There was just no place for it to fizzle. But it could just as easily blow over to the eastern seaboard and skitter off into the Atlantic. You just never knew about storms. They reminded me of the unstoppable, unpredictable force of life with the power to change everything or nothing.

Honora had often talked about Hurricane Camille, how she'd tied up the draperies, then pulled everything out of the dresser drawers, stuffing underwear and pajamas onto the highest closet shelves, but it all got ruined anyway. Muddy water filled the house, buckling parquet floors and bursting out the windows.

Gladys used to say that storms carried gossip from other towns. The story of a heartbreak, the sound of a baby's cry. The tears of a hundred lovers. "Close your eyes and listen," she'd say. "Can you hear the voices?"

I thought they sounded like a woman weeping; other times I heard music. Blues and jazz pouring up into the night, the notes swarming like mosquitoes. The coast was a different world, a jambalaya of the senses. Full of danger and dampness and desire. Heat and hazards and heartbreak.

I leaned across the counter and switched off the television. Then I clicked on the little radio beside the toaster. Old Dick Haymes was singing "The Very Thought of You." He was probably dead by now, but his smooth voice lived on.

Reaching into my pocket, I pulled out the article. I'd heard the grown-ups whispering about Mama's accident, but when I'd pressed for details, they'd clammed up. "Your mama just got cold, is all," Gladys said. I thought she meant that my mother had an illness, a cold virus, and it never occurred to me to ask more questions.

Gladys stepped into the kitchen, swiping the feather duster along the counter. "What you reading, baby?" she asked.

"How did my mama end up in a frozen bay?" I held out the article.

"It was half froze," said Gladys.

"She told you about it?"

"No, I was there."

"And?"

"How many love-gone-wrong stories must I tell?" She shook her head.

"Until there are no more?"

"They'll always be love stories, baby," she said. "Even if the world stops spinning, there will always be more."

Chapter 24

⬤ ⬤ ⬤

RESCUE

If you dream of putting roses in your hair, then you will be deceived by someone you love. If you dream of your hairdresser, you will soon be entangled in a family scandal or moral dilemma. I am making this up. But this one thing is true: nobody ever leaves a warm bed for a cold one.

All I remember about that winter was ice and cold. The man on TV said a arctic front had swooped down from Canada, and temperatures shot down into the single digits. All over the Gulf Coast, water pipes bursted and azaleas froze solid. It was mighty strange weather for this part of the country, and I thought it was a sign of worse things yet to come.

Then Shelby decided to drive over to Perdido Key, Florida, and check on her daddy's old beach house. "I'm worried about his pipes," she said.

"Will Louie be coming, too?" I asked, trying to be sly.

"He's on duty. It'll just be me, you, and Renata."

During the drive to Point Clear, Shelby didn't stop talking. Her thick hair was stylishly brushed into a one-sided ponytail, and I wondered if she'd fixed it herself, then shook the thought from my mind. The rest of her was shabby—her black wool pants were all beat up, and that moth-bit gray sweater looked like rats had been sucking on it. She wasn't a slouchy dresser. She and Louie didn't have much money, even with all that extra hospital work he did. But that baby wore a pink snowsuit that Honora and Isabella had bought at an exclusive children's shop in Mobile. Honora believed that money didn't make people happy, but it sure was a blessing when you had a beautiful grand-child. She had the bestest time buying clothes for that baby. Although she was really a toddler.

When we pulled up to Honora's house, she flung open the door and let out a whoop, then she clapped her hands. Shelby set the child down, and she ran straight to her grandmother, the snowsuit whisking.

"Come into the kitchen where's it warm," Honora said. She dished up steaming bowls of red beans and rice, then opened a bottle of red wine. I didn't get suspicious until Kip showed up, smelling of cold air and hairspray. He and Shelby started drinking and talking, having a little too much fun. Honora opened another bottle of wine. I had all but forgot about the danc-ing and flirting at Dr. Nigel's birthday party. Kip had gone back to Fairhope, coloring hair and giving permanents, and Shelby went back to Covington. But now, listening to them talk and watching the sparks that shot out of their eyes, I realized that their calf-love hadn't ended in the Carolinas, it was just getting started.

A dirty aura hovered near the ceiling, gray smoke all shot through with brown. Part of itself had glued itself to Kip; the other part was curled around Shelby, only it didn't look like smoke, it was peaked and foamy, just like the water in the Pontchartrain before a hurricane hits.

Keeping my eyes on them, I spooned up red beans. Kip's hairstyle was loose and free. He'd growed it out into a long, glossy ponytail, and it ran like dark water down between his shoulders. He weren't no hippie, but he verged on being one. His eyes lingered on Shelby, and I felt tender waves rolling all around the room. Some of those waves crashed into the aura, mixing it all together.

Honora didn't seem to notice. She was all wrapped up in that baby, carry-ing her around the kitchen, trying to feed her oatmeal cookies. Shelby brought out pepper cheese and crackers and made a pot of coffee, but they switched to gin and tonics, talking about the cold snap. "I heard the bay is frozen," said Shelby.

"Not solid," Kip said. "Just the top."

"Ain't that bad enough?" I asked. "Them poor shore birds' feets got stuck to the ice and people tried to save them, but they had trouble getting them free."

"Speaking of trouble," said Shelby, glancing at her Timex, "I should check on Daddy's place."

"You're not going alone, are you?" Kip stood up, then fell back into his chair. He stared at his empty glass and laughed. "Hell, I'm drunk."

"Me, too," said Shelby.

"Y'all shouldn't drive," said Honora, handing Renata a box of crayons and a Cinderella coloring book. The toddler picked a orange stick, then sprawled on the floor. "Just stay here tonight, Shelby," Honora added. "You can check on your daddy's house tomorrow."

"He's worried sick," said Shelby, and glanced over at me. "Gladys, you're sober. Will you drive me?"

"I reckon I could," I said, silently cursing rich people and their beach houses. I wondered why Shelby's daddy couldn't tend to his own house. He'd bought it for fishing trips with his buddies.

"It's too cold to go anywhere," Honora said.

"I'll go with y'all," said Kip.

"Great!" Shelby clapped her hands.

"No, that's all right," I said. "Just us girls will go."

"I'd better go along in case you all have a flat tire," he said.

"It could happen," said Shelby.

"Humph," I said.

"Drive carefully," called Honora, then she got down on the floor and began coloring in the book with her granddaughter.

*B*y the time we drove up to Perdido Key, it was sunset, and I was half crazy from all the whispering and giggling in the backseat. We passed the fire department and a condominium complex. I turned up the sandy driveway, then herded Kip and Shelby into the house. While they mooned at each other, I checked the faucets. Don't ask me how, but the pipes hadn't burst. But the house had been built in the 1950s, and it was solid, with knotty pine ceilings.

Kip found a bottle of Wild Turkey in the pantry and poured a round of drinks. "Y'all put that away," I said, thinking of how much they'd already drunk, and of the long drive back in this cold. "Come on and join us, Gladys," said Kip.

"Ain't got time." I turned up the heat and flung open the cabinets under the kitchen sink. I pushed back the yellow curtain. Outside, the moon was rising over the dark purple ocean. The sky and water were empty; even the shorebirds had the sense to stay out of the frigid air.

"Let's go see if the bay is frozen," Shelby said.

"Yes, let's," said Kip.

"No!" I whirled around. "Don't you dare!"

"We're just going across the road." Kip was helping Shelby into her coat. She staggered, and I saw how drunk she was. Kip, he saw, too, and grabbed her arm.

"Just lean on me," he said, pushing her out the door. Then, over his shoulder, he said to me, "We'll be back in ten minutes."

"Make it five," I snapped.

I walked around the house, making double sure the faucets were dripping. I even checked the hot water heater. I kept looking out the windows, hoping I'd see them hurrying back. The long sandy driveway was empty. I turned on the TV and listened to the Pensacola evening news. But I couldn't stop worrying. Shelby was acting plain silly. She was in the grip of a crush, but was it love? I didn't think it had gone past the smooching stage. When we were in Pinehurst, I will bet you that kissing had took place. I knew the "why" of her crush, just not the when, where, and how.

Louie's doctoring was too huge for Shelby. Many a time I heard her say that she'd married a man just like her father. Then here came Kip—no ringing phones, no beeping—and he couldn't take his eyes off her. She perked up like gerbera daisies you'd forgot to water. So, that was the why of Shelby and Kip. But I just didn't know how far they'd took it, or what all had gone on since Pinehurst.

This was a fact: Shelby wasn't a loose woman, and Kip wasn't a home wrecker. However, Isabella had been dead right about one thing: he was a self-centered mama's boy. When the Pensacola weatherman came on, promising warmer temperatures, I said Amen, then I peeked out the kitchen window. The sky had turned black, all speckled with cold stars.

A little voice started up inside my head, and it was saying, Gladys, girl— this has gone on too long. You better go after them.

I buttoned my coat and stepped outside, my shoes crunching on the froze sand. I darted across the street to a ugly condominium complex. In the back of those apartments was a dock where the people kept yachts. Some of the boats was hoisted up, the others jutted crookedly from the frozen water, icicles hanging from the sides.

A light at the end of the dock shown down on the froze water. It reminded me of rumpled sheet metal. I saw something moving in the middle of the bay. It was two people, and they were sprawled out on the ice, clothes flung off everywhere. They were bouncing, giving off steam and a humming noise, more like a chant or a prayer, real pretty noises, what Honora would call "beguiling."

I walked toward the sounds. Miss Shelby's blond hair fanned on the ice. Kip's trousers hung low, wrinkled around his knees, his lower body circled by Miss Shelby's long, white arms. Her fingers dug into his fleshy buttocks. Their froze breath hung in the air.

I went red-hot with anger and covered my eyes. I wanted to grab her ankles and drag her back to her daddy's cottage. They hadn't seen me. So I stepped onto the ice. I heard a pop, and my shoe sank down a little. It scared me bad, so I lifted my foot and stepped back to the shore.

But the damage done been done. I heard a crackling sound, loud as a shotgun. All around them, just under the surface, twig-shaped lines spread through the ice, making a popping noise. The piece of ice they was laying on broke, floating for a moment, with black water lapping onto Kip's legs and Shelby's nakedness. They rose up, then pulled apart. He reached for a solid chunk, but his arms broke it to pieces. His hands splashed into the water. Then he lunged to a large, solid layer and heaved himself out of the water, his wet trousers tangled and soggy around his ankles. Shelby crouched on the ice, then she stood up and gingerly took a step. The ice shattered, and she fell screaming into the water.

"Get her!" I screamed. "Kip, she's gone under, she'll drown."

He lay motionless on the ice floe, his face hidden in his arms, and couldn't—or wouldn't—look up. Behind him, Shelby's head broke through the surface. She gasped for air, flailing at the ice, her arms churning water.

"You, Kip Quattlebaum!" I yelled. Still, he did not move. I whispered a Hail Mary. Then I pulled off my shoes and shrugged out of my coat. I crossed myself and slogged forward, not caring if I fell. I grew up on a bayou, and while I didn't know anything about ice, I knew how to swim.

Shelby screamed again. "Hold on," I said. "Gladys's coming." Halfway to her, I stopped. The ice looked thinner. I took a small step and cracks zigzagged around my shoe like when you hit a hard-cooked egg with a fork. I hunkered down, then scooted across my stomach until I was close to the gaping hole where Shelby was flailing. I stretched out both hands, but she was still too far away. I could hear her praying to Saint Jude and Mary Magdalene. From the condominiums, terrace lights snapped on and people looked through sliding doors. A man hollered, "Help is on the way."

"Shelby?" I called. My voice sounded tight and raspy. "Dog-paddle to me. And do it gentle, or we'll both go under."

She glanced crazily over the ice toward Kip. Her arms moved in slow motion, real clumsy, and I saw that she was too froze to swim. Her lower jaw moved like she was singing hymns, but her lips were dark blue, almost purple. I glanced back at Kip. He was breathing, but he still wouldn't look at me. I wondered if he'd passed out—not from the drink or the cold, but from fright.

Then I heard a siren, and a minute later, a rescue truck roared up. The siren snapped off. Red lights wheeled over the boats and the glossy bay. Two police cars swerved into the parking lot, tires crunching over icy gravel. Right then, I knew they were going to make a fuss. So did Kip.

"Shit," he said. He rolled over and yanked up his trousers. From the water, Shelby began to shriek. I raised my hands and waved to the rescuers. They hopped out of the truck, gripping a big orange inner tube, a rope dangling down.

"Over here," I yelled, then I whispered a prayer to my Jesus. " 'Death and life are in the power of the tongue: and they that love it shall eat the fruit there of. Proverbs 18:21.' "

An ambulance screeched into the parking lot, followed by a TV news van.

One of the rescuers led me off the ice and wrapped a blanket over my shoulders. Somebody else draped a blanket around Kip. Two others crawled onto the ice, tossing a rope ladder out to Shelby. Each time, she glanced up, her eyes unfocused. She looked dozy-headed, like she'd just woke from a hard sleep. One arm clutched a large chunk of ice, the other floated in the water. "C-cold," she stammered.

"Don't bump her or she'll slip under and drown," said one man.

"Just grab the rope, honey," said another.

Shelby's hand rose up, shaking and mottled, then crashed back onto the ice, breaking off a chunk. Another fellow disappeared into the truck, and minutes later he came out wearing a black skin diving suit. On his hands were gloves, and on his feet was rubber fins. The fins slapped onto the ice. All around him, it cracked like gunfire.

"What's her name?" he asked Kip, but before he could answer, I said, "Shelby. Her name is Shelby."

He slid into the black water and kicked past ice chunks. A sheet broke off and floated dangerously close to Shelby. I watched the rescuer swim over to her. Ice was stuck to her chin and ears, and all caked in her hair. "Okay, Shelby," he said. "You're going to be fine, you hear? I've got you. You're safe."

The diver swam up beside her. From the ice, one of the men threw out the rope. The diver tied it around Shelby, forming a harness under her arms and between each leg.

"Steady now, pull her out," shouted the diver. The police grabbed the rope and helped the rescue men. They dragged Shelby out of the hole. She was naked from the waist down.

One of the men wrapped her in blankets, then carried her to the ambulance. I did not see what happened after that, except I heard the door slam and watched the ambulance blast out of the parking lot, into the road. I shut my eyes and listened to the siren. A news reporter asked me if I'd give a statement. I pushed them aside.

"We won't show your face," he said. "We'll just show your shoes."

"Everybody know what kind of shoes I wear," I snapped, then I grabbed Kip's arm and led him toward the road. "Just keep walking," I said. "And don't open your mouth unless you want it sewed shut."

Kip pressed his lips together. I shut my eyes and quoted Song of Solomon 8:7: "Many waters cannot quench love, neither can the floods drown it: if a man would give all the substance of his house for love, it would utterly be condemned."

And it sure enough was.

Chapter 25

◎ ◎ ◎

Just Outside the Garden of Eden

I stood on the pier, the wind snapping my blouse, wondering how many other secrets my mother had taken to her grave. No matter what she had done, she could have told me; at least, I wanted to believe that if she had, I wouldn't have judged her the way I'd judged my father. I didn't have all of the puzzle pieces, but even so, I felt a little sorry for him. If only I could talk to him about Mama. If only he could tell his side of the story.

Reaching up with one hand, I wiped my eyes. I missed my mother. I missed her throaty laughter, and the way she'd hug me whenever she passed through a room. I wanted to think that Daddy missed her, too.

The wind shifted, and the surface of the bay rippled: the tide was going out. Growing up on the water, I'd learned how to read the weather. Unfortunately, I'd always lacked the talent to understand the psychological currents of the people I loved.

Behind me, I heard footsteps on the dock. I glanced over my shoulder and saw Honora. She gripped a brown leather scrapbook. Cracking it open, she pointed to an invitation. "I want to show you something. When Chaz turned fifty, I gave him a big party over in New Orleans. He specifically requested a faux funeral, so that's what he got."

I tilted the book, squinting at the cursive print.

Dr. Louis Charles "Chaz" DeChavannes
• Cordially Invites You to His Faux Funeral •

St. Louis Hotel
211 Rue Beinville
New Orleans, Louisiana
Seven p.m. to Midnight
September 6, 1975
RSVP

"I remember that party," I said.

"Well, you should. It was the day you started talking again."

"Again? When did I quit? I was a chatterbox."

"You were until your mama fell though the ice."

"I don't remember that."

"You've probably repressed it. All the screaming between your daddy and mama probably left a mark on you. You just buttoned your lips and refused to talk."

"For how long?"

"The first time? Almost a month," said Honora. "Then you got over it. Children are resilient, thank heavens; but only to a point. Each time your mama and daddy fought, you'd lapse into silence. The longest time you went without talking was during the summer of '75. But you snapped out of it after the faux funeral."

Honora dumped the scrapbook into my arms. "I've got to fry chicken. You just stay out here and ponder awhile."

I sat down on the edge of the pier and balanced the scrapbook on my lap. A plastic sheet covered the invitation. I peeled back the plastic, then pulled out the card. I remembered a hot June night in 1975, when I was catching fireflies in the Covington yard. Inside, Mama and Daddy started yelling. I didn't know what had started the fight. I just heard the word "Kip," or maybe it was "Chip." Right before the fight, Mama had eaten Lay's potato chips, so I figured that was it. I ran onto the porch and crouched beside the screen door, listening to them fight.

"I *said* I was sorry," Mama yelled. "I've killed myself, trying to please you."

"I'll never forgive you," Daddy said, "especially when you exaggerate."

Daddy flung open the screen door, and I went flying across the porch, down the wooden stairs. I landed on my chin, biting through my lip and tongue. They drove me to the hospital for stitches. Because I wouldn't stop kicking and yelling, the doctor and nurse wrapped me in a papoose.

On the way home, Mama held me in her lap. Daddy kept rubbing my arm, saying, "Baby girl, I'm so sorry. Do you believe me?"

"She can't talk, Louie," Mama said through her teeth. "She's got five stitches."

When Mama said, *She can't talk*, it struck a chord. The way I saw it, my family talked so much, I didn't need to. In the past, when I'd given them the silent treatment, it always got my daddy's attention. He'd bring me coloring books and candy, and he'd talk real sweet to Mama. So I decided I'd stretch it out, make the silence last.

Three months later, I still hadn't talked, but my family had gotten used to it.

The day of Papa Chaz's faux funeral, I sat on the front porch in Covington, waiting for Mama and Daddy to get dressed. Daddy couldn't find his onyx cuff links, and Mama's hair was conspiring against her. She stood in front of the pier mirror, trying to pin her hair into a chignon. It made me sad to watch her. If she knew what the gossips were saying, she would stop primping and break that mirror over my daddy's head.

Early this morning, Gladys had dropped me off at the New You Salon, where Mr. Pierre was supposed to sausage-curl my hair, then glue on little white flowers. It was torture in more ways than one. Pierre turned me over to a sad-eyed girl. While I got a shampoo, I also got an earful of slander. On this particular morning, it was directed at my family.

"Are you going to that faux funeral over in New Orleans? It was written up in the paper as the event of the season," said a woman with black pointy eyeglasses. I did not recognize her. She was having her hair frosted, and wet purple strands protruded from pinholes in a tight rubber cap.

"Indeed not," said a woman in pink curlers, who reeked of permanent solution. I didn't know her name, but I'd seen her at the library, ripping out dessert recipes from Betty Crocker.

"The gall of Dr. DeChavannes," said the woman with purple hair. "Didn't his mother die an appalling death?"

"Wait, which Dr. DeChavannes are you talking about? There's a whole slew of them. But Dr. Louie is the cute one. He lives right here in Covington."

"I'm referring to the brain surgeon, the one who lives near Mobile. I don't see why he has to come all the way to New Orleans to throw this ridiculous party. Why can't he do it in Mobile? Anyway, it was *his* hoity-toity mother who died."

"It was shocking." The frosted woman leaned forward. "A botched hemorroidectomy. That's what killed Solange DeChavannes."

"Killed by a pain in the butt."

"I wonder if Judge and Mrs. Stevens will be attending the party."

"The judge might go, but Emma won't. Not the way she shuts herself up in that house. Why, I think she's ashamed to show her face."

"She ought to be."

At this, I raised my head and blinked. What had Grammy Stevens done? Water and suds streamed down my neck. These fool women were talking about my people! What did they mean, botched hemorrhoids? What was that? My great-grandmother, Solange DeChavannes, had died before I was born. She'd died on the operating table. Daddy said her heart had stopped beating.

The frosted girl peered into the mirror, nodding at her reflection. "Wonder if that actress is invited. What's her name?"

"Isabella D'Agostino McGeehee," said the woman with purple hair. "I was visiting my auntie at the Ochsner Clinic last week, and I saw her and young Dr. DeChavannes kissing in the parking lot. *In* broad daylight, too."

"Are you talking about our very own Dr. Louie DeChavannes? The one who's married to Judge Stevens's daughter?"

"Yes."

"But she's gorgeous."

"So's Isabella."

"Were they kissing or . . ."

"Why, alley cats have better sexual etiquette. Louie had his hand up her blouse. And *her* hand was heaven knows where."

"I bet *I* know."

"Tacky, tacky, tacky."

"I'll *never* use Louie DeChavannes for a doctor."

"Not unless you need a heart surgeon."

"Honey, *he* needs one."

"Maybe he should see a gynecologist."

The women giggled, and I rose all the way up. Suds skidded down the plastic cape, pattering onto the tile floor. Before I could eyeball the women and tell them to shut the hell up, the shampoo girl firmly pushed my head down. Her fingers were wet and cold. She got right into my face. "Move again and I'll break your little neck," she hissed, eyeballing me. "You're getting crap all over me."

I tilted back my head. My eyes smarted with tears. They fell down the sides of my face, mixing in with the shampoo. The girl twisted the faucet, and water spewed out of the hose, pounding onto my hair, drowning out the women's voices.

Now, inside our living room, a crystal bowl shattered, followed by my mama's cries, and I spun around, pressing my face against the screen door. "That was Waterford!" she sobbed.

"I know it," Daddy said. "And I'm sorry. I'll buy you another."

"It's irreplaceable," she said in a heartbroken voice.

"Stop being dramatic, Shelby."

"Stop breaking my crystal."

He ignored her and yanked out a desk drawer, flipping it upside down. Coupons, stamps, pencils, and money pattered to the floor. "What did you do with my caduceus cuff links?" he said, slinging open another drawer.

"Look in the bedroom, on my dresser. And stop throwing things on the floor!"

"If Gladys kept things in order, I wouldn't have to. What am I paying her for, anyway?"

"You won't be paying her much longer," Mama said through her teeth.

"Hey, this move to New Orleans was *your* idea," Daddy said. "Not mine."

He rushed down the hall, turning into their lavender bedroom. A minute later, he charged out with the cuff links. He got them a thousand years ago for being in medical school. In our house precious objects dissolved into the air and irons burst into flames. We were always rushing, yet we were always late.

Mama grabbed her pocketbook from the table and hurried onto the porch. Her high heels clicked over the planks. Two years ago, after she'd fallen through the ice and caught that bad cold, her appetite had perked up. Her green dress was a tad too tight, and her hips were lumpy beneath the silk. From behind she looked like a parakeet that's eaten too much millet, and it hurt my heart to look at her.

"There you are, Renata." She smiled down at me. "You look so pretty! Mr. Pierre outdid himself, didn't he? Let's go wait in the car for Daddy."

I stood up and shook out my petticoat. Then I walked bow-legged down the oyster shell driveway.

"Shelby?" Daddy's head poked out of the door. His eyes were the color of burnt caramel. "You got my car keys?"

"Never saw them," she called, then crossed her arms over her chest. She squeezed herself into the passenger seat. I climbed into the back, my organdy petticoat frothing around me. A few minutes later, he hurried out of the house with the keys and jogged down to our blue Thunderbird convertible. He wanted to put the top down, but Mama wouldn't let him.

"Can I at least roll down my window?" he asked.

"Suit yourself." Mama shrugged.

Daddy drove through a tunnel of live oaks, past white raised cottages with galleries, past yards full of crape myrtles, blue hydrangeas, and banana trees. From the radio, a jazz station was playing somebody called Miles Davis, "I Fall in Love Too Easily."

The T-bird was Mama's car, and it didn't have a decal on the windshield. She didn't like to drive across the causeway. It was the longest, scariest bridge in the South. If your tire flattened or your engine stalled, you were out of luck, unless you made it to a crossover. It used to be one bridge, but now there were two, running side by side—one went into New Orleans, the other headed to St. Tammany Parish. If you stared cross-eyed at the farthest point on the horizon, the bridges ran together.

Daddy pulled up to the tollbooth, lowered his window, and handed the man a dollar. "Y'all have fun in Sin City," the man said, winking at me.

"We'll try," said Daddy. In the seconds before he closed his window, I breathed in the heavy air—salt, catfish, shrimp, sunlight, and pine trees. Louisiana was in the middle of a dry spell: long, broiling hot September days, the heat pressing down like a fist.

Traffic was light today; but the empty Causeway seemed to buckle and writhe, shimmering at the edges. The choppy water spread around the bridge in a dizzy pattern, the waves slapping against the concrete piling. Across the water, New Orleans was hidden in frothy, low-lying clouds.

I sat up on my knees and stared out the rear window. St. Tammany Parish dropped away into a swirl of green-black pine trees, the edges blurred like the watercolors I painted at school. I turned around and flopped onto the seat, then I started playing a game called I-Am-Blind. I'd learned it at school. My teacher, Miss DuBois, had blindfolded everyone in the class, then passed around mysterious objects. "Smell them, children," she instructed us. "*Feel* them." Into my small hands she dropped something cold and bumpy—was it a guava or a dead bullfrog? I couldn't tell.

"Think hard, Renata," Miss DuBois said, her knees popping as she squatted beside my table. "Put yourself in a blind person's shoes. Your object is green. What does that color smell like? Does it have a flavor?" I knew what she was getting at; she was hoping to increase our appreciation of the world and to stimulate our imaginations—something I myself did not need. I squeezed the object. My thumbnail sank into ripe flesh, and I felt something cold and squishy ooze out. With a gasp, I dropped the horrid thing. It hit my desk with a sickening thud. Miss DuBois sighed and pulled off my blindfold. She held up an avocado. "Is that what you imagined?" she said. "Well, is it?"

I shook my head.

"Things are not what they seem," said Miss DuBois.

*D*addy steered with one hand resting on the bottom of the wheel; the other hand reached back to smooth his hair. It was very dark, with a bluish tinge—European hair, Mama called it, the dreamy kind that was evermore falling into his eyes. He cracked the window, and warm air poured into the car.

Mama's bun came loose, and her hair blew forward. "Please, Louie," she said.

"What you pleading for, baby?" Daddy's voice was kind, but it was an act.

He knew what she wanted—for him to slow down and roll up the window and unbreak her Waterford bowl.

He swung the Thunderbird into the passing lane and accelerated around a yellow Cadillac. Hunched over the wheel was a hook-nosed, white-haired woman who honked her horn and gave us all a dirty look. I wanted to say, It's not my fault, lady. He's a wild man. We can't do a thing with him.

"Please roll up your window. I'm about to blow away." Mama clawed hair out of her eyes. "I give up," she said. "I just *give up*."

"About time," said Daddy. He sighed as if she'd asked him to give up something precious—gumbo, po-boy sandwiches, bourbon in his Coca-Cola. He pushed a button, and the window buzzed shut. "Satisfied?" he asked.

"No, but it's a start." Mama slapped her dress, trying to knock out the wrinkles. She wouldn't look at him.

Daddy hit his brake, swerving around a dead seagull. One white wing flapped up and down in the wind. Mama shut her eyes, and I knew what she was thinking. Every time we crossed the Pontchartrain, she worried that our car would skid out of control, then burst through the guardrail, trailing a plume of smoke. I imagined the trajectory of our car—a flash of baby blue metal hanging in the sky for an instant before it smashed into the water. The car would sink slowly to the bottom, spinning around and around. Inside, the three of us would be trapped, trying to stem the flow of water as it poured in through the vents. We banged our fists on the glass and screamed. By the time they sent divers, it would be too late, we'd already drowned.

*H*alfway across the Pontchartrain, I saw blinking red lights. Daddy tapped the brake, and the Thunderbird slowed down. I stood on my knees and looked out the rear window. The bridge stretched out into the haze. Then I saw a green dot creep down the bridge as if pulled by string. It got closer, and I saw that it was a station wagon. It was moving fast.

I whirled around, looking at my daddy. He wasn't paying attention to what was behind us, and neither was Mama. They looked straight ahead as a wooden rail swung down, blocking the road. On the other side of the rail, the traffic was starting to pile up. Then our highway broke apart, rising straight up into the sky. A sailboat glided through, listing to one side. Down on the boat, a man in a red-and-white shirt turned around and waved at the cars, as if to say, Thanks for being patient, guys.

Turning back to the window, I saw the green station wagon barreling toward us, and I sucked in air. I thought I saw the driver, a woman with a beehive and eyeshadow that matched her car. One arm dangled out the window, her cupped hand playing with the wind. Singing to herself, not a care in the world. If I could see this car coming, then surely my parents could see it, too. I twisted my head and looked back at them. They were watching the sailboat. I opened my mouth to warn them, but I remembered I'd taken a vow of silence. I wasn't sure I could talk if I wanted. I coughed, then made a low humming noise. Still, my parents didn't turn around.

"Daddy!" I screamed. "Look out!"

I spun around and sprang forward, my arms extended, and landed on the padded console. Mama jumped. Daddy stared down at me and said, "What the—"

"Behind you!" I yelled. He twisted around. His eyes widened when he saw the station wagon. Mama turned, too, then she screamed and pulled me into her lap. "Holy Mother of God," Daddy said. The little man who operated the gate ran out into the road, waving his arms above his head. I heard tires squeal, and the station wagon skidded sideways, stopping inches away from our bumper.

The beehive lady got out of the station wagon and staggered. From inside her car, a baby started to scream. She put her hands on her head. "Oh, shit! Are y'all all right? I'm so sorry!"

Daddy leaned out his window. "You almost hit my car," he yelled. "You could've killed my family."

"I said I was sorry," yelled the woman.

The little man rushed forward. "Lady, get back in your vehicle and tend to your baby."

"Damn, that was close," Daddy said, rubbing the back of his neck.

"Renata," Mama said, putting her hands on my face. "You talked."

"It's about time," Daddy said.

I arched my neck, toward the windshield, and watched upside down as the bridge snapped back together. Then I sat up. Daddy pressed his shoe against the accelerator. The T-bird started moving down the Causeway. Lake Pont-chartrain spread out gray and choppy, full of sailboats and pontoons. Daddy said it was shallow, but it looked bottomless to me. Mama shut her eyes. Her lips moved as if she was whispering a secret to herself. I wondered if she was praying; although she might be cursing. She sometimes did that when she thought I wasn't listening. She shifted in her seat, green silk against blue leather. I looked past her, toward tollbooths and flashing lights, and some-thing broke loose in my chest. The Causeway was ending. Mama peered out the window at the dusky, churning water. "I wish we didn't have to cross it again."

"Well, you've got to," Daddy said without looking at her. "No two ways about it. Just drink lots of funeral champagne, darlin'."

He glanced over at me and smiled. "Hey, Renata, girl. You ready for this silly old funeral?"

I nodded. Just as long as it wasn't a real one, I thought.

"Oh, come on now," he said. "Don't clam up. Let me hear that pretty voice of yours. Now, I'm going to ask you again. Are you ready for the party?"

"Yes, Daddy," I said.

"Well, let's go," he said, and the car lurched off the Causeway, plunging through sunlight and dappled shade, curving toward the dark heart of New Orleans.

Now I shut the scrapbook and ran into my grandmother's house. I couldn't wait to tell Honora what I'd remembered. She was in the kitchen, hanging up the phone. "Don't panic," she said, turning to me, "but that was the police. They want to interview you this afternoon."

"You mean interrogate," I said.

"Come on." She grabbed my elbow and steered me upstairs. "We've got work to do."

Two hours later, I walked into the police station with Honora on one side, Gladys and Isabella on the other. I wore an old-fashioned hat because they insisted that someone with a punky haircut might appear capable of blud-geoning their future stepmother-in-law.

Detective Bass led me into a blue room and gestured to a white Formica table, all surrounded by metal chairs. A young man in a white polo shirt was setting up a video camera, pointing it in the direction of the table. As I sat down, I noticed an acoustic tile ceiling and a small mirror on the left-side wall. With a sigh, the detective sat down in a chair and opened a fat notebook. "Ready?" he asked. I nodded. He read off questions in a stilted voice, and I truthfully answered each one. I felt calm, and for the first time in weeks my hands weren't shaking. During my years in Hollywood, I'd attended meetings at MGM, Caliban, and VanDusen, and I suppose listening to studio executives had toughened me a bit. A police interrogation seemed rather banal.

After it was over, and we were headed back to Chateau DeChavannes, I started to crow about my calmness. "I can't believe how cool I was," I told them. "I even impressed myself."

Isabella laughed. "You weren't so brave," she said. "I slipped you an Inderal."

"A what?" I cried.

"Oh, don't look shocked. It's just a little old blood pressure pill. I put it in your Diet Coke. It will cure stage fright every time. But you can thank me later."

Chapter 26

◎ ◎ ◎

MÖET IN THE MORNING

*T*he tropical storm hit during the night, but the next morning sunlight spilled down the beach. I walked down to the Grand, to drop off several designer handbags for my grandmother—a lilac Chanel and a straw Kate Spade. I left them in the Birdcage Lounge, and as my eyes adjusted to the darkness, I glanced around, hoping I'd see Isabella. She often came down to the Birdcage during happy hour. But this morning the bar was empty except for two men in knit golfing shirts.

I walked outside, to the end of the pier, and sat down. Gulls flew in and out of low clouds. Behind me, the pier shuddered as children ran back and forth. Suddenly I remembered something my father had once said, that Mobile Bay was a big, old nursery for oysters and baby shrimps. He'd even said that mermaids were born in these brackish waters. Once, my father had been whimsical. And I'd never even noticed.

Reaching in my shirt pocket, I pulled out a yellowed obituary that I'd found in the trunk.

Point Clear *Gazette*
OBITUARIES

Richard Lance McGeehee, Jr.

Services for Mr. McGeehee will be at 1 p.m. Monday,

September 9, 1975, at Woodlawn Funeral Home in Fairhope, with the Reverend Earl McAfee officiating, followed by interment in the Fairhope Cemetery. Mr. McGeehee, 60, died at home early Saturday morning, September 7. The Point Clear native was born July 20, 1915, to Martha Neville McGeehee and the late Richard Lance McGeehee. Survivors include his wife, Isabella D'Agostino McGeehee, and his aforementioned mother, Martha Neville McGeehee, both of Point Clear.

In Honora's study, she had a framed picture of Dickie Boy. He had a large, red face, the broken capillaries running across his cheeks like tiny estuaries, and his stomach jutted out so far he couldn't button his jacket.

One of the children bumped my elbow, knocking the clipping out of my hand. It caught the wind and twirled, then skidded down into the bay. I leaned over, reaching into the water, but the paper darkened, then melted into a wave.

"Sorry, lady," said the kid.

I walked back toward Honora's, leaning into the wind. Blue clouds were piling over the horizon, edged with polished nickel. The bay was thirty-one miles long and twenty-four miles wide, but its deepest part was only ten feet deep. When I reached Isabella's beach, I stopped. Over the years she had brought in truckloads of white sand, and most of it had washed away during every hurricane season; but ivory traces still gleamed in the scrub pines and sea oats. I cut up the path, stepping onto her terrace, and pressed the bell beside her kitchen door. It rang out the first six notes of what sounded like "Hooray for Hollywood."

Isabella's maid, Joquina, opened the door and gave me the once-over. "You probably don't remember me, but I'm Renata, Honora's granddaughter," I explained, pointing next door.

"Come on inside, then. I'll see if she's up to receiving."

Receiving? I thought, and rolled the word around on my tongue. I followed the maid into a large rectangular room that overlooked the water. This near the beach, I had expected spare, contemporary decor, but Isabella preferred a baroque style—heavy inlaid furniture, Flemish tapestries, puddled draperies. The maid disappeared into a hall, and a moment later I heard a hoarse, tobacco-drenched voice complaining about misplaced jewelry. A glass shattered, followed by a muffled curse.

Thinking it might be several minutes before my hostess appeared, I hunkered down to examine a marble-topped Bombé chest with inlaid wood and gold-leaf trim; I had grown up with similar frippery at Chateau DeChavannes, but I preferred a more laid-back, casual style. I walked over to the terrace doors and stared out at the water, where a prop plane flew across the sky, towing a banner advertising happy hour at the Grand.

Isabella appeared in the hallway, wearing freshwater pearls and a green voile pleated dress, which showed off bare, shapely legs. She reached up, adjusting lightly tinted Valentino sunglasses, then stepped over to me.

"Renata, darling, so sorry to keep you waiting. Would you like some champagne?" Without waiting for a reply, she glanced over her shoulder and called, "Joquina? Fetch that bottle of Möet, and make it snappy."

I saw a shadow and glimpsed Joquina passing through the room. She opened the kitchen door, and I saw a vase of white tulips sitting on a black granite counter. The cabinetry was white and heavily carved. Amber medicine bottles were lined up in the window. Moments later Joquina appeared holding a champagne bottle, two flutes trapped between her knuckles. Without spilling one drop, she tilted the bottle over the glasses. She handed one to me, then to Isabella, who said, "That'll be all, Joquina," then saucily crossed her legs and tossed her head. "Wait, come back here, Joquina!" she called. "Why don't you turn on a little music?"

I gripped the champagne flute, studying the bubbles, wondering what else was in there. A moment later, the music started up, Jimmy Buffett singing "Stars Fell on Alabama."

"Is this a social call, or did you want more juicy gossip?" She lifted one manicured eyebrow and smiled, showing the barest glimpse of teeth. Her pupils were huge, eclipsing the green irises, whether from excitement or from the pharmacopoeia I'd spotted on the kitchen window, I didn't know.

"Both," I said. "I found Dickie Boy's obituary today, and I started thinking about our little talk the other night."

"It wasn't little."

"May I ask a personal question?"

"Certainly. Those are my favorite kind."

"Did you sleep with my father before or after Dickie Boy died?"

"Beat around the bush, why don't you." She took a sip of champagne. "I adored your father, and I always will. We did have an affair-ette while he was married to your mother, but it didn't mean a thing to either of us. Especially not to him, but he saved my life. I guess I did love him a little. Without his help, I wouldn't have gotten away with murder."

She leaned forward, the pearls swinging. "Do you want to hear about it? Wait, pour us more bubbly. This is one of those sad tales that goes perfectly with Jimmy Buffett songs and alcohol. One must be drunk to appreciate the twists and turns of a love-gone-wrong story. If you're sober, Renata, you'd have to kill me or jail me, so drink up, baby doll. Drink up. You're going to be here awhile."

Chapter 27

◎ ◎ ◎

TILL DEATH DO US PART AND ALL THAT JAZZ.

*D*ahlin', sit down and get comfortable, because I'm getting ready to tell you about love and death, and the best sex I ever had. Do you want something besides champagne? A piece of Mississippi Mud cake? Just tell me what you want, and if it's a legal substance, I will make Joquina get it.

Dickie Boy and I had gone to Chaz's faux funeral over at the St. Louis Hotel in New Orleans. I sat in the courtyard, nursing a glass of tepid champagne, watching Chaz and Honora hold court in the Robespierre Room. The chandelier reflected in the mirrored walls, throwing light onto the guests in the receiving line. All of them were laughing and talking and sipping champagne. In the crowd, I picked out notable faces: a state senator, two famous artists, the *Times-Picayune* food critic. Enough doctors to raise the dead, and Chaz's Civil War reenactment friends.

Chaz's horrible sister, Aunt Na-Na, stood on the far side of the room, sipping the planter's punch and examining the gift-wrapped boxes on a long banquet table. Year-round, she wore black crepe and orthopedic shoes. She glanced my way, so I stood up and wandered around a spurting fountain, where a circular buffet had been set up. Do you want to hear about the food? I'll tell you anyway. Iced Gulf shrimp. Miniature quiches. Finger sandwiches. Puff pastry shells with crabmeat. *Champignons farcis de Paris.* A sheet cake decorated like a tombstone. Lording over it all was an ice sculpture of an enormous melting casket. I remember the food because I'd poured a bottle of Benadryl into the planter's punch. It was nonalcoholic, of course. I'd picked it because it was evermore fun to watch the teetotallers act like they were drunk.

Naturally that's where I found Dickie Boy, over by the punch bowl. He mopped a white handkerchief over his ruddy face, then ran his hand through that wild shock of lemon-colored hair. After he drained his punch glass, he sashayed over to the buffet and picked up a plate. He hadn't yet seen me, but he looked positively jovial. He lived by stock market fluctuations, you know. At a party the previous August on Dauphin Island, I'd heard him talking about the Federal Reserve. He was standing with three silver-haired men, and they were all drinking champagne.

"Even though I partially blame Abraham Lincoln for the Civil War," Dickie Boy said, "the man did say a few wise things. Like, 'Little men do not gain by bringing down big men. And the Federal Reserve is full of midgets.' "

The men laughed politely, then they got the hell away from Dickie Boy. I couldn't believe he'd said such a thing. I mean, really. It was 1975. Plus, he was a Republican and aspired to the Fortune 500; but he was totally henpecked by his mother, Miss Martha. Later, I tried to attach myself to a group of her ritzy-fitzy Dauphin Island friends. Miss Martha, who'd been sipping champagne all night, cocked one eyebrow and finally introduced me as Isabella Lee McGeehee. Well, Miss Martha damn well knew that Bennett was my maiden name. I don't know where she dreamed up Lee. But I decided to play along until a woman with gigantic diamond earrings said, "You aren't by chance named for the Lees of Virginia?"

"No, but I'm kin to the Leroys of Bayou Crapeau." I smiled. I'd never said the word *kin* in my life. I turned to my mother-in-law and said, "So, which Martha is in your family tree—Washington or White?"

That shut her up but good.

Now Dickie Boy walked over to me and held a shrimp by its tail, offering me to bite it. I didn't want fish breath at Chaz's party, so I gave my husband a chilling look, then hurried off to the powder room. I locked myself in a stall and lit a cigarette. I'd met Dickie Boy in 1967 at one of Honora's infamous dinner parties. She'd seated me between a portly, red-faced man and his bejeweled wife. The wife would not speak to me, but the husband told me his name was Dickie Boy McGeehee. His voice just reeked of oil money, and it turned out he was into offshore drilling and I don't know what-all. In between the tomato aspic and the snapper en croûte, I saw a way to fix my life.

We ran off to Mexico and lived in an apricot-colored villa while we waited for his divorce to come through. A few years later we bought the house next door to Honora, and I hired an architect to revamp it. Then Dickie Boy and I flew off to Italy. My marriage to Dickie Boy was a job, not an adventure; although sometimes it was a little of both. We were together because of my beauty and his money. Sex was just thrown in for a bonus. But that was all right; when it worked, it worked. Dickie Boy's didn't work half the time. But he'd gotten everything he'd paid for, and I got what I needed. We kept each other up, if you get my drift.

When I stepped out of the powder room, Louie grabbed me from behind me and put his lips against my ear. "Hey, gorgeous."

"Well, if it isn't the son of our dear, departed guest of honor," I said, trying to sound bored. "Nice funeral."

"It's not mine." He laughed. I just loved hearing that laugh, and he had the most expressive dark eyebrows, shaped rather like magpie wings. "Let's run off together," he added.

"Depends on where we're going." I glanced behind me, worried that a busybody from the faux wake would step out of the powder room and see us. Ever since Shelby had fallen through the ice, Louie had been drinking hard. When he visited Honora and Chaz, he'd walk over to my house, and I'd tell him about Dickie Boy's ruined liver. Then I'd lecture him about the evils of alcohol while I mixed him a martini. Finally, I'd take him upstairs to my bedroom and screw the hell out of him. I knew he was sleeping with me to punish Shelby, but I flat didn't care.

"I can get us a room at the Royal Orleans." He blew into my ear. "Or is the Big Easy not exotic enough for you?"

"I've already got a room there. Oh, I just adore New Orleans. Do you know what I call it? The Big O, in honor of all the orgasms I've had in this city."

"Get ready for another one." Louie grabbed my wrist and guided me around the corner, into the men's restroom. Cold air blew around my face, and I smelled pine disinfectant and urine. He led me into a stall and latched the door. When he turned, I picked up his left hand and stared at the gold ring.

"Why don't you find Shelby and kiss her and put an end to our little affair? Why don't you—"

He silenced me with a kiss. Then he lifted my dress and put his face under it. After a few seconds, or maybe it was minutes, I laced my fingers through his dark hair. I'd always heard that bald-headed men had the highest sex drives, but Louie's thick black curls were abundant. I suspected that more than testosterone flowed through his blood. Or maybe it didn't flow there, but stayed in his nether regions.

"Louie, honey," I said. "You'd . . . better . . . stop . . ."

He shook his head, and I gasped. The stall began spinning. I gripped his ears for balance and shut my eyes. From beneath my dress came Louie's muffled voice. "Still want me to stop?"

"Not unless you want me to kill you," I said. "Wait, you and Chaz can have a father-son faux funeral. Any last requests?"

"Stop talking," he said.

Earlier that year at Mardi Gras, we'd all come down to New Orleans. Shelby stayed home with the baby, although I suspected that she was still brooding over Kip. When push came to shove, he hadn't saved her. If Gladys hadn't been there, Shelby would have drowned. Anyway, back to Mardi Gras. Louie and I had the darlingest quickie in an elevator. He slid his hands under my dress, and we crashed against the control panel. Each button clicked, and I imagined them lighting up. He bit my nipple a tad too hard, and my elbow hit the emergency stop. While a bell trilled over our heads, he peeled down my panty hose. His fingers moved between my legs, and I thought the man's talents were wasted on heart surgery. He would have been a world-class gynecologist.

Now, he grabbed my hand and pushed it against his nether regions. I slid my hand back and forth. "What you got in there? A boa constrictor?"

He flipped up my dress, and his head was framed by Italian silk. I felt like a teenager on prom night. Well, that's not true. I never got to be a teenager, but I had a rather lengthy childhood. My daddy was a barber, but he used to chase fires. He kept a police radio at his shop, and whenever there was an inferno in Baldwin County, he'd run out of the shop, leaving a customer half shaved, and follow the engines. I loved to go, too. We'd stand across from the burning building, the heat pressing us back, and gallons of water streaming down into the blaze. There's something real masculine about a fire—all those men lugging hoses, being hoisted up in mechanical buckets, thrusting into rooms with burning ceilings. The firemen looked small against the flames, and I remember hearing my daddy say that "pissing in the wind" took on a whole new meaning. After I became a famous actress, I specialized in setting men on fire and then putting out the flames with gasoline. Well, not literally, but you get my drift.

The door to the men's room boomed open. I held my breath as footsteps clapped across the floor. I heard a zipper unzip, and a man's sigh, followed by the pattering of urine. I shook Louie's shoulder. In one swift motion—and without dislodging my dress—he lifted me up by the waist. I balanced my high heels on the toilet, as if I'd gotten caught in restrooms a thousand times. This just galled me. Never in my life had I set foot in a men's restroom; I had no idea how large those urinals were. Why, I didn't even know they had cubicles. Yet here I was, making out with my best friend's son in a commode room. It was crazy, and mean and exciting. I thought, Oh, my *God*. What am I doing?

As soon as the man left the restroom, Louie unzipped his trousers. I slapped his hand, and he stepped backward, his shoulders striking the door, sending a shudder through the metal. With as much dignity as I could muster, I climbed off the toilet. Then I unlatched the door and walked out the door, my heels clattering on the tile. I stepped into the cool, empty hall. Nothing thrilled me more than playing hard to get, especially when the guy was hard.

"Isabella? Baby?" Louie's voice echoed against the tiled walls. I thought about hiding in the powder room until the wake was over; but then, farther down the hall, I saw a door leading to a lush green courtyard. I hurried toward it and stepped gratefully into the pungent darkness. It smelled of lilies, tuberoses, and Mississippi River musk.

I pulled off my high heels and walked in my stocking feet around the fountain. From inside the hotel, the band was playing one of Honora's favorites, "Wonderful, Wonderful!" From here, I could see her on the dance floor, dancing with Shelby.

Now, I will just tell you. That was the strangest relationship I'd ever

witnessed. You would think that any mother would turn against her adulter-
ous daughter-in-law, and for a little while she did, but after Shelby did the Big
Nasty with Kip, she took up Catholicism, and Honora forgave all.

They were more like a mother and daughter. I was a little jealous of them
until Dickie Boy and I stopped off in Covington and I met Shelby's family;
then it all became clear. Her father was a judge, but all he did was kill poor
little animals. Her mama was a faded beauty queen and a defecater. That's
right—I said *defecater*.

Louie tried to get along with that wild, voodooing tribe. Mrs. Stevens
may have been a former Miss Louisiana, but she was an abomination to
humanity. I'd always heard that she wouldn't leave her house, but thanks to
modern medicine, she snapped out of it. She started traipsing around Covington in a blond wig. Well, she was practically bald from abusing Miss Clai-
rol. Then she'd defecate in people's yards. They'd be washing their supper
dishes and glance out their windows, and in the dusky light, they'd see Mrs.
Stevens squatting in the flower beds. It's the God's truth, I swear it. When I
tell this story to people, they accuse me of making it up. "That's just unreal,"
they say.

Mrs. Stevens wasn't but fifty years old. They say the hair dye seeped into
her brain. Whatever the cause, that woman had a big problem, and nobody
tried to help her, least of all Shelby. Then Gladys got it in her head that it
might help Mrs. Stevens if she spent the Easter holidays over in Point Clear.
They carried that poor woman to the car, with her kicking and screaming.
Louie gave her a sedative. After that visit she seemed to perk up, and Honora
invited her back for a July Fourth picnic.

Mrs. Stevens fell in love with Chateau DeChavannes. And do you want
to know why? I'll tell you why. Because the yard she loved to defile best was
Honora DeChavannes's. Once Chaz tried to call the police, but Honora
stopped him. "Put that phone down," she'd said. "There are no statutes for
pooping in someone's yard. She's family, and we have to overlook certain
things. Besides, it's good fertilizer."

Now, watching Honora and Shelby dance across the room, I felt dizzy, and
yes, I'll admit it, a little jealous. Honora was my best friend. I slipped on my
shoes and turned away. Not that I was always a party pooper—pardon the
pun, dahlin'. Just last month, I'd been to an Irish wedding, and I'd danced

until my hair was wringing wet; I stamped my feet to heart-thrumming songs like "Drowsy Maggie" and "MacLeod's Reel." I adored parties.

On my way out of the courtyard, the music broke off. I could see into the ballroom where a few couples kept on dancing. Way off in the distance, I saw Chaz talking to an unfamiliar brunette. The band began to play "Autumn Leaves," and Louie picked up his little daughter and led her to the dance floor. She put her little feet on top of his feet, and they shuffled around the room. He looked dashing, and I wished I'd stayed with him in the men's room. Louie was a big talker, but I could have shut him up with kisses. Well, it was too late now. People were starting to gather at the edges of the dance floor, smiling at Louie and Renata.

I left the pretend funeral and walked toward the Royal Orleans. Over the buildings, I saw a three-quarter moon, but it hadn't set. I turned into a candy shop to buy pralines. When I made that movie with James Darren, I'd tried to describe these confectionaries to him. "What is a praline?" he asked. "Describe how it tastes."

"Oh, honey, they're sublime," I told him, holding out my hand and taking a pretend bite. "Imagine a crunchy explosion of sugar and pecans on the tongue. It makes you think of fabulous sex, world peace, and bull markets."

Inside the candy shop was a bald-headed man wearing a gold-leaf crown. A white sheet was draped over his shoulder. He held out his hand while the clerk counted change.

"Are you pretending to be Julius Caesar?" I said.

"No, Augustus," the man said, giving me a withering look. He marched out of the shop, scurrying across the street to Antoine's, his sheet flapping behind him. I doubted they'd let him in, but they did. My head throbbed. Champagne and sex always gave me a migraine. I needed coffee, but I was too tired to walk back to the hotel. Besides, I might run into Honora. If only I could find Dickie Boy. Sweetie baby, I'd tell him. Run on down and get me a café au lait and two Bufferin, please. And he would go, thrilled to do my bidding, although he liked doing his mama's errands best of all. But I wasn't one bit jealous. No, I was glad they had each other.

After I bought pralines, I walked back to my hotel. I reached into the candy sack, broke off a piece, and slid the fragment into my mouth. Coming down the street was a man on a giant yellow tricycle, wearing a purple and green

Harlequin suit. On his head was a pointed hat with a bell at the end, chiming along his shoulders. I turned my face up to the sky, my arms spread wide, and shouted, "I love New Orleans!"

Soon as I got to my room, I stripped and filled the tub with hot, bubbly water. I soaked for a long time, washing off the scent of lovemaking. Sugar, I thrived on being bad. I invented the word. But I was also sweet, thoughtful, brave, and intuitive. I didn't think Dickie Boy suspected a thing. I'd die if he had. Because I am not a cruel woman.

I'll tell you who's cruel. Dickie Boy's mama is cruel. One time she called me a "wanton woman," and I swear I didn't hear her correctly. I thought she'd said "wonton," like what you'd order in a Chinese restaurant. You see, about a hundred years ago, she took elocution lessons to lose a hereditary lisp. My mother-in-law was a fe-male, with emphasis on the first syllable. All *fe* and no *male*, like a hormone imbalance. There was a whole lot wrong with the McGeehees, flaws that made you think of incest. Their genes probably looked like runes. Not only that, I hated to disappoint her, but I was neither hussy nor noodle. I just enjoyed sex—and not with Dickie Boy.

I stayed in the tub until the water was cold and scummy, and I was puckered all over. Then I climbed out and wrapped myself in a towel. When I stepped into the room, a naked man lay stretched out on the bed, a haze of blue cigarette smoke drifting above him. For one second I thought it was a pervert, and I screamed. Then the naked man laughed.

"How did you get in here?" I opened the French doors, and a breeze tousled my damp hair. It was one of those perfect moments, the kind that only happens in the movies.

"I was just in the neighborhood," Louie said. "Actually, I told the clerk that I was Mr. McGeehee, and he gave me a key."

"Well, I'm so glad you came."

"But I haven't." He bit down on the cigar and grinned. "Not yet, anyway."

"We'll just have to remedy that, won't we?" My voice sounded deliciously sultry. That's because of formal singing lessons. My poor fire-engine-chasing daddy sacrificed a lot for me, but it all paid off in the end. Unfortunately he died while I was making *It Happened in Venice* with that damned Doris Day—she was overrated, if you ask me. Anyway, my daddy died and I never got to buy him a nice brick house like I'd promised.

"Isabella, get over here, baby," Louie said.

I loved how he divided my name into four separate syllables—I believe that's what they're called. Anyway, he said it with a deliciously soft "I." Hearing him say my name was like biting into a praline. I'd had lovers of nearly every nationality, and they spoke all kinds of languages, but with the exception of Dickie Boy, I liked the southern accent best.

I let my towel drop. Louie crushed his cigar in the ashtray and opened his arms. A long while later, we got dressed and tried to figure out what to do next. Louie stood by the French door, brushing wrinkles out of his pants. Street noise drifted up, and I smelled fried oysters.

"Why go anywhere?" I said. "But what about your wife? She's probably worried sick. Maybe you should call."

"And tell her what?"

"She doesn't suspect anything, does she?"

"Not one bit," he said. "Let's go outside and walk around."

"Are you crazy? A walk in New Orleans after dark?" I lit a cigarette, then tilted back my head and exhaled a plume of smoke. "Honey, listen. It's not safe. You can get killed out there. It's not like Europe."

"Every place has its wicked parts."

"Sweetie, this en-tire city is wicked."

"We'll be fine."

"I can't let you go out there alone. Just let me throw on some clothes. Don't look like that. I'll hurry."

I walked over to my Vuitton suitcase, riffling through silk dresses, blouses with plunging necklines, and skirts with deep slits up the side. "I wish you'd skip the walk and let's just go to the bar and get gin and tonics."

"I can fix you a drink now." He started toward the dresser, where I'd set up a minibar.

"But there's no fresh lime." I swatted a mosquito.

"No problem, we'll buy one." He lifted his jacket with the crook of his finger, then slung it over his shoulder.

"Where you going to get a lime at this time of night in New Orleans?" I asked. But I was really thinking: What if we ran into someone from the party and they told Shelby and she hired a hit man? You can hire one in New Orleans for practically nothing. Although that was more Dickie Boy's style.

"I'll get it from the bartender." He winked, then stepped over to the door and opened it. "Listen, you don't have to go. Just keep the bed warm till I get back."

"Louie?"

"Yes?" He turned, one hand on the doorknob, his eyebrows raised expectantly.

"I love you, sweetie. I just want to make sure you know."

"Go ahead and fix your drink. I'll see you in a bit with the lime." He stepped into the hall. The door clicked shut behind him. I got up from the bed, leaned against the French doors, and gazed down into Royal Street. A taxi sped by, stirring up trash. A newspaper skittered over the sidewalk toward the antique shops. I saw Louie walk out of the hotel, into the street. I guessed the bar was out of limes. Or maybe he was leaving me. I wish I hadn't slept with him. Well, I loved him. And I wished he was mine. I just had a flair for attracting men and mosquitoes. They both just ate me up. This was my gift, and my curse. But insects and beautiful women just couldn't help what they did. We were driven by the instinct to survive. One was drawn by the smell of blood, the other was drawn by money. Somebody always got bit, and I felt sorry for them. Well, not too sorry. In fact, I didn't feel one bit bad. Like a famous person once said, I forget who, If you can't stand the mosquitoes, then get out of the swamp.

*L*ouie never came back. When I returned to the St. Louis Hotel, the party was winding down. I looked everywhere for Dickie Boy, but I couldn't find him. We all thought he'd gotten mugged, even murdered. Then he showed up at midnight without one word of explanation. Naturally I didn't ask, seeing as I'd done what I'd done. He was all swolled up and yellow from his liver problems. A doctor at Ochsner said it was cancer, but Dickie Boy and his mother preferred the diagnosis of cirrhosis by a general practitioner in Fairhope.

Chaz suggested we have a round of drinks and do a party postmortem. Louie begged off and drove his wife and child across Lake Pontchartrain. Everything was fine until we wandered out to the pool, and Dickie Boy fell into the deep end. Okay, he didn't fall. I pushed him. But it was an accident. Nigel and Chaz grabbed a giant net and fished my husband out of the water. Then everybody jumped in and began splashing, and before I could say Jack Robinson, the pool was full of drunken fools.

I dried Dickie Boy with a tablecloth, then waited out front for the valet to bring our Mercedes. I squished Dickie Boy into the passenger seat, then sped away. He stared out the window as if downtown New Orleans was the most fascinating thing he'd ever seen in his life, like he was trying to memorize it.

"Where did you go, honey?" I asked.

"Hmm?" he said, opening one eye.

"Where did you go tonight?"

"I don't know," he said, and rubbed his eyes. He seemed slurry-drunk. Then I remembered he'd been drinking the planter's punch. "I went for a walk and got all turned around."

"That can happen in New Orleans," I said and did not add: especially when you're drugged.

He put two fingers in his mouth, whisked them around a bit, and then pulled a hair off his tongue. I leaned over, trying to see what color it was. My hair was dark ash blond.

"Hey, watch the road," Dickie Boy cried. He nudged me toward the steering wheel.

"*You* watch it." I shot him a warning glance. "And don't change the subject. I asked where you ran off to."

"I ran off?" His forehead wrinkled. "When?"

"At Chaz's funeral," I prompted.

"Chaz died?" His eyes rounded. "When?"

"It was a party, and you know it. One minute you were eating oysters Rockefeller, and the next you were AWOL."

"I was no such thing." His eyes opened wide. His irises were dark as chicory coffee, but the left pupil was off center, drifting back and forth. I hadn't noticed this before.

"Did you know you have a wandering eye?" I said, studying his face.

"Oh, God. I'm so sorry, Isabella. I never meant for it to happen."

"That's all right," I said, genuinely touched. "Don't apologize. You were probably born with it."

"I was?"

"Wandering eyes can be hereditary."

"I guess they are. My daddy had one, too." He settled against the leather seat. "You aren't mad at me?"

"Why, no." I patted his hand. "It's no big deal. It can be surgically corrected."

"Surgery?" He gasped.

"Of course. See, the wandering is due to a short muscle," I explained. I'd read all about this in *Redbook*. "The surgeons just pull the skin back, then they cut and splice. Somehow they lengthen it. I'm not sure how. You could ask Chaz."

"But he's a brain surgeon . . . And you say they . . . make it *longer*?"

"It's the only way, dahlin'."

"Oh, my God," Dickie Boy said, one hand rising to his mouth. "Pull the car over now!"

"What's wrong?" I guided the Mercedes into the breakdown lane, but he wouldn't answer. As soon as I stopped, he flung open his door, leaned out into the road, and vomited. I began trembling, afraid the smell would trigger my gag reflex. (I had a weak one.) A few seconds later the smell drifted over, forcing me to fling open my door and vomit onto the pavement. If anyone passed us on the road, they'd think we were a matched set—the wife upchucking on one side, the husband on the other.

After we got home, I helped Dickie Boy into the house. He kept weaving, banging along the stairway. "We're almost there," I said in a comforting tone. With my free hand, I flung open the door to the master bedroom, then guided him to the four-poster bed. I had designed this room to resemble Scarlett O'Hara's lair in *Gone With the Wind*—I just loved that movie, even though my passion was French films with English subtitles.

"I'm so sorry, Isabella," he muttered, then fell backward against the mattress, his eyelids fluttering. Almost immediately he began to snore.

"*N'importe*," I said, pulling off his shoes, letting them drop to the burgundy and bone needlepoint rug. Then I took off his tuxedo. It was still just a little damp and smelled ever so faintly of chlorine. The whole time I undressed him, I whispered endearments. "*Ma petit crouton*," I said, unbuttoning his shirt, dropping his cuff links into a crystal bowl on the night table.

"*Ma petit écrevisse,*" I whispered, drawing the sheet over his naked body. "*Ma chère amour.*"

"I love you, too, Mandy," he said.

My hand froze to the sheet. "You *what?*"

He answered with a snore—he was out cold, drunk on champagne.

"My name is *not* Mandy." I viciously shook his arm. Tears pattered to the bedsheet. I brushed them away. He hadn't heard me, he was sleeping and looked so innocent. They all did when they were sleeping: little boys grown into men, now at the mercy of their wives. I stared at the outline of his body against the cotton sheet. I thought about snipping his penis at the root or maybe shoving a dried pepper down his urethra. But he might come up swinging.

Again, I shook his arm. His right eye peeped open. "Dickie Boy," I began, "who is Mandy?"

He didn't answer. He just stared at me with those coffee-bean eyes, so much like Miss Martha's, I wanted to cry.

"Dickie Boy?"

He answered with a snore. I shook him again, and he said, "Oh, yes, Mandy."

"Wake up and talk to me." I pushed his shoulder. "Who the hell is Mandy?"

"A hooker," he said. Then he nodded off again. His mouth sagged open, and a ragged snort emerged from the back of his throat.

Oh, my God. A hooker, I thought, pacing the room. I took a sleeping pill, then got into my nightgown and pulled back the covers. But I could not fall asleep. I leaned over and sniffed his hair and neck, but he only smelled faintly of chlorine. And if he'd truly been with a hooker, wouldn't I have smelled cheap perfume? I didn't have room to talk. Louie's fluids were all over my body. I stretched out on my side of the bed and tried to collect my thoughts, but Dickie Boy's snoring was earsplitting.

I got up, rummaged in my gift-wrapping closet for strapping tape, and tore off two wide strips. Then I returned to the bedroom and, straddling his chest, I placed the tape over his mouth. Once more, I stretched out beside him and forced myself to relax. Dickie Boy rolled onto his side, away from me, and released a muffled snort. I'd just have to deal with him tomorrow. I shut my eyes and waited for sleep, but it didn't come for a long time.

When I opened my eyes, I smelled something sour, like poor-quality goat cheese. The gold hands on the Meissen clock pointed to ten a.m. It wasn't unusual for me to sleep late, but Dickie Boy was an early riser. I pulled up on my elbows, then glanced over at him. He was lying on his back. As long as I'd known him, he'd had a yellow cast to his skin, but today it resembled tarnished silver. One hand rested on his swollen stomach. The tape was still on his mouth, but foam and spittle had dried around the edges.

"Wake up." I shook his arm. His hand slid off his belly and hit the sheet. I blinked. Was he breathing? I didn't see his chest move. I wasn't a doctor. I was an actress. But I knew dead when I saw it. I leaned over him, and the stink of old cheese rushed up my nose, only it wasn't cheese, it was vomit. And the only thing keeping it inside his mouth was tape. Dickie Boy wasn't just dead, I had killed him. My stomach heaved, and I barely made it to the bathroom.

For a long time I just lay there on the marble floor, trying to wrap my brain around the situation. Then I started to cry. Poor old Dickie Boy didn't deserve this. Had he suffered in the night and reached for me? Thanks to champagne and Nembutal, I was out cold. If Dickie Boy had flailed, I wouldn't have known. But why hadn't he woken up, yanked off the tape, and vomited on the floor the way he always did? His mama had never trained him to puke in a toilet. No, she'd just let him vomit wherever he pleased and send a maid to clean up after him.

Maybe Dickie Boy had passed out on champagne. Then he might not have woken up. I imagined the party food shooting out of his esophagus and hitting the tape, backing up in his throat until he stopped breathing.

And it was all my fault. I had accidentally murdered him. Oh, if only I'd just let him snore. But now he was dead, and I couldn't live with myself. As a murderess, I'd never have another peaceful moment. On the other hand, Dickie Boy had a rotten liver. He would have died anyway, and I had just hastened it along. But no, that was wrong. I wasn't God, even if I *was* a bit of a goddess.

I lay very still on the floor and drew up a plan. The police would call this a suspicious death, maybe even a homicide. It would make all the papers. They would turn it into a three-hankie story. I simply could not go to jail—not that I didn't deserve it. But behind bars, I would shrivel up and die. And that would make two unnecessary deaths.

Pulling myself off the floor, I reached for the telephone on the marble bathroom counter. Dickie Boy had a phone in every room so he wouldn't have to rush to answer it if he was on the toilet. I dialed Louie's house in Covington. He loved me. He would know what to do. He would smooth this over. When he answered, I made my voice sound light and airy. "Dahlin', I need to ask a favor."

"What's up?" he said.

"Can you come to my house?"

"Now?"

"Yes, it's an emergency."

"What's wrong?"

"I can't tell you over the phone. You'll just have to trust me. Louie, you know I wouldn't ask if it wasn't a life-or-death matter. Please hurry."

I hung up and checked on Dickie Boy. His body was turning darker by the minute, and rigor mortis was setting in. Soon, his whole body would harden. I wondered if his penis might be affected, and I lifted the sheet. Dickie Boy's privates were buried in fleshy grooves, his manly parts resembling a bird peeping out from its nest.

I was waiting on the front porch, smoking my thousandth cigarette, when Louie's blue T-bird pulled into the driveway.

He got out of the car—he bought a new one every year. "What's going on?"

"It's hard to explain," I said. "Let me just show you. Come on inside."

He followed me into the house, up the carpeted stairs, into my Scarlet O room. Dickie Boy lay motionless in the bed. Two pieces of tape still covered his mouth. Well, I hadn't known what to do with it.

"Is he sick?" Louie crossed over to the bed. He felt for a heartbeat, then pressed his ear to Dickie Boy's chest. Finally he raised up and pulled the tape off Dickie Boy's mouth. Vomit oozed down his chin.

"I didn't mean to hurt him," I said. Funny, but with the tape gone, Dickie Boy looked peaceful and not like a victim, like he'd died natural.

"Hurt him?" Louie lifted Dickie Boy's right eyelid. His pupils were huge. "He's dead. What the hell happened?"

"He, he, he—" I broke off, my chin working up and down. I was fixing to discombobulate. It was hard to believe that a little piece of tape could cause so much trouble.

"Why is there tape on his mouth?" Louie asked.

"He was snoring."

"It looks like he might have choked on vomit."

"My thoughts exactly," I said, and nodded, wondering if I could hire a smooth-talking lawyer and get out of it.

"Should we call the police?" I asked. "Jail will be horrid, but I deserve punishing. Unless I can find another way to pay my debt to society."

"You'll look good in stripes." Louie squeezed my hand.

"That's not funny. Oh, this is terrible." I pulled my hand away and clapped it over my face. No matter what I told Louie or the police, I knew they wouldn't understand. They would look at the dead man and know he didn't put that tape on his own mouth. They'd wonder if it was premeditated murder or second degree. During the trial they would show pictures of how the tape had left a sticky sheen around Dickie Boy's mouth. When they put me on the witness stand, I'd tell how his snoring had kept me awake. The jury wouldn't know that he'd done worse to me, that he'd taken up with hookers. They would see only a spoiled white woman in pearls and a Hattie Carnegie suit who didn't want to lose beauty sleep.

"If only I hadn't taped his mouth," I said. "If only I'd slept in another room."

"It's too late for if-onlys," Louie said.

"Hand me that phone," I said. "I'm calling the police."

"You won't necessarily go to jail. This is involuntary manslaughter. You might get a suspended sentence, maybe a few years probation."

"Probation?" I sucked in air. "Maybe if we just cleaned him up a little. Then it won't look so bad."

"Are you asking me to be an accomplice?" Louie asked. "To help you stage things?"

"Better to reshape the truth than go to prison. I'd just as soon die! And besides, Dickie Boy was a sick man. I don't know for sure that he choked on vomit."

"*I* know," said Louie.

"If you're not going to help, then you might as well leave. I'll clean him up myself. But if I go to jail, I am telling all that I know, and I *do* mean all. Got it?"

"You wouldn't," Louie said.

"Desperate people do all kinds of desperate things," I said.

I sat in the last row at Eastern Pines Funeral Home, watching Dickie Boy's mama hold court beside her son's casket. The lid was open, showing his upper body, but I couldn't look at him. Louie didn't come to the funeral. I hadn't heard from him since the afternoon he'd helped me with Dickie Boy. The funeral home was crammed with too many flowers and mourners. Miss Martha greeted each one. Over the humming air conditioners, I heard snatches of conversation.

"Died in his sleep."

"Went peaceable."

Fools, I thought. If it was this easy to get away with murder, then the end of the world was near.

Two months after the funeral, while I was getting my roots touched up at Salon le Mer, I heard that Louie and Shelby were getting a trial separation. Kip was just tickled to pieces.

"Honora is threatening to cut Louie out of her will," Kip said, teasing my hair. "It's all because of me, you know."

I made no comment. The little braggart was the best colorist on the Gulf Coast, and I couldn't afford to alienate him. But I was just stunned that he knew all about Louie. Honora hadn't mentioned it to me, and I was just next door. I felt like she'd had a party and left me off the guest list.

After Kip combed me out, I tipped him and drove over to the bakery and bought Italian cream cake. Then I hurried over to Chateau DeChavannes. "I just heard about Louie and Shelby," I said, putting the cake into her arms.

"That g.d. Kip," said Honora.

"Are they really getting a separation?"

"I'm afraid so. I would've told you, but you've been distraught over Dickie Boy's passing."

I let that pass. "But didn't they just buy a gorgeous house in New Orleans?"

"Yes." She set the cake on the counter, then pulled a knife from the drawer.

"What happened? Did they have a fight?"

"Shelby caught him having a fling."

"Oh?" I said, trying to resist the impulse to put my head between my knees. That damn Louie. He'd told Shelby all about us. I wondered if he'd mentioned Dickie Boy. If Shelby knew the truth, she would call the police. And they'd exhume my husband's body. I'd get slapped in jail with check forgers and hookers. Maybe Dickie Boy's hooker, Mandy, would be my cell mate.

"It was a patient's wife." She cut a slice of cake and plopped it on a Limoges dish.

"*What?*"

"I was shocked, too. The patient was from McComb, Mississippi. Louie was sleeping with his wife. She was quite young and pretty. Shelby walked into his office and caught him on an exam table with the woman."

Tit for tat, I thought. Or should I say tit for tit? I was furious with Louie. He'd been two-timing both me *and* Shelby. But I shouldn't complain. Louie had changed the course of my life, and even though he was a rat, I owed him my freedom. I might never find love, but then again, I'd never be forced to wear stripes unless they were in fashion. And dahlin', that means a lot, if not everything.

Chapter 28

○ ○ ○

SHANGHAIED

Point Clear *Gazette*
EASTERN BAY SOCIAL BUZZ

by Miss Mary Katherine Jamison

Mrs. Honora DeChavannes will host a garden party on Saturday, June 21, 1978, honoring the recent marriage of her son, Dr. Louie DeChavannes, to Bitsy Wentworth DeChavannes. Dr. Louie is a noted cardiovascular surgeon at the Ochsner Clinic in New Orleans. The bride, a native of Crystal Falls, Tennessee, is an interior designer. After a belated honeymoon trip to France, the couple will reside in Jefferson Parish, Louisiana.

I flopped down on the bed, reading the article, hoping it might open up and convey the details I had forgotten—and the ones omitted by Miss Jamison. I did know that my parents got a divorce after Papa Chaz's faux funeral. In February 1978, Papa Chaz himself died. At the real wake, I'd heard whispers that he and my grandmother had been arguing the day he'd died, and to this day Honora would not speak of it; but during the funeral my mama and daddy reconciled. They would have remarried if Bitsy Wentworth hadn't come along the following spring.

It had been years since I'd thought about Bitsy; I could remember my dislike for her better than I could recall her face. But I did have a memory of her long, swirly blond hair. It was striking and unforgettable. Almost all of Daddy's women were light-headed.

I carried the article downstairs and started looking for my grandmother. I couldn't remember the garden party, but she'd kept detailed records of every event, right down to the canapes and vintage of the wines. I found her in the sunroom with Gladys and Isabella. My grandmother tipped a watering can over a blooming dendrobium, its bowed stem heavy with white blossoms. Gladys and Isabella were discussing Grandmother Stevens again. "The first time she pooped in Honora's yard, we all thought a Saint Bernard had done it."

"She always did eat too much bulk," said Gladys.

"I don't believe this," I said. "Y'all are making this up."

"Well, it's true," said Isabella. "If Emma Stevens were alive today, we could DNA her poop; but she's dead. You'll just have to take my word for it."

"But it doesn't make sense," I said. "How could an agoraphobic ex-beauty queen overcome her fears and traipse around people's backyards?"

"She did more than traipse," said Isabella.

"It was drugs," said Gladys. "Those doctors in Mandeville gave her strong medicines."

"It's true," said Honora. "One pill made her sleepwalk."

"And one made her defecate," said Isabella.

"Well, it made her overcome certain inhibitions," said Honora.

I walked over to my grandmother and handed her the article. She tilted her head and made a humming noise. "I was wondering when you'd find this."

"What was so special about Bitsy? Why did he dump my mama for her?"

"It was the circumstances that surrounded your father at the time— surrounded all of us. It had been a rough few years. First, your parents went through that tumultuous separation and divorce. Then Chaz . . . died. And I don't know, it just did something to Louie. He worshipped his father."

"But I thought Mama and Daddy got back together at the funeral."

"They did." She set down the can and walked over to the wicker sofa. She patted the cushion, inviting me to sit beside her. "Those two had a star-crossed thing about funeral parlors."

She leaned toward the coffee table and opened a shell-covered box, then pulled out a cigarette. She didn't light it—fifteen years ago she'd quit smoking—but she just held it between her fingers. "Your mama and daddy helped me settle Chaz's estate. Aunt Na-Na was causing trouble. She wanted to sell this house and divide the money amongst the surviving DeChavannes. But Louie made her back off."

She laughed, shaking her head. "He and Shelby couldn't keep their hands off each other. I was thrilled. I babysat you a lot that winter. They spent a weekend in Destin, and Louie asked your mother to remarry him. In the middle of this tentative reconciliation, they planned a trip to Jamaica.

"I think they were going to get married on the beach. Gladys and I were going to babysit you. Anyway, right before your parents left, you took bronchitis, and Shelby backed out of the trip. So Louie went to Jamaica alone. And got shanghaied."

"I sort of remember that," I said.

"Yes, but there's more." Honora gave me a penetrating stare. "Do you want me to continue? Because it's painful."

"I can take it." I nodded.

"All right. But when I'm finished you may never speak to me again. You may think I'm too crazy to be your grandmother—and in a way I probably am. Yes, I probably am."

Chapter 29

⊙ ⊙ ⊙

HONORA & THE CIVIL WARS

The day Chaz died, I found out that he was having an affair with a woman Civil War enthusiast he'd met at one of those reenactments. Her name was Francis Baylor. She called me long distance from Valdosta, Georgia, and broke the news that she and Chaz were lovers.

At first, I thought she was referring to another Chaz—Dr. Chaz Breaux, a Point Clear gynecologist—but he wasn't interested in the Civil War. When I caught my breath, I said, "Why are you telling me this? Do you hope I'll leave my husband? Or has he promised you that he'll leave me?"

"No, I thought you ought to know the truth," said Francis Baylor.

"No, you didn't," I said. "What's the real reason? Is he trying to break it off?"

"I'm not saying," Francis snapped.

"Well, maybe he'll change his mind. I'd love to chat, but I've got something burning in my oven." I hung up and wandered in a daze out to the garden. When I spotted the red wheelbarrow, I knew what I had to do. Grabbing the handles, I pushed the wheelbarrow into the house, leaving a muddy swath up the back staircase. When I reached Chaz's closet, I gathered all of his custom-made Confederate uniforms, including his antique guns and newspapers and doodads. His collection was the finest in Alabama, if not the entire Southeast. It had cost thousands of dollars and had been written up in *Southern History Illustrated*. When I'd found every last thing, I pushed the wheelbarrow onto the far side of the terrace and piled all of the pricey costumes and artifacts into the old, shell-lined barbecue pit. Next, I doused everything with Jack Daniel's and lighter fluid, then I struck a match.

It was a cold, crisp February afternoon, and the sun hung low over the water. The flames were reportedly seen from several points on the bay, including the USS *Alabama* over in Mobile. Fire engines roared up to the gate, but I wouldn't let them in. I told them I was barbecuing a pork roast, and the last time I'd checked, it was perfectly legal to cook in one's backyard. I demanded they leave at once. Then I went into the house and poured single-malt whisky into an iced tea glass. I was Catholic, and the idea of divorcing Chaz was abhorrent; but I didn't think I could live with him.

Somebody called his office and reported the flames. He rushed home, took one look at his charred relics, and his face turned purple. "Damn you, Honora! What did you do?" he screamed.

"What did *I* do?" I raised my eyebrow, watching as he took the pool net and tried to fish out a jacket with gold bouillon fringe. Then I hurried into the house and locked the door.

An hour later I peeked out the kitchen window and saw him lying facedown on the terrace, still clutching that incinerated jacket.

One good thing came out of that funeral: Louie and Shelby fell back in love. Then, like I already said, he went by himself to Jamaica and dropped off the face of the earth. He called a few weeks later and said he'd gotten married to a woman he'd met on the trip.

"Hurricanes give more warning than you," I said, but he just laughed. If he and Shelby had been on the verge of reconciling, how—and why—had he jumped up and married someone else?

The phone call had originated from Las Vegas, of all places, and in the background, it sounded like a party was going on. "But I thought you were in Jamaica," I said.

"I was. But I took a little side trip to Vegas," Louie said. Then, to someone in the background, he whispered, "Stop that, Beauty."

"Stop what?" I asked.

"Not you," said Louie. In the background a women shrieked. Actually, it sounded like two women, possibly three, but I couldn't be sure.

"Honey, you're scaring me," I said. "Who'd you marry?"

"We met in Montego Bay."

"But I thought you and Shelby were back together."

"I know, I know. My plans changed. That's just how life is."

"You're not still punishing her over that thing with Kip?"

"Hell, no," he said a beat too fast. "Listen, I've got to run. I'll call you back."

I fixed a large glass of sweet tea and gulped it down. Then I walked upstairs into my shuttered bedroom and stretched out on the chaise, a wrung-out washcloth over my eyes. I wondered if I'd imagined the call. For weeks after Chaz had died, I'd imagined all sorts of things. One time I thought I heard something pass under the bedroom window—burglars, or even a peeping Tom. I climbed out of bed and opened the shutters. Five thousand frogs were madly hopping across the grass, scampering to the bay. The next morning I looked everywhere for those frogs, but I couldn't even find tracks in the sand. I wondered if I'd dreamed it.

Now I prayed I was suffering an auditory illusion, that I had misunderstood the whole conversation with my son. Perhaps Louis had said *carried* rather than *married*. No, I'd heard correctly. An impromptu announcement from Las Vegas, accompanied by screaming, could mean only one thing: my baby boy had been nailed by a hustler.

I wondered how Louie would explain this so-called marriage to Shelby. I had no intention of breaking the news—or her heart. Lust was one thing, love was another; but a Las Vegas wedding to a stranger was pure-dee insanity. He'd been raised better.

I waited two days for my son to call, the whole time imagining his new wife. Naturally I envisioned a woman with parakeet green hair. When he was in medical school, he had dated a woman like that. The more I pondered this matter, the more heartsick I became.

To make matters worse, an early spring heat wave had settled over the coast, and the air turned thick and scalding. When I stepped outside to fetch the mail, the sun poured over my head like melted shortening. A shimmering haze collected over the bay, and I couldn't see ten feet in any direction. Mobile Bay felt like the edge of the world, a repository of craziness. I knew trouble was brewing for Louie, but I couldn't stop it, any more than I could stop this weather.

Rather than walk next door, I called Isabella, thinking she would have better insight into the matter; but she wasn't home—or else she wasn't taking calls. Like me, she was a widow, and sometimes bad weather made her anti-social.

I didn't know who else to call. I thumbed through my address book, but I couldn't think of a soul who'd share my angst over Louie's marriage. Then it hit me, Na-Na DeChavannes, my husband's sour sister. Na-Na's real name was Mary Agnes, and she was an old maid with cold blue eyes and the DeCha-vannes nose. She wore brown lace-up orthopedic shoes, and her hairstyle hadn't changed in fifty years—parted in the middle, then pinned into a bun. Na-Na had no use for me, more on that later, but she loved Louie and would be interested in the marriage; she'd understand why I was fretting.

Picking up the phone, I dialed her number over in Pass Christian. Years ago, when I realized that she was meant to be an old maid, I felt sorry for her; I tried to be nice. She took that as an invitation to move into our lives. She treated my Chaz more like her boyfriend than her brother. We butted heads over him, fighting over his clothes, meals, and leisure time. When Louie was born, I softened, and Chaz begged me to let Na-Na be the godmother. I thought it was a terrible idea, but he just insisted. Against my better judg-ment, I agreed, but I secretly made up my mind that I just couldn't ever die, not until he was grown.

Na-Na assumed the role with a vengeance. When Louie and Shelby got married, Na-Na tried to force her way onto the front pew with me, as if Louie had two mothers. That was one time I put my foot down—quite literally. I dug my three-inch spiked heel into her orthopedic shoe, and under my breath I said, "Go away."

I rarely phoned Na-Na, even in emergencies. When Chaz died, I was too crazy to make the necessary calls, even though everybody assumed I had, and Na-Na had read about his funeral in the obituaries. She never forgave me. Well, she lived over in Pass Christian, near James and Nigel, and I just as-sumed they'd tell her. I assumed wrong.

"Hello?" said Na-Na in a sour voice.

I started to hang up, but then I heard her shriek. "Who is this?" she cried. "Why won't you speak? What kind of pervert are you?"

"No, it's just your sister-in-law," I said, trying to sound cheerful.

"Oh, crap," she said.

"Well, that's not very nice."

"I don't have to be nice at my age. Look, you called me. What is it that you want? And please, don't ramble. It's too hot."

In the background, ice tinkled in a glass. In Na-Na's youthful days, her drink of choice was iced coffee; now she drank lime Kool-Aid because caffeine made her heart race—all of the DeChavannes had weak hearts.

"It's Louie," I said.

"Yes?" Na-Na's attention was caught. "Is he okay?"

"He got married."

"To Shelby?"

"No, somebody else."

"You are lying! They're about to remarry, and you know it. You have an evil soul, Honora."

"Sorry to disappoint, but it's true."

Na-Na fell silent, and I knew she was crossing herself—forehead, chest, shoulder, shoulder. "When did this happen?"

"I don't know."

"You *don't know*?" Na-Na scoffed. "Isn't that's just like you. Why didn't he call me?"

I let that pass. In the back of my mind I heard Louie's woman, or women, screech.

"How can this be?" Na-Na cried.

Before she caught her breath again, I filled in the details. When I finished, Na-Na said, "Poor little Renata shouldn't have to put up with a stepmother. Louie could've married a nut! You say he called from Las Vegas—did he mention which hotel?"

"No. Why?"

"No reason. Well, I've got to take my heart pill."

"Don't start calling every hotel in Vegas and bribing the operators."

"You can't tell me what to do! Oh, go fix yourself a Land O'Lakes sandwich," Na-Na said, and slammed down the receiver.

I settled on the chaise and opened a photograph album, flipping pages until I found a picture of Na-Na's house. It was a gray-shingled bungalow that faced the Gulf of Mexico. Built in haste after World War II, it was reputed to be haunted by the daughter of its original owner. Local legend claimed that the daughter had shriveled up and died while waiting for her one true love to return from the war. Na-Na swore that the girl's ghost paced the front porch, and sometimes it heaved the wooden glider. "I saw the chains *lift*," she'd say. "The wind doesn't do that."

Years ago the house had attracted Louie, but the ghost appeared only for Na-Na. Even so, he would beg me to let him spend the night with his aunt. "Please, Mama," he'd whine, jumping up and down on one foot. "Please let me go to Pass Christian."

I did not want my son to spend one night in Na-Na's haunted house. "The ghost could be dangerous," I told him, but I really meant Na-Na. Louie would cry, and I'd let him have his way. Now I was reaping the whirlwinds of soft parenting.

A watched pot never boils, I told myself. And a watched phone never rings. Still, I could not drag myself from the house, even to fetch the mail. I wanted to call Shelby to see if Renata was feeling better, but I knew she would hear trouble in my voice. Better to seem neglectful of my grandchild than to break shocking news.

To keep busy, I made cheese straws, lemonade, and icebox pies. I dragged the phone into the kitchen, propping it on a green stool, straining to hear above the whirring KitchenAid mixer. "Ring, damn you," I told it. "I dare you. Ring!"

The waiting stimulated my appetite, and I found myself craving foods I hadn't eaten in years. For supper that night I ate an avocado and mayonnaise sandwich, laced with crumbled bacon. At eleven p.m., when I got ready for bed, I checked the dial tone—yes, it was working. It hummed in my ear. I settled against the pillows. But it was a long time before I felt sleepy. In the deepest part of night I could hear the mosquitoes buzzing. Sometimes they sounded like drunken women, the type who cried in bars and restaurant powder rooms and told their life stories to perfect strangers. I wondered if Louie's woman was like that.

The next morning, while I experimented with key limes, the kitchen phone rang. I snatched it up, not caring if I sounded anxious. When I heard Louie's voice, I said, "Well, it's about time! How dare you leave me hanging? You should've called sooner."

"Oh, Mama."

"Don't you 'oh, Mama' me. You only went to Jamaica two weeks ago. How could you marry a woman you barely know?"

"I just did."

"Well, aren't you ashamed?"

"Look, don't be upset, Mama. Be happy for us."

"Louie, don't take this wrong. But I've known you to take more time picking out golf balls."

"Do you believe in love at first sight?"

"No."

"Well, then, I can't explain."

"Try."

"I saw this gorgeous woman standing on the diving board. Her ankles were dainty like handles on a Dresden vase. And I don't know, I just fell for her. That's the end of the story."

"I'm afraid it's just the beginning," I said, rubbing my tired old eyes.

"You'll like her, wait and see. We're flying back to New Orleans in a few days. How about you throwing us a party next month?"

"Honey, I can't get a caterer in this short of time. I doubt I could order a fruit tray from Winn-Dixie."

"You'll pull it off just fine, Mama."

"As long as you don't expect much," I said, but I shook my head. In the old days I had thrown spectacular parties. I'd bring out flaming ducks, all surrounded with rum-soaked sugar cubes, and my guests would stand up and applaud. But widowhood, not to mention the relentless coastal storms, had sapped my energy; I lacked the strength to host a parasite, much less a party. And it would rub this sudden marriage into my daughter-in-law's face. *Ex*-daughter-in-law, I reminded myself.

"Louie?" I said into the phone. "You still there?"

"Yes, Mama."

"What in the world are you going to tell Shelby? That poor girl will be heartbroken."

"Don't you go telling her, you hear? I will do it."

"What do you take me for?" I said. "A meddler?"

"You've been known to do it." He laughed.

The rest of the day, I moved in a daze. I told myself it was a combination of the news and the heat. Right before the sun went down, I mixed a gin and tonic and carried it out to the screened porch. The surf had picked up, and the breakers were edged with foam. Dirty clouds were packed on the water. Somewhere way out on the bay, it was pouring rain, and it was headed straight my way.

I sipped my drink, shaking the ice in the glass. A breeze stirred the shell chimes, and rain began to fall, lightly at first, ticking through the trees. Louie's bride was bound to be pretty, but he was bound to disappoint her. There was something in him that made him act thoughtlessly. His love life was a minefield, requiring finesse and sure footing.

In the old days, when he was small, I took measures to protect him. Even if I sensed no danger, I took precautions. I tried to stop him from camping out at Na-Na's. I'd gripped his tiny hand whenever we walked down the beach. The shallow bay had a muddy, grassy bottom, and you could walk a long way before the bottom sloped off. When Louie waded out into the water, I would call out, "That's far enough!" He'd pretend not to hear. His head would dip down into a wave, and he'd swim like a kingfish, his tanned body gliding through the water, then arching deeper where I could not see and could not reach, no matter how hard I tried.

Chapter 30

⊙ ⊙ ⊙

HOLLYWOOD INFORMER

After Honora finished talking, she picked up the watering can and drenched another orchid. "That's really all I know," she said.

I sat there a moment, trying to absorb the information. "How did my mother react to the news?"

"She cried her eyes out and lost fifteen pounds—but she looked fabulous."

I started to ask another question, when Isabella breezed into the sunroom, tucking an Hermès equestrian scarf around her head. "Y'all look depressed," she said. "What the hell happened?"

"Oh, we've just been talking," said Honora.

"Maybe y'all should do less talking and more drinking." She walked over to the sofa. The article was still lying on the cushion, and she picked it up. "I remember that party," she said.

"Don't we all," said Honora.

"Louie got married. Then he started having an affair with his ex-wife. What a glorious scandal!" Isabella curled up on the sofa.

"It wasn't a scandal," said Honora.

"No, just the talk of New Orleans. Louie was caught between two wives, one old and one new. I thought it would settle down when Bitsy turned up pregnant."

"It's a wonder I'm not crazy," I said.

"Don't be so quick to judge," said Isabella. "Adultery is complex and misunderstood. Personally, I think it's something the Old Testament prophets thought up to control the masses. Don't get me wrong. I'm sure it's no fun if you're the one being cheated on. Although that isn't my realm of expertise. No man ever strayed from my bed."

"Because you chained them," said Honora.

"Only when they begged for it." Isabella's lips parted, showing her teeth. "You know what, Renata? You should call Aunt Na-Na. She was at the party. She was there when you tried to drown yourself."

"I never did that!"

"Yes, you did," said Isabella.

"It's true. You did it to scare Louie," said Honora. "In your little mind, you thought he would leave the new wife and go back to your mama."

"I'd remember something like that," I said.

"Maybe." Isabella tilted her head, watching me with those green eyes. "Maybe not."

"Okay, fine. I'll call Aunt Na-Na," I said. "I'll ask her to clear this up."

"Let's not involve Na-Na," said Honora. "We haven't spoken in years. I didn't invite her to Louie's most recent soiree, and she'll be furious."

"Too bad you didn't," said Isabella. "Then the police would know who hurt Joie."

"She's at Bay Manor over in Pass Christian," said Isabella. "That's an assisted-living facility. If you go, remember to flatter the old bird. That's the key to Na-Na."

"Did I really try to drown myself?" I asked the women.

"Yes," said Honora, and Isabella nodded.

"Well? Did it work? Did I disrupt his new marriage?"

"Tricks don't work with Louie DeChavannes," said Isabella. "He is impervious to tricks."

"Do I need to call before I visit Aunt Na-Na?" I asked. "What are the visiting hours?"

"Oh, please don't go. It's a long drive. Why don't you just sleep on it?" Honora suggested. "I'll make us some crab cakes and home fries, and then, in the morning, if you still want to see Na-Na, you can borrow my Bentley."

"Can I stay for supper, too?" Isabella said. "I just love your fries."

*   *   *

The policemen returned to the house, this time with an engineer who measured Honora's garage steps, trying to calculate the angle and trajectory of Joie's alleged fall. That's what they called it—alleged.

When I finally went to bed I couldn't sleep. I kept remembering how, after my father married Bitsy, I turned evil. One weekend they brought me to Daddy's apartment, and I got tired of watching Bitsy sit in my daddy's lap, whispering and making him laugh. So I wandered to their bedroom and stood in front of her dresser, touching all of her crystal perfume bottles. I poured them into the bathroom sink and refilled them with vinegar.

Not an hour later, my crime was discovered when Bitsy doused herself with cider vinegar, thinking it was Robert Piaget. Daddy jerked my arm and said I was a cruel child, that I should be nice to Bitsy and leave her things alone. After he punished me, I didn't speak to him for weeks. I wanted to hate him, but I couldn't. When I got over being mad, I called him up, asked if he'd take me out to lunch at Morrison's Café, just me and him. He laughed and said he'd be right there. But he never showed up. He had broken my heart and mama's. I felt hard toward him; but I still loved the man that I wanted him to be. For years, I clung to that hope. When he couldn't become that person, I felt orphaned, as if my real father had died, leaving behind an inferior replacement.

At daybreak, I finally drifted off, only to be awakened by nesting birds. I lay there until eight a.m., then put on my clothes and went downstairs. I got into the Bentley and headed over to Pass Christian, Mississippi. Honora had owned a beach house here until Papa Chaz had died, but now strangers were living in that house.

I pulled into Bay Manor's parking lot and hurried into the building. A receptionist with a nose ring pointed left and said, "Room 231." As I turned down the tiled hall, the smell of Clorox, urine, and boiled cabbage washed over me. Cupping my hand over my nose, I took shallow breaths. A white-haired woman shuffled past me, bent into an S over a metal walker.

Thumbtacked to my great-aunt's door was a poster of an upside-down orange kitten. *Hang in There!* read the caption. I knocked on the door, and a crabby voice called, "What now?"

I peered inside. The walls were bright yellow, and scattered around the room were carved Mediterranean antiques that I remembered from her old house. My great-aunt was sitting at a round table, surrounded by breakfast dishes. Lifting one bony hand, she stirred milk into oatmeal. She wore a two-piece black velour jogging suit, and on her feet were white Reeboks. Her gray hair was braided and pinned on top of her head.

"Aunt Na-Na?" I said

"Yes?" She glanced sideways and straightened her polka-dotted glasses. "Are you the new dietician?"

"No I'm Renata DeChavannes, your grandniece," I said, then added, "Louie's daughter."

"Speak of the devil!" She sucked in air, swiftly crossed herself, and whispered a Hail Mary.

"I didn't mean to surprise you," I said.

"No, no, come on in." She waved her hand. "Just come on in. I read all about you and that Hollywood man. I cut out the articles. Do you want to see? Or would you rather have some oatmeal?"

"No, thanks."

"Is that why you're in Alabama—boyfriend trouble? Tucked your tail and ran! And what did he do? He went jewelry shopping for a hooker!" She laughed and pushed a spoonful of oatmeal into her mouth. Then she leaned sideways and reached into a stack of papers. She pulled out a *Globe*, then threw it down and reached for a *Hollywood Informer*. Licking her finger, she began turning pages. Then she held it out.

March 28, 2000
The Hollywood **INFORMER**
World Exclusive!

Ferguson Lauderdale Shops for Engagement Ring

While Ferguson Lauderdale's romance heats up with Esmé Vasquez, the H.I. has learned that he made a secret trip last week to Weir and Sons on 96 Grafton Street, a landmark

jeweler in Dublin, to peruse diamond rings. Meanwhile, on
the other side of the ocean, his former girlfriend, screenwriter
Renata DeChavannes, was spotted at Atlanta-Hartfield Airport dressed in refugee garb (see page 17, "Freaky Photo of
the Week"). An unnamed source said that Mr. Lauderdale
looked at several diamonds before settling on a 3 carat pear-
shaped stone, which should complement the equally pear-
shaped Esmé.

"Oh, don't cry!" Aunt Na-Na patted my arm. "Men are rats. I can see why you
ran home."

"I came to see you, actually," I said, remembering Isabella's advice.

"Me?" She lifted her spoon and preened. "Really?"

The article, plus the smell of oatmeal, was making me queasy, so I got to
the point. "Do you remember when my father married Bitsy Wentworth? And
Honora threw them a party?"

"That day is cemented in my memory." She tapped her head with the
spoon, leaving a comma of oatmeal in her hair.

"Did I try to drown myself?"

She drew in a deep breath, then dropped her spoon into the bowl. "Yes.
But it wasn't my fault."

"I don't remember it. If you feel like talking," I said, "I'd like to hear the
details."

"I bet you would," said Aunt Na-Na, fixing me with hooded eyes. "I just
bet you would."

Chapter 31

* * *

The Patron Saint of Water

You want details? I got details. I may be old, but I remember everything about that cursed party. It was for my godchild, Louie, and that blond bimbo he'd up and married. The news had drove up my blood pressure. I went to confession and told the priest I had black thoughts in my heart. My favorite godchild had married a blond Baptist, a divorcee with a child. But just try and tell that to Honora. She lived for her parties.

I sat in a white Adirondack chair, in the shade of a hundred-year-old live oak, watching her play hostess with the mostess. A warm breeze rose up from the bay, tinkling the wind chimes along the patio, ruffling blue water in the swimming pool. Votive candles burned everywhere, even though it was still light enough to see. Guests crowded around the barbecue pit, where a caterer was turning a piglet. It was the same barbecue pit where my brother Chaz had collapsed and died—no, he didn't die *in* the pit, but next to it. I don't know what Honora was making him cook. But they say it was burned to a crisp.

Thanks to her bad cooking, she had clogged Chaz's poor heart with butter. Now she was throwing parties, serving high-cholesterol shrimp. She stood next to the barbecue pit, her yellow dress fluttering around her calves. Why, she didn't even have the decency to wear black. It was a disgrace. Somebody should call the police, because Honora killed my poor brother. Her weapons were butter, bacon grease, and Crisco. That unholy trio will kill you every time.

Ruined hearts run in the DeChavannes family, and I'll tell you, I feared for my life. Plus, I was allergic to sunlight. I'd chosen the Adirondack because of the shade. Me and the live oak were soul mates. When I was a girl, I'd thrown tea parties under the oak's low, gnarled branches. We had endured hurricanes, lightning, droughts. Now, all of this belonged to Honora.

The party had been arranged at the last minute to celebrate Louie's marriage. His bride was pretty. Curly blond hair drawn back with a silver clasp. Blue eyes rimmed with black lashes, each one longer than my little finger. A short white dress showed way too much leg—not a skinny leg but a curvy one. Louie kept one hand on her waist, his fingers cupped just shy of her breast. She lifted her arm, and silver bracelets clinked. Her charm bracelet caught my eye. It had a silver mermaid, lighthouse, and conch shell. Her fingers were unadorned except for a thin silver ring. It looked cheap, like the bride herself.

Renata sulked around the edges of the party. Her blond bangs hung in her lovely gray eyes, and her arms were painfully thin. She kept her distance from the bride; but she watched her through narrow eyes, as if she were thinking, Who will get the love, if there is any left to go around?

When the child thought no one was looking, she skulked over to the buffet table, then she picked up a huge platter of raw oysters and boiled shrimp and flung them onto the grass. With a self-satisfied smile, she flounced off, marching around the pool, her arms swinging back and forth.

The caterers ran over to the buffet table, calling to Honora. A black-haired caterer knelt down and picked up the oysters and shrimp, tossing them into a plastic trash bag. Louie, oblivious to everything, found Renata and hoisted her into the air. He could open raw oysters like nobody's business, and so could my brothers; but his daughter couldn't be beat throwing them.

On the other side of the pool, the bride sat on a low brick wall, sipping champagne. Even in the failing light, I saw that she was a beautiful woman. Her eyes briefly met mine, and there was an instant clash. Electric sparks flew into the air. I smelled ozone and sulfur. Then I crossed myself, asking the Blessed Virgin to give me strength.

As I uncoiled myself from the deep wooden chair, my black dress rustled like crow feathers. Walking stiff-legged, I crept around the pool. My intention was to interrogate the bride, to trick her into saying something she'd regret.

Halfway to my victim, I was stopped by the groom, who shifted Renata to his shoulder and gave me a one-armed hug.

"Here's my little godmother," said Louie.

"It's about time you noticed me," I said, pretending to bristle.

"You're my favorite aunt," Louie said.

"Listen to you." I poked his shoulder. "I'm your only true aunt. My sister-in-laws don't count."

"You were so good with children," he said, then glanced over at Honora, who was throwing shrimp into a garbage can. "Better than most people," he added. "If you get my drift."

"I was, wasn't I?" I smiled.

"As a matter of fact, you'd be the perfect one to take Renata to the beach." He swung the girl down and gave her a little push toward me. "You all have a good time."

"Now?" I blinked, horrified at the prospect of leading this child to the water, slogging through the sand in her good Sunday shoes. The child scowled up at me with evil eyes. She was dressed all wrong, in babyish clothes: a short dress, hand-smocked shirt with rabbits, the sort of suits little children wear to church here in the Deep South. Renata needed a sedate black dress and sensible shoes.

"You take her." I pressed the child's shoulder, guiding her back to Louie. I hardly knew Renata. Honora had made certain of it. "I'm too old to beach-comb," I added.

"That's impossible, Na-Na. You can't be a day over forty-nine."

"You really think so?" I straightened up, preening a bit, and my black dress stirred.

"If Mama went down to the beach, she'd break her hip or faint. She's in horrible shape."

"And slow," I pointed out.

"I'll bet it wouldn't take you ten minutes." Louie steered the little girl back to me.

"Oh, all right," I said crossly. I peered down at my godchild's evil child and smiled, showing all my teeth. On purpose. The girl stepped backward, bumping against Louie's leg.

"It's all right," Louie said to her. "Aunt Na-Na is a sweetheart."

212 ● MICHAEL LEE WEST

As we headed across the lawn, I clasped the girl's hand, causing her to cry out. "You don't want to get eaten by a pelican, do you?" I scolded, baring my teeth. The girl shook her head. Before we stepped down the rickety steps, I crossed myself. Forehead, chest, shoulder, shoulder. When we stepped down into the sand, the girl twisted her hand and broke free, running toward the water.

"Don't go too far!" I called to Renata. Then I glanced up and down the beach. It was a little after sunset, a dangerous time to be out and about. I could see disaster lurking in the shadows. While the child dawdled, the night would thicken. In my widow-black dress, I would be virtually invisible. The girl would walk into the bay and meet a horrid end, but not me. I hadn't lived this long to become shark food.

"Come on back, girl!" I cried, but the wind pushed the words down my throat. "Come back this instant!"

The child ran along the water, then squatted to pick up a shell. She had sturdy legs and flyaway dark hair that was starting to grow in blond. Just like Shelby. With a weary sigh, I lifted my skirt and shuffled through the sand. I was already breathless, and I could feel my old heart pumping the blood to my brain. Straight ahead, the long wooden pier was empty. I prayed the child wouldn't see it and get ideas. Children were that way, always sticking their pudgy fingers into dangerous things.

I hadn't been to the beach in years, mainly because of the sun and the stink of fish. And I hated the local teenagers who came down here to drink beer and smoke that dope. I knew what-all they did. I read the papers. I had spent my girlhood here with Chaz and our friends, waiting for the wind to change, and then someone would shout, "Jubilee!" Crabs and flounder would jump out of the water. And we'd get buckets and run down to the beach and bring it back to the house. The maid would open a cabinet and take out the crab boil. A Jubilee happened only once in a while, but almost every day I went sailing with my brothers in their rickety boat. Those were joyous days, long before Honora came along and spoiled everything. I moved to Pass Christian to be near my brother James, who eats dinner with me every night and leaves his silly wife at home; but it's not the same.

Now I gazed past the sandbar, where gulls were crying. I strained to see what was exciting them. The sky looked empty, except for a few thin purple clouds drifting east. I looked back at the sandbar. Several yards beyond it, in a streak of dark gray water, a human head bobbed up and down. I heard the gulls again, but it wasn't birds, it was a little child crying for help.

I gathered up my black skirt and trudged through the ribbed sand, leaning into the wind. There, in the water, I saw Renata. "Daddy!" she screamed. "Get my daddy!"

This seemed like an excellent idea, fetching Louie, but when I turned back and faced those rickety steps and all that godforsaken sand, my heart started thumping. Behind me, Renata screamed and flailed in the hazardous waters. I raised my skirt, revealing bony ankles, and waded out into the water. The warm waves lapped around me like chicken stock.

"Float, Renata!" I called. "Don't fight the current! Float until I get there!"

"No! Get Daddy!" Renata let out an agonized cry. All around her the water churned. At that instant, I remembered another reason I'd stopped coming to the beach—it had happened right after I saw that awful movie *Jaws*. I pictured a toothy shark ripping into my grandniece. I glanced down into the water, thinking I spotted a shadow. I screamed, then waded back to shore. Wringing out my dress, I whirled around and waved at Renata.

"Help is coming!" I called. I scuttled over to the base of the terrace and yelled up at two guests from Tennessee, who were placidly gazing out at the bay. "A child is drowning!" I yelled. "Get Louie!"

The startled guests ran off, and I slogged back down the beach to check on Renata. Behind me, I heard footsteps on the wooden stairs. Louie and two men ran down to the beach. Above them, on the lawn and terrace, all of the guests had gathered, still holding champagne flutes. Renata let out a garbled cry when she spotted her daddy. Then, with a wicked little smile, she slipped under the water. Again, I crossed myself, praying to Saint John the Baptist, the patron saint of water.

Poor little Renata. First, she overturned a bowl of shrimp, then she got into shark-infested waters. I pictured the little girl stretched out in a youth-sized casket. Then a funny thought hit me. Why was Renata smiling? Maybe this wasn't an actual drowning. Maybe the girl was forcing her daddy to choose—the bride or the daughter, the party or a rescue.

Louie rushed past me, pulling off his shoes, flinging them into the sand. He ran down to the bay in his sock feet. When he was little, he had been horrified of the water. Well, I hadn't meant to scare him. All I did was tell him that a cyclops lived under the lighthouse, and it would snatch bad little boys. Children drowned every day, and I didn't want that to happen to Louie.

Nigel and Chaz got sick of Louie acting like a girl. But Honora made him that way, not me, I didn't coddle him. I was visiting that day, and I knew the men were up to something. They waited until she went off to play canasta. Then they trapped Louie and carried him to the end of the pier. The whole time, he bit and screamed and kicked. Chaz and Nigel swung him back and forth like a rolled-up rug and threw that child into the water. I just knew he'd drown, but Louie surprised us all and swam.

Now I shook my finger at him and yelled, "This is all your fault! You up and married that woman, and Renata wants to die."

He wasn't listening. He ran into the shallows, his legs churning up foam. The two men charged in behind him, and I thought what a pity, they've ruined their nice pin-striped suits for nothing. Just before Louie reached the sandbar, Renata's head shot out of the water. She gasped, arms waving.

"Da-dee!" she called in a pathetic voice. She rose up on the backside of a wave, then slid over it.

"Baby, I'm coming," Louie cried hoarsely. "I'm so sorry, baby."

In three steps, he crossed the sandbar, then lunged out. The water instantly rose to his hips, then his chest. The bay flattened, and Renata splashed toward Louie. From shore, I watched the two heads come together. When they stumbled into the shallows, Renata leaned against her father, her arms around his waist, his arms clutching her shoulders. Her party dress billowed behind her, floating in the water, the sheer cotton forming a pink bubble on the water. I waved them ashore, feeling absurdly happy, as if I'd saved them both.

Chapter 32

● ● ●

HALF AN OYSTER SHELL

I drove home and went straight upstairs to my mother's trunk. Something that Aunt Na-Na had mentioned kept rolling around in my head, something about my father and oysters. I reached into the bottom of the trunk and scooted my hands over the bottom, dislodging papers and little trinkets. I pulled out an oyster shell, then a stubby knife with a wooden handle.

I sat down on the bed and pulled the phone into my lap and dialed my father's cell phone.

"What?" he said.

"Daddy, it's me." My hands started shaking.

"Yeah, your name popped up on my caller ID. I can't talk long. Joie woke up."

"That's wonderful, Daddy! When did it happen?"

"Yesterday. Faye stuffed Billy into a beach bag, then sneaked him into the ICU. The minute he started licking Joie's face, her nose twitched, then she opened one eye."

I laughed. "Oh, Daddy, I'm so happy for you."

"I thought I was imagining things until she waved one hand and said, 'Enough kisses, Billy.' Then Faye screamed and ran into the hall, 'Call 911!' she screeched. 'My baby is awake!'"

"You do a fabulous imitation of Faye," I said, *and Joie, too,* I silently added.

"Coming from you, I'm not sure that's a compliment. Why are you calling? You never call."

"I found your old oyster knife, and half of a shell. An oyster shell."

"Really? I've been looking a couple of decades for that knife."

"Mama had it. It was in an old chest that she left at Honora's. In fact, I've found all kinds of things. If you want the knife, I'll give it back."

"Well, thank you for returning my own property. How can I repay you?"

"Just tell me one thing. After you and Mama were divorced, did you ever come over to our house and open oysters?"

"Your mama didn't have a house, she had a floating shack. And yes, even after the divorce, I continued to open her oysters."

"Did y'all have an affair? While you were married to Bitsy?"

"No comment. Not now, not ever."

"But Daddy—"

"Go tell it on the mountain," he said. "Or better yet—tell it to the *National Enquirer*. I don't know who is putting you up to this excavation, or what you hope to accomplish, but when you dig up old bones, it's a foul, smelly process. Stop puzzling over those damn artifacts. Dive headfirst into the present."

"I can't. Not yet. I'm hoping you and I can have a long talk about Mama."

"There's nothing I can tell you that you don't already know."

"Oh, yes, there is, Daddy."

"Listen, I really have to go. Catch you later."

The line clicked. Still holding the phone against my ear, I sat cross-legged on the floor, forcing myself to breathe. Was I expecting too much from my father? On some level, had I been waiting for Ferg to abandon me the same way Daddy had? I slowly replaced the receiver. A moment later, I snatched it up and dialed Ferg's hotel. The operator put me through to his voice mail. I started to tell him where I was, and that I loved him—but I had an image of Esmé hearing my heartfelt message, then keeling over laughing. So I hung up, then lay back on the bed, studying the oyster knife.

Pushing all thoughts of Ferg and Esmé out of my mind, I scraped up an old memory. It was a Sunday afternoon in 1978, when I'd been visiting Daddy and Bitsy. When they brought me home, my mama waiting on her dock. She'd cleaned up, I noticed—her hair was all fluffed out around her shoulders, and she was dressed in cutoff jeans and a tight T-shirt.

"I bought fresh oysters," she called to Daddy. "And guess what? I can't open them."

"Do you have an oyster knife?" he asked.

"Your old one. But I can't seem to pop them open."

"Do you want me to?"

"Oh, would you?" Her lips parted. "I'd be so grateful. But it's too hot for your wife to sit in the car. Tell her to join us."

Daddy hunkered down, and I climbed on his back. He swung me around. I grabbed Mama's hair, drawing her into the circle. Minutes passed before we noticed Bitsy standing on the dock.

"The oysters are in here," Mama said, lifting me off my daddy's back. She opened the screen door and carried me into the house, bending under my weight. Inside, it was cool and dim, smelling pleasantly of seawater. She set me down, and I followed her into the minuscule kitchen. Everything was tidy, almost astringently clean. Off the kitchen was a square porch, haphazardly screened, leading out to a small dock. Next to the sink was a blue cooler filled with ice and oysters. A fat knife lay on a battered pine table. Two unopened oysters sat in the middle of the table, all surrounded by hard gray chips where Mama had tried to pry them open.

When Daddy and Bitsy walked into the room, Mama said, "I've seen you do this a thousand times. It looked so easy. But it's impossible!"

"There's a trick to it," he said.

"An art," said Mama. On the pocket of her shirt, "THE RAW BAR—NEW IBERIA, LA" was printed in blue letters. When she turned around, the back of the T-shirt was plastered with a 1940s cartoon woman—a big-breasted blonde in pink high heels. Above the blonde's head, in bold red letters, was "Give It to Me Raw."

"It's no big deal." Daddy laughed, then shrugged.

"No big deal to you, maybe." She threw him a pair of man-sized gloves.

Using my elbows for leverage, I hoisted myself onto the table and watched my father pull on the gloves.

"I get the first oyster," I said, swinging my legs back and forth.

"She likes to suck them from the shell," Mama told Bitsy. "Of course, *I* do, too. On Sunday afternoons Louie used to shuck a whole sack of Louisiana oysters. And I swear I ate them as fast as he could open them."

Daddy gave Bitsy a guilty glance, then picked up the knife. Bitsy peered into the ice chest, then stepped back when Mama threw in a handful of corn-meal.

"To make them happy," she explained. "Do you eat them raw?"

"Actually, no," Bitsy confessed.

Mama's eyes blinked open wide. "We've got to fix that. Don't we, Louie?"

"Mmm-hm," Daddy said, not looking at either woman. He laid one hand over the oyster, anchoring it, then pressed the knife into a seam, rocking the blade. His wrist flexed up and down, and the hinge gave way. The oyster opened, and Daddy ran the knife under the glistening oval, cutting the thick cord of muscle. Then he presented the oyster to me.

"I'm starved," I said, touching my lips to the shell. With a greedy slurp, the oyster disappeared.

"Look at that child." Mama laughed.

"Mmm," I hummed. Then I stretched out my hand. "More," I demanded.

"No, this one's for Bitsy," said Daddy, already cracking open another oyster. "Got any sauce, Shelby?"

"Coming right up." She opened the ancient humpbacked refrigerator, set-ting out a lemon, a jar of horseradish, a plastic jug of catsup. Standing on her bare toes, she reached into a cupboard and snatched a bottle of Tabasco and a box of saltines.

Daddy strained, and the shell popped apart. He ran the knife around the edges, then held it up for his new wife. "With or without sauce?" he asked.

"Wait, how do I do it?" Bitsy laughed. "I won't choke, will I?"

"Nah," I said, holding my empty shell up to my mouth like a doll's teacup. "Just suck it up like this."

"She's not going to do it," Mama said, giving Bitsy a doubtful look. "Here, put it on a cracker for her."

"That's the sissy way," I said.

"No, it's not," said Daddy.

"Is too," I said, poking him with my shell. "You said it at Granny Honora's. You said it when I was a little baby girl."

"You still are," Mama said.

Daddy was still holding out the shell. Bitsy touched her mouth to the oyster, then hesitated, her silver charm bracelet tinkling.

"Go on," Mama said.

"If you don't eat it, I will," I said.

Bitsy opened her lips and tried to draw it into her mouth, but the oyster didn't budge. She tried again, making an exaggerated slurping noise, and this time it slipped halfway into her mouth. The rest of it hung on the edge of her lip, dripping juice onto her white blouse.

"It looks like a booger," I said, then fell sideways on the counter, laughing. "Oooh, look at her."

"She looks fine," Daddy said, then he reached out and pushed the whole oyster into her mouth. She chewed, her eyes watering, but she didn't spit it out.

"Atta girl." Daddy patted her shoulder. Still chewing, she tried to smile. Then she held up her arm, clenched her fist, and made a muscle.

"My turn!" I yelled.

"No, this one's for your mama." He held out another oyster. Mama snapped it right up, then wiped her lips with the back of her hand. She hopped up on the counter next to me, entwining her legs with mine, and picked up an un-shucked oyster. "Remember that spring we were in Destin and a crazy man robbed McDonald's? He was disguised as a giant oyster."

"I remember that," I said. I took a cracker and dipped it into the sauce. "Daddy, give me another one."

Daddy grabbed another oyster out of the ice chest and opened it. He waved the shell in front of my mouth. I leaned forward and the oyster disappeared. Then I turned to Mama and held out the shell. "Here's your prize," I said.

"Thank you." Mama took the shell and turned it over and over.

"Can you show me how to open them?" she asked Daddy, then hopped off the table. She stood very close to him, their arms touching.

"Okay," he said, stripping off his gloves. She pulled them on and wiggled her fingers, laughing because her hands were so small. Daddy handed her the knife. "Lay the oyster on the table, and press your palm over it, like this." He stood behind her, pushing his large hand over hers. A troubled look crossed Bitsy's face. The knife rocked back and forth, as Daddy showed my mother how to work at the sealed edges.

"I've got it, I've got it," Mama said, her tongue touching her upper lip. Daddy let go, and she awkwardly ran the knife under the lid, severing the cord. The oyster broke apart—one half empty, one half full.

"Like a pro," said Daddy.

"Wait," Mama said. She yanked off the gloves and reached for the Tabasco, unscrewing the green cap. A red drop of hot sauce hit the oyster dead center. She held out the shell, smiling up at him. "Just the way you like it," she said.

Chapter 33

❀ ❀ ❀

THE MERMAID BADGE

*H*onora bought a mermaid weathervane and hired a man to put it on top of the boathouse. To celebrate the new doodad, Gladys served lunch on the terrace—artichokes vinaigrette, shrimp étouffée on white rice, French bread, and pecan pie. While the mermaid spun on the roof, the wind blew away the clouds, and sunlight bounced on the waves. I ate two helpings, causing Gladys and Honora to laugh. "You sure don't eat like somebody with a broke heart," said Gladys.

"That's not one hundred percent," said Honora, reaching for another slice of bread. "After Dickie Boy died, Isabella lived on pralines and champagne. And gained eighteen pounds."

"But was her heart broke?" Gladys laughed.

"I'm just pointing out that we all react differently to stress." She slid another piece of pie onto my plate. Then she bit her lip. "I wasn't going to say anything, but—"

"You want to know if I've weighed myself lately?" I laughed. Lord, but it felt good to be around Gladys and Honora, where the most pressing problems were calories and cocktail time.

"Actually, no," said Honora. "Have you seen the engagement ring story in the *Hollywood Informer*?"

I nodded and set down my fork. "Na-Na showed it to me."

"Why, that old witch," said Honora. She leaned forward, her sapphire necklace swinging. "Honey, have you heard from him?"

"No," I said, failing to add how many times I'd called but failed to leave a message, or that when and if I did, I was going to break up with him.

I picked up my fork, cut into the pie, and stuffed the hunk into my mouth. I wondered if I could be a food writer.

"Well, he can't call here," said Honora. "My phone number has been unlisted ever since Chaz died."

"Were you scared of perverts?" asked Gladys.

"No, Confederate widows," said Honora, smiling at me. "Don't fret over your beau. You've only been here a few weeks. That's not long."

"Long enough to put Joie into a coma and to dig up unbelievable dirt on my mother," I said. "And for my boyfriend to buy his new love a diamond."

"There you go again," said Honora. "Dame Doom. You shouldn't dwell on the past or the future; rather, live in the moment."

"How very Zen," I said.

"It works. It's one of life's secrets, and it will get you through many a crisis. I always think of it like rock climbing. You move from stone to stone. Minute to minute."

"I can't do that," I said. "My mind goes off in a hundred directions."

"You must cultivate it, darling. And it doesn't happen in a day, or even a year. It's a process. It takes practice to not focus on the bad."

"I like to embrace the dark side."

"Are you not even allowing the possibility of a positive outcome?"

"No."

"Silly girl." Honora got up from the table and clicked to the dog. "I still think you should call him—if nothing else, just to hear the truth. Sometimes not knowing is the worst. Well, if y'all will excuse me, I'm just going next door to check on Isabella. I haven't heard a peep from her today. Anyone want to join me? "

"I'm still working on this pie," I said.

"I might have me another piece, too," said Gladys.

"Save room for supper, my piglets," she said, scooping Zap into her arms, holding him like a human baby. "We're having my famous crab cakes with disgustingly dangerous home fries and bittersweet slaw."

"I'll have room," said Gladys.

"Catch y'all later," said Honora, walking around the pool house. Gladys reached into her pocket and drew out a small fabric disc. She slid it across the table. It was aqua and showed a mermaid diving into the ocean. Stitched above her in bold red letters was "CHAMPION SWIMMER."

"Does this jog your memory?" asked Gladys.

"Not a bit. Was it Mama's?"

"No, yours. Louie gave it to you."

"Daddy? That's odd. Looks like I'd remember." I rubbed the badge between my fingers.

"You would have, but you had a accident, baby. A swimming accident. I want to say brain damage—that's what everybody thought, but praise the Lord, you got all right. When you got better, you didn't remember anything that happened before. That's why everything's so sketchy. And because we shielded you."

"Brain damage," I said, pushing away from the table. "That explains why I'm such a goofball. What happened, Gladys?"

"Let's just call it a lack of oxygen," she said. "Pure and simple, a lack of air."

Chapter 34

⊙ ⊙ ⊙

GLADYS TELLS A STORY CALLED "SIRENS"

After Bitsy turned up pregnant, Honora invited me, Shelby, and Renata to come stay in Point Clear with her. I got the Mardi Gras room, which reminded me of Emma Stevens's kitchen, and Shelby and Renata took the "Bay View," which was all done up in blue and white. Years ago, long before all this trouble happen, Shelby used to sit in Louie's lap, and he'd rub his face in her hair and say, "You're a siren."

The first time Renata heard him say this, she went around the house making police and fire engine noises. She was just a child, she didn't know it was driving everybody crazy. She did that when she got upset. Now she was doing the same thing at Point Clear. Going around the house, making noises and calling herself a siren.

Honora pulled that child into her lap and said, "Baby girl, let's get one thing straight. A siren isn't just a loud sound, it can be a beautiful sea nymph."

"What's a nip?" asked Renata.

Honora put the child down and rummaged in the shelf. She pulled out a thick picture book that had mermaids in it. "This siren has a woman's head and the body of a crow," she explained. "It certainly isn't their beauty that lures men, is it? No, it's the sweetness of their song."

Renata looked up with those huge gray eyes, then lowered her eyebrows. Now that her hair was turning blond, it made her dark eyebrows look unnatural.

"The word *siren* means 'entangler.' " Honora tapped a picture of two mermaids. "It says right here that they are daughters of Achelous, a river god, better known as the old man of the sea. The siren represents the danger of being lulled and distracted. The danger is a loss of attention, a lapse in concentration."

Renata nodded.

"Because sailors needed to pay attention to the rough seas," Honora continued, as if the child understood. "Water can be dangerous or dull," she added. "But the real danger is not falling in love."

I was listening to all this, and I blurted out, "Falling overboard is a danger, too."

"Only for the poor swimmers." Honora laughed. "But the worst thing of all is the siren's song. If it gets you, then you risk becoming so entranced, you'll lose consciousness. The water nymph embodies all of the qualities of the sea when it's out of control."

I just rolled my eyes. If I lived to be a hundred, I would never understand rich people.

Days went by, and Shelby was too heartbroke to get out of bed. Renata, she wouldn't stay in her bed on account of her sleepwalking. We made her sleep in a life jacket, but she just untied it. Next thing we knew, she'd be out of that bed. We'd rush out of the house and find her standing on the diving board.

When Louie drove up to see Renata, Shelby told him that she was scared Renata would fall into the bay, or even Honora's pool. He didn't want the child to be frightened of anything, and neither did Shelby. Hoping to get to the bottom of the sleepwalking, they took her over to a doctor in Mobile. He put the child on a mild sedative and said she was reacting to all the changes in her life.

Then they called a pool company and had them put a plastic cover over the pool. Next, they put a lock on Renata's door and a fence around the pier. Louie thought it was a good idea to put the little girl in swimming lessons two mornings a week at Miss Lane's Water Academy. During the first lesson the child learned to swim.

One morning Shelby and Honora were in Mobile, so I drove Renata to her lesson. Miss Lane had curly red-blond hair and was built like a linebacker. Her pool was shaped like what you'd see on TV. It had blue tile, black lines on the bottom, a big diving board, and two kiddie pools. She divided the students according to age. The toddlers were called starfish; the three- to four-year-olds were shrimps; ages five to six were dolphins; everybody over age six was a mermaid.

One of the students, a dark-eyed little boy, didn't want to be a mermaid; he wanted to be a dolphin. His name was Robert Whitman, and he wore baggy blue swim trunks. The other mothers talked about Robert's mother and suspected the woman had dumped the child in the swimming academy while she went shopping.

"But mermaids are the very best swimmers," Miss Lane explained to Robert, putting her thick arm around him. "Younger kids are dolphins!"

"I don't care," said Robert, shrugging away from her hands. "Boys can't be mermaids."

"Sure they can," Miss Lane said. "Mermaids are sirens of the sea. No one really knows if they were male or female, you know. They sang to sailors, and their voices were so sweet, they caused major shipwrecks."

"I won't be one." He folded his arms and jutted out his chin.

"Then you can be a merman."

"There's no such thing." He glared at Miss Lane.

"You never know what's in the ocean, Robert. You just never know." Miss Lane pointed at the wrought-iron table. "I guess your lesson's over for today. Have a seat."

He walked around the table and sat down on the patio, his bony legs sticking out of his blue swim trunks. Miss Lane marched to the pool, clapping her hands. "Okay, students, line up in the deep end. We're going to practice our breath holding."

She slid into the blue water and swam over to the children. Treading water, she explained what she wanted them to do. It was her own version of dead man's float. The reason I knew is because one of the other mothers quizzed her about it, and Miss Lane said that she was writing a book about how to improve upon the basic strokes. And while she was at it, she'd renamed them.

"Watch me," she told the students. She inhaled, her cheeks filling, then her head dipped into water, face-first. Her hair fanned out, moving around her shoulders. Bubbles gathered on the surface, but Miss Lane kept her head down.

One of the kids said, "Is she alive?" I didn't know; I couldn't hold my breath that long. Another game they played was called Tea Party. This is where the children took a really deep breath, then tried to sit on the bottom of the pool, holding imaginary teacups and pretending to drink. The last one to come up for air was the winner. I did not like Renata to play, even though she loved that game best of all. In just a few lessons, she'd learned every stroke and could hold her breath forever.

Miss Lane raised her head, and water streamed down her face. "Now," she said, eyeing the children. "Now, it's y'all's turn."

When the lesson was almost over, she let the kids splash and play. When Robert's mama showed up, Miss Lane took her aside and said they needed to talk. "He was a little uncooperative today," Miss Lane said. "I've divided the class according to age and ability. Robert's such a good swimmer, I put him in the mermaids. And that's where the conflict comes in. He wants to be a dolphin, but he's too advanced for them. I told him he could be a merman, but that didn't work, either." Miss Lane smiled, showing how patient she was.

"Robert?" Mrs. Whitman called. She shielded her eyes with one hand. "Is this true? You don't want to be a mermaid?"

He shook his head, and he shot Miss Lane a hateful stare. I wondered if she would tell Mrs. Whitman how Robert bullied the little kids.

"I'm sorry about this," Mrs. Whitman said. "But I wonder, is it really necessary to use labels?"

"Well, yes," Miss Lane said. "It is. This way the children aren't pigeonholed as good or bad or intermediate swimmers."

Mrs. Whitman nodded, but it was clear that she was upset. "What could it hurt if he's a dolphin?"

"It's really not fair to Robert or to the younger swimmers." Miss Lane gazed at the pool. A few of the advanced students were playing Marco Polo, and the ringleader was little old Renata. Her body moved underwater like wrinkles. I was so proud of her.

"I've got to have some kind of order in the class," said Miss Lane. "Otherwise, it breaks down. And they don't learn anything."

"I'll talk to him," said Mrs. Whitman, herding Robert out the back gate, into the driveway.

At the next lesson, when Miss Lane put Robert with the mermaids, he climbed out of the pool and sat on the patio.

"Robert, come back," said Miss Lane.

"I want to be a dolphin," he growled, staring at her from under his eyebrows.

"Okay, fine. You're a dolphin. Now come over here with the mermaids."

"No." Robert folded his arms. Miss Lane turned to her students. "Okay, everybody. Practice your breath holding for a minute. Starfish? You guys just blow bubbles. When I get back, we'll do the butterfly." She walked over to Robert and squatted beside him, talking in a soft voice. He wasn't her kid: she had to be nice. She sat there for five minutes at least. Then she threw up her hands. All the other mothers stared and began to whisper.

"Okay, Robert. You win. Go swim with the dolphins."

He scrambled to his feet and ran to the edge of the pool, where the toddlers were gathered. Robert leaped in, his hands clasped around his ankles, landing in a perfect cannonball. Water splashed all over my purple dress. After a second, Robert's head shot up, his mouth spurting water, and he climbed out of the pool. He did another cannonball, causing the pool water to sway. The dolphins shrank back, holding on to the sides of the pool. Two of the little girls began to cry.

"Little devil," Miss Lane muttered. She put her hands on her hips and stared down into the pool. Robert squatted on the bottom, looking up at her, bubbles curving over his head.

"Come out of there, Robert," she called, but he shook his head. "I mean it, Robert."

He climbed out of the pool and jumped back into the water, sending a wave over the sides, spilling water onto the concrete. I saw him swim over to Renata. She stuck out her tongue, and pushed water into his face. He started kicking, sending droplets spinning into the air.

I scooted my chair away from the pool, and so did the mothers. I don't know how much time passed as I bent over the pillowcase I was embroidering, only half listening as Miss Lane turned back to the mermaids and clapped her hands. "Okay, class. Let's all get in the water and—"

"Miss Lane?" asked one of the dolphins, a black-eyed girl who'd just learned to swim.

"Yes?" Miss Lane smiled.

"One of the mermaids is on the bottom of the pool, ma'am." The girl pointed. "Over in the deep end."

"Robert was holding her underwater," said a dolphin.

Her? I thought. Miss Lane put one hand over her eyes and scanned the water. I stood up and looked all around the pool for Renata. Then I looked in the deep end, and there she was, her hair moving above her like seaweed, arms stretched out along the bottom as if she was reaching for something. I screamed. Miss Lane raised her arms and dove into the water, her big legs moving like scissors. Then she surged upward, holding Renata's body. It looked heavy, like Miss Lane was dragging a bag of cement to the surface. One of the mothers ran into the house to call an ambulance.

"Somebody help," Miss Lane cried. "Help me!"

It took me and all of the mothers to heave Renata out of the pool. We set her down on the cement. Water streamed from her ears and mouth, it ran through her hair, out of her bathing suit, gathering in a puddle under the small of her back. Her eyes were closed, her lips were dark, almost smeared, as if she'd been eating blueberries. Miss Lane yelled for someone to call an ambulance, then she placed a trembly finger on Renata's neck, feeling for a pulse. She got on her knees and put her mouth over the girl's and breathed.

"Is she all right?" asked one of the mothers. Miss Lane didn't answer. I don't think she heard. Suddenly Renata choked and spit out a plume of water. She sucked in a ragged breath. Then she began to cry.

"Thank the Lord," I whispered. Then I fell to my knees, hugging Renata. She felt cold and smelled of chlorine. The sirens cut through the air, moving closer and closer, blotting out the light, the other children's voices, the half-drowned child. I was conscious of small things: the rise and fall of the siren, Renata's flat chest moving, Robert Whitman's screams as his mother switched his legs, my own lungs expanding and shrinking, drinking in air and never filling up.

Chapter 35

◉ ◉ ◉

HONORA SAYS, QUE SERA SERA

From inside my boathouse, I stared down at the empty beach, waiting for Renata to come back from her morning walk. She'd left her tennis shoes on the steps, and the red tin shell-collecting bucket was missing. Pelicans floated on the waves, the bay stretched out around them like a wrinkled ball gown. Zap pressed his nose against the screen, watching those pelicans.

The wind shifted direction, and on the roof, the copper mermaid began to turn, the metal pole screeking. A breeze swept through the screen mesh, ruffling the envelopes I'd left stacked on the wicker table. Louie had dropped them into my lap this morning. "Where's Renata?" he'd asked. "Getting her beauty sleep?"

"No, she's taking a walk. She'll be back in a minute."

"I can't wait. I've got to get back to the hospital. But since you and Gladys are hell-bent on dragging up the past, I decided to make a little contribution. Just make sure I get them back."

I fingered the blue ribbon that held the envelopes together. I didn't ask him to explain; I recognized Shelby's handwriting on the pale aqua stationery.

"How's Joie?"

"She's conscious." He stared out at the water. "But she's having trouble moving her left arm."

"Do they know if—"

"If she's got permanent damage?" He shook his head. "Not yet."

"I'm sorry this happened," I said. "If only I hadn't thrown that damn party. You aren't still blaming Renata, are you?"

He shrugged. "The police called. Your caterers passed their lie detector tests. The waiters, too. So I don't know. I guess we'll just have to wait and see what Joie tells us."

"Renata has nothing to hide," I said, trying not to bristle.

"Hope you're right." Louie stood up. "Well, I've got to run. Just give her those letters."

Now, the screen walls shuddered as a salty wind swirled through the boathouse. An envelope fell, and Zap ran over and gently bit one edge, then trotted over to me.

"Such a little gentleman!" I said. He lowered his ears, inviting a pat. Years ago, Isabella had owned six Yorkshire terriers, and after Dickie Boy's death, while she renovated her house, she stayed off and on in the Mimosa Room here at Chateau DeChavannes. It was named after the tree that bloomed outside her window. After she left, I had to send the rugs to New Orleans for fumigation. Those uncivilized dogs had ruined them.

For many years she sold puppies to the crème de la crème of Gulf Coast society. Not that she'd ever intended to be a backyard breeder. She refused to spay or neuter any of her babies, so her Yorkie population grew. She charged outrageous prices for the puppies. She loved pitting the prospective owners against each other, creating a competition. Isabella lapped up the attention, making them court her with phone calls and letters and visits.

Never in my wildest dreams did I suspect I would end up with a descendant of that tribe, or that Isabella would be dogless. Zap was born on December 21, 1998, the last puppy that Isabella bred. His ears wouldn't stand up, and neither would his tail. Plus, he had a cottony coat. Isabella almost had him put to sleep, but I took one look at those intelligent brown eyes and that hairy face, and something hard melted inside my chest. I convinced her to give him to me.

My wind chimes clinked, and the wind sent the papers spinning. Bending down to collect them, I heard my knees pop—old age and the ailments that go with it aren't for sissies. Although I shouldn't quibble. My eyesight is 20/20, and while I have a touch of the rheumatism, I'm able to open tiny jars of capers and sun-dried tomatoes.

I set the letters on the table, anchoring them with a conch shell, then glanced at the beach. There, in the shimmering haze, I saw a tiny figure in a gray hooded sweatshirt. She was holding a bucket, and when she bent down, the sun glanced off the metal. She didn't seem to be in a hurry, so I figured I had a little while longer to work up my nerve. I leaned against the screen, praying for strength. I wasn't sure what to say, or how much more she could stand to hear.

I had a clear memory of those days after Bitsy turned up pregnant. Shelby and Renata moved back to New Orleans, leaving Gladys with me in Point Clear. It was a strategic move on Shelby's part, to keep herself available to Louie. I struggled with my emotions, and my tendency to meddle; my loyalties were divided between Renata and my unborn grandchild. The adults could damn well take care of themselves.

Now, all these years later, I didn't feel right bringing up Shelby and Louie's affairs. In fact, I was tempted to gloss over that crazy period. I stepped over to the table and lifted the shell, gathering the damning evidence. I could toss everything into the bay. I could dig a sandy hole and stick the letters inside. I could burn them in the barbecue pit. Instead, I sat down on the sofa, and the cushion gave off a sour, salty smell. The letters were out of order, and I began to rearrange them by postmark, when a small clipping fell to the ground.

Covington *Citizen*
December 15, 1978

EMMA STEVENS

Services for Emma Stevens will be at 11 a.m. Thursday, December 16, at Bond Memorial Chapel at Gaston-Edwards Funeral Home, with Reverend Daniel McPeak officiating. Visitation will be from 5 to 9 p.m. at the funeral home. Mrs. Stevens, 57, died December 13 at her home. She was a local author. She is survived by her husband, Judge Thaddeus Stevens, of Covington; a daughter, Shelby DeChavannes; and a granddaughter, Renata DeChavannes, of New Orleans.

The obituary had left out a few pertinent facts. Judge Thaddeus Stevens had been driving Emma to her weekly appointment with the psychiatrist at Mandeville. A bee flew in the window and stung Thaddeus on the neck. He lost control of the car and smashed into a hundred-and-seventy-year-old live oak named Angelina. It didn't hurt the tree or Thaddeus, but they were shaken up and bruised; since no bones were broken and no one was bleeding, they called a cab and went home.

A week later, while Emma sat at the kitchen table peeling shrimp over the society pages of the *Covington Citizen,* she fell face-first into the shells. The doctor said it was most likely a blood clot. Gladys and I drove over to the funeral home. Louie and Bitsy were sitting in the back row. She was barely into the pregnancy, and already her face had thickened. Renata was sitting on the other side of the room with her mama and grandfather.

Gladys and I walked up to the casket and paid our respects. I'd heard from Louie how he and Shelby had to buy a wig to cover Emma's baldness. Her penchant for abusing hair-coloring products had taken a toll. She hadn't just washed away the gray, she'd killed hair follicles. Now, the wig was crooked, and Gladys reached down and straightened it.

We drifted over to Thaddeus and told him how sorry we were for his loss. Gladys started to cry, and he put his arms around her. "She was just getting better, too," he said. "She'd stopped prowling around at night, doing what she was doing. And she'd joined Lakeside Baptist."

I drifted over to say hello to Louie and Bitsy. Then Renata ran over and grabbed my hand, dragging me to the row behind her mother. She wanted to know about Christmas, how many trees I'd set up, and if I'd put one in her room.

The entire Sunday school at Lakeside Baptist walked in and surrounded the casket. Thaddeus got up to talk to them, and Gladys drifted over to me and Renata. From the corner of my eye, I saw Bitsy walk into the refreshment room and reach for a sugared doughnut. After a minute, Louie eased out of his row and sat down next to Shelby. He put his hand on her knee. I half-expected her to move it. She didn't.

Over my granddaughter's chatter, I heard Louie say, "She insisted on coming, I tried to stop her."

"Don't worry about it."

"I love you."

"Please don't." She bowed her head, and a tear hit the back of her hand.

"I will always love you."

"Stop it," she whispered.

"I was drunk when I married her."

"Maybe, but somehow you got from Jamaica to Las Vegas."

"I never meant for it to be anything more than a fling. We got to Vegas and sat down to play blackjack. Those free drinks kept coming and coming. And I woke up married."

"I don't want to hear this," she whispered. "You could've gotten an annulment."

"I was so drunk, I wasn't thinking straight. In my confusion, I worked it all out: my marriage to Bitsy canceled out your affair with Kip. I'd get a quick divorce, send her packing, and try to win you back."

"Didn't work." She looked up at him. "Did it?"

"I'm sorry. I've got plenty more to tell you, but not in public."

"Why? Nothing you can say will fix this."

"Just hear me out. That's all I'm asking." He squeezed her hand. "Please. It's all I'm asking."

She looked at a staircase that curved up into darkness. "It's quiet upstairs," she said.

"You go first," he said. "I'll find you."

No! I wanted to shout. She stood up and tugged at the hem of her black dress. It showed her curves without being vulgar. Louie's gaze dropped to her hips, then back up to her face. He squeezed her hand, and she walked past me without making eye contact. Her shoes brushed against the carpet.

Renata was telling us about seeing Santa Claus at Maison-Blanche, but I couldn't listen.

Louie got up and glanced into the refreshment room. I looked, too. Bitsy had a beignet in each hand and was licking powdered sugar from her wrist. Louie walked in the opposite direction, then ran up the stairs.

I lost track of time while I sat there, listening to Renata's chatter. Over the child's head, my eyes met Gladys's. She shut her eyes, then shook her head, as if to say, *What's the use?* From the ceiling, I heard a rhythmic bumping, and prisms on the chandelier trembled.

Bitsy stepped into the room, wiping the corner of her mouth. She looked around for Louie, then walked over to my row and sat down next to Gladys. "Hello, Renata," she said.

"Hi," Renata said.

Louie entered the room, his cheeks flushed. I gave him a quick once-over, looking to see if he was unzipped or unbuttoned, but his clothes were immaculate. He sat down next to Bitsy and kissed the back of her hand. On the other side of the room, two Sunday school women stood in front of the staircase, chatting about the Christmas parade. Behind them, I saw Shelby duck into the powder room.

Sometime after New Year's Bitsy started spotting, and her obstetrician ordered her to bed.

Her mother, Dorothy McDougal, drove down from Tennessee, and she was the strangest woman I'd ever met in my entire life, and that was including the late Emma Stevens.

Then it was April, and Bitsy was not only out of bed, she was decorating her new Garden District house. Louie and Shelby were the talk of New Orleans. They had been spotted by my dear friend, Sister De Benedetto, at the Court of Three Sisters, feeding each other shrimp creole. Afraid the gossip would reach Bitsy, I invited Shelby and Renata to Point Clear; but my son drove over every week—sometimes more—and each time he left, I got a migraine headache.

Bitsy showed uncommon strength after I received a poison pen letter that exposed her past. I want to say that Aunt Na-Na sent that letter, but I didn't have a shred of proof. And if Shelby had known about Bitsy's crimes, she would have told me. My new daughter-in-law's old crime spree had been chronicled in several newspapers, including the *Mobile Register* and *Times-Picayune*, so anyone could have sent it. I won't get into it, but the letter said that Bitsy had tried to kill her first husband with a package of frozen baby back ribs. I feared for my son, so I drove over to New Orleans to confront his new wife.

I came away from that encounter respecting that girl. She'd been railroaded by her rich in-laws and had lost custody of her daughter, but she'd found Louie. She had high hopes for this baby. It was a second chance. She told me about a newfangled test, something called an ultrasound, and it had shown the baby's sex. She and Louie were having a son. Louis Charles DeChavannes III. They were going to call him Trip for short.

"I am so thrilled," I said, and I meant it, even though I knew this news would break what was left of Shelby's heart, and it wouldn't set good with Renata, either. I followed Bitsy upstairs, and she showed me the baby's nursery, blue walls, watered silk draperies, a simple but elegant white crib, an antique rocking chair with deep cushions, and a French armoire already filled with sailor suits and hand-smocked blankets.

On the way home, I swung by Shelby's house and picked up Renata. I did not mention Bitsy or Louie. I invited Shelby to drive over to Point Clear when she was ready to collect her daughter.

The sun was setting over Mobile Bay when I pulled up to my house. I found Gladys in the kitchen, fixing jambalaya. "Shelby loves Louie," I said, "but it's time for her to move on."

"I was thinking the same thing," she said.

"If only I could introduce her to a fabulous man."

"Just as long as it ain't Kip," she said.

The next morning, Isabella and I sat in the boathouse, surrounded by cookbooks, planning my annual Easter Egg Hunt and Brunch. We drew up a guest list that included her old Hollywood crowd. We drank champagne and told dirty jokes and gossiped about everybody in Point Clear, all the while smoking low-tar cigarettes.

"Do you think our little plot will work?" Isabella lit a cigarette.

"Don't call it a plot," I said, glancing out at the water. It was strangely quiet. "And when Shelby gets here tomorrow, don't you breathe a word of this party."

"Maybe we shouldn't be hasty. What if she's meant to be with Louie?"

"If she was, that time has slipped away. I know my son. And even if he left Bitsy and remarried Shelby, he would never forgive that dalliance with Kip."

"But why?"

"Hubris."

"Excuse me?"

"Excessive pride. That's Louie's problem. And before it's over, he will have punished Bitsy for Shelby's crime. He will punish all of the women who will come after her. And there *will* be more."

"So, what are we doing, exactly? Matchmaking?" Isabella blew a smoke ring. "Or is Shelby a sacrificial lamb?"

"That's a harsh way of putting it," I said. "But yes, she's a sacrifice. That said, she will be free to love another man."

"You don't know this for a fact," said Isabella.

"Oh, yes I do."

"Then where's your crystal ball?"

"Hidden," I said "Quick, let's change the subject before we're overheard."

I looked past Isabella's shoulder, and through the screen mesh, I saw Gladys and Renata coming up the sandy path, their metal buckets full of shells. Renata ran up the wooden steps and raced down the pier, toward the boathouse, her small heart-shaped face split into a grin.

"Granny, look what I found," she cried.

"Come here, my precious darling," I said, and crushed my cigarette. Then I leaned over and opened my arms. "Show me everything."

$\mathcal{S}$helby was sunbathing on the terrace, her taut brown legs glistening with oil. I mixed two stiff vodka tonics, then carried them outside. "Hey, there you are," she said, cracking open one eye. I handed her a drink, then pulled up a chaise longue and sat down. I didn't know where to begin. I'd had a difficult relationship with my mother-in-law. I didn't know if the trouble was Solange or me; but I had to face the possibility that it was me, that I was the type who recognized the smell of her own pack and hated all others. I thought this might be a good place to begin. I took two breaths and plunged ahead.

"I love you, Shelby."

"Ditto." Her hand moved into the space between our loungers. She grabbed my hand and squeezed it. I shut my eyes, trying to find the strength to continue. In my head, I'd practiced this speech, but now it seemed manipulative. If I mentioned her ill-fated relationship with my son, she would know I was up to something. If I held my tongue, our friendship wouldn't suffer any damage, even though Shelby herself was headed for certain disaster. If I spoke my mind, she might never forgive me. I adored her and Renata, but I also loved my future grandchild. It behooved me to balance my love and loyalties, because I was also growing fonder of Bitsy.

No one could possibly know the outcome of this love triangle. I could make predictions based on the personalities and histories of those involved; but there was much I didn't know. I wasn't a psychologist. But Louie was the last DeChavannes male. He would not let the name die. On one hand, I was meddling, big-time, and that usually led to regrets. On the other hand, if I remained silent and all of these precious lives spun apart, I couldn't live with myself.

So I pressed on.

"We need to talk about Louie," I said.

She hugged herself and smiled, sloshing a bit of tonic onto her leg. "What about the magnificent Louie?"

"Bitsy had an ultrasound," I said, rattling the ice in my drink. "Have you ever heard of that test?"

She shook her head.

"I'm not sure what it is, either. But apparently it shows the baby's sex." I paused. "They're having a little boy."

Shelby flinched. Then she took a long sip of the vodka tonic.

In the softest possible voice, I said, "He won't leave her."

Shelby lowered her head. A tear fell into the vodka tonic. "You don't know that he won't."

"And Bitsy won't leave him. Well, not for a while. She strikes me as the sort of girl who doesn't give up easily. She's more of a fighter than you."

"What are you saying? Why are you telling me this?"

"Because I love you and Renata. And you are headed for an unhappy place if you keep things going with Louie."

"I'm sorry about all the gossip." Shelby rubbed her eyes. "The last thing I wanted was to turn out like my mother."

"You're not like Emma," I said, but then again, maybe she was. Around here, radiation would dissipate quicker than gossip, and the damage was just as insidious.

"Don't worry." I squeezed Shelby's hand. "We'll sort it out one way or another."

My annual Easter Egg Hunt and Brunch was an astounding success. Isabella's idea of inviting Randolph "Andy" Filbert VanDusen III had been a stroke of genius. Andy was divorced and wealthy. "He's well endowed in more than one way," said Isabella. "If you get my drift."

Gladys and I dyed 988 eggs. It would have been 1,000 if she hadn't accidentally sat down on one carton and crushed it. Then Isabella and I drove over to Mobile to rent an adult-sized bunny costume. It was the cutest thing you ever saw. Pink faux fur, tall ears held up with wire, and a gorgeous, phallic-shaped carrot attached to one paw.

The day before the party, we purposely sent Shelby and Renata over to her daddy's beach house in Perdido Key, Florida, with explicit instructions to work on her tan and not to return to Point Clear until the day of the party. Then Isabella and I rushed to the Mobile airport and picked up Andy VanDusen. We got him settled at the Grand, then bought him a drink in the bar. I had plenty of guest rooms, but we wanted to keep him hidden, in case Shelby turned up.

On Easter Sunday, right after mass, I drove over to the hotel and fetched Andy, then Isabella and I fixed him some drinks. After three mimosas and one Cuban cigar, we cajoled him into dressing up in the costume. I was pretty sure that Shelby would be a sucker for any man who'd put on a stupid rabbit suit. Even with that cigar, Andy looked adorable. Isabella laughed, then whispered in my ear, "If Shelby doesn't want him, I might just keep him for myself."

A buffet was set up on the terrace and featured garlic cheese grits, grilled sausage, beaten biscuits, fruit platter, made-to-order omelets, and eggs Benedict. And you could get anything you wanted to drink, but we also had huge pitchers of mimosas set up on the buffet. Isabella's job was to keep the Easter Bunny sober. He was still reeling from a rather nasty divorce. Also, she'd sworn up and down that she wouldn't tamper with the food. At the last moment, I tossed jelly beans on the table, then checked on the lawn decorations. We'd set up dozens of colorful egg-shaped balloons along the driveway, and giant, papier-mâché eggs in all colors.

When Shelby arrived, clutching her small daughter's hand, Isabella broke away from the bunny and ran over, kissing the air on either side of Shelby's face, the way she does everybody. Shelby wore a lilac sundress that showed the barest hint of cleavage, and I wondered if she was hoping to see Louie at this party. I walked up and slipped my arm around her small waist.

"Nice tan," I told Shelby, then I turned to Renata. "And just look at your pretty dress!"

My granddaughter curtsied, and the yellow hand-smocked dress grazed the stone path. She patted her hair, then adjusted the thick, lemony ribbon. She had beautiful little hands, Louie and Chaz's teardrop nose, and Shelby's eyes.

We chitchatted a minute, then I pointed Renata toward the side yard, where the empty Easter baskets were lined up. She scampered off, her ribbon floating behind her. Then I turned back to Shelby. My plan was to introduce her to the Easter Bunny, and, as they say, let nature take its course. If they clicked, fine. If not, well, as Isabella's old nemesis, Doris Day, once sang, que sera sera.

"Dahlin', there's somebody I want you to meet," Isabella told Shelby and dragged her across the egg-strewn yard. I followed at a discreet distance. Isabella said, "He's rumored to have one of the biggest you-know-whats in Hollywood."

"Rumored?" Shelby laughed. "Haven't you checked it out for yourself?"

"The father, yes, but not the son. Come on, dahlin'. He's right over there in the bunny suit." Isabella paused, waiting for a reaction. Shelby just blinked. Isabella made the introductions. Andy took one look at her pretty blond hair and her dimples, and he bit his cigar in half. It fell to the ground, red sparks arcing over the grass. Shelby stepped back, laughing.

I folded my hands under my chin and thought, This is just brilliant. They will fall in love and move to California, and Louie can concentrate on his marriage and new baby.

After the party, while the caterers packed up their gear, I found Shelby standing on the pier. She faced the bay, the wind lifting her hair. The tide was coming in, and far out on the horizon, a blue sailboat listed to the right. "You okay?" I asked.

Shelby nodded, then dabbed her eyes with a napkin.

"You look ready to throw yourself into the water." I squeezed her shoulders. "Whatever is the matter? Why all these tears? Did the bunny hop off and leave you?"

"No, he's inside, changing. He wants me to go sailing this afternoon."

"Well, are you going?"

"No. I don't know." Her voice cracked. "What if Louie calls? Why wasn't he at the party? I've tried calling him for days. I'm worried."

"He's in Pass Christian for the holidays. He bought Bitsy a little beach house."

She sucked in air. "But why didn't he tell me?"

"Please don't take this the wrong way, but that man is gone. Not now. Not this minute. But soon." I drew in a deep breath, wishing I had a mimosa, anything to bolster my nerves. What I was about to say was harsh, but true; at least, it was the truth as I saw it.

"Shelby, honey," I began, "I'm not a mind reader, and I've never been able to predict the future, but I know my son. The minute that baby boy is born, Louie will fall desperately in love. You cannot compete with a namesake. He will never leave Bitsy. So, unless you're willing to be his long-suffering mistress, putting yourself and Renata through untold misery, I suggest you get on with your life. And the Easter Bunny is a good place to start."

She kept staring out at the bay, tears hitting the purple dress. Isabella walked up, holding a silver tray with three mimosas. As she handed Shelby a glass, she took in her blotched cheeks and swollen nose but made no comment. Shelby took a sip of her mimosa, then threw it into the water, and said in a wavy voice, "What's L.A. like? Traffic? Smog? Gossip and glitz?"

"You've got all that in New Orleans," Isabella said.

"Yes, but is California a horrid place to raise a child?"

"Heavens, no," said Isabella, "it can be whatever you want it to be."

At that moment, I began to regret my scheme. I almost said, *Can't she have that here?* But I didn't say anything.

"It's not me I'm worried about," Shelby said.

"Then who?" Isabella frowned. "What's going on in that head of yours?"

"Exactly what y'all put there," Shelby said. And I knew she was going to make Andy VanDusen fall in love with her.

O n May 21, 1979, she and Andy were married on my terrace. Andy's parents were thrilled to see their son marry such a cultured, beautiful woman, and they kept thanking me and Isabella for introducing them.

Isabella stepped over to me. "I would have let Andy's father thank me in a more personal way," she said, "but his manly parts aren't working properly. Apparently he's lost his big toe to sugar diabetes."

Renata was the flower girl and seemed excited about moving to Malibu. Andy's house overlooked the Pacific. It had once been the Disney compound, and it even had stairs leading to a little beach cottage. Although the child's sleepwalking had stopped, and Louie had gotten the child over her fear of water, Shelby wasn't keen to live on the ocean. I pointed out the pluses. She would attend premiers and hobnob with Hollywood royalty, like Goldie Hawn, who'd been invited to the wedding, along with James Caan. It wouldn't be a bad life.

Personally, I think she saw what was inside that bunny suit. Well, who wouldn't? Only a fool, that's who. Just before the bride and groom left for their honeymoon, Gladys passed out beribboned packages of birdseed. The guests lined up along the curved walkway and untied the packets. Then Andy and Shelby were running down the path, dodging the seeds. Andy suddenly stopped and swept his bride into his arms and bent her backward dramatically.

"Just look at that." Isabella's eyes misted. "Rock Hudson did that to me in a movie."

Andy swung Shelby to her feet, and they dashed off to the limousine. Little Renata put her hand in mine, and in the cutest voice said, "Well, they're gone."

"They'll be back," I said.

"We're going to miss them, aren't we, Granny?"

"Yes, dahlin', we will," I said. "We surely will."

*N*ot two months after the wedding, in early summer, Renata came down with a strange stomach ailment that she'd caught at a camp in Colorado. I offered to nurse the child back to health, and the VanDusens brought her to Point Clear. That whole summer, Bitsy taught Renata how to stencil, and together they spent hours on the porch, their heads inclined together. Bitsy gave the child her silver charm bracelet, and Renata wore it everywhere. When Renata got well, Andy and Shelby flew down to Mobile and spent a few days lolling on the bay. Then the three of them flew straight to Maui for a month of beachcombing and whale watching.

In the hottest part of July, Bitsy lost her baby. When I reached the hospital, I insisted on seeing my grandchild, and I was awestruck by his beauty. Swirled brown hair, a cherub's mouth, a beautiful head, and the DeChavannes nose. His eyes were squeezed shut as if he'd glimpsed something frightening. I imagined the three mythical Fates—spinning, measuring, and cutting the threads of life. The Fates sang with the sirens, their voices singing in unison of things in the past, present, and future.

Louie teetotally collapsed. I was afraid to leave the hospital, but then Bitsy's mother showed up and started acting crazy, so I drove back to Point Clear. I waited to see if Bitsy would divorce Louie.

She didn't. They managed to stay together five more years before she caught him *en flagrante* and left the country, cutting off all contact with us. Not that I blamed her, but I'd never seen Louie that upset, and I was beside myself with fear. I just knew he'd drink and end up in a car wreck, or accidentally overdose on tranquilizers.

After Bitsy left for good, Louie formed no lasting attachments, but that didn't mean he'd turned into a monk. I happened to know he'd been writing letters to Bitsy, professing his undying love, but he still managed to date an astounding number of floozies; I knew he would never change.

Now, gripping the letters that Louie had brought, I gazed down at the beach. Renata stood at the bottom of the wooden steps, brushing sand from her feet. She set down the pail, then reached for her tennis shoes.

"Did you have a pleasant walk?" I called.

"Lovely," she said. "Wait till you see my shells."

"I've been waiting for you." I pushed open the screen door, and Zap stepped out, wagging his stubby tail. "Your father was here."

"Is anything wrong?" A frown creased Renata's face.

"No more than usual," I said, and handed her the letters.

"What are these?"

"Something from your father—and your mother. Something that might change everything."

Chapter 36

EMPTY NEST

$\mathcal{I}$ sat cross-legged on the floor, fanning the letters around me. The stationery was pale aqua engraved "Shelby VanDusen," with a little shell motif in the top center. I picked up the first letter, and the paper made a crinkly sound. The faded red postmark said 1979, approximately two months after she'd married Andy. I remembered that Bitsy had lost her baby after she'd caught Daddy in their private courtyard, fixing mint juleps for a naked woman. The woman was in the pool, not that the details mattered, but Bitsy had not been well, and the shock was too much.

I squinted at the return address, blinking at my mother's back-slanted handwriting. I raised the envelope to my face, thinking it still smelled like her—violets, tea roses, Chanel No. 5. Then I opened the envelope and pulled out the aqua paper.

July 24, 1979

Dear Louie,
Honora told me about Bitsy losing the baby. I am so sorry. I know how much you wanted a son. I have not told Renata. I figured you'd want to

tell her yourself. If you'd like me to fly her down to New Orleans, just say the word. Again, I send my prayers to you and Bitsy.

Love,
Shelby

May 1, 1980

Dear Louie,
Andy and I will be spending the summer here in Nags Head, North Carolina. I'm sending you our address and phone number. Renata is doing fine. She is a strong swimmer. You'd be so proud. I remember how, after the swimming accident, you took her into the water and helped her get over her fear. I will always be grateful. Hope you and Bitsy have a lovely time in England this summer.
Love,
Shelby

I leaned over to the night table and picked up the mermaid badge, scraping my fingers over the red letters. Something about that badge nagged at me, but I couldn't remember anything. Then I sat down and opened the third letter. When I recognized my loopy, childish handwriting, I sucked in my breath.

November 2, 1981

Dear Daddy,
I am writing to thank y'all for inviting me to New Orleans for Christmas. I would love to go but I'm spending the holidays in Italy

with Mama and Andy. Maybe next year? Mama is helping me mail
y'all's presents next week. I will call you on Christmas Day, so don't
leave the house, okay?

Love,
Renata

P.S. Thank you for the beautiful Swatch you and Bitsy brought me back
from Switzerland. It is so cool.

February 2, 1984

Dear Louie,
I'm sorry that Bitsy left you, but these late-night phone calls have to
stop. I can't decide if you don't remember that California is in a different
time zone or if you're drunk. I am also sorry to hear that you are on
tranquilizers and antidepressants. In some ways I think you have
reverted back to the little boy with big eyebrows. I just want to shake
you! I want to say, Stop wallowing in self-pity and bitterness. I know
these are tough words, but Louie, maybe this is a chance for you to evolve
into the man and father you were meant to be. I have faith in you, buddy.

Shelby

October 3, 1985

Louie,
The next time you call Renata and burden her with your problems, I will
be forced to take drastic measures. No little girl should be forced to listen
to how you literally screwed up your marriage to Bitsy. Renata doesn't

understand, and when you cry, it worries her. She is having nightmares.
So if you can't help yourself, think of your daughter.

Shelby

January 14, 1986

Louie,
No, I will not divulge the location or phone number of Renata's new
school. You'll just get on a plane and fly over and continue being a
disruptive force. She wouldn't **be** *at this new school if you hadn't shown*
up drunk at the old one, blabbering about lost loves. Why must you keep
dumping our burdens on her?
  I have talked to Honora about this, and she says you have lost your
mind. And no, I haven't told her where Renata is going to school. So
please stop badgering her! If I told her, you would charm and beg it out of
her. Go on, keep threatening to take me to court, but you've got to know
that you helped create this situation. It isn't permanent unless you want
it to be. I will not keep Renata away from you forever. I'm not trying to
punish you. I am just protecting her. You know how I feel on this subject.
  I am counting on you to pull yourself together. In the meantime, I
will send your birthday cards and presents to her. Please get help.

Shelby

June 21, 1986

Dear Louie,
Honora tells me that you are just about back to your normal self, and
I thought I'd write you a little note. We will be spending the summer in
Nags Head. So, if you'd like to drive up and see Renata, you are welcome

to stay with us. Just let me know. I have already invited Gladys and
Honora, and Isabella may join us, too.

  I'm sorry that I had to get tough, but I didn't know what else to do.
I hope you don't blame me. Anyway, I'm so happy that you're feeling
better.

All best,
Shelby

I stretched out on the bed, trying to piece it all together. My thoughts were
chaotic. It was as if I had assembled the ingredients for a layer cake, but someone else had whipped it together. I hadn't known that my mama had banished
my daddy. I'd just assumed that he wasn't interested in me. After Mama married Andy and we moved to L.A., I felt odd and out of place. My southern
accent not only set me apart, it turned me into a spectacle. When Andy took
us out for lunch at the Polo Lounge, I tried to order grits.

"Grist?" asked the puzzled waiter.

"Well, what about iced tea?" I asked him.

Andy VanDusen leaned across the table and in his nasal voice, said, "Just
bring the little lady a Shirley Temple—no, bring her two."

I showed up at school wearing a hand-smocked lilac dress, all em-
broidered with little grapes. "It's so Napa!" Honora had said when she
presented me with the going-away outfit. She also gave me black patent
leather Mary Janes. This was the late 1970s, and all the girls were into
vintage mishmash, better known as the Annie Hall look. The only Annie
I knew about was from a cartoon, *Little Orphan Annie*. I had never seen a
Woody Allen film, much less heard of him. Mama bought me a new, hip
wardrobe that included one of my stepfather's vintage ties and a little
turned-up felt hat; but around my school, I was known as Baby Jane and
the Grape of Wrath.

Hoping to turn me into a California girl, Mama sent me to an exclusive
girl's camp in Colorado. I returned with a stomach ailment, giardia, a pear-
shaped protozoan. They said I got it from drinking contaminated water.
Honora insisted that I recuperate at her house, because my father was a

doctor, and even if he didn't practice pediatric medicine, he had access to the finest brains in the South.

I recuperated on Honora's side veranda. My father visited weekly, bringing Bitsy, who was enormously pregnant. She taught me how to stencil ivy and morning glories on the wooden floor. She would sit on the floor beside me, pillows tucked around her stomach, and show me how to hold the paintbrush. Her hands were swollen, and it must have been difficult, but she never let on. She gave me her charm bracelet and braided my hair. Halfway through the project, I was well enough to leave Alabama and go whale watching in Maui with Mama and Andy.

When we got back to L.A., I heard that Bitsy had lost her baby. It was Honora, not my father, who'd broken the news about my half brother. She told me that an emergency cesarean had saved Bitsy's life, but it was too late for the baby.

That Thanksgiving, Andy's private jet flew me down to New Orleans. Whenever I'd step into the living room, Louie and Bitsy would abruptly stop talking. I wondered if all the painting we'd done had hurt the baby. Years later, it was almost a relief to find out that she had caught him with another woman, that I had not killed my little half brother.

After Bitsy left him, I had no recollection of any phone calls, or of my father coming to my school; however, I did recall that my mother jerked me out of the private school in Malibu and sent me to a new one on the Mendocino coast.

A year passed, and I still had not heard from him, and I begged to visit him. For reasons my mama wouldn't make clear, she refused to send me to New Orleans, insisting that I spend my summer vacation with Honora and Gladys. I never saw my father, and whenever I mentioned him, Honora changed the subject and took me around her gardens, walking through dappled sunlight, the ice tinkling in her gin and tonic, cigarette smoke curling above her head. "Dahlin', if you want your hydrangeas to produce lush blue flowers," she'd say, "then you need to take rusty nails and hammer one at the base of each plant."

I didn't care about hydrangeas; I wanted to know when my father was coming over. But she just pulled me over to her herbs and, pulling scissors from her pocket, demonstrated how to snip chives ("Fabulous when sprinkled over alfredo"), and then we'd move into the oregano bed ("Marvelous in marinara"). Finally, our pockets bulging with fragrant greenery, we'd head back to the house.

Years later, Honora, Gladys, and my father flew out to California for my high school graduation. Mama and Andy had a party at the Malibu house, with its sweeping views of the coastline. They got on my nerves, telling everyone how I'd been accepted by six colleges, including UCLA and Stanford. They were disappointed that I'd chosen the University of Mississippi, but it was the best place for a writer. My father made a toast to Ole Miss and rabble-rousing women, and everyone cheered.

Mama's eyes met Daddy's, then he raised his champagne flute. It could have been the shifting coastal light, but I could have sworn that something passed between them. She swept her fingers under her eyes, then flung open the glass doors and hurried out. I set down my glass and squeezed through the crowd, onto the terrace.

"Oh, Mama." I put my arms around her. "Please don't be sad. I'll be in Faulkner country."

"I'm not. Really, I'm happy for you. It's just that I'm losing my best friend."

"It's the empty nest syndrome," I said.

"It's more than that." Mama's bottom lip trembled.

Daddy came outside and squeezed my mother's hand. "Don't worry," he said. "I'll take good care of her."

"Please, Mama," I said, pressing my cheek against hers. "It's time for me to leave the nest. Please let me fly away."

Now, I stuffed the letters into their envelopes, then walked on my knees over to the trunk. Stuffed into the right pocket was a travel itinerary—a deluxe guided tour to Egypt. The outer envelope was dated "October 31–November 18, 1999." Inside, I found an aqua note.

Dear Honora,
I am still trying to get Renata and Ferg to go with us to Egypt, but

he's stuck in Ireland, and she's having trouble with her screenplay. Personally, I think she's overworked. But she told me she was thinking of coming down to Point Clear to spend a few days with you and Gladys. Andy says to tell you that he knew Ferg would be famous even before he won that Oscar. But he is also the most levelheaded young man we've met. He will be a loving, steadying force in Renata's life. I went to all those extremes to protect her, but she managed to absorb the negative vibes. I never said anything negative about Louie. Renata would have felt it as a criticism of herself, and that poor girl doesn't just have low self-esteem, I don't think she has any at all.

Right now we're at Nags Head. We're flying out of JFK on Halloween. Won't that be fun? When I get back from Egypt, I plan to spend a few weeks with Renata at Nags Head, filling in the missing pieces—painful as it will be, it's time for her to know the truth so she can bond with Louie. He needs someone to look after him.

I hope all is well with you and Gladys. I am hoping Ferg and Renata get married soon, because I am looking forward to being a grandmother. I am predicting that Louie is going to make a fabulous grandpa.

Love,
Shelby

P.S. Enclosed is our itinerary, with dates and a list of our hotels and phone numbers in case of emergency. Naturally there won't be one—but you never know.
XX OO

Chapter 37

⚬ ⚬ ⚬

GLADYS SAYS, I DREAMED OF BLACK WATER

Last Halloween, Renata flew from Raleigh to Point Clear. Honora and I met her at the airport, then we went out to lunch at the Grand. That evening Louie came over and opened oysters on the dock, tossing the shells into the water. We ate on the terrace, all surrounded by orange candles. We'd dressed Zap in a bear costume, and I swear, he knew it. He strutted around that patio growling and carrying on.

"Mama and Andy should be boarding their plane in about an hour," Renata said.

"I've never been to Egypt," said Louie. "And I don't want to go, either."

That night I dreamed I was on a jet plane, flying over black water. The tail fell off, and then the plane dropped. Instead of sinking, it floated, water lapping onto the carpeted blue bottom of the plane.

Next morning, I got up and turned on the TV to hear the Sunday news. It was All Saint's Day in New Orleans, and I wished I could've been there. While I was making coffee, a man on CNN interrupted the program. Wolf Blitzer started talking—just his voice came on, mind you, not his woolly cuteness, and in the background they showed a picture of the ocean, a helicopter flying over dark gray water, its shadow rolling over waves and debris.

I looked out the window. Honora was still out in the bay, taking her morning swim. I reached behind for a chair, telling myself to hold on, no need to panic, plenty of airplanes flew to Egypt from JFK. From the TV, Wolf Blitzer kept on talking, but I only heard *"All 217 passengers feared dead."* And they wouldn't know what happened until they found the little black box.

Honora walked up to the back door and pulled off her rubber swimming cap, what they don't sell anymore. Then she raked her fingers through her hair and wrapped a towel around her bosom, tucking it under her armpits. She stepped barefoot into the kitchen, leaving a trail of water. When she saw me, she stopped.

"What's wrong?" she asked. Water ticked against the floor. "Why are you crying, Gladys?"

All I could do was shake my head. From the TV, Wolf was still talking, his voice circling like a white death moth. Honora sat down on the sofa, listening to Wolf. One hand rose to her mouth, and her eyes filled. "What was Shelby's flight number?" she asked. "I don't know where I put that itinerary."

"Renata might know," I said.

"Where is she?"

"Upstairs sleeping," I said. "Should I waken her?"

"Not yet. It may be the last decent sleep she'll ever have." Honora got up and crossed the room in three steps, her bare feet slapping against the tile. She turned up the TV. "We've got to find out if Shelby was on that flight. And even so, people miss flights all the time."

Please, Lord, please don't let them be on that plane. Don't take Shelby and Andy. Don't take anybody. You don't have to, Lord, not that I'm trying to tell You how to do Your job, but I can't take this.

Honora heaved herself onto a bar stool, leaned across the counter, and dragged the French-style phone into her lap, along with a notepad. In Renata's handwriting, "Flight 900" was wrote down in bold black letters. It didn't say Egypt Air, but I had heard Renata say that name. The VanDusens were going from New York to Cairo, and they'd hired an Egypt specialist, something with an *ologist* at the end of it, to show them around the pyramids.

Honora stared hard at the pad. I leaned over, put my arms around her wet self. She started shaking and pushed her face into my neck. "This is not happening."

The phone jangled, startling Honora so bad, she spun around and knocked it to the floor. It hit the tile and jangled. From the receiver came Louie's voice, "Mama? Renata?"

Honora slid off the stool, lifted the receiver, and let out a ragged sigh. "Oh; Louie," she said, then her mouth sagged open, but no sound came out. I couldn't hear what he said, but on the TV Wolf was talking to a bald-headed man from the FAA and he showed a diagram of a 767. They were speculating about the crash.

"Gladys?" Honora held out the phone. "He wants to talk to you."

I pressed the receiver to my ear. I said, "Yes, sir?" but what I meant to say was: I am so sorry. This is wrong, a nightmare, it shouldn't of happened. But maybe we shouldn't give up hope.

"Where is my daughter?" he asked.

"Sleeping, sir."

"All right, then. I can tell that Mama's getting ready to be hysterical," he said. "Can you give her a pill? There's Valium in the medicine cabinet. Give her two, now, then put her to bed. And turn off that damn television."

"Yes, sir. But what if Renata wakes."

"Don't say anything. Don't let her watch the news. Just hold everything together until I get there." He paused. "What is Mama doing now?"

I cut my eyes at Honora. She was stretched out on the floor, her eyes closed. She had that pale, Irish skin. I used to tease her, used to say she was the whitest lady I ever saw. It looked like she'd painted her face with milk. You could not be that pale and live. But I said, "She's laying down."

"Well, give her that Valium, and I'll be there soon."

I did what he said. I shut off the TV, then reached around back and unplugged it. Then I drugged Honora and laid her out in her dark bedroom. Renata never did wake. She always was a hard sleeper, she craved it. All around me the house was quiet, except for the tick-whoosh of the ice maker. From outside I heard shorebirds and the ringing buoy.

I went into the kitchen and straightened the cookbooks, nothing like a good cleaning to keep my mind's eye from wandering. But some things were hard to tamp down. You could straighten your house a lot easier than you could tidy up your life. And Renata's life—all our lives—would never be the same.

It was almost eleven a.m. when Louie arrived. His face looked haggard, eyelids all puffy like they'd been chigger-bit. I had kept my promise not to watch the news, but I was champing at the bit to find out. "Have they found any survivors?" I asked.

"Not yet." He dropped into a chair, covered his face with his hands, and began to squall. All this time, he'd loved Shelby. He thought he'd get her back one day, maybe when they were old and ready for the retirement village. I pulled his dark curly head to my bosom, and said, "You go on and cry, Louie, just go on and cry."

Two weeks later, Renata rented a car and drove back to Nags Head. I didn't blame her for not wanting to fly anywhere. She'd told her boyfriend to stay in Ireland, but he flew to North Carolina and met her at the cottage. I was glad she wasn't alone. Me and Honora were having a tough time facing up to Shelby's death. We could not believe that she and Andy was gone. I kept thinking they would walk through that kitchen door and holler out, "What's cooking, Gladys?"

Louie was obsessed with the crash. He told us that two flight recorders showed a normal flight until the autopilot was turned off. The plane had took off from Kennedy, then rose up to 33,000 feet, and flew normally for about thirty minutes before it fell into the Atlantic. Louie said it crashed about sixty miles south of Nantucket. It simply dropped off the NY radar screens. At daylight, a merchant marine training ship spotted a cushion and human remains.

Louie said—and I'm quoting—the plane had experienced trouble during a previous flight with the hydraulic system. The relief copilot had disengaged the autopilot and pushed the plane into a steep dive, praying to Allah at supersonic speed. The captain returned from the lavatory and yelled at the pilot. "I rely on God," said the copilot without one trace of emotion.

"Those poor people," I said. Renata had lost her mother and stepfather, but she had also lost her past and future. All those things had gone into the ocean with Shelby.

"At least Andy provided for Renata," said Isabella. "She's an heiress. She won't have to work again."

"She don't care about money," I said.

"Don't be silly, Gladys." Isabella laughed.

"What she wants," I said, "can't be got."

She wasn't the only one. Louie stopped by and told us about three other flights that had crashed: TWA 800, Swiss Air 111, Egypt Air 999. All three had tooken off from JFK. "How can three seemingly intact jetliners leave JFK," he said, "and except for Swiss Air, meet their doom in exactly the same spot, all within a few years? Makes you wonder if someone is loosening bolts."

I didn't know about that, but I knew one thing. No matter who that man married, no matter what he said, he still loved Shelby and always would. I want to call them star-crossed, but they only crossed themselves. Whenever I looked into that man's eyes, I saw a torment that wrenched at my heart, and all I could do was look away.

Chapter 38

⊙ ⊙ ⊙

LOUIE FACES THE MUSIC

*N*ow that Joie was out of the ICU, Faye began to decorate the private room. Vases of carnations and roses were lined up in the window-sill. Cards from Joie's third-grade class were taped to the wall. Humming to herself, Faye plugged in a blue boom box and slipped in a Coldplay CD. Then she bustled around Joie's bed, straightening sheets and rearranging the IV tubing, her bracelets jangling. Even though Joie was sleeping, Faye talked nonstop about diet, skin care, nail polish, and the season's hottest color. In excruciating detail, she recited details of Billy's day, along with a recap of soap operas that Joie had slept through.

"There, that's better," she said, folding Joie's blue Ralph Lauren comforter at the foot of the bed. Faye opened her gigantic pocketbook and pulled out eight-by-ten photographs of Joie in all of her precomatose glory—dimples, turned-up nose, lush blond hair spilling over her shoulders. Those pictures were misleading, making her seem tall and independent, not a petite, babi-fied girl who'd never been allowed to drive a car. Now that I'd had a chance to see Faye in action, I realized that her pampering had all but crippled her daughter.

When Faye wasn't orchestrating Joie's breakfast or decorating her bedside, she called the police for updates. After I'd gotten over the shock of seeing Renata's pearls, I knew that she wasn't capable of hurting Joie and I regret-ted all that I'd said. Faye, however, wouldn't discuss it. "Joie is all I have," she told me. "She's my best friend and daughter rolled into one." Her unshakable belief that Renata had injured Joie seemed ludicrous, and I resented it, but I wasn't sure how to handle my rising distaste for Faye. I loved Joie, but there was no possibility of limiting my exposure to her mother.

Mother and daughter were a package deal.

From the bed, Joie was stirring. She looked like a sixteen-year-old, and I felt obscurely guilty for loving her. Her neurosurgeon, Austin Brewington, had assumed that she was my daughter. Austin had a long, glossy blond ponytail and a scruffy beard. He wore a white lab coat over ripped blue jeans. Every other word out of Faye's mouth was, "Austin said" or "Austin thinks." She gave him tiny boxes of Whitman Samplers and beribboned packages of Mayfield's Crab Boil.

"Water," said Joie. She had great difficulty moving her left hand, and not just because an IV was affixed to it.

I tipped the pitcher over a plastic cup, then held it to her lips. She drank greedily, her throat making high-pitched squeaks. She'd been off the ventilator for sixteen hours; they'd taken off the bulky bandage over her nose, replacing it with a butterfly strip. She pushed away the cup, then I helped her lie down. Faye sprang over to the bed with a pink makeup bag and pulled out a tube of lipstick.

"Now, pucker up." She pursed her own lips. "Let's get ready for your cute doctor."

"Don't use the navy blue mascara." Joie pushed Faye's hand away. "Use the waterproof black."

While they discussed mascara and blush, they seemed to forget that I was sitting in the chair. I'd barely left her side since the engagement party.

"Have you remembered anything?" Faye held her breath as she painted her daughter's eyelashes. "Do you know who hit you? Was it Louie's daughter?"

"Louie?" Joie blinked.

"Why, your fiancé, of course." Faye waved at me.

"Oh," said Joie. When she spoke, the left side of her mouth didn't move. If I didn't know better, I'd say she'd had a stroke.

"Don't press her," I told Faye. "It'll come back to her."

Faye ignored me. "Sweetie, try to remember who hit you. Think. What's the last thing you remember?"

Joie licked her lips. Then she turned her face toward her mother. "I was at some party," she said in a slurry voice. "Drinking champagne. Eating strawberries. They were real juicy."

"Yes," said Faye, "but who attacked you?"

"Nobody. I was sitting in the kitchen. Licking chocolate from my fingers. I started for the powder room. But I was drunk. I must've opened the garage door. Next thing I knew, I was flying down the stairs. That's all I remember."

"What about Renata, Louie's daughter? She says *you* grabbed her pearl necklace and broke it."

"Oh, yeah. That happened earlier. I stumbled down a few steps. But I didn't get hurt. Well, I banged up my knee."

"She—she didn't push you?"

"No. I jumped her. From behind, I think. Don't ask why. Because I can't remember."

"Are you sure?"

"Yes. And, Mama?"

"What, my precious?"

"Can I have some strawberries? Or a Hershey's bar? I'm starving."

"Coming right up," said Faye, grabbing her pocketbook.

"She can't have solid food yet," I said. "Not till her IV comes out."

"If my baby wants chocolate, then she's getting it," said Faye.

The door opened, and Austin Brewington swept into the room, his boat shoes squeaking on the tile. Joie struggled to sit up. Even with the little shaved patches on her head, she glowed with a dewy luminosity.

"Hey, Joie," said Austin, and with a nod in my direction, he plopped down on her bed.

"Morning, Austin," she said. Morning sun spilled through the window, falling in patterns across the bed. She looked up at him with those long lashes, and one side of her mouth curved into a smile. He smiled back, then touched her droopy lips.

"You're much better," he said. "Don't you think so?"

She nodded. Something fell inside my chest, and right then, I knew that she was going to fall in love with him. In a way, I was relieved. Every woman I'd loved had a crazy, overbearing mother. It wasn't a coincidence; it was a pattern. I needed to stop falling in love and figure out why I attracted these types. Maybe I needed to look at my own mother, and at my daughter, to understand why all my romances fell apart. Hell, it was worth a try.

Chapter 39

⚬ ⚬ ⚬

IN THE BIRDCAGE WITH ISABELLA AND FERG

Under normal conditions, I would never travel to coastal Alabama. To be precise, I had my doubts that Point Clear even existed. However, when the engagement ring story appeared, showing a picture of my bedraggled sweetheart at the Atlanta airport, I booked the next flight out of Dublin.

I had no idea where her grandmother lived, but I knew her name. *Honora* made me think of rue du Faubourg Saint-Honoré, with its narrow balconies looking down on the posh boutiques of flowery Parisian streets. Renata had said the town was barely a town at all, a mere blip on the map.

Twenty-four hours later, I was standing in a lush, semitropical resort town, populated by southern bluebloods and a flock of brown pelicans. I checked into the Grand Hotel, a Deep South version of the Grande-Hôtel du Cap-Ferrat, but instead of overlooking the Mediterranean, this hotel faced a dark, dirty, brooding bay. I selected several brochures from the rack, then followed the bellman into the lift. He was middle-aged, with faded blue eyes, and he wore a red suit and a matching hat, resembling an organ grinder's monkey. "Is this your first visit to Point Clear?" he asked.

"Sorry?" It took me a moment to understand the gentleman. I thought he'd said, "Pon't Claire."

"I said, is this your first visit to Point Clear?"

"Yes, yes, it is," I said.

"You sure do got a funny accent," said the man. "What are you, Italian?"

"Hardly," I said, repressing a smile.

"You come here to play golf?"

"No."

"Sail?"

"Afraid not. You wouldn't possibly know a woman named Honora DeChavannes, would you?"

"Nope," said the bellman.

I crushed several American dollars into the man's stubby hands, then fled into my room.

After I unpacked and changed into a polo shirt, I wandered down to the Birdcage Lounge and ordered a gin and tonic. The bartender spoke with a Brooklyn accent and wasn't familiar with anyone named DeChavannes, but he pointed to a pinch-faced older woman with green eyes, who was sitting alone at a table. "Ask Isabella McGeehee," he said. "She knows everybody."

I turned. The woman looked to be in her late seventies, prosperous and demure, wearing a pink linen suit and a pearl necklace. When I approached her table and introduced myself, she gestured at an empty chair. "Sit down, honey. Are you from England?"

"Scotland, actually," I said.

"You look familiar." She narrowed those green eyes, then leaned forward, smelling of tobacco, vodka, and gardenias. "How long have you been in town?"

"I just arrived."

"Ever been here before?"

"No."

"Well, I guess I don't know you, after all." She smiled. "Although I used to be a famous actress, but now I'm just a private citizen. My best friend's granddaughter has a Scottish boyfriend. He's a director, and he looks a little like you. It's been in all the gossip magazines."

"Has it?" I said.

"It's the juiciest story. The boyfriend has been on the cover of every gossip magazine. He got caught with some foreign-looking actress. I don't recall the name. Anyway, Renata—that's Honora's granddaughter—has come home to lick her wounds."

"Sorry, did you say your best friend's name is Honora?"

"Yes. Why?" The woman smiled, revealing extraordinarily straight teeth, whether from orthodontia or genetics, I didn't know. My own teeth were crooked, rather like roof shingles blown astray after a storm.

"Actually, I need to get in touch with her." I stared down into my gin and tonic.

"What's your name?" she asked, and tilted back her head, blowing a smoke ring.

"Ferg Lauderdale."

"No!" She slapped the table, jostling my drink. "Not Renata's Ferg!"

"Well, I was."

"Tell me, did you seduce that actress?"

"No, no." I waved my hand. "I've been unable to reach my girlfriend to explain. She won't answer the phone. I couldn't reach her father, and I didn't know how to find her grandmother—"

"Honora's phone number is unlisted," she cut in.

"A colleague from Caliban Films called and said Renata's picture was in the *Globe.* Apparently it was taken in the Atlanta airport. I didn't think she was headed to Ireland, so I took a chance and decided to fly here."

"You picked right." The woman winked. "Renata is here."

"Here?" I glanced over my shoulder.

"Not in this bar. I'll draw you a map." She fumbled in her purse, pulling out a pen. She reached for her napkin and started drawing lines and X's. "Okay, here's how you get to Chateau DeChavannes."

As I drove the Hertz Roadster down a blacktop road, I glimpsed hidden estates, *grandes maisons* through pines and Spanish oaks. I rolled down my window and smelled sour, brackish water mixed in with sun-baked pine needles. In the distance I saw a wrought-iron gate set into tall stucco pillars. The gates stood open, and they were beautifully embellished with what appeared to be a coat of arms. A closer look revealed hairless donkeys, which seemed odd and out of place next to the elaborate grillwork. On the left pillar, "Chateau DeChavannes" was carved into a stone plaque.

I turned down the curved drive, past tall hedges where statues were set into niches, reminiscent of the sunny estates on the Côte d'Azur. On my right, I saw an allée with a winding crushed gravel path that led to the water. Then I saw the house. The architecture was definitely French, a three-story beige stucco with green shutters and a tiled mansard roof. Casement windows stood open, lace curtains stirring in the breeze. The front walls were covered in red climbing roses. Balconies with ornate iron railings poked out here and there, each one embellished with a naked donkey.

Turning into a circle drive, I parked in the shade, then started up the long flagstone path, through a grove of Spanish oaks and oleanders. I stepped past an ornate three-tiered fountain, and farther down, I paused beside a koi pond, admiring a statue of Circe tilting her bowl, the magical elixir spilling over the lily pads. I passed through a rose-covered trellis, where the air was so fragrant, I felt drugged as I climbed the porch steps, pausing to grip the limestone balustrade. When the dizziness passed, I lifted my arm and rang the bell.

A square-built, green-eyed woman opened the door, her pale yellow housedress ruffling around her legs. She was quite old, but her small face was unwrinkled, with freckles scattered over her nose. In the background, I heard shrill barking.

"Isabella just called. You must be Ferg." She stood on her toes and kissed my cheek. "I'll tell Honora you're here."

Without bothering to introduce herself, she disappeared around a corner. But I knew she had to be Gladys Boudreaux. I clasped my hands behind my back. Sunlight fell in diamond patterns on the parquet de Versailles floor. A dramatic iron staircase curved up three stories, toward a domed ceiling painted with clouds and floating cherubs. It reminded me of my family's home in Scotland.

The green-eyed woman reappeared and led me down a hall, which culminated in a large kitchen, where a pot of something delicious bubbled on the stove. A tall, gray-haired woman in a tweed suit stood beside the counter, mixing champagne and orange juice.

"Hello, Mr. Lauderdale," she said, extending her hand. "I'm Honora, Renata's grandmother. She's out on the beach. Would you like a mimosa?"

"Er—" A loud bark startled me, and I looked down. A Yorkshire terrier peered from under a bar stool, showing its teeth.

"Where's your manners, Zapper?" Honora asked the dog. He sat down and put his head on his paws, but continued to eye me with considerable suspicion. Honora handed me a crystal flute. The fizz tickled my nose. I have an extremely long nose; it always ends up in a wineglass, as if dredging for plankton.

"I'm so pleased you're here," she said, sipping her mimosa. "Thank goodness Isabella recognized you."

"Yes, it was quite fortunate." Through the French doors, I saw a terrace and an oddly shaped swimming pool. Farther out, a wooden walkway led to a pier with a boathouse at the end. An extraordinary-looking woman stood at the end. She was barefoot and wore a black floppy hat and a gauzy white dress. She turned and my pulse ticked in my neck.

Behind me, Honora DeChavannes ran her finger over the rim, making the crystal squeak. "I'm trying to place your accent. Renata told me you're Scottish, but if I didn't know better, I'd say you were from London."

"Actually, I was born in Scotland," I said, then paused, trying to decide how much, and how little, to divulge.

"Whereabouts?" She lifted one eyebrow.

"The Borders," I said, praying this wasn't the beginning of an ancestral inquisition, and that she was merely performing the southern tradition of "placing me." Renata's mother had done this long ago. Interpol couldn't have done a more thorough job. However, if Honora had any Scottish connections at all, and I suspected that she did, a few well-placed calls would reveal my lineage—but that was all.

"That explains your accent." She smiled. "But how did you end up in London?"

"Well, after Eton, I attended King's College," I said. "My family has a flat in Knightsbridge. So, after university, my relocation to London was inevitable."

It wasn't a lie, even though I'd carefully omitted certain details, like my family's estate in Lauder, twenty kilometers south of Edinburgh. The Lauderdales and Maitlands had owned Thurstelane since the late 1300s. I hadn't wanted it; I'd unceremoniously removed the silver spoon from my mouth, preferring to make my own way. My father had threatened to disinherit me, but my mum had talked him out of it. Americans loved historical gossip, but I didn't know how much Renata had already told her grandmother. Thurstelane's most famous overnight guest was Bonnie Prince Charlie, who was, incidentally, related to us by blood; my other distinguished forebear, William Maitland, had faithfully served as Mary Queen of Scots's secretary of state.

He had married into the Thurstelane fortune, but after Mary's half brother had seized the crown, Maitland poisoned himself in Edinburgh Castle. A charming legacy, wouldn't you say?

We owed Maitland our ugly teal-blue tartan, along with our clan name (a rarity in the Borders) and certain renovations to Thurstelane, such as the knot gardens and the tiered, embellished wedding-cake ceilings. The latter were something of an architectural peculiarity and must have depleted Scotland's coffers. In any event, these unusual features lured tourists by the thousands. I'd spent my childhood dodging guides and obnoxious travelers, and in later years, I was pressed into service in our cellar tearoom. My father, viscount of Lauder (Tr. Hon. the Earl of Lauderdale; Chief of Clan Lauderdale, etc.), had added the building in the early 1970s, along with an adjacent gift shop, where my mother and sisters sold tea towels and mugs, pencils, and whatnots, all printed with either a picture of Thurstelane, the family crest, tartan, or motto: "Consilio Et Animis." Naturally, I never explained what it meant ("By wisdom and courage," if you care; I never did). I possessed neither virtue.

Honora picked up the mimosa pitcher. "I know you're eager to see Renata, but first let me refresh your drink, and then I'll show you around the house. It's on the historical register, and it served as a hospital during the Civil War—it's practically new, compared to castles in the UK. But I don't have to tell you." She tipped the pitcher over my glass, then led me through the high-ceilinged rooms, the little terrier trotting behind us, shooting malicious glances.

From the center hall, a curved staircase rose up to a Palladian window. The glass panes were old and bubbled, distorting views of the live oaks and sago palms. "Lovely," I said.

"Yes, but my late mother-in-law used to say this house is haunted." She peered into the dining room, then turned and smiled. "I've never noticed any ghosts. And I've looked."

I laughed.

"The house *has* been unlucky. But please, don't tell Renata." She stood in front of two long windows, backlit by afternoon sun. I longed to ask why the house had been unlucky, and for whom, but my nerve faltered.

"It's a gorgeous house," she continued. "Although I must confess, I had little to do with the decor. That was my mother-in-law's doings. I used to laugh at the way she fussed over the gardens, agonizing if the blue delphiniums clashed with the purple hydrangeas. When she had chandeliers and chiffo-niers shipped from Austria and Normandy, I thought she'd lost her mind. The sheer pretentiousness of this house galled me."

"It looks like a small chateau," I said. I kept twisting my head, trying to peer out the back windows to catch a glimpse of Renata. But I had a feeling that Honora DeChavannes would not be rushed. So I added, "And it's so . . . fragrant."

"Well, that's because of the flowers. I don't normally have vases set about, but my granddaughter is here visiting. Well, you know that. Dahlin', you look like you need a refill." She pointed to my glass.

I followed her into the kitchen, the terrier clicking behind, sniffing my trousers. While Honora refreshed our mimosas, I wondered how I might gently turn the subject to her granddaughter. However, if I asked straight-away, she might start quizzing me about the lurid tabloid articles.

"Let's go outside and see if we can find Renata," she said, handing me a glass. She picked up the mimosa pitcher, and we stepped through French doors, our footsteps clapping on the stones, and turned down a path, where, at the end, ornate iron chairs faced the water. The terrier trotted ahead, toward a wooden dock, pausing to sniff the air. The wind blew from the southeast, smelling of seaweed. I looked around for Renata, but she had vanished.

Honora and I sat down, sipping our drinks; but I couldn't concentrate. The sun was dropping, and the water glowed with a coppery sheen. I spot-ted the dim outline of a red sailboat; I squinted, but it was too hazy to see the opposite shore. The wind shifted direction, and I heard a buoy clang. With one hand I groped in my pocket for my prescription sunglasses and put them on.

"Well, it's not Brighton or Southampton." She smiled. "But the mosqui-toes aren't out, and it *is* lovely, don't you think?"

"Exquisite." I raised my glass.

"I'm just thrilled you located Renata. I've no idea where she's gone." She leaned back her head. "Just look at those clouds. Sometimes Alabama just breaks my heart—it's so pretty, it just breaks my heart into little pieces."

I heard Renata before I saw her. Her footsteps pattered up the steps, then she came into view, pausing to brush sand from her feet. Her blond hair was abnormally short and wind-tossed. She glanced up, and I had a sense of falling into those eyes, silver with pewter lights. And those cheekbones—they were exotic. All my life I'd had a weakness for gray-eyed blondes. Unlike most women in the film industry, she wasn't rail-thin; rather, she was small-waisted and quite curvy. If I were to pull this woman into my arms, she would feel soft and solid, not like fish cartilage.

I grasped the chair to steady myself. Suddenly I couldn't get my breath.

"There you are," called Honora, facing Renata. "Guess who just happened to be in the neighborhood?"

Chapter 40

PLANTING ZINNIAS

W hat the hell are you doing here?" I asked.

"Honestly, Renata," said Honora, squeezing Ferg's arm. "Where are your manners?"

"Drowned," I said, keeping my eyes on Ferg.

"That's not funny," said Honora.

"It wasn't intended to be," I said, trying not to look at him.

Ferg stood up and pulled off his sunglasses. "What the bloody hell happened to your hair?"

"A lady cut it off."

"On purpose?" he asked.

Honora leaned over and picked up the Yorkie. "Time for us to scoot," she told the dog. Her shoes clicked along the pier as she headed back to the house.

"How did you find me?" I said.

"I saw your picture in the *National Enquirer*."

"Well, you can just turn around and go back to Molly Bloom."

"I don't want her," he said. "I don't even particularly like Ms. Vasquez."

"That doesn't mean you didn't jump her bones."

"I didn't." He stepped toward me. "I've been calling you nonstop for weeks. I've called Nags Head and your cell phone over and over."

"I lost my phone."

"Your grandmother has one, doesn't she?" He swept his hand to the side, gesturing at the grounds. "I was out of my mind with worry. You could have called *me*."

"I did. Several times. The hotel always put me through to your voice mail."

"I never got your messages."

I stared down at the pier, the orange water slapping against the barnacle-crusted pilings. "That's because I didn't leave any."

"But why not?"

"Because I didn't get my picture taken with Esmé Vasquez's hand on my leg. I didn't buy an engagement ring. *I'm* not involved in a new Taylor-Burton affair."

"Things aren't how they appear, Renata."

"The entire free world thinks you're screwing her. A picture really is worth a thousand words. It's worth more than your denials."

"It's fiction," he said.

"I don't know what to believe, Ferg. I've had it with lies and secrets." I drew my finger across my throat. "Do you take me for a fool?"

"No, Renata, I do not think you are a fool. But I cannot control the paparazzi."

He sat down, running one hand through his hair. It was just a little shorter than mine. "I've been true to you since the first day I saw you at your mother's house. You were wearing diamond mermaids in your hair, and a black dress with a slit up the side. Look at me, darling. I love you. I would never betray you. But I cannot prove a negative. I can't prove something that didn't happen."

"I think the tabloids have unearthed a fundamental weakness," I said.

"In society?"

"No, in you! When I saw that picture, I thought, What's going to happen ten, fifteen years from now? Your midlife crisis will be in full swing."

"I only know that I adore you, and I wouldn't risk losing you."

"Yeah, right." I folded my arms. "So, how did the ring shopping go?"

"Rather well, actually."

"That's what the tabloids said." I put my hands on my hips. "You know how I found out? My great-aunt showed it to me. She's in a nursing home, and yet she knows all about you. I hope Esmé loves the ring."

"No, no, I bought it for you." He stood up, digging one hand into his pocket. He dragged up a small black box. Then he dropped to his knees, opened the box, and plucked out a pear-shaped diamond.

"Marry me, Renata," he said.

"Stop." I shook my head and took a few steps back. Then I turned and jumped off the pier, into the old rowboat. It tilted to one side, and I grasped the sides. Two pelicans lifted gracefully from the water, into the tea-stained light. Leaning forward, I hastily untied the rope and slung it into the water. Then I picked up the oars and rowed until I was several yards from the pier.

Ferg stuffed the ring back into the velvet case, shoved it into his pocket, then crouched down and started to jump into the boat. As if realizing that I was too far away, he turned toward the steps and ran down to the beach. He watched me for several minutes, then sat down cross-legged in the sand. "You can't stay out there," he called. "You'll get hungry."

"That's too bad," I called. "I need to diet anyway."

I lifted the oars, water pattering down. The boat skidded over a wave, then slowly began to revolve. Ferg picked up a stick and began to write in the sand MARRY ME. Then he turned. "So? What's your answer?" he yelled into the wind.

"Give a girl a minute," I said.

"If you don't say yes in two seconds, I'm coming after you."

"Don't do this," I yelled. "You'll lose your damn ring."

"*Your* ring." He sprinted forward, kicking sand over the M in MARRY ME, then he charged into the water. A wave slapped over his knees, wetting his trousers. Then he dove. The water took him with a slap.

I grabbed my oars and tried to maneuver into deeper water. He swam over to the boat, then heaved up, grasping the side. The boat tipped violently, then he rolled over the edge. He shook his head, and water sprayed onto the metal bottom. He lay there a moment, breathing hard, then he pushed his hand into his pocket and tugged at the box, working it out of the wet fabric. With two fingers, he opened the box and grabbed the ring. He walked over to me on his knees, the boat swaying.

"Say yes, dammit. Say yes."

"Is this what I'll have to tell our children?" I asked. "Will I have to tell them that Papa used profanity when he asked me to marry him?"

"That sounds like a yes to me," he said. He tossed the box over his shoulder. It splashed into a wave. Then he pulled me into his arms and slid the ring onto my finger. "I, Ferguson Lauderdale, promise to love you, Renata DeChavannes, for the rest of my life. And to always tell the truth." He broke off and began kissing me. He drew back, water dripping into my face, and stared down at me. "Nothing but the truth, so help me God."

We sank down to the bottom. My foot hit something solid. I heard a clunk, followed by a splash. I wondered if I'd knocked an oar into the water. But it was a long time before we bothered to look.

I awakened to the sound of whistling. It sounded like "Drowsy Maggie." I sank deeper into the featherbed and remembered that Ferg used to whistle that song back in L.A. Then I remembered he was in Point Clear; but just in case I was dreaming, I felt the ring on my left hand. Then I grabbed the notepad beside my bed, uncapped my pen, and made revision notes for *Hydrophobia*. I wrote until my fingers cramped, and then I wrote more. Words fell down like water. I could swim in these words. I laughed, stretched my arms, and kept writing.

The window was open, and the smell of pine and lilacs blew into the room. I heard Honora's tinkly laughter, followed by Isabella saying, "Hollywood hasn't changed one iota, except that the special effects are better."

I threw back the covers. I was still wearing my bathing suit from last night's romp. Pulling on my jeans, I paused in front of the dresser mirror and licked my hands, trying to flatten the cowlicks. Tucked into the mirror's rim, I saw the mermaid badge. I had the impression that Honora and Gladys knew more than they were telling, but I wasn't sure how to extract the truth. I was pretty sure those two would not respond to badgering.

Badgering, I thought, and reached up to the mirror, touching the little mermaid's tail. Maybe I just needed to take another approach. I may have ruined my screenwriting career, but I could try and bait the women with a bad-ass story; I could make up one that put my daddy—or them—into a bad light. Honora would leap to his defense and set me straight.

I slipped the badge into my jean pocket, then reached inside my tote bag for my mother's old packet of zinnia seeds. I could still hear Ferg singing; but before I joined him, I had to do something. I hurried downstairs, into the conservatory. I found a clay pot, filled it with dirt, then opened the envelope and poured Mama's seeds into my hand. I pressed them into the soil, sprinkled a little water over the top, and set the pot on a sunny table, next to the orchids.

"There you go, Mama," I said, and turned out of the room, into the hall. In the living room, the French doors stood open. The whistling was louder, and when I stepped onto the terrace, I saw Ferg. He was standing next to the iron table between Honora and Gladys, holding a platter of French toast. Tied around his waist was Gladys's yellow ruffled apron. As he moved over to Isabella, she held up her plate and smiled at him.

"Another piece of toast?" he asked her.

"I'd love one."

He slid the French toast onto her plate, then stepped over to my grandmother. Behind them, a buffet was set up on a glass table with dolphin legs— a stack of gleaming china plates; silverware jutting up from crystal glasses; a platter of cantaloupe and strawberries, all studded with soft wedges of brie. Steam curled over two silver chafing dishes, and I smelled buttered grits and smoked sausage, the thick, spicy type that can't be found outside the Deep South. On the other end of the table stood a bottle of Veuve Cliquot and a pitcher of orange juice, beaded in moisture.

Zap barked, then shot out from under the table and ran over to me, jumping on his hind legs, putting his paws on my knees, his stubby tail a blur. Ferg turned. He stopped whistling and smiled. "Look who's up," he called.

"Get you some of this delicious French toast," Gladys said.

"Isn't he marvelous?" Isabella set down her plate and clapped her hands. "He can direct, he can write, he can cook!"

With his free hand, Ferg pulled out a chair, its iron legs scraping over the stones, then bowed. When I sat down, he tilted back my head and planted an upside-down kiss on my lips. Honora and Isabella clapped, and Gladys put two fingers in her mouth and whistled. "Encore, encore!" Isabella cried. Ferg kissed me again, then grabbed a china plate from the buffet and set it down in front of me with a flourish.

274 MICHAEL LEE WEST

"French toast, madame?"

"Please." I smiled up at him.

"We need more bubbles." Isabella held up the empty bottle of Veuve Cliquot.

"And music," said Gladys, spooning grits into her mouth. "But not the New York harmonica!"

"Philharmonic," said Isabella.

"Be right back." Honora bustled into the house, trailed by the dog. A few minutes later the outdoor speakers crackled and I heard Lena Horne singing "Love Me or Leave Me."

"Perfect," said Isabella, watching Ferg pile sugar-crusted French toast onto my plate. Gladys leaned forward and pushed the cane syrup across the table.

"Grits, madame?" Ferg asked, biting my ear. "Coffee, tea, or—"

"Me?" Isabella said, resting her chin on her hand, glancing flirtatiously at Ferg. "I take it y'all kissed and made up? Tell us *all* about it before Honora gets back."

"I heard that," called Honora, walking out of the house with the champagne. She gently pinched Isabella's cheek and added, "Can't you leave anything to the imagination?"

"Not a chance," said Isabella, looking over at Ferg. "I'm at that stage in life where my imagination has a PG rating."

"Don't look at me. I'm not telling," he said.

"Me, either." I laughed and poured syrup over the toast. My hand wasn't shaking. "You'll just have to wonder."

"Such a pity." Isabella sighed. Then she watched as I picked up a fork and cut into the French toast. She squealed and reached for my left hand. "Oh, my God," she cried and grabbed my hand, holding it up. "It's the infamous pear-shaped diamond. And to think I believed that damn *National Enquirer*."

"Told you not to," said Gladys.

"I didn't believe it for a second," said Honora, handing the champagne bottle to Ferg, then she stepped back when he popped the cork. She bent over to look at my ring. Isabella leaped from her chair and squeezed in for a closer look.

"Goodness, Ferguson, how many carats?" said Honora.

"Three." He smiled.

"The perfect stone," Isabella said reverently. "Not too dinky, and nowhere close to vulgar."

"My, look how it sparkles," said Gladys.

"What sparkles?" asked a deep, masculine voice. I turned, and my father stepped through the French doors.

"Why, your daughter's engagement ring," said Honora. "Get over here and take a look."

For a second, a confused look crossed my daddy's face, then it was replaced by a sardonic grin. He shook Ferg's hand. "I'm Louie DeChavannes, Renata's father."

"So nice to meet you," Ferg said.

"Nice apron," Daddy said.

"Yes, isn't it?" Ferg lifted one lacy edge. "Would you like to try it on?"

"I like this guy already." Daddy laughed. Then he put his arm around Ferg's neck and pulled him into a bear hug. "But I want to get one thing straight. You better take good care of my little girl. You hear?"

"Yes, sir."

"Any truth to those articles, boy?" Daddy tightened his grip. Ferg shook his head.

"Didn't quite hear that," Daddy said, pressing his arm against Ferg's Adam's apple.

"No, sir," Ferg croaked.

"Any news on Joie?" asked Honora.

"She's out of the hospital," he said. "She's still got some left-sided weakness. She has to walk with a cane."

"So sad," said Gladys.

"Faye took her to a rehab that specializes in CVAs."

"CVA?" asked Gladys. "She had a heart attack?"

"No, CVA is a cardiovascular accident," said Daddy. "It's medical jargon for a stroke. All CVAs are strokes, but not all strokes are CVAs."

"Now I'm thoroughly confused," said Isabella.

"She didn't actually have a stroke, but her head injury caused a brain hemorrhage," he said. "The damage was the same damage as a stroke."

"Will she recover?" I asked.

"The prognosis is good." Daddy sank down into a chair.

"I'm so happy for you both." Honora patted his arm.

"I don't think there will be an *us* much longer." Daddy sighed.

"Why not?" asked Isabella.

"Well, Joie doesn't know it yet, but she's falling in love with her neurosurgeon." Daddy shrugged. "Any more French toast? And what's in those chafing dishes?"

"Sausage and grits," said Gladys. "Grab a plate and join us."

"Don't mind if I do." He got up from the chair and walked over to the dolphin table, then glanced over his shoulder at Ferg. "Hey, you in the apron. How about fixing your future father-in-law a mimosa?"

The speaker crackled, and the music changed to a Count Basie song, "Rusty Dusty Blues."

"Why don't you stay and have supper with us tonight?" said Honora. "Renata and Ferg are leaving day after tomorrow for Ireland."

"Ah, Ireland," Daddy said. "Haven't been there in years."

"You ought to fly back with us," said Ferg, handing my father the mimosa.

"With y'all?" Daddy laughed, then raised his flute and sipped the drink.

"Why not?" Ferg said. "You can show Renata the sights—she's never seen Blarney Castle."

"Can we come, too?" Isabella laughed. "Come on, say yes. It'll be like a family vacation."

"Put that thought right out of your mind," said Honora. "That little island isn't big enough for us. We'd drive Ferg crazy."

"No, you wouldn't." He laughed. "I come from a big, messy Scottish family. I'm a member of Clan Lauderdale. I'm used to big gatherings."

"See?" Isabella spread her arms. "I just hope we can even book a flight on this short notice. I won't go unless I can sit in business class."

"I'm not going, period," said Honora.

"Humph, you don't want to leave that dog," said Gladys.

"She can take him along," said Isabella. "She can get a pet passport from the vet. Just stick him into a Vuitton bag—the dog, not the vet. Unless he's cute. Oh, it'll be a blast! I'll hire a limousine to drive us around."

"Isabella," Honora said, "it takes you two weeks to pack an overnight bag. You'll never be ready by tomorrow."

"Then I won't pack," she said. "I'll just buy what I need."

"What you need is a good, stiff drink," said Honora.

"Maybe not a drink," said Isabella, "but something stiff would be divine."

"Come on, Gladys. Let's give the others a little breathing room." Honora grabbed Isabella's hand and towed her into the house.

After they left, I remembered the mermaid badge. I reached into my jean pocket, then slid it over to my father.

Ferg leaned over my chair. "What is it?"

"Some kind of badge," I said, turning to my daddy. "What does it mean?"

"Could be anything." Daddy picked up the badge, then turned it over.

He looked toward the bay. I couldn't read his expression, but I got the feeling that he was coming to a decision. He turned the badge over and over, then glanced at Ferg. "Mind if I have a private word with my daughter?"

"Certainly," Ferg said, and started to go inside. He looked toward the house, where female voices drifted out. The music changed, and Shirley Ellis began singing "The Name Game." From inside the house, Isabella sang, "Renata-botta-bo-botta-banana-nana-bo-notta-fee-fi-fo-dada, Renada!"

"I wouldn't go in there just yet," said Daddy. "It'll be like a minnow swimming into a shark tank. I'll just take Renata-bo-botta for a walk over to the pier, if you don't mind."

"Not at all, sir." Ferg pulled out my chair, and my daddy took my hand and gently pulled me to my feet.

Daddy looked over his shoulder, winking at Ferg. "Be right back, buddy."

"Yes, sir," Ferg headed toward the house. "I think I'll take on the shark tank—er, the ladies."

"Don't let 'em bite," Daddy called. "Open a bottle of Dom, and they just nibble."

We walked to the end of the pier and sat down. The bay resembled a bowl of dishwater, and dirty waves slapped against the pilings. We sat there, our shoulders touching. Then I said, "Are you going to Ireland with us?"

"Would it shock you if I did?"

I nodded.

"I'm thinking about it," Daddy said. "I want to keep my eye on Mr. Hollywood. And I wouldn't mind meeting the notorious Esmé Vasquez."

"Is it really over between you and Joie?"

"We'll see what happens while I'm in Ireland."

"What about them?" I glanced back at the house. "Can you handle Honora and her coven?"

"With one hand tied behind my back and both legs tied," he said.

"If you can pull that off, you ought to be bronzed."

"They're easy." He held the badge up to the light, and the aqua fabric turned a lighter shade.

"Tell me about it, Daddy."

"I'll try." He tucked the badge into his shirt pocket, then smiled down at me. "I'll try, baby girl."

Chapter 41

❀ ❀ ❀

LOUIE SAYS, IT'S THE CHAMPAGNE TALKING

*A*fter Renata nearly drowned at the swimming school, she couldn't look at water. It just broke my heart. See, I wanted her to be fearless, not scared of a damn thing. Mainly because I had this great big yellow streak running down my back. I spent that whole spring driving between New Orleans and Point Clear, helping my daughter overcome hydrophobia.

First, I got her to sit on the edge of the swimming pool, dangling her feet into the shallow end. Another visit, I coaxed her down to the beach, and we built a sand castle a few feet away from the breakers. "Can't make a decent castle without water," I told her, handing her the pail. She shook her head. So I carried the pail to the water and filled it. "Didn't even get wet," I said.

It took a few visits before she would fill the pail. Sometimes we'd walk along the beach and stand in the shallows, letting the waves break over our legs. Then I went to the French Quarter, and in a dusty old shop on Royal, I found a blue badge with a mermaid on it. The next weekend, I drove over to Point Clear, thinking I'd hit on a solution.

First, I tried to persuade Renata to swim in Honora's pool, but she screamed and kicked me. Hell, she even bit my thumb. Left a scar. She squirmed out of my arms and ran down to the beach, skipping along the sand. The small waves were green, edged with brown. Farther out, the water churned as gulls fed on baby shrimp. The light was hard and pure, solid as the wind. I remember she wore a pink polka dot suit with ruffles on her hind end. And her hair was banded into pigtails.

I hurried after her, pausing at the bottom of the steps to watch the pelicans. It was unusual to see them this time of year. They wheeled along the dark line dividing sky and water, disappearing for an instant as they cut through a cloud, then emerged in a V pattern, each bird separate and yet together.

Down at the water's edge, Renata skipped barefoot, stopping now and then to pick up a limpet. I reached down and lifted her above my head. Then I tossed her into the air. When I caught her, she screeched and said, "Do it again, Daddy."

That got me to thinking. "Baby," I said, "when I throw you into the air, aren't you scared I'll drop you?"

"No, Daddy." She shook her head. "You'll always catch me."

"That's because you trust me, right?"

"Truss? Is that what Gladys does to the Thanksgiving turkey?"

"No." I explained the difference between *truss* and *trust*. Then I said, "Renata, can I talk to you like you're a big girl?"

She nodded.

"This fear you've got," I began, "we've got to make it go away."

"What fear, Daddy?"

"The fear of water. I might know how to fix it."

"How, Daddy?"

"Let's me and you go into the water and play toss-up. And maybe you'll see that the water isn't a scary place."

"It is scary, too. Let's just stay right here, Daddy. I like the sand."

"I thought you were going to act like a big girl. And a big girl would go with me into the water."

"I'd rather be little."

"We'll just wade out a little bit. I won't go deep. It'll be just like playing toss-up on the sand—"

"No!"

"I will catch you. Come on, now. Don't be afraid."

Renata burst into tears, whipping her little head around, the pigtails trembling.

"If you trust me to catch you on the beach, then you should trust me to catch you in the water. It's the same thing, Renata."

"It's not." She balled up her fist and hit me in the chest. She looked so much like Shelby when she was mad.

"I will catch you no matter what." I scooped her into my arms, holding her legs still so she couldn't kick. Then I started toward the water. She went limp, and crumpled over, dangling sideways out of my arms, gagging and coughing.

"I can't breathe! Daddy, put me down."

So I put her down, and she took off screeching for her mama and Honora. She pounded up the steps, over the pier, those pigtails twitching up and down.

I sat there a long while, wondering how it all got so tangled. All I had to do was look at Shelby, and I'd get excited. If she blew in my ear, I'd just about lose consciousness. If only I'd tried harder to forgive her, but it was more than that thing with Kip. Their affair had exposed fears that I didn't know I had.

I didn't know if craziness was in the genes; but even if it wasn't, I knew that little fears had a tendency to pile up like trash on the beach. Pretty soon you can't walk without stepping on something sharp. Next thing you know, you're taking baby steps. You're breathing, but you're not alive.

As I stared up at the sun, I watched the pelicans etch across the sky. I felt light-headed, as if my soul had left my body. It soared above the little beach, into the clouds, and was swept along by the Gulf Stream, all the way to Miami, veering over to Dolphin Stadium, where it hovered over the press box and watched the first day of spring practice.

I knew that Honora and her witches had their own theories about my sudden marriage to Bitsy. The truth was, I'd fallen hard for her. I'd seen her around our hotel in Montego Bay, but I hadn't really paid attention until she climbed onto the diving board. The sun was in my eyes, and for a minute, I thought she was Shelby—they had the same small-boned, dainty features.

If we hadn't been in Jamaica, we might not have rushed into marriage, but she was headed back to Tennessee, and I knew I'd never see her again. We went to dinner, and I explained about wines and cuts of meat, and the final days of Vietnam. Bitsy folded her hands and watched me with adoring eyes. And I knew she didn't see any trace of the man who'd accidentally shot Judge Stevens, or who'd vomited in quail feathers. Bitsy saw me as a sophisticated tough guy, a hotshot cardiovascular surgeon who saved lives, a man who had the capacity to save *her* life, rescuing her from an intolerable situation in Crystal Falls, Tennessee.

I didn't want those good feelings to end, so I begged her to fly off to Las Vegas—just a few days of gambling, I told her. Then we'd take it from there. We checked into the MGM and went down to the casino to play blackjack. A skinny waitress took our orders, a piña colada for Bitsy, a Long Island iced tea for myself. Bitsy had never gambled, and I had fun explaining it.

Whenever I touched her, I didn't feel the jolt that I always felt with Shelby; but I felt something else. She needs me more than Shelby, I thought. But the truth was, I needed to see myself through her eyes.

Next thing I knew, I was honeymooning in Las Vegas. I didn't plan it; I just went gambling and woke up married. I had no recollection of having left that casino. The following morning, while Bitsy sang a Barry Manilow song in the shower, I drank black coffee and sobered up long enough to call Honora and break the news. Bitsy stepped out of the shower, her hair curling in wet ringlets.

A while later I went back to the casino and told the gal to bring me a boilermaker. Then I strolled into the lobby and called Shelby. She burst into tears, then threw down the phone. When I finally returned to New Orleans, I stopped by her floating house to see Renata. "She's at school," Shelby said. She wore white shorts and a loose muslin blouse, and she stood against the wall, one foot tucked behind her leg, and she wouldn't look at me. I didn't blame her. I hated myself for what I'd done to her.

"Well, I'll stop by another time," I said. I bent over to kiss her forehead, and at the same moment she looked up. Our lips grazed for just a second, but I felt an electrical jolt. My body was hot, almost thrumming. Spots whirled in front of my eyes. I stepped back, trying to catch my breath and hoping my erection wasn't straining against my trousers. She'd felt it, too. She pressed against the wall, her chest rising and falling. Her nipples jutted against the muslin blouse. She lowered her eyelids, looking between my legs. My trousers formed a tent, and it bobbed in a rhythm that matched my pulse rate. My testicles swelled and ached.

"You'd better go," she said.

"Yeah, I better."

We sprang together, lips crushing, hands roughly groping and kneading.

We barely made it to her bedroom doorway, collapsing on the floor. Buttons popped and rolled along the tile. Her hands tugged at my belt. I peeled off her shorts and threw them over my shoulder. She stretched out on the floor and bent down. I climbed on top of her, my pants hanging around my knees.

"I'm not going to last long," I warned her. I licked one finger and traced it over her pubic bone, then farther down. Arching her hips, she sucked in air, and I thrust into her. She hammered against me, then pulled away, teasing. Again, I pushed into her. She began to shiver and call out my name, "Louie, Lou—" She dropped the "ie" the way she always did before she came. I shuddered and moaned into her hair.

She curled up against me, exhaling tiny, stabbing breaths. I traced my finger through her damp hair. Our lovemaking had always been tender and satisfying, but during our time apart, it had undergone a metamorphosis into something urgent and addictive. She looked up at me, and her irises darkened. "Louie, we can't let this happen again."

"Too late," I said, and in one smooth motion I pulled her on top, and I fit myself between her legs. She gasped and her eyes widened, then she locked her hands behind my neck.

While I sat on Honora's beach, I realized that I'd made a mess of things. I picked up a shell and tossed it into the bay. The sun hung low over the water. A crab skittled sideways, its claws extended like a surgeon holding up freshly scrubbed hands, hurrying off to an operating suite. A copper wave broke on the sand, washing over the crab, engulfing one of Renata's abandoned sand castles.

A little while after sunset, I walked back to the house. Gladys was standing in front of the sink, capping strawberries. Reaching in my pocket, I pulled out the badge and laid it on the counter. "Do you think you could sew this on Renata's bathing suit?" I asked.

"Sure." She glanced at it. "It's pretty. What is it?"

"A little something I found in the French Quarter. I'm hoping it'll give her confidence."

Honora stepped into the room, wearing a black-and-white silk pantsuit.

On her head was a white turban with a rhinestone clip. Hell, for all I knew it could've been a diamond. "Next time you visit, bring Bitsy," she said, then she lit a cigarette and watched the smoke spiral above her head.

"If she's feeling up to it," I said.

"She's up to it," Honora said. "But you're not."

"I'm up to anything," I said. "If I want an opinion, I'll see a shrink."

"Before this is over, you'll have squandered ten years and a hundred thousand dollars—that's what it would take to shrink your head. And the problem is perfectly clear: you love both women."

I shoved my hand into my pocket, fingering the loose change. I hated how she had the knack of seeing straight through me. She was a voodoo kind of mother. Instead of biting off chicken heads, she went straight for mine. "So what if I do love them?"

"Dammit, Louie, it's wrong. You are not a Mormon. You can't have them both. Too many innocent lives are threatened by your selfish wants."

"Too many innocent lungs are threatened by your cigarette smoke," I said. I left the kitchen and stepped onto the terrace. I hurried around the path, then stopped to pick a handful of zinnias. They were Shelby's favorite flower. A long time ago, I'd given her a seed packet, and she'd planted half of them, saving the rest in a tiny envelope as her good luck charm.

When I stepped off the path, I saw Shelby standing in the side yard, throwing rose petals into the koi pond and the Circe statue. Her short blue dress clung to her hips. One hand rose up, smoothing back her shiny blond hair. It was twisted up with mermaid clips, each one encrusted with sparkly stones. A dozen votive candles burned on the railing, throwing light into her mermaids. She sipped her drink, ice cubes tinkling, and threw another handful of petals.

"You've got mermaids in your hair," I said.

"They're Honora's." She patted them. "How'd it go with Renata?"

"Not good." I shook my head, then held out the flowers. "I'll just try another time, I guess."

"You going back to New Orleans?" She buried her face in the bouquet.

"I was, but I'm starved. Let's go over to Gulf Shores and eat some raw oysters."

I took her dancing at Coconut Zed's, where we drank two bottles of

mediocre champagne and ate two dozen raw oysters. When it started rain-
ing, we drove down the beach and rented the bridal suite at Sugar Sands.
There was a mirrored wall behind the bed, reflecting the jade green walls and
whitewashed furniture. I pulled her onto the bed and pushed her hair from
her eyes.

"It's not like this with anyone else, Shelby," I said.

"It better not be," she said.

We sat down on the king-size bed, admiring each other in the mirrors,
performing the strange, compelling rituals of courtship. Later, she sat cross-
legged in the bed and spoon-fed me frozen daiquiris. Then she fed me pepper
cheese and bacon crackers. I opened my mouth like a baby bird, blind and
trusting. "Marry me."

"But you're already taken," she said.

"I'm leaving her," I said. "Soon as the baby's born, I'm leaving."

"It's the champagne talking," she said.

"Do you believe me?" I asked. "I don't feel this way about Bitsy."

"If you keep talking, I'm going to leave. I just feel terrible about your wife.
She loves you, Louie."

I ran my finger up and down her arm, making her shiver; but deep inside,
I felt like a shitbag.

"I have no business being here with you," she said.

"The hell you don't. We're different from other people."

"All love affairs are different." She shrugged. "All love affairs are the same."

I pulled her into my arms, and she tucked her foot around my leg until we
resembled a pretzel, the way she always did. Gossips from New Orleans to
Covington to Point Clear thought I was heartless, but Shelby took the brunt
of their judgmental wrath. The president of the Covington Iris Society said,
"She's just like her mother. Those women just take who and what they want."
The Jefferson Parish Medical Auxiliary marked through Shelby's name in the
address book, calling her a danger to all married women.

In less than a month, I would lose her for good. She would remarry and
build a new life, and mine would crash down around me. But I never gave
up hope. Every morning when I was shaving, I'd look in the mirror and say,
"Shelby will come back to me." But she never did.

After a while I said, "I'll stop talking, okay?"

"Good idea," she said.

"Let's just enjoy the moment."

"And the daiquiris," she said, sliding out her leg. She sat up, reached for the daiquiri, and tipped another spoonful of the rum-limeade mixture down my throat. "I know what's good for men," she said, smearing cheese onto another cracker, fitting it into my mouth.

"Yes, Miss Shelby," I said, my voice muffled by the cracker. "You sure do."

Later that night, we drove to the Florabama Lounge and ordered boiled crawfish, sucking the heads with a devilish flourish, while out-of-towners looked on in mute horror.

"Where you from?" Shelby asked them.

"Kentucky," they answered.

Shelby twisted a crawdaddy, then noisily sucked its head. She smiled, her lips curving around the crawfish's red body.

"Those things you're eating," said the tourist, gesturing with her fork. "They look like something that lives under my sink."

*T*he next morning when we drove up, Renata was waiting on the front terrace. She was wearing her pink swimsuit, and Gladys had sewn the badge right in the center. "Daddy!" Renata cried and flew down the limestone steps. She grabbed my hand and started dragging me toward the bay.

"I been waiting for you," she said.

"Waiting for what?" I asked.

"I'll let you take me swimming," she said, then grabbed the front of her swimsuit and stretched the fabric. "See this badge? Gladys said it's magic. It might not help me to swim, but it melts fear! So let's go try it. Now!"

"Oh, that's wonderful, baby," I said, turning back to Shelby. "Hey, Shelby, come on—"

"No," Renata snapped. "Mama can't go. This is between me and you. Got it, buddy?"

"Got it," I said.

We headed down to the beach. My daughter ran ahead, outlined against the blue sky, all backlit by the sun, her screams lost in the noise of pelicans and a distant pontoon boat. She curved in a wide circle, and ran back to me. "Okay, Daddy," she said, putting her hands over her eyes. "I'm ready."

"You sure?"

She nodded.

"You're not going to bite this time?"

She shook her head. I picked her up and waded into the water up to my knees. Way out on the bay, pelicans seemed to watch us. I tried to raise her, but she grabbed fistfuls of my shirt.

"Wait, Daddy. Not yet. Stop, I see a shark!"

"Ain't no sharks out there," I said. "But there might be a mermaid. She'll come up to watch you. She'll give you a prize."

"She'll eat me! Let me go!"

"Wait, I think I see a mermaid," I said.

"Where?" Renata twisted around, blinking at the water. "Where is the mermaid, Daddy?"

"She's with the pelicans. Don't you see her? She's waving to you." I lifted my hand. "Wave to the pretty mermaid, Renata."

She shook her head. "No, I'm too afraid." Her face puckered, then her eyes filled.

"But I'm right here, baby. Nothing will happen while I'm here."

"You weren't at Miss Lane's school. And I nearly drowned."

"I'm here now. And I want you to trust me. So let go, and I'll toss you just a little ways. And then I'll catch you."

"But what if you drop me?"

"I won't, but if I did, you could swim."

"I can't. I forgot how. But I don't need to swim. Mama says I don't have to."

"Well, she's wrong. One day me or your mama won't be around, and if you accidentally fell into the water—"

"I won't."

"But you could. And I don't want you to be helpless. I want you to be brave." I kissed the top of her head. It felt warm and tasted salty. "Now, I'm going to do one little toss-up. And I will not drop you. Repeat after me, Renata—Daddy will not drop me."

"Daddy will not drop me," she kept saying, then she squeezed her eyes shut. Her eyelids twitched; she was thinking hard, trying to find a way to escape, and whenever that child plotted, she had a tendency to stretch out her fingers like she was reaching for something in her thoughts. I waited until her fingers relaxed, dropping my shirt. Then I said a quick Hail Mary and tossed her up into the air—just a few inches is all. She let out a scream that probably carried all the way to Mobile. She screeched so loud that the pelicans flew away.

I caught her and said, "See? I didn't drop you. Why, you didn't even get wet."

"Put me down." Her chin was trembling. "That old badge didn't work."

"Before your accident, you were an expert swimmer. You could outswim any shark—you were better than the mermaids."

"No, take me back."

"Renata DeChavannes," I said. "If you don't swim today, this is it. I'm done. I'm through trying."

She hung her head, scraping her fingernail over the badge. Then she looked up. "Okay. I'm ready now."

Before she had time to think about it, I hunkered down and gripped her waist. Then I gently set her into a wave. She whimpered, but I said, "Trust me, Renata. I will not let go."

She screwed up her face, struggling not to cry. "Daddy will not drop me," she said. "My daddy will not let go."

She stretched out her arms and began to move them in the water. Beneath the surface, her legs frog-kicked. "Hold me, Daddy," she cried.

But I'd already turned her loose. I didn't mean to, she just slipped away. Her small arms cut through the water, churning foam. "There she goes," I cried. "The brave and mighty Renata! I knew you could do it; I knew it the whole time."

Chapter 42

⊙ ⊙ ⊙

SWIMMING WITH MY FATHER

I put my arm around his neck, then pressed my forehead against his cheek. "Your tactics might be questionable," I said, laughing, "but they worked. I love you, Daddy."

"Love you, too, baby."

"I'm still not the world's best swimmer," I said.

"Says who?" He laughed.

For a long time we didn't speak. A speedboat cut across the bay, sending waves crashing under the boathouse. "I wish my mother were here," I said.

"She is, baby." He paused. "I wish it wasn't so hard for me to show love."

"You're showing it," I whispered.

"So, do you remember the badge?" His forehead wrinkled. "How I put you in the water?"

"No, Daddy. I don't. There's so much I've forgotten or repressed. But would you mind taking me swimming again?"

"Now?"

"Yes." I grabbed his hands.

"All right, then." He kicked off his shoes, then I led him down to the beach, stepping around a glistening jellyfish, into the cold surf. Daddy's trousers billowed up, floating on the water. I felt, rather than saw, him hovering just inches away. Then he put his hands on my waist, and I leaned over and began to move my hands in the silky water. As it lapped gently against my face, I couldn't tell if he was still holding me, but it didn't matter. I lifted my arms, dove into a wave, and it all came back. I remembered my terror. I remembered the badge and how strong my daddy's hand had felt and how, when he loosened his grip, I surged into the water, the same way I was doing now. *I will always love you*, my mother whispered. *I will always be with you.* I kicked deeper into the murky bay, grateful that the Fates had brought my father back to me. He was somewhere on the surface, watching and waiting, a tall, dark-haired man with a teardrop nose, and he loved me. My daddy loved me. *Take care of him*, my mother whispered.

Yes, I said, yes, I will.

April 2, 2000
The National *ENQUIRER*
Exclusive report!

Director Ferguson Lauderdale
Lip Syncs with Old Lover

Sometimes love really is lovelier the second time around. These tender photos seem to echo that old sentiment, because Academy Award–winning director Ferguson Lauderdale, 38, has obviously made his choice between the two women who have been vying for his affection. Just weeks ago, Lauderdale was juggling lovers, Esmé Vasquez and Renata DeChavannes, 33. But the *National Enquirer* has learned that Lauderdale has not only reunited with DeChavannes, he has given her a 3-carat pear-shaped engagement ring. The exclusive, candid snaps show the director in perfect lip sync with his screenwriter-love. The couple were spotted in the Atlanta airport, en route to Ireland, with an unnamed bodyguard. A source close to the couple says a summer wedding is being planned.

Acknowledgments

I owe a debt of gratitude to Ellen Levine, Carrie Feron, Tessa Woodward, Lydia Weaver, Miranda Ottewell, Mahlon West, Trey Arnett, Tyler West, Carla Arnett, Ary Jean Helton, Darnell Arnoult, James Ralph Helton, Brittany Ann Helto, Mary Gay Shipley, Nancy Nicholas, DeAnn and Craig Floyd, Allison Arnett, and all my friends and family who put up with me when I'm in the grip of a book. The Yorkie in the book was inspired by the real Zap, who slept on my feet while I wrote, except when he retrieved countless balls of wadded-up paper.

I'd like to thank Kathy Patrick of Beauty and the Book for selecting my books for her Pulpwood Queens' book clubs. If you are interested in starting a club, I highly recommend her book, *The Pulpwood Queens' Tiara-Wearing, Book-Sharing Guide to Life*. And check out her "Girlfriends' Weekend," too. While working on the book my editor, Carrie Feron, sent a marvelous audio book, by Mary Pope Osborne, *Tales of the Odyssey*, vol 2, HarperAudio. I was inspired by movies, poetry, art, picture books, legends, and myths. My sources include works by Emily Dickinson, whose poem inspired the title, along with John Keats, T.S. Eliot, Homer's *Odyssey*, Hans Christian Andersen, Jane Yolen, Oscar Wilde, Sir James George Fraser, Beatrice Philpotts, Lucretius, Maria Rainer Rilke, Theodore Gachot, William Shakespeare, W.B. Yeats, Lord Alfred Tennyson, Elizabeth Ratisseau, Carl Jung, John Donne, and the films *Splash* and *Miranda*.

I dedicated this book to my darling red-headed, one-year-old granddaughter, Annabel Lee, who not only happens to live by the sea, but whose name was inspired by Edgar Alan Poe's poem, and also my own name, beating out my mother's middle name, Ary, which was in the running for a while. Love you, Mom. You may be the pits when it comes to naming girls, but you—and your cooking—are irreplaceable.

A⁺
AUTHOR
INSIGHTS,
EXTRAS, &
MORE...

FROM
**MICHAEL
LEE
WEST**
AND
AVON A

THE LEAVING STEP:

At Home with Michael Lee West and Her Yorkies

Many hundreds of years ago, when I was a small girl and "acted up," my mother would roll her eyes and say, "It's not my fault. Michael Lee was raised by a dog—quite literally. She was raised by an eighty-five-pound Weimaraner named Cindy."

Cindy had abandoned her own puppies and sat diligently beside my crib, watching me sleep. My mother had to bottle feed all twelve puppies, painting their toenails to keep track. The moment I woke up, Cindy bolted out of the house (back then in North Louisiana, no one ever locked their doors). She found my mother, bit her dress, and towed her back to my nursery.

So all these years later, it's no surprise that my Yorkies found their way into *Mermaids in the Basement*. Honora's dog, Zap, was a composite of my three boys—Murphy, Mr. Big, and the real Zap.

Writing a novel can be a long and lonely process. It is a comfort to be surrounded by all of those beating hearts. Nothing is finer than having one of the boys flop down on my feet, or to make me laugh when I toss a crumbled piece of a work-in-progress into the air and they chase after it.

Actually, my Yorkies fit perfectly into a southern novel. Murphy is the father—and the brother—of the boys. An accidental breeding between Murphy and his mother resulted in the birth of what my husband calls "the illegitimate Yorkies." My sons remind me that it's straight out of the film *Chinatown*, with Zap and Mr. Big saying, "He's my father, he's my brother."

My husband told me I'd have to sell them; but I'd already fallen in love. The puppies were born on December 21, 2003— hamster-sized, sleek black, with their tan ears folded back like tiny limpet shells. Mia kept escaping the utility room to be with me (because that's a trait of Yorkies—they just want to be with you), so I spent many hours sitting cross-legged on the tile floor, coaxing Mia to nurse. This is where my B.S. in nursing came in handy. I set my alarm clock and got up all during the night to make sure Zap and Mr. Big were properly nourished, and that Mia wasn't alone.

When their eyes squinted open, I was right there. Zap, especially, would sit at my feet, gazing up as if to say, "You are my mother. Mia is my sister." My husband said a nurse at the hospital wanted to buy a puppy, and I told him to back off. There was no way I'd give up these Yorkie boys.

Now, when I go out of town, my son always teases the Yorkies—and me—saying, "Watch it, boys—she's doing the 'Leaving Step.'" He explained that "the leaving step" came from the film *Restoration,* when Meg Ryan's character explained why she kept doing a squatty dance. It was based on how her character's husband "stepped over her" in the night and left for good.

My own "Leaving Step" turns the normally quiet house into a tearjerker—mostly my own tears. My son tells me that the boys sit beside the front door, keeping watch, just the same way I'd watched over them, and it requires bacon tidbits to lure them away.

Sometimes the Leaving Step is a lasting one. We lost Mia last year after a sudden illness. And, as a mutual dog fancier once said, "As much as you appreciate them while they are here on earth, somehow it's never enough." And it never is.

RECIPES FROM

Mermaids in the Basement

HONORE'S EASY CHEESE STRAWS

1 box Pepperidge Farm frozen puff pastry sheets
¾ cup grated Gruyere cheese
Pam (cooking spray)
parchment paper

Preheat oven to 400 degrees. Place frozen pastry sheets on a large sheet of aluminum foil, lightly greased. After they thaw, sprinkle cheese over the sheets. Using a wooden rolling pin, firmly press the cheese into the pastry, keeping the rectangular shape.

Cut into long strips about ¾-inch wide, larger if you like—a pizza cutter works beautifully. Now, twist each strip into long corkscrew curls. Place on a parchment paper–lined cookie sheet and bake 10 minutes, or until the straws "puff" and turn golden. Place on your best silver platter and serve to guests, or eat them in secret on a paper napkin.

GRAND MARNIER-INFUSED
CHOCOLATE-COVERED STRAWBERRIES

Serves 4 to 6, or 1 Extremely Hungry Chocolate Lover

1 box of giant strawberries
1 bag Swiss Castle Chocolate Fondue (available at groceries like
  Publix)
1 syringe with 20-gauge needle
¼ cup Grand Marnier

Wash the berries and set on a paper towel to dry. Meanwhile,
fill a syringe with Grand Marnier and inject about 1 cc ino each
berry. Melt the chocolate in a glass bowl, according to directions,
and do not make an estimate and then get distracted, as I did last
New Year's, filling the house with smoke and setting off the fire
alarm just as my guests were arriving. After dipping each berry,
set it on a wax-paper-lined baking sheet. Chill about an hour.

GLADYS' SHRIMP CREOLE

Serves 6

2 pounds large shrimp, fresh or frozen
1 cup chopped yellow onion
1 tbs flour
1 cup chopped bell pepper (green)
1 tbs tomato paste
2 cans chopped tomatoes (reserve juice)
3 cloves garlic, chopped
3 tsp chopped fresh parsley
1¼ tsp Hungarian paprika
1 bay leaf
1 stick butter
salt and freshly ground pepper (to taste)

If your shrimp are frozen, defrost and shell. For fresh shrimp, just rinse, shell, and devein. Into a cast iron skillet, melt ½ stick butter and add 1 tbl flour, stirring with a wire whisk until you think your hand might fall off. Stir until the roux is the color of a copper penny.

Sauté onions and pepper. When the vegetables start to look translucent, add tomato paste and stir. Sprinkle the paprika over this. Keep stirring. Now pour in the tomatoes with juice. Add the other seasonings (reserve 1 tsp of chopped parsley for garnish). Cover and simmer for 1 hour or so.

In another pan, sauté the shrimp in the remaining butter. Cook 3 minutes, turning shrimp on all sides. They will quickly turn pink. Do not overcook. Add shrimp to the sauce, allowing a little of the butter to drizzle in. Serve over extra long–grain rice with a green salad on the side and crusty garlic French bread (to "mop" up the sauce). Key lime pie (see *Consuming Passions* for recipe) with a nut crust and topped with whipped cream is divine.

FERG'S FRENCH TOAST

Serves 8

10 slices Texas-style bread (thick-sliced)
5 large eggs
¼ cup cream
¼ cup Grand Marnier
½ cup white sugar (granulated)
¼ tsp ground nutmeg
1 tsp real vanilla flavoring
tiny pinch of salt
½ stick butter (more, if necessary)
1 cup chopped pecans or macadamia nuts (an interesting
  variation is Corn Flakes)
powdered sugar
mint sprigs (garnish)
maple syrup

Procedure:

Into a bowl add eggs and whisk until frothy. Add milk and Grand
Marnier. Whisk until blended. Now add sugar, nutmeg, salt, and
vanilla. Melt butter onto a griddle. Dip bread one slice at a time
into the egg mixture, then quickly roll in the chopped nuts. You
will make a huge mess, but never mind. It's worth it. Place slices
onto griddle. Brown on each side, adding extra butter if necessary.
Remove to a paper towel–lined platter and sprinkle slices with
powdered sugar. Drizzle with real maple syrup. Garnish with a
fresh mint sprig. Serve with huge piles of sausage and bacon and/
or fresh fruit.

READING GUIDE FOR
Mermaids in the Basement

1. *Mermaids in the Basement* is a story about fathers and daughters. Renata DeChavannes returns to her family's home in Alabama to discover the truth about her parents' failed marriage and to reconnect with her estranged father, Louie. How did Renata and Louie drift apart? Do they reach an understanding? How does divorce impact their relationship? Why was Renata shielded from the truth? Discuss the father/daughter relationship and how it differs from mothers and daughters.

2. The novel opens and closes with faux tabloid articles; the chapters are short and each one had a "title." Discuss the use of tabloids as a metaphor. Can ordinary lives be more outrageous than stories in the *Star* and *Globe*?

3. Honora and Gladys present Renata with a trunk that's filled with artifacts—puzzle pieces to her parents' tumultuous marriage and divorce, and also clues to secrets from Renata's childhood. Discuss how each artifact (newspaper clipping, obituary, jewelry, etc) solves a bit of the mystery.

4. After Renata returns to Alabama, she tries to reconnect with her father, but before she can make headway she is accused of attacking his fiancée, Joie, sending the woman into a coma. Discuss how Louie and Renata became estranged. How does divorce affect the parent/child relationship?

5. Why did Renata's mom, Shelby, conceal the truth? Who was she really protecting? What happened in her past to make her want her daughter to have a "normal" childhood? Did Shelby succeed? Should parents shield their children from painful truths?

6. The novel's title was inspired by an Emily Dickinson poem. The title serves as a metaphor for Renata's depression and for the hidden past, bringing the truth out of darkness, into the light. How many secrets were hidden? Which one had the most impact?

7. Central to the novel are the relationships between the women—Renata, Honora, Gladys, and Isabella. How are the women alike and different? How do their actions define character? For example, Honora has a large collection of designer handbags that she regularly "sets free" in public places; and the flamboyant Isabella has a penchant for lacing the food with laxatives and tranquilizers. These women are capable of forgiving each other—but not the men in their lives. What is the significance of their friendship? How has it sustained the women?

8. During the course of the novel, Renata learned the true history of her family. Which "secret" did you enjoy the most? Which one had the biggest impact on her? Do you think she and Ferg will have a successful relationship?

MICHAEL LEE WEST is the author of *Mad Girls in Love, Crazy Ladies, American Pie, She Flew the Coop,* and *Consuming Passions.* She lives with her husband on a rural farm in Tennessee with three bratty Yorkshire terriers, a Chinese Crested, assorted donkeys, chickens, sheep, and African Pygmy goats. www.michaelleewest.net

Michael Lee West